BROKEN BONDS

Published by:
1517 Publishing
PO Box 54032
Irvine, CA 92619-4032

Publisher's Cataloging-In-Publication Data
(Prepared by The Donohue Group, Inc.)

Names: Mantravadi, Amy, author.
Title: Broken bonds : a novel of the Reformation / Amy Mantravadi.
Description: Irvine, CA : 1517 Publishing, [2024] | Series: Reformation novel series ; part 1 | Includes bibliographical references.
Identifiers: ISBN: 978-1-962654-75-3 (paperback) | 978-1-962654-77-7 (hardcover) | 978-1-962654-76-0 (ebook) | 978-1-962654-78-4 (audiobook)
Subjects: LCSH: Reformation—Europe—Fiction. | Church history—16th century—Fiction. | Luther, Martin, 1483-1546—Fiction. | Erasmus, Desiderius, -1536—Fiction. | Melanchthon, Philip, 1497-1560—Fiction. | Fear—Fiction. | Hope—Fiction. | LCGFT: Christian fiction. | BISAC: FICTION / Religious. | FICTION / Historical / Renaissance.
Classification: LCC: PS3613.A5825 B76 2024 | DDC: 813/.6—dc23

Printed in the United States of America.

Cover art by Zachariah James Stuef.

AMY MANTRAVADI

BROKEN BONDS

A NOVEL OF THE REFORMATION
BOOK I OF 2

Contents

Primary characters

In Wittenberg:

Philipp Melanchthon, Professor of Greek
    Katharina, his wife
    Anna, their daughter
Martin Luther, Professor of Theology
Justus Jonas, Provost of the All Saints' Foundation
Johannes Bugenhagen, Pastor of St. Mary's Church
Famulus Koch, Live-in assistant to the Melanchthon family
Wolf Seberger, Live-in assistant at the Black Cloister
Eberhard Brisger, Former prior and housemate of Martin Luther
Lucas Cranach, Artist and Court painter
    Barbara, his wife
    Anna, their daughter, one of several children
Joachim Camerarius, Professor of Greek
Katharina von Bora, Former nun

In Basel:

Desiderius Erasmus, Scholar also commonly known as Erasmus of Rotterdam
Johann Froben, Publisher
    Gertrude, his wife
    Hieronymus, their elder son
    Justina, their daughter
    Johann Erasmus, their younger son
Christoph von Utenheim, Bishop of Basel
Margarethe, Housekeeper to the Frobens

Karl Harst, Assistant to Erasmus
Johannes Œcolampadius, Vicar of St. Martin's Church
Guillame Farel, Reforming preacher

Elsewhere:

Friedrich, Elector of Saxony
Andreas Bodenstein von Karlstadt, Pastor in Orlamünde
Johann von Staupitz, Benedictine Abbot of Salzburg

Timeline

1440: Johannes Gutenberg of Mainz creates his moveable type printing press

1453: Constantinople falls to the Ottoman Turks, ending the Eastern Roman Empire

1466: Desiderius Erasmus is born, mostly likely in Gouda (modern-day Netherlands)

1483: Martin Luther is born in Eisleben (modern-day Germany); Erasmus' parents both die of plague; The Battle of Bosworth brings Henry Tudor to the throne of England

1488: Erasmus becomes a monk in the Order of Saint Augustine

1492: Erasmus is ordained as a priest, but soon receives a temporary dispensation from his vows on grounds of poor health and desire for study; Christopher Columbus lands in the New World

1497: Philipp Melanchthon is born in Bretten (modern-day Germany)

1498: Portuguese explorer Vasco de Gama navigates the Cape of Good Hope and arrives in India

1502: The University of Wittenberg is founded

1505: Luther becomes a monk in the Order of Saint Augustine; The Swabian League lays siege to Bretten; Leonard DaVinci paints the *Mona Lisa*

1507: Luther is ordained as a priest

1508: Melanchthon's father and grandfather die, leaving his education to be overseen by others; Michelangelo paints the Sistine Chapel ceiling

1510: Erasmus begins a five-year period teaching at Queen's College, Cambridge

1511: Erasmus' immensely popular satirical work *The Praise of Folly* is published

1512: Luther becomes chair of the theology department at the University of Wittenberg

1516: Erasmus publishes his Greek New Testament with a new Latin translation of the Bible

1517: Luther posts his *Ninety-Five Theses* criticizing the indulgence trade

1518: Melanchthon becomes Professor of Greek at the University of Wittenberg

1519: Luther and his colleague Andreas Bodenstein von Karlstadt debate the Romanist theologian Johann Eck in Leipzig; Melanchthon's supreme work of systematic theology, the *Common Topics*, is published in its first approved edition; Charles of Hapsburg becomes Holy Roman Emperor Charles V

1520: Luther is officially excommunicated; Melanchthon marries Katharina Krapp

1521: Luther appears before Emperor Charles V at the Diet of Worms, then lives in hiding at the Wartburg Castle for almost a year

1522: The reform movement in Wittenberg faces a moment of crisis due to the teachings of Karlstadt and others, forcing Luther's return; Melanchthon's daughter Anna is born; Ulrich Zwingli heads a new reforming movement in Zürich

Preface

Dear Reader,

Before you begin this book, it seems best that you should know which type of literature it is and what kind of author has written it.

First, this is not chiefly a work of historical analysis. If it were, I would include far more details about contemporary trends, bolstered by statistics and an intense dissection of primary sources. My aim is not to teach you what the years 1524-5 were like, nor what their significance was for the broad scope of human history.

Second, this is not chiefly a work of theological or philosophical analysis. Numerous books and articles have been written exploring the political thought of Erasmus, the theological statements of Luther, and the educational principles of Melanchthon. If that is your interest, then seek out those works, for some things which were heavily emphasized by these three men receive little or no mention in my novels.

Third, this is not a biography. Numerous events occurred in the lives of these men which I have completely ignored. There are many relevant details from their pasts that ought to have been mentioned if my main goal was to tell you who they were as persons. That was not my goal, and those details must be sought elsewhere. If you desire a good introductory biography, I recommend *Erasmus and the Age of Reformation* by Johan Huizinga, *Melanchthon: The Quiet Reformer* by Clyde L. Manschreck (though he was not particularly quiet), and *Martin Luther: A Life* by Martin E. Marty.

This book is, first and foremost, a parable: a story intended to communicate timeless truths. When deciding what to include,

I generally gravitated toward material that would enhance the narrative and support the overall points I was attempting to make. One could quibble with the way I have portrayed the characters and events, but if there are elements that seem out of line with your own perception, ask yourself, were they meant to support the parable? The answer is likely, "Yes."

Now, as for the author, I am a person of no renown. My academic credentials are minimal, and I am tragically monolingual. I composed much of this book while watching my toddler sleep on the baby monitor. So, you should not confuse my work with that of an actual scholar. There are many good ones out there, and I encourage you to support their efforts.

I am, in the final analysis, merely a sinner saved by grace, and it is in that spirit that I offer to you this work of my hands and heart, in which I pray that the Lord may be glorified.

Grace and Peace,
Amy Mantravadi

For my father
In whose love I feel secure

"Work out your salvation with fear and trembling, for it is God who is at work in you, both to will and to work for His good pleasure."

—St. Paul, *Epistle to the Philippians*[1]

"For he who strove with the world became great by overcoming the world, and he who strove with himself became great by overcoming himself, but he who strove with God became greater than all."

—Søren Kierkegaard, *Fear and Trembling*[2]

---

[1] Philippians 4:12b-13. All quotations from the Christian Scriptures in this work are taken from the following translation: *The New American Standard Bible* (LaHabra, CA: The Lockman Foundation, 1995).

[2] Søren Kierkegaard, *Fear and Trembling*, trans. Alastair Hannay, Penguins Classics Edition (London: Penguin, 2003), 50.

"The dove descending breaks the air
With flame of incandescent terror
Of which the tongues declare
The one discharge from sin and error.
The only hope, or else despair
Lies in the choice of pyre or pyre—
To be redeemed from fire by fire."

—T.S. Eliot, "Little Gidding"

Prologue

He should never have traveled this night.

Only a fool would have made such a choice, and he is no fool. Something else has driven him to this point: fate, God, the devil? Who could say?

The sky was red at break of day. He smelled the vapor in the air—felt the sweat upon his skin. Ungodly heat! The clouds have gathered, storing up their wrath of thunder, preparing to throw down their bolts. There will be no rocky cave or hole in the ground to shelter him when that fire comes down from heaven to earth. *I knew it, and yet I set out*, he laments.

He remembers the storms of his youth. In his bed at night, lying between his younger brothers, bodies pressed together for want of space, mouths agape in sleep, he would hear the distant cataclysm— the upheaval of the elements. Ever closer it would creep. How the wind would lash that house! Then the momentary glow: the lurid flash of white. Again, again, again! His brothers would sleep through it all, but he would lie flat on his back transfixed, staring up at the rafters, his heart threatening to bolt from his chest—lips trembling, limbs rigid.

"O Maria, salva me! Sancta mater, salva me!"[1] Even so, he would whisper into the void—the dark abyss of terror.

This is one such storm. He has watched it take shape upon the western horizon as he urges his horse one mile, two miles, three miles from his former life and toward another. Is he spurring the beast, or is some beast spurring him? It fills him with angst to see the great

---

[1] "O Mary, save me! Holy Mother, save me!"

cloud rise like a bird of prey taking its stand, unfolding its vast wings, engulfing the hills beneath it. Now he passes over flat earth with nothing to shield him, utterly alone upon the road. Reason herself forbids him continue, but he is compelled by something stronger. He traverses the lower sphere—the realm of fire—as the heavens pass in circuit above him, set in motion by the unmoved mover.

So great is his dread of storms that he could only have been driven to this point by something worse than death.

In his thigh resides a memory that enlivens his fear. Not three months hence, as he was placing a blade in his belt, it pierced through cloth, skin, and flesh, severing an artery. A one in a thousand chance, or perhaps one in ten thousand, but it happened sure enough, and before he had time to contemplate the fact, his life was hanging by a thread of fate. The blood was loosed from his veins, pouring down his leg, covering the hands that rushed to stymie the flow. He was pulled into darkness, unable even to call for help. Only the skill of a surgeon had saved him from the grasping fingers of death. Never had he felt such terror, and since that moment, he has done nothing but consider what would have happened had the good surgeon failed in his task.

For in that darkness—that dread catharsis of the mind—he knew the full horror of damnation. He weighed his deeds in the balance and found them desperately wanting. He felt the wrath of God as keenly as the cowherd's brand. He came within a breath of hell, and he can never be the same.

So, when his strength was recovered and his mind firmly set, he made for the home of his youth, there to inform his parents that he could no longer afford to waste his time learning the particulars of the law, for his soul was in deadly peril. His life might be snatched from him any day: that much was clear. The burden of his sin was crushing, and he could see no remedy but to devote the remainder of his life to the God before whom he had cowered all his days. Yes, he would pursue a career in the Church. Perhaps in seeking salvation for others, he might find it for himself.

In any case, he had long since tired of legal texts, which seemed to bury truth under great heaps of words, and found himself drawn instead to the Holy Scriptures, where the truth struck one free and clear like a blade to the heart, dividing joints and marrow, soul and spirit. This is what he had hoped to explain to his parents when he arrived at their home two days earlier.

His father's reaction was immediate and violent: far worse than anything he could have imagined. He watched that immense body quake with rage, face contorting wildly. Even now, he hears the deep voice rising, issuing from lungs racked by soot, bursting forth like the torrent that will soon fall upon his head.

"I bet my life on you—all our lives! What didn't I do for you?!"

How his father's words pierced him! From his earliest days, if there was anything he knew, it was that he was the eldest son: the pride, the hope, the legacy of his parents. As such, they had molded and shaped him, pouring themselves into him, sparing no expense for his advancement. It was only upon his return, as he informed his father that he could no longer become the lawyer he was meant to be, that his elders realized just how thoroughly their son had been shaped by others—how little their own efforts had counted in the end. But his father was not a man to simply accept hard truths. When his son explained his desire to pursue the things of God rather than the things of man, it drew forth a stream of venom: the offense of years released in a moment.

"That's nice! The pot giving it back to the potter!" the older man bellowed, his words clipped and biting. "Do you condemn your father?"

"I do not condemn you!" he protested, trembling inside.

"Your every word condemns me. You've rebelled since birth!"

Even as he thinks of it now, he struggles not to give way to tears. Only five miles lie between him and Erfurt: city of scholars, city of his future. Within those walls, he will find refuge from the storm, but where can he hide from the wrath of his father? Not for the first time, he tugs on the reins and bids the horse to pause—looks back in the direction he has come. He feels the frantic longing: the inescapable urge to run back to his father. The weight of that disapproval threatens to drive him into the dust. *How can I bear it? But how can I bear the wrath of the Almighty?* No, he has come too far, and the storm is too near. He has crossed the Rubicon of his soul. There can be no turning back.

"You forget your duty to this house!" his father had charged, spitting the words as much as speaking them. "You forsake us in our hour of need!"

He could think of no reply except to utter softly, "I also owe a duty to my heavenly Father."

The sky is utterly black as he urges his horse forward. In the distance, a church bell rings: an attempt to combat the power of the storm. Off to the west, he sees the first streak of light move from heaven to earth—hears the ripping of the air. Seated upon his horse, riding past treeless fields, he is the tallest object for half a mile in any direction and may well be a target of the thunder's wrath. His Saxon ancestors would have said Thor was having himself a fine romp in the clouds, but he does not fear the old gods. Something far more alive haunts him.

As he presses on, the rain begins to fall: first a light pattering, then a ferocious torrent, pelting him from head to toe, breaking up the earth beneath him, filling his eyes so he can hardly see. The wind catches his cloak and whips it to and fro. The sound of the bell is drowned by the din of rain and peals of thunder. Less than four miles to go, but it seems an eternity.

As the water presses into his nostrils, he thinks of his friend, Paul, like himself a student on the brink of something great. Four months earlier, this fellow pupil stepped into a boat to cross the Gera: a boat that was not entirely sound. Unable to swim, Paul drowned within fifty feet of the bank. Standing over his friend's newly cut grave, he was struck dumb by the cruel turning of fate. Why should he live and breathe while Paul was set to become food for worms? The priest had approached him, placed a hand on his shoulder, and spoke unbidden:

"The hidden purposes of God are strange beyond all measure, and we are fools who seek beyond the bounds."

For a moment, he was torn from his grief, or perhaps provoked into a deeper level of agony. He looked the man of God in the eye and spoke accusingly: "Is that supposed to comfort me?"

"Men in general set too much store by comfort," the priest replied without shame, "or perhaps they seek the wrong kind of comfort. I tell you now, there are words which must be heard whether you are prepared to receive them or not."

Two miles left before the city walls, and all around him the lightning strikes. His hands clutch the reins, striving to maintain control. The horse's chest expands and contracts, its breath labored as he drives the beast forward at a vicious pace. *Is the fate of Paul about to be my own?* He knows he must cry out to God, but he cannot find the strength. He is held back—no, held down. He is crushed by the sin in which he has lived and moved and had his being. In sin his mother conceived him,[2] and he has breathed it in and out, in and out. How then can he expect the mercy of a holy God? Who can see that face and live? His thoughts are spiraling, turning inward, dragging him down into a darkness more real than that which fills the sky. And still the words of his father haunt him.

"You're trapped inside your own head," the old man had claimed. "Too smart for your own good—always were."

"I just feel…" And then he hesitated, afraid of the reaction his words would provoke.

"Yes. Spit it out, son!" his father demanded.

"I just can't help feeling that God wants me to serve his Church," he answered, and even to him the words seemed weak.

"He's got an army of priests to serve his Church, boy! I only need one lawyer! What does God need with one more priest?"

But his heart was already captive. He could not move by any power of mind or soul, and so he stood his ground, not in bravery or defiance, but from a simple inability to do otherwise. And then came the final judgment: the revocation, the parting of the ways.

"If you do this thing, don't you dare call yourself my son!"

In the middle of the storm, with the specter of death before him, he weeps at the memory of these words. He is broken, body and soul. For the first time in his life and quite possibly the last, he has been thrown out by his father, forsaken to the darkening world. He was granted no money for the journey upon his expulsion, so he rode until he was too weary to continue, making his bed beneath a tree, sleeping rough beneath the star filled sky. Arising from fitful sleep, he has continued throughout this day despite the warning signs of nature, riding beneath the burning sun, watching the clouds rise to torment him even as the demons rack his soul.

Before he crossed that threshold for the final time, he had turned to his mother: the woman who taught him to fear God. If anyone could understand him and restrain his father's fury, it would be her.

---

[2] Reference to Psalm 51:5.

"Mother," he pleaded, "speak to father for me. I have lost his love. I beg you, help me regain it!"

She took his face in her hands, her eyes as moist as his own. He saw love within those spheres, but a firmness in her jaw: an unwillingness to press beyond the bounds of her husband's will.

"You burn too fiercely, son. You will destroy yourself," she told him. An accusation or an act of love? Who could say?

As she began to shut the door, cutting him off perhaps forever from his childhood home, he cried, "Mother, please! I'm afraid."

To his shock, she laughed softly, but with eyes infinitely sad. "Oh, my son! Only the dead are free from fear."

He is close to Stotternheim now. Less than a mile to the city wall and a kind of salvation. He thinks to himself, *Perhaps I am wrong after all. Perhaps there is another way. Might I please one father and also another? Must I force the breach and destroy what we have worked to build? I can still be a lawyer. After all, wouldn't God want me to obey my father? Is that not one of the chief commandments? But what of my soul? And how can I stand before the holy one? Who am I before God?!*

Even as these questions torment him, a strange silence breaks overhead: a sort of dampening of sound. Perhaps against his better instincts, he looks up—and then it happens.

The clouds are kindled and lightning issues forth, severing the air, rushing toward the ground. The sky begins to whirl and spin above him even as the earth beneath. He realizes he is being thrown from his horse. Suddenly he thinks of old Heine, the cripple of Mansfeld who lost his mount and had his neck snapped, never to walk again. Denied a quick death, he lingered on for years confined to his bed, unable to feed or dress himself, longing for release from his lifeless body. *Will that be my destiny? Have I already walked for the last time, held a book for the last time, known joy for the last time?!* These thoughts pass by in a flash as brief as the lightning.

The next sensation he feels is pain as his body collides with the ground. He is lying flat on his back, staring up into the storm, the fall of rain merciless, the shock moving from the core of his body to the extremities. Then he hears the loudest sound he will ever hear in his life, as if God had once again rent the heavens and come down. The earth beneath him quakes. His ears ring—his head feels as if it will split open. His heart is pounding with the force of a fighter's fist. His very existence is terror. He is not certain if he is injured. The fear has so overwhelmed him that he can do nothing but—scream! Yes, the cries are issuing from him now: violent, desperate, pleading.

"Help me! Someone, help me! Please!" he yells into the void, but there is no reply. He is alone, without comfort in life, exposed before the elements and the wrath of the Almighty. He senses that this is it: the moment that will define all he is. *I must do it. I must make the breach.*

So, Martin Luther cries to the saint whose image graces the wall of that home he loves so well, who blessed the days of his youth and perhaps, if he is the most fortunate of men, will hear him now.

"Help me, Saint Anna!" he begs. "I'll become a monk. Yes. I will become a monk. I swear it! Just please, spare me!"

As the heavens wheel above him, he feels himself broken: chastened from head to toe, longing for absolution. And somewhere deep below, in the secret caverns hidden from man, comes a response, like the rolling thunder around the throne. A crack spreading in splintered veins, branching out across Christendom, driven toward an end beyond imagination. For not only he, but the earth itself will never be the same.

19 years later...

Spring

14 April 1524
Wittenberg, Electorate of Saxony

Philipp Melanchthon sits at the oak desk in his study, shoulders bent, one hand pressed against his temple, the other holding a pen. The hour is late, and the light has long since faded, but he is unable to find his rest. Thus, it was the previous night, and the night before that, and stretching back for weeks unending: the bliss of sleep withheld from him, his mind stretched to the breaking point, his body a hollow shell with nothing left to give. When he cannot sleep, he thinks—he remembers. The shadows of the past impose themselves on his existence: the questions without answers, the droning of anxious thoughts, the things once lost that can never be restored. Therefore, he sits alone in his study, waiting for the words to come, for the written word is the final recourse of mourners.

The blackened nib of the pen still hanging in suspension, his eyes wander to a book sitting on his desk: a Greek grammar gifted him by the late Johannes Reuchlin, his great-uncle and adoptive father. On the first page is a note scrawled by that aged hand—a message he has read a thousand times but can no longer view without pain. He feels a sharp pinch in his stomach. *It is out of my control: the man is dead,* Philipp tells himself. *I must carry on.*

He presses nib to paper, directing the flow of ink, shaping it according to the measure of his mind.

Dearest Mother—

We depart for Bretten tomorrow. I have matters to attend to here, and we must stop along the way. Camerarius accompanies me. You will find him amicable. I shall remain for about a month and take my rest. The Elector[1] has graciously permitted me this absence, and may the good Lord restore my health. I long to see you and the land of my birth once again. My Katharina sends her greetings, as does young Anna. Forgive me these years apart. They will soon be at an end.

Your devoted son,
Philipp Schwarzerdt

He signs it using his birth surname: Schwartzerdt, "black earth," the name dignified by his late father, armorer to the Count Palatine of the Rhine. Only with the woman who bore him does he use the German form. To the world he is Philipp Melanchthon, renowned scholar of the Greek language, champion of the New Learning and, since his arrival at the University of Wittenberg, theological brother-in-arms of the most infamous man in Christendom.

He thinks of a necessary addendum: he has not mentioned the possibility of visiting Basel. Joachim Camerarius, his dearest friend and fellow professor, is continuing on to that city and has invited him along. There he could be reunited with Johannes Œcolampadius, whom he knows from their student days at Tübingen. He thinks of the hours they passed late at night together, devouring Greek manuscripts with a ferocious energy. How much simpler life was then! He would love to see Œcolampadius, but if he is honest with himself, he would also like to meet another resident of Basel: the scholar of scholars, defender of letters, and beacon who has lit the way in the recovery of biblical studies.

---

[1] The Electorate of Saxony was ruled at this time by Elector Friedrich, often known by the sobriquet "The Wise." The title 'elector' indicated that he was one of the select group of officials who could vote in the election of the Holy Roman Emperor. There was at the time a separate Duchy of Saxony ruled by Friedrich's cousin, Duke Georg, as part of a complicated political arrangement.

Erasmus of Rotterdam! How I long to see you in the flesh, but I fear I must not, Philipp thinks.

He dips his quill in the pot again, then moves it to the bottom of the page, a single drop falling along the way. He begins to write.

Now a crash shatters the silence of night. A chorus of piercing screams rises to the heavens like a flock of birds in petrified flight. In the shock of the moment, he presses too hard: his pen slides, leaving a dark trail on the page, and the shaft of the quill cracks. He looks with disapproval upon the black streak which has sullied his parchment. *I will have to start again.* He mutters to himself, sets the broken instrument down, and rises to discover the source of the clamor, which seems to come from outside.

As he covers the few feet between his desk and the window, troubled thoughts race through his mind. The simplest explanation is that some students have been too much at the drink, but there are darker possibilities. The screams continue unabated, and he cannot help but think of the riots two years previous, when the students of Wittenberg were caught up in a fervor of expectation and driven to fits of iconoclasm, breaking into churches and smashing everything in sight, abandoning their classes, proclaiming the coming of Christ to earth in the Electorate of Saxony. *Karlstadt, is this your doing?* Philipp wonders.

He reaches the window but finds little to satisfy his need to know. It faces the road, not the buildings of the Leucorea—the Greek name for the university. He sees one person passing by on Colleges Street, lantern held aloft, but that could mean anything. Hearing another crash, Philipp has no choice but to investigate. The shouts are unrelenting, and if his two-year-old daughter is woken by the noise, his wife will be a mess of anxiety.

He strides to a rack in the corner that holds his scholar's cloak and cap, then pulls the black robe over his shoulders, sliding each arm into place. As he does so, the pain in his back flares—a deep ache clinging to the base of his spine—and he lets out a momentary groan. Recovering, he takes his cap in hand and departs the study, descending the stairs to the lower level, the wood planks creaking with every step.

Hold together, old house, he prays. *We cannot afford another.*

The "Poor House," as his wife Katharina affectionately calls it, holds not only them and their daughter Anna, but also their assistant

Famulus Koch and four students renting rooms. Here they live one on top of the other, a leaky roof above. He must leave them all to the slumber he is denied. Approaching the front door, he stoops to lift the lantern that sits there in case of emergency. There are a few inches of wax left—good enough, he hopes, for the need of the moment. He lifts the lantern with his left hand and uses his right to secure his cap in place. Then he opens the door and enters the world of night.

Stepping onto the cobbles, he sees heads emerging from open windows, all staring in the direction of the main Leucorea buildings. The street is lined with half-timbered houses on the opposite side, most bearing thatched roofs like his. They are lit by a faint glow, which fills him with concern. He has never enjoyed the dark of night, but the alternative—an eve lit by unexpected flame—is a truly fearsome thing.

"Fire!"

The word sends his pulse to flight. Did he think it or did someone else scream it? *Someone else, surely.* He looks left down the street, in the direction of the town center, and spies a group of shadows whom he takes for men. They are running around or perhaps dancing, torches held aloft. He guesses they have set a fire in the courtyard. *Could they also have weapons?* As his vision adjusts further, he sees that one or two of them have metal implements in hand, though how deadly he cannot discern. They cry out not in terror, but fierce exaltation. *I ought to go back inside,* he thinks. After all, he is unarmed and doesn't want to forfeit his life in a pointless fight.

As he attempts to calculate the relative strength of himself and the dancing figures, a voice from another age echoes in his mind like the shock of some distant eruption: *Don't you know that fire purifies?*

It was Andreas Bodenstein von Karlstadt who said that to him— his former colleague at the university. The words were spoken in the dark days of 1521, when Martin Luther was kept far away in the Wartburg Castle for his own protection, leaving those in Wittenberg to carry on alone. In that chaotic hour, Philipp Melanchthon found himself pulled this way and that, uncertain which path to take— indeed, uncertain of much of anything. How he longs to forget that time, for he was called upon to take up the mantle, and he failed. Events spiraled out of his control, and were it not for Luther's return, they would all have been finished and the work of reform ended. But rather than ending the threat, Karlstadt's departure has only spread his poisonous teachings—errors that Philipp neglected to recognize at the first. That failure and the fear it induced are a constant weight he carries, and as he watches the scene unfolding, he worries that the menace has returned. It is bitter in his throat.

Now a new figure enters the street on his left, approaching the swarming band of shadows and yelling, "You there! What do you think you're doing?!"

It is the booming voice of Philipp's colleague Justus Jonas, provost of the Castle Church and professor of canon law. Had the tone not revealed his identity, the broad shoulders would have. There is a sudden tightness in Philipp's chest—a constriction of breath. *I cannot let him face them alone,* he thinks, and summoning up his courage, he begins to walk toward Jonas, still holding the lantern aloft.

Even as he does so, he hears the distant noise of hoofbeats: a pair of shadows in the distance are moving toward the disturbance. They are guards from the Elbe Gate, and not a moment too soon. The prospect of a serious fight puts the fear of God in the agitators, who immediately drop their torches and scatter in different directions, cutting down alleyways or running back toward the school. There cannot be more than seven or eight in total, and one of them makes the mistake of running in the direction of Jonas, who without hesitation pushes him to the ground and pins him.

As Philipp walks forward to aid his friend, he hears Jonas cry, "You thought you would come back here and play a little joke, did you?! Well, let me tell you, boy: destruction of university property is not funny and I'm not laughing!"

"Who is it, Justus?" Philipp calls.

His colleague abandons the interrogation to greet him. "Ah, Philipp! Good evening!"

"Please let me go!" the young man begs. "We didn't mean anything by it."

"Didn't mean anything indeed!" Jonas scoffs. "I know your face: you're one of Karlstadt's disciples. Did he send you here to make trouble?"

"No, Herr Professor! Brother Andreas knows nothing about it!" the man on the ground insists, using Karlstadt's preferred title.

Reaching their position, Philipp bends over and casts his light upon the young man's face. "Conrad Voller!" he exclaims, recognizing his former student. "What are you doing here?"

"They broke the windows of the lecture hall, tore up the books, turned over the chairs, left obscene messages on the board, and pissed all over," Jonas complains, "and that was before they set the fire outside!" Looking down at Voller, he bellows, "How do you plan to fix it all on your non-existent salary?!"

"Forgive me, Herr Professor!" the young man begs. "They put me up to it!"

The provost shakes his head in disgust. "Just like your father Adam: passing the blame!"

One of the guards runs toward them, sword at his side, and Jonas pulls Voller to his feet, holding him by the collar of his dark coat.

"Who's this?" the guard asks.

"Good evening, Hans," Jonas begins. "I have here one Conrad Voller. He has perpetrated acts of vandalism on university property and is now subject to the Elector's justice. I place him in your keeping."

"Very good," Hans replies, grasping the prisoner by the arm.

The guard and his charge march off in the direction of the Elbe Gate, where Voller will spend the remainder of the night in custody before paying a hefty fine—or worse—in the morning.

"Off he goes into the waiting arms of justice," says Jonas softly.

"It pains me to see him brought to this point," Philipp replies. "He was a good student, back in the day."

"Back in the day? You mean back before Karlstadt convinced him that education was worthless and property was meant to be destroyed? Before they tried to bring down this university and all of us with it?!"

"Do we know for certain that Karlstadt is behind this?" Philipp asks, not wanting to cause trouble where none exists. After all, the man has just been subject to an administrative hearing, and there will be another in a few days' time. *I would hate to poison things further.*

That recent meeting featured an endless string of complaints, all of them tearing at Philipp's sense of self. "Who are you to judge me, boy?! You poured approval on all my acts, then left me to the wolves! What hold does that sorcerer have over you?!" Karlstadt had charged, granting the power of necromancy to Martin Luther. Philipp was forced to sit across from his former colleague and withstand this barrage for a full three hours. Yes, the situation is clearly precarious. Philipp cannot afford to make a false accusation when his honor has already been called into question.

Jonas places a hand on Philipp's shoulder. "You must not fear to read the signs, even if their revelations pain you. But I am glad you are here, for I will be spending the next few hours seeing to this, and I need someone to walk over and inform Martin."

"What—you mean now?" Philipp's asks incredulously, voice quivering slightly.

"Yes, of course. We may need to cancel the morning's lectures."

"He won't like that."

"Tell him anyway. Wake him if you must."

The thought of waking Martin Luther from his sleep is enough to fill Philipp Melanchthon with dread. *I would sooner wake a bear from hibernation,* he thinks, but realizing he has no choice, he begins to walk east along the road, passing his own house as he does so. He blows a kiss to his wife and daughter. *I hope you are still asleep, Anna. This world is not fit for babes to rest.*

Not far to his destination: the former Augustinian monastery, known as the Black Cloister on account of the monks' dark vestments. Founded by the Elector to provide a constant supply of tutors for his university, it is almost empty now. The revolution begun by Luther led the brothers to renounce their vocation, forsaking the path of righteousness by works. Nearly all of them found new homes, but the former prior, Eberhard Brisger, remains, along with the most famous Augustinian of them all. Here Martin Luther, the bestselling author in Christendom, condemned excommunicate and hero of the Germans, lives in far more humility than most would suspect, lecturing students and preaching sermons, and here Philipp will find him on this April night, hopefully in a state fit to see.

The cloister is in truth a dormitory seated back from the road, rising three stories above the ground and with little in the way of ornamentation. As Philipp pulls open the front gate and traverses the gravel path, he can barely make out the chapel on his right. It is a mere wood hut, its new stone foundation having been abandoned when the money ran out. In such a place, Luther mounted his campaign against the sale of indulgences: the one that would make his name known to pope and peasants alike. That was before Philipp's arrival in Wittenberg, but he came shortly in its aftermath and heard words that inflamed his soul and altered his destiny. *Sorcery? Yes, perhaps it was, but a rather white magic at that.*

He reaches the main building and walks to its eastern side, making out the green door with the light of his lantern. On the lintel above are written the words, "Ergo noli quaerere intelligere ut credas, sed crede ut intelligas," a quote from Saint Augustine's tractates on John's Gospel.[2] *Do not seek understanding to believe, but believe to understand,* Philipp translates loosely. The Augustinians have always loved such pithy sayings. He takes hold of the simple brass knocker and pounds it thrice.

A reply is long in coming. When he has just about convinced himself to knock again, the door swings open and a man holding an oil lamp stares back. It is Wolf Seberger, the only servant residing in the house. A man no older than himself, Wolf nevertheless appears grizzled, neither his cheeks nor his head having seen shears in the past year—perhaps not even a comb. There is a general pallor about his face, and he wears a simple gray tunic belted at the waist, a hole or two in his hose.

"Do you know what time it is?" Wolf inquires, an edge to his voice.

"Past midnight, if I am any judge."

"And yet you come calling."

"I must speak to Doktor Luther as a matter of urgency," Philipp emphasizes, annoyed that any lesser motive would be suspected.

Wolf grumbles something inaudible, or else his accent is too thick for comprehension.

"May I see him?" Philipp asks pointedly.

"Doktor Luther's in his tower battling the devil," Wolf finally explains, very matter of fact.

"If that be so, then perhaps I should assist him."

Wolf rolls his eyes and steps aside to grant entrance into the small reception room. Once the door is shut, he points toward the spiral staircase on the left and says, "Up you go then. You're a braver man than me."

---

[2] Saint Augustine of Hippo. *Tractates on the Gospel of John,* XXIX.

With a nod of thanks, Philipp climbs to the second level, exiting into the long hallway outside the lecture hall. He walks down the corridor, a row of windows on his right and a blank wall on his left. This used to be a gallery of icons—Saint Augustine, the Evangelists, and even shockingly Saint Francis—but when Karlstadt decided that all images were a violation of the Second Commandment and an abomination to God, there was a trial by fire in the courtyard and none of the saints survived their ordeal. Philipp briefly enters the Aula: the lecture hall where hundreds of students used to listen to Luther teach, though the numbers are now greatly diminished thanks to Karlstadt's agitations. Out the exit and into the common area he walks, passing rooms that have been out of use since the last of the escaped nuns moved out a few months earlier. *How did you get away with filling your house with women, Martin?* he laughs to himself, shaking his head.

Finally, he reaches the entrance to the tower: an addition to the southwest corner of the building that was previously the privileged space of the abbot. Around the time of the indulgence furor, it was granted to Martin for use as his study. *Was he drawn by the shelves of books or the private toilet?* Knowing Martin, it could have been either. Philipp knocks on the door and gets a quick response.

"I told you, Wolf, I'm busy!"

"It's not Wolf. It's Philipp," he says.

A brief pause, and then a directive: "Come in."

Philipp pulls the door open, revealing a circular room with dark stone walls and a wood floor. Immediately before him is an open spiral staircase enclosed by an iron railing, which could carry one up to the attic or down to the privy below. Save for two windows, the walls of this study are covered entirely by shelves, each displaying rows of books: the *Sentences* of Lombard, the commentaries of Aquinas, two copies of Erasmus' Greek New Testament, works by the Church Fathers, Greek and Hebrew grammars, Summas upon Summas, mystical works by Tauler and Eckhart. On and on they go, volume upon volume, a collection worth more than most men earn in a lifetime. But even this is too little, for there are stacks of books and papers on the floor, some scattered haphazardly. A line is strung from one end of the room to the other, and on it several handwritten pages are hanging to dry. On the far side of the room, sitting on a plain wooden faldstool before an oak panel desk, sits Martin Luther in nothing but his shirt and braies, his back to Philipp, poring over some document.

Without turning around, Martin says, "If you're here to tell me about the break in, I already know."

"They vandalized the hall. I was meant to lecture there at six. Justus thinks we may have to cancel. What do you think?" When his colleague fails to respond, he asks again, "Martin? What do you think we should do?"

With a sigh, Martin drops his pen and turns to face Philipp, rubbing his face with his hands. "Forgive me. My mind is elsewhere," he mutters, looking at Philipp with the piercing eyes of a bird of prey. He is no longer the man of skin and bone who stood before the Emperor at Worms, but some decent meals would do him no harm. His dark hair needs tending, and he has the general look of a man who has been under siege for far too long.

"Wolf said you were at war with the devil," Philipp recounts.

"Well, close enough. I'm writing a letter to your good friend."

"Camerarius?"

"No, Camerarius is no devil. I speak of the eel in Basel."

This is the title Martin has bestowed upon Erasmus due to the latter's tendency to squirm his way out of unfavorable situations, or perhaps on account of the difficulty of pinning him down on anything. Philipp swallows hard, the muscles of his throat constricting, for he has had premonitions of a dreadful collision to come: the two men who have shaped him most may soon break each other to shards. To avoid that strife is his dearest wish of the moment. Knowing Martin's general disdain for the Dutch scholar, Philipp fears what the contents of the letter might be. Erasmus prides himself on courtesy of form in all his correspondence and will surely take offense at any failure to return the favor.

"And is that how you intend to address Erasmus in your letter? 'Dearest eel, I have a petition to make of you'?" Philipp inquires, suggesting a lightness of spirit he does not feel.

"No, no," Martin insists, chuckling. "The niceties must be observed. I am not so crude as all that, no matter what people say." He turns back toward the desk, recovers his pen, and begins scribbling again.

Philipp sets his lantern on the floor and moves closer, ducking beneath the hanging papers and attempting to avoid the mess on the floor. *I would never leave my study in such a state*, he thinks, but he would never do half the things Martin does. When he is close enough to look over Martin's shoulder, he asks, "What are you writing to him?"

The reply is curt. "I am urging him to stay out of our affairs and leave the theology to theologians."

"He'll love that," mutters Philipp, his insides clenched. The last thing they need is to anger the most respected scholar in Christendom when they could very much use his support.

"You should know—you who are such good friends with him."

There is more than a hint of accusation in this statement, and Philipp finds it entirely unfair. After all, Erasmus is hardly the only person who has failed to embrace their calls for doctrinal reform, and unlike many others, he has steered clear of openly condemning the Wittenberg movement.

"You do know I've never met the man, right?" Philipp asks.

"If only I could receive such heaps of praise from men I have never met! Yet even the ones I do meet find something to complain about."

"Well, that's the answer then: stop meeting people. Keep that sharp wit to yourself."

Martin ceases writing again and looks up. "How long have you known me, Philipp?"

Philipp knows what his colleague means: *He cannot help himself. It is who he is.* It is a truth Philipp is loath to accept.

"Fair enough," Philipp concedes. "I wish we could get through to him—to Erasmus. I believe him to be a man of good character, and he is as devoted to the recovery of biblical studies as anyone."

"Yes," Martin muses, his voice trailing off along with his gaze. "What a pity he should lead us to the Jordan only to succumb to fear. I suppose it is his fate to languish in the wilderness."

"Can you not simply see him as I do: a great scholar, a man of letters, the one who called us back to the sources?"

Martin's eyes latch onto Philipp's again. He speaks with great conviction. "I do not deny his role in shaping our fortunes, but there comes a time when every man, be he great or small, must take a stand—must find something to believe in. I think your friend does not believe in anything."

"He is not my friend," Philipp insists, growing annoyed, "but he is taking a stand. My spies tell me he will argue in favor of free will."

Martin scoffs loudly. "Then he will have a hard time making his case from Scripture. Tell me one place—one place, Philipp—where Scripture says anything about this so-called 'free will'."

"Do you actually wish me to answer?"

"I don't speak merely to amuse myself."

Bracing himself for a verbal blow, Philipp replies, "Very well. 'Behold, I stand at the door and knock. If any man hears my voice and opens the door, I will come in to him and sup with him, and he with me.'"[3]

With this, the storm descends. Martin slams a palm on the desk, then gestures with both hands.

"That's not what that means! Of all the ridiculous things—"

"I beg your pardon, but you asked me for an argument. I did not say that I agree with it."

"I should hope not! That's the same shit Biel used to peddle: 'Do what it is in you, and God will not deny you grace.' But there is nothing in natural man but foulness and decay. No, no—I see that look in your eye! You must not chastise me for my treatment of Biel."[4]

Philipp smiles broadly. "I didn't say anything."

"If these people carry around shit in gold vases, pretending it smells of rose water, it's still shit, Philipp! I am not afraid to call the thing what it is. If this is how Erasmus intends to come at us, he is bound to be disappointed. He will suffer the same unhappy fate as the rest of the Pelagians."

Now it is his turn to scoff. "I hardly think that Erasmus deserves to be compared with Pelagius."[5]

"Call it what it is, Philipp. You will sleep better at night," Martin concludes, rising from his seat to see to the piles on the floor.

"Yes, well, that implies that I sleep at all."

---

[3] Revelation 3:20.

[4] Gabriel Biel was a late 15th century German theologian.

[5] Pelagius was a teacher in the late 4th and early 5th centuries AD/CE who denied the doctrine of original sin and argued that human beings have free will to avoid sin and behave righteously even without divine intervention. Augustine of Hippo was one of his chief opponents. Pelagius was ultimately declared a heretic at the First Council of Ephesus in 431 AD/CE.

Philipp stoops to help Martin, but is greeted by a cry of, "No, no! I have a system!" Unable to imagine what this so-called 'system' could be, he takes the chair so recently vacated by his colleague and accepts an upbraiding.

"How do you expect to sleep when you spend every waking hour helping students, never saying 'no' to anyone?" Martin asks, making something like a good point. "I should be with you constantly if only to slap these incessant petitioners across the face and bid them help themselves!"

"If I do not see the trouble, then why should you?" he asks.

"I dare say your wife sees the trouble."

He pulls his head back in surprise. "Why? Did she say something to you?"

"She didn't have to," Martin explains, tossing some of Chrysostom's homilies to the side. "Honestly, you can't keep this up, Philipp! If I were to admit every person who wanted to speak with me, there'd be no end—No, actually, I'd be dead. But what is this insatiable need you have to never say 'no'?"

"If I choose to help my students, where's the harm in that?"

"Yes, well, with you I think it's a compulsion more than a choice. That's what concerns me. I must protect you from yourself! But what is that wife of yours doing? I made her promise me when you were wed that she would put a stop to this."

"Perhaps she is more compassionate than you."

Martin rises, his arms full of books, and begins returning them to the shelves. "Philipp, if they're only going to pay you a hundred a year, you must only do a hundred worth of work and devote the rest of your time to your family."

"I spend time with them! I do!" he insists, resenting the implication.

"In body, yes, but not in spirit, I fear. When I convince our dear Elector to double your salary, then and only then may you work yourself to death—when your family is well fed." His burden unloaded, he flicks his hand and instructs, "Up, please. I must continue."

Exasperated, Philipp stands again, feeling very much as if he has accomplished nothing with this conversation. Then as he watches Martin settle back into place, staring down at the letter, he asks himself, *What is this really about? What does Martin fear?* Philipp thinks of the offers of employment he has received from universities across Germany, the way he tends to speak of his homeland with longing, the praise he has heaped upon Erasmus in the past, and the trials he has faced since arriving in Wittenberg—difficulties from which most men would prefer to flee. His fellow professor knows these things full well, and Philipp senses the true cause of Martin's poor mood: he is afraid.

"You know you're not going to lose me," Philipp says quietly. "I'm not leaving Wittenberg."

"I know that," Martin replies, not bothering to look up. "My whole life is here: everything I believe in."

"Of course."

"So, I'm not leaving, even if someone were to come along and offer me five hundred. You must know that."

Finally, Martin looks him in the eye, smiling gently. "Well, I am glad to hear it, for the Elector would hate to be robbed of his Grecian."

Philipp nods in acknowledgment. "So, what are we going to do about this mess?"

"Erasmus?"

"No, the lecture hall."

"We're not cancelling," Martin states emphatically. "Tell them to clean it up. Otherwise, they may use the hall here when I'm finished. We're not cancelling."

He nods. "I figured as much. I should go home now. Try to get some sleep."

"I'll sleep better when this is finished," Martin insists, readying his pen to write.

"Suit yourself."

Philipp makes to leave, then hesitates. He looks back at his friend hunched over the desk—hears the nib scraping against paper. He fears what it might be writing. More than that, he fears what a clash with Erasmus of Rotterdam would mean for the movement. Once, Philipp had dreams of what it would mean to have Erasmus fully on their side. Now, he has nightmares of what it would mean for Erasmus to become a deadly enemy. If Erasmus does write against them, it may well carve a breach forever unbridgeable. *And I have lost so many already,* he thinks. *So many...*

"Will you not let me read it before you send it off?" he asks a bit timidly.

"What are you afraid of?" Martin responds, pen still scratching.

"Nothing. Good night, Martin."

"Good night, Master Philipp. Steer clear of the mob! The Lord didn't make you for fighting."

This final retort galls Philipp, but he accepts it in silence and makes his departure from the Black Cloister, mind spinning with anxious thoughts. He is glad—even deeply relieved—to be leaving the university for a spell, but he senses the time away may do little to ease his tension. There has recently been a Great Conjunction in the heavens: not only Saturn and Jupiter, but all the planets of Pisces were aligned. Some say it means flooding on a scale not seen since the days of Noah, when the heavens and the earth were moved. Whatever it heralds, he senses that change is near, and change is rarely for the better.

What will become of us, Lord? he wonders. *Does the dream live on? Do they remember us when we've gone?*

14 April 1524
Basel, Swiss Confederation

In the publishing capital of Christendom, Desiderius Erasmus sits in his study, contemplating the state of the world. He is perched on a silk cushion from the Orient, his hands sprawled over the arms of an immense high-back chair carved in the workshops of Florence. The night is halfway gone, and he stares at the fire in front of him: a blaze which burns within a massive hearth decorated with tin glazed tiles, each displaying the Basel staff that is the symbol of the city. Beneath his feet is a Persian rug, and behind him the walls are lined with shelves bearing volumes from Venice and Cambridge, Paris and Rome, each purchased by the sweat of his brow. Here is a linenfold cabinet, there the desk at which he composes letters to send to every corner of Christendom.

As he sits in his thick ermine coat watching the fire crackle and spark, a phrase echoes in his mind: *All this could be lost.*

It is a thought that has troubled him for several years—a burrowing whisper that inflames the fibers of his brain. *How did this tragedy come to be?* First, a brief scent upon the northern wind, noticed only by the most observant. Now, an overpowering putrefaction poisoning all of Christendom: the rotting of society itself.

His eyes scan the room, taking in the colors and textures—the products of a civilization that has only reached such glorious heights after centuries of devastation. Everywhere he looks, he sees evidence of his life's work: bringing the peoples of Christendom together, recovering the wisdom of the past, forging a new and brighter future.

All this could be lost.

He shuffles in his seat, searching for the fine point at which his joints and muscles will be brought into balance. *When did I first hear the name Luther?* It must have been around the time the friar took issue with the indulgence trade. A common complaint in this part of the world—so common that he, Desiderius Erasmus, did not judge the moment correctly. He saw in Luther a fellow campaigner against the abuses of corrupt churchmen: another Augustinian aiming to restore the pure teachings of the Doktor. Every man of sense supported Luther then. But oh, how that name haunts Erasmus' every waking moment! How it has come to dominate his life! The battle lines are drawn—teeth and weapons are bared. Soon the Emperor and the French king will be at war, and what then for Christendom?

I need a drink, he concludes.

Rising from his seat in pain, nearly sixty years old and feeling every minute of it, he shuffles over to the dark oak cabinet in a pair of slippers procured from a Genoan merchant: far and away the most comfortable things to ever caress his calloused soles, but terribly unfit for outdoor wear. He opens the double doors and retrieves a glass decanter full of Burgundy wine, the liquid of choice for his over sensitive stomach. The decanter is not his any more than the cabinet. They belong to the master of the house, the celebrated printer Johann Froben, whose hospitality he has enjoyed these past few years. Together they forged one of the greatest partnerships in the history of printing: an alliance that saw him become the bestselling author in Christendom. Then came that ill-fated year when the world changed. *So ruthlessly fast!* He can hardly believe how quickly it happened, his friends and fellow scholars deserting him no less than the Roman Church, and all to follow a band of raving madmen who would bury the world beneath an avalanche of pamphlets.

Once he has filled a glass and returned the decanter to its nook, he walks over to his desk: a relatively simple piece of furniture with a raised writing surface and two shelves beneath, more useful for reading and correspondence than serious research. A few of his papers are still lying upon it. He takes a drink and sets the glass down, reaching with his other hand for a drawing of himself recently made by the artist Hans Holbein. In it, he stands at this very desk, a backdrop placed behind him, writing a letter to someone—Wolsey, perhaps.[6] He cannot remember. A large, painted version hangs in the parlor downstairs, but this is one of several sketches meant for friends who have never seen him in person. This version, he thinks, is far kinder than that in the parlor, for one cannot tell that his blond hair has gone entirely gray.

Will the recipient of this drawing know me any better after seeing it? he wonders.

No one holds a firmer opinion of him than those he has never met. The whole of Germany despises him, as do the schoolmen of Louvain and Paris. Perhaps worst of all, enemies plot against him daily in the Roman curia, filling every corner of the Lateran with their slander. He is reminded of the words of Petrarch: "The utterances of men concerning me will differ widely, since in passing judgment almost every one is influenced not so much by truth as by preference."[7] Anything he says to please the Lutherans angers the schoolmen, and anything he says to please the Pope has the Lutherans demanding his head. Not only his head, but his writings are in danger of destruction.

What friends he has see a better Erasmus: the man of letters and citizen of all Europa, the pilgrim unceasing and scholar ever teaching. He is the embodiment of his era—the name on every man's lips. They picture him at some great dining table with bishops and kings, regaling them with his intellect, conversing as easily in one language as the next, his fingers clad with jewels and his neck hugged by costly fur. He is every man's friend, a lover of peace, promoter of good education, humorist without equal—in short, the best of his generation.

Popes answer to him. Kings kneel before him and beg. Universities and the scholars therein are dependent upon his work

---

[6] Thomas Wolsey, Cardinal Archbishop of York and Lord High Chancellor of England.

[7] Petrarch, "*Epistola ad Posteros,*" in *Petrarch: The First Modern Scholar and Man of Letters*, ed. James Harvey Robinson and Henry Winchester Rolfe (New York: J.P. Putnam's Sons, 1898), 59.

to complete their own. At the dawning of a new age, he is the sun giving light to all. Blessed is the man who sired him and the woman who gave him birth! What can he not do and what can he not be—Erasmus of Rotterdam?

But he sees a version of himself unknown to friend or foe: one who barely set foot in Rotterdam. The bastard son of a priest, his childhood marred by poverty and plague, forced into a monastery against his will. Constantly striving, eternally wandering in search of a friendly home. Living on an empty purse, fleeing disease and war, pursuing knowledge only offered at great expense. Forced to tolerate the vices of the aristocracy and the arrogance of the monks, he works endlessly to gain the protection he needs to speak out against them. Plagued by a bad stomach and recurring battles with the stone,[8] seeking one cure after the next, feeling often more dead than alive, praying for one more year to restore good learning.

Few of his friends are true friends, and the less said about his family the better. He is lonely, stateless, illegitimate, and now the chief witness to a bloody tragedy: the destruction of all he holds dear. Some days he begs for money, others for companionship, but mostly he finds himself longing for a quick and easy death, the sooner the better to spare his eyes the sight of the evil done under the sun. What is more, he fears the revelation of all he is. In the dark of night, when none are there to witness it, he clasps his hands and whispers a prayer, wondering if it will ever be answered and fearing the answer he will receive.

With a sigh, he sets down the drawing and takes his drink in hand. He steps toward one of the windows facing the street, pulling back a red damask curtain to reveal the scene. The moon hangs silently in the ebony sky, casting its silver light over the earth. He hears the distant call of a barking dog—takes another sip of the fruit of Burgundy.

All this could be lost, and who will be left to remember it?

The self-styled reformers hack at the body politic with crude weapons of iron, not so much reforming as utterly destroying. He fears the outbreak of war, and what if these are mere birth pangs of

---

[8] Erasmus suffered from kidney stones on many occasions, which he typically referred to as a singular menace: "the stone."

an age of blood to come? How the taunts of those men reverberate in his mind!

Antichrist is drunk on the blood of the saints! A curse on all who support his rule! Even so he has heard them cry. *Erasmus of Rotterdam: coward of cowards! You set your hand to the plow but look back on Sodom with longing! You will share in that fate!* What exactly were they implying by that? Is he to be transformed into salt, burned with sulfur, or both? Were they aware they were mixing biblical metaphors? Likely not. *We will tear that mask off your face and show men who you truly are! We know your weak spots, and we will expose them!*[9]

He can almost hear them now, beating their drums and shouting their prophecies. *I actually do hear them!* he realizes. *Or at least, something very like them.* It sounds as if a great crowd is marching this way. He glances down the road in the direction of the noise, but his view is blocked by the neighboring roofs. The chants are growing louder—drawing nearer by the second. He grips his glass more tightly.

Here they are come into view: a band of twenty or so marching along Nadelberg, several of them carrying torches, one beating a drum, and the leader holding a book that Erasmus suspects is a copy of his Greek New Testament. The man is wearing a dark cloak with the hood raised. Even so, Erasmus can make out a long beard beneath it, and by the sound of his Gallic-tinged shouts, it is possible to identify him: Guillame Farel, an enthusiast who has taken to preaching a message of judgment on street corners, warning of imminent disaster if the city does not cast off the Roman yoke. There were rumors of protests this night, and Erasmus can guess their aim well enough: like their fellow radicals, this mob hopes to bully him into submission. *They will be disappointed.*

He glances down at his right hand, which holds the silver goblet in an ever-tightening grip. There on the smallest finger is the signet ring he forgot to remove after finishing his correspondence: a gift from a former pupil inset with a Carnelian seal. In the dim light, he can barely make out the features of the ancient god Terminus, guarder of boundaries, as immovable as the earth itself. *And yet the earth has*

---

[9] These final comments are a paraphrase of Otto Brunfels' words to Erasmus in a letter dated December 1523.

been known to move. For years, he has treasured the thing, taking it as his emblem and his charge, for it is Erasmus' dread fate to speak the word of the Lord: *Here you may come, but no further.*[10] He scowls out the window at the Frenchman. *You have crossed the bounds.*

Now comes a knock at the door, and he turns to see Johann Froben enter the room still wearing his clothes from the day before, a candle in his right hand. He is a man of medium build, the hair he still possesses long and dark. Not two years previous, Froben fell down a flight of stairs and suffered significant injuries; therefore, he limps slightly as he moves to join his compatriot.

"Still awake?" Froben asks.

"Yes, sadly."

"I came to see what was happening, but it seems you have beaten me to it."

Erasmus looks out the window again. The mob has stopped directly in front of the Froben properties. So close are they now, he can see the spit flying from Farel's mouth as he gesticulates wildly, waving his Bible about and yelling at the top of his lungs, "They ban the works of godly men! They persecute the prophets like the Israelites of old!"

Froben joins him at the window and asks, "What is all this rabble? A man can hardly hear himself think."

"There will be no need for you to think, Johannes," he replies, his voice thick with irony. "They have not come to reason with you." Even as he says this, he pulls the curtains together, leaving only the smallest crack through which they can watch.

"Who is it this time?"

Erasmus watches the man now pointing at their house with a crazed look on his face. "Guillame Farel, the latest gift of the French: a scholar of little note who managed to radicalize himself. When Paris finds a plague, they send it out to infect the rest of the world."

Froben snorts in derision. "I've never heard of him. Is he a Lutheran?"

"Lutheran...Zwinglian...Who can say?[11] Every man has his own spirit now and will be led by nothing else. This one has taken to gathering his friends and marching through the city at sundown,

---

[10] Job 38:11.

[11] Ulrich Zwingli was a major religious reformer in the town of Zürich.

brandishing his Bible like a real sword of the Spirit, proclaiming the wrath to come."

They watch the unfolding scene in befuddled horror, faces pressed close together. One of the protesters produces a small effigy of the Holy Father and sets it alight.

"What do they hope to accomplish?" Froben inquires.

"They are marching by all the printers hoping to make a conquest of them."

"How? By smoking us out?"

"Paper does have a tendency to burn, or so I've heard. But if there is one man they hope to cast in the fire more than any other, it is myself. Not a day passes when I don't receive abuse from these spiritual men. We are not safe here, Johannes. Not nearly as safe as we would like to be."

The agitators are dancing in a circle now, holding the effigy aloft. One of them lifts his tunic and displays himself to the burning doll, then turns to provide a full view to the house.

"Good Lord!" Froben cries in disgust. "Thank God the women are asleep! I had hoped you would find your peace in Basel, but it seems the whole world is intent on war."

Erasmus sighs deeply. "Louvain hates me, Paris hates me, and now the whole of Germany takes up arms against me while the princes laugh.[12] They had best be wary. There will be no end to the flow of blood once it starts."

"Erasmus against the world!" Froben proclaims, then places a hand on his shoulder. "Christendom doesn't deserve you, friend. Is there anything I can do to help?"

"Publish good books and hope the right people read them," he replies solemnly. "Education may be our only hope, and a faint hope at that. One struggles to believe in such times."

"Certain men may be more dangerous with books in their hands than without."

---

[12] Erasmus had previously spent time at both the University of Paris and the University of Louvain, two stalwarts of the more conservative wing of the Church. These universities were known for their strong support of the old scholastic methods of study developed during the medieval era, while Erasmus was chief among those promoting new education and research methods. Therefore, the antipathy was somewhat inevitable and mutual.

"If the man in question is Farel, I agree with you. I wish he would spend more time reading his Bible instead of using it to beat others! Truly, he is a public menace. I must have a word with the town council if any of us are to sleep again."

Froben chuckles grimly. "Perhaps he does us a favor, for if he did not keep us awake, our fears would."

"In my case, they are one and the same."

Farel is still holding court on the street. Though he surely cannot see them, the Frenchman cries in his thickly accented voice, "Froben, you coward! Be a man! Why do you censor the works of godly men?"

"Don't I have a right to print what I choose?" Froben inquires, pulling back from the window. "They have their own presses. They hardly need mine."

"They will say you are passing up a fortune," Erasmus notes wryly. "Nothing sells like libel and sedition."

"I printed Luther's works before it became untenable to do so. I have a reputation to protect and a family to feed. They may have no shame, but I still intend to be a man of honor!" Froben concludes, marching off in the direction of the hearth.

The mob has apparently given up. They are moving past the house and on to the next printer to be robbed of slumber. Satisfied that they will have peace for the moment, Erasmus moves to join Froben, who has taken one of the seats by the fire. Placing himself again on the silk cushion, he consumes the remainder of his drink and sets the empty goblet on the floor, then leans back against the carved wood panel, crossing his arms and staring at the crest above the hearth. In truth, it is no crest at all but the printer's device that appears on all Froben's publications: a staff with two crowned serpents entwined around it and a dove perched between them. He drops his gaze and stares into the flames, his exhausted eyes losing focus and crisscrossing, turning the image into an orange blur.

"Perhaps you should get some sleep," Froben offers.

Erasmus ignores this suggestion and laments, "They say I laid the egg that hatched all of this—Luther, Zwingli, Œcolampadius, Pellicanus.[13] They would even blame me for Farel!"

---

[13] Johannes Œcolampadius was vicar of St. Martin's Church in Basel and reader of holy scripture at the university there. He assisted on Erasmus'

Froben laughs softly. "I've heard of geese laying golden eggs, but you, my friend, are a rare bird indeed."

"Everyone credits me with far more influence than I possess. If men were truly heeding my words, we would all be sitting at the table of fellowship, feasting upon pearls of divine wisdom. Instead, they bite and devour one another, and soon we will all be consumed."

"I'm afraid the list of guests at that table grows smaller by the day: you, me, Pirckheimer, your English friends.[14] Who else?"

He shakes his head sadly. "I wish I could say Philipp Melanchthon, but he is too much in the clutches of the boar if his writings are any indication."[15]

"The boar? You mean Luther?"

"Yes, although in truth there is something of the mule about him. He's far more stubborn than the Pope—though they say Luther has moderated of late. That explains why all the radicals are flocking down here."

Silence falls. Soon the fire will be naught but embers. Froben asks the question that is on both their minds.

"Have you decided yet whether you will write against him?"

This is the matter that has consumed Erasmus' thoughts for at least a year. As long as the Elector Friedrich of Saxony continues to protect Luther within his territory, neither papal bull nor imperial edict can bring an end to him or his movement. There is always someone willing to print Luther's pamphlets, and always a legion of Germans happy to buy them. Therefore, the pressure has long been placed on Erasmus' shoulders, as the most respected scholar still loyal to Rome, to oppose Luther publicly and refute his arguments. The English king was among the first to admonish him in this regard, and the late Pope Adrian joined the chorus. Given that scholars of biblical languages and readers of ancient poems tend to be condemned

translation of the New Testament before adopting Reformation ideas. Conrad Pellicanus was a Franciscan friar and scholar of biblical languages who assisted on many of Froben's translations before coming to sympathize with Luther's ideas.

[14] Williband Pirckheimer, a lawyer and humanist scholar living in Nuremberg. He frequently corresponded with Erasmus.

[15] In the papal bull *Exsurge Domine*, Leo X famously referred to Martin Luther as the "wild boar from the forest" trampling the vineyard of the Church.

along with Luther, there is good reason to fear that the destruction of the troublesome Saxon could lead to the persecution of the New Learning itself. *And if I attack Luther, Melanchthon may turn against me, and any hope of preserving my work will be lost.* Erasmus' spirit is torn asunder, for he fears the consequences of any choice he might make. Day and night, they implore him—"Make the breach!"—but must the bridge be burnt? Can nothing escape the purgation of the hour?

"No final decision," he answers. "I implied that I would write against him to King Henry, but as I am no Englishman, he cannot set my head on a spike like Buckingham's."[16]

Froben smiles weakly. "You know I am happy to publish anything from your pen, but you may accomplish nothing more than angering everyone involved."

"Oh, that is a certainty, or as certain as anything can be in this life. But this much I have learned from Luther: whether in success or failure, living or dying, I shall be myself. I shall do things my way."

"If that were true, you wouldn't be writing."

"Wouldn't I?" Erasmus retorts, his tone grasping. "In the end, every man does what he desires. I desire not to meet my end at the whim of fools. Therefore, I write: I survive. That is my choice—I have very nearly made it. And when I write, I shall not do it to please the king of England, or the pope of Rome, or the devils of Louvain, for I cannot. Nor will I attempt to please Luther, or Œcolampadius, or Pellicanus and all the rest. Their disdain for me was sealed long ago. I shall do it according to my temper, in line with my usual manner, although there is nothing usual about it. I know well enough that Luther will be himself, and I envy him that freedom even as I despise his use of it. But perhaps if I too am myself, if I appeal to whatever good may exist in him, then perhaps he will be the best version of himself, whatever that might be."

"Ha!" Froben cries. "It would still be crude—that's for sure."

"Yes, it is his singular talent to mock and disparage," Erasmus acknowledges, nodding sadly. "He has no regard for my self-control. Before one God do we stand or fall. He will take his stand on his

---

[16] King Henry VIII of England, who had Edward Stafford, 3rd Duke of Buckingham, executed for treason on 17 May 1521.

vision, and I on mine. We will see whose spirit is true, if indeed we are not both sons of perdition. Terminus did not yield to Jupiter.[17] I yield to no one."

They fall silent again, both staring ahead, the weight of the moment a crushing burden upon them. In this quiet, he thinks, *You are not being yourself. You have never been yourself, for if you showed the world who you truly are, then you would learn what it is to be marked as a son of perdition.* And to himself he replies, bitter and defiant, *Only God knows what I truly am.*

15 April 1524
Wittenberg, Electorate of Saxony

Martin Luther opens his eyes, barely aware that he is doing so. A dark haze obscures his sight, then clears to reveal a wall covered in papers. No, not a wall—a pile. Yes, it was a pile on the floor, and now the papers are scattered. He realizes he has fallen asleep on the floor, perhaps for a few minutes but he suspects a few hours, and somewhere in that time he knocked over the stack.

Rising wearily to his feet, his limbs stiff and aching, he reorients himself to the room. Outside his window, the stars are still gazing down from the black expanse. The tallow candles on his desk have lost a few inches since last observation, but his note to Erasmus of Rotterdam remains illumined. It is his final attempt to avoid open conflict: a war long in coming, but inevitable nonetheless, in which he has felt himself as much pawn as player. A war that threatens all he has worked to create in this place so dear to his heart! The dark letters are coated in an orange glow that flickers slightly, as if the words themselves were things of fire.

The silence is broken by the bells of St. Mary's: one…two…three…four…five rings. *So it is five in the morning then,* he thinks. *Less than an hour before my students arrive.* He slumps into his chair, rubs his eyes, lets out a yawn, and recovers his pen. *Where was I last?* He scans the two pages he has already written, nodding each time he

---

[17] There is a common tale that the Capitoline Hill in ancient Rome was home to a temple to the god Terminus, and when the Romans sought to replace it with a temple to Jupiter, Terminus would not be moved.

is satisfied. Then comes the point where he left off mid-sentence, got down on the floor to read something, and promptly fell asleep. Here it is: "I say all this, excellent Herr Erasmus, to prove my earnest wish that the Lord may give you a mind worthy of your great name."[18] *But what was meant to come after that?*

He rubs his eyes again, kneading the lids this way and that. Colors burst and spark across his field of vision, igniting his mind. He thinks of Erasmus sitting on his high perch in Basel, surrounded by sophist volumes, no doubt eating the flesh of some waterfowl and sipping wine from the stores of Dionysus, showering the common folk below with biting witticisms. Such is his wont. The man has said it himself: Christendom is caught up in tragedy, and he has no intention of taking the field of battle simply to drown in the blood. He will make speeches in the Senate house but never descend into the gladiator's pit. *Well, go back to Rome then, if you love it so much,* he thinks. *Go dine with Cicero and leave the real work to us.* It seems his fate is to live boldly and perish in flames, while Erasmus will suffer a long rot of body, mind, and spirit.

He puts pen to paper and writes, "I beg of you only to be a spectator of our tragedy and not unite with our opponents, nor write against me, seeing I shall not publish anything against you," then scrawls out a few more lines for good measure, signing his name at the bottom.[19]

After making a copy for his personal records—a necessity in this case, he thinks, given the likelihood of false reports—he opens the lower drawer of the small cabinet on his desk, looking for wax to seal the letter. It is only then that he remembers he used the last of it for his letter to Duke Johann.[20] Always, he must write, defending the cause, preserving the fragile peace! Sighing deeply, he departs his study and steps back into the main building. Faint moonlight seeps through the southern windows, guiding his path. Passing through

---

[18] "CII: To Erasmus of Rotterdam, April 1524," Martin Luther, *The Letters of Martin Luther*, Volume 1, trans. Margaret A. Currie (London: MacMillan and Company, 1908), 122-4.

[19] Ibid.

[20] Duke Johann, often called "The Steadfast", was the brother of Elector Friedrich and his heir, as Friedrich had no children.

the common area and into the small lecture hall, he turns left and
knocks on the door of the prayer closet, where he suspects he will
find Eberhard Brisger.

"Eberhard? Brother, are you there?"

It is his old prior's usual habit to lock himself inside before students arrive, and sure enough he opens the door, candle in hand and
frowning. Holding the flame aloft to reveal a clean-shaven face full of
sharp edges and points, he asks, "What is it? I was only halfway done."

"Do you have any wax? I need to seal a letter."

"No, and our delivery doesn't come until next month. You'll
have to buy some."

"But the stores are closed," he mutters, mostly to himself. So
urgent a matter is this business with Erasmus, so critical for the work
of reform, that he cannot brook the slightest delay. He must seize this
final chance to avert a collision.

Brisger scrunches his brows in confusion, his weathered skin
pressing into peaks and valleys. "They'll be open after your lectures.
Can't you wait until then?"

Tension in Martin's limbs, flowing into his chest. *No, I cannot
wait! I cannot wait one instant!* But it is only a feeling, and what are
feelings in comparison with facts?

"Yes, of course. Thank you," Martin concludes, leaving Brisger
to his prayers.

Now he returns the way he had come and enters his bed chamber
to prepare for the day. *The world may be ending, and the emperor may
seek my life, but I must still change my clothes!*

'Bed chamber' is perhaps too grand a title for this space. The bed
is a simple pallet of straw covered in sheets that haven't been laun-
dered since Advent. The walls are bare save for a single window that
hints at a more colorful world beyond. The only other furnishings
are a basin and mirror, an oak chest far older than him based on the
number of previous owners who have carved their names on the side,
and a chair barely fit to hold a human frame. These are all cast offs:
items prized so little that they were donated. Such is the existence of
an Augustinian.

He retrieves a clean shirt from the chest and makes the swap,
tossing the dirty one in a corner he has appointed for the purpose.
Next, he lifts a porcelain pitcher, still filled with water from the day

before, and dumps the contents into the basin. He immerses his hands, rubbing them one against the other, allowing the friction to do its work. *Harder! Harder!* his mother used to chide him. *We may live in soot, but we don't have to look it!* He cups his hands and brings the water to his face, the chill seeping into his pores. Eyes closed, he uses his sleeve to wipe them, then looks in the mirror.

For a moment, Martin stares at himself, taking in the curves and angles of his face, the shadows beneath his eyes, the nose given him by his father. As familiar to him as the earth itself, they strike him to the core.

Ten years ago, no one cared what he looked like apart from Brother Hildebrand. Seventy years old, a self-appointed defender of the old ways, and as cantankerous as they come, Hildebrand would take one look at Martin's face after he had returned from a fourteen-hour workday with stubble on his cheeks and declare, "It's a disgrace to the order!" *If only he had lived long enough to see what a disgrace to the order really looks like*, Martin thinks, smiling to himself.

Now he has the most famous face in Christendom, his likeness printed in books and stamped onto fliers that cover the Empire as surely as the winter snow. Like it or not, what he looks like defines him in the eyes of others. This is an unsettling fact that he prefers not to ponder if he can help it. He has long since given up maintaining his tonsure, in the interest of saving time if nothing else, but he learned during his time in hiding that he hates having a beard, so he has become friends with his barber. *I hope you're pleased, Brother Hildebrand, wherever you are,* he muses.

He opens the chest again and retrieves the black cowl gifted him upon his return to Wittenberg. The rough cloth of the Augustinians is a second skin to him, but lately he feels himself torn by it. Pulling the robe over his body and tying the belt, he wonders how long he will continue to wear it. After all, the game is up. The monasteries are empty, their former occupants having taken on wives and taken up trades. Only he, the one who went before them all, is now held back. It must be so: if he abandons the cowl for good, it will open him up to criticism as never before and possibly alarm his congregants as well. *I cannot do what other men do.* At some point, he stopped being a mere man to others, though personally he feels his flesh more keenly than ever, and not only because he is fully middle-aged.

There is something hauntingly sad about this liquidation of his old life, not in the loss of the world so much as the people in it: the fellowship of souls. It hangs like a weight upon his frame, this silence, this loneliness. His name is on everyone's lips, but he feels forgotten—the last remnant of a dying age, a winged beast incapable of flight. *I alone am left.* But enough of that. There are lands to conquer! Since his return to Wittenberg he has done nothing but preach and translate the Bible, but this semester he is teaching students again, and they tend to show up regardless of what else is troubling him.

The next three hours are spent lecturing on the Book of Hosea, that strange prophet commanded by God to marry an adulterous wife as a symbol of Israel's harlotry. His audience is fifty men, many of them young and eager to marry, and he notes the horror on their faces as he describes Gomer's unfaithfulness: the line of bastards emerging one by one. *Surely, not I, Lord!* their eyes cry. *Spare me the fate of the prophet!* Meanwhile, he struggles to keep his own mind on the topic at hand and away from the prince of Basel. He is usually happy to speak to students afterward, but today he is restless, eager to seal his letter at the first possible moment and get it to Joachim Camerarius, who will serve as his messenger.

At last, he gains his freedom and marches out into a beautiful April morning, purse at his waist, ready to make his purchase. The sun streams down from a cloudless sky, but his mood is dreary. The letter is as likely to provoke Erasmus as dissuade him, and while he does not personally fear the arguments of a man who is no theologian, he knows how deeply the Dutchman is respected in Wittenberg and beyond. The Elector himself is said to be quite devoted. Then there is Melanchthon. *Oh, Philipp!* he gripes internally. *Why can't you see through the mist that man creates?* If he loses Philipp, the game is up. What the emperor has not managed to accomplish with his edict,[21] his colleague's departure would surely achieve: the work of reform would be ended. He knows it, and it terrifies him.

---

[21] The Edict of Worms was decreed by Emperor Charles V after Martin Luther's appearance before him in 1521. It called for not only Luther himself, but also those who taught his doctrines unrepentantly, to be arrested and subjected to the civil penalty for heresy: execution, quite possibly by burning.

As he walks by the old broken-down chapel and toward the street, he passes a pear tree now just past blossom. His thoughts are torn from the feud with Erasmus—there is a biting pang in his chest. *Staupitz!* Yes, it was here that his old mentor, Johann von Staupitz, convinced him to become a Doktor of Theology, directly under this tree. *Why? Why?!* The grief wrings his heart, releasing a flow of lament. It has been long since they were joined in communion. Recently, he received the first letter from Staupitz in ages: sadly, not an attempt at reconciliation. Like a second father, Martin had revered him, learned from him, confessed to him, relied on him. They went to war together. They shook worlds together. *I loved you,* Martin thinks. *I still love you, but I have lost your love.*

He pulls himself away, entering onto Colleges Street, heading west toward the marketplace. He passes Philipp's house. *How we will miss you these next few weeks!* His younger colleague needs the rest, but the university can ill afford such an absence. And what will become of Philipp while he is gone? *They will come to him in his wanderings. They will attempt to draw him in.* Martin trembles at the thought, but he must let the man go to receive him back again. He must have faith.

Now on his left, a flood of students pours out of the Leucorea buildings in a frenzy of conversation, some on their way to the library, some back to their dormitories, some heading out for a beer. *Don't make eye contact,* he urges himself, increasing his pace. He manages to skirt past them without being engaged, his mind very much on one object. *Every ruler must have his fool, and you are that fool, Erasmus. Ah, to be blessed with such knowledge and waste it on frivolities!*

Now he is in the center of town. The shopkeepers are sweeping the covered walkways while pots are emptied from windows above. He veers right to avoid a cart full of onions, then left around a trio of girls playing some form of jumping game. The blacksmith Ulrich ceases beating shoes long enough to greet him, and Martin offers a "Good morning!" in return.

Here is the town square, less packed than it would be on a market day, but nonetheless full of life. On the south side stands the town church, St. Mary's, its twin towers shining in the sun. At their base is a painting of the Virgin—a rare survivor of Karlstadt's purge. She looks down serenely as the residents of Wittenberg go about their business. Across from him is the city hall, which was partially demolished the previous year to allow for expansion. *Always breaking and remaking!* They say some day it will be a thing of beauty, but presently the construction is taking up half the square, and no one is very pleased about it. The pastor, Johannes Bugenhagen—or as Martin prefers to call him, Doktor Pomeranus—complains that the noise distracts the congregants from his sermons. *They seemed attentive enough the last time I preached*, he thinks. Perhaps the noise isn't the problem.

He crosses over the Lazy Stream, one of two waterways routed through the town walls. It helps filter the water, sure enough, but this is a university town, and in the cold, dark nights of winter, it becomes an open-air privy. He has made his way across the cobble-lined square. Five paces from the door. Then he is stopped.

"Herr Doktor! Herr Doktor!"

He turns to see the owner of this voice, a young woman with three gray kittens in her arms. She is Elisabeth von Mersitz, and with her are her constant companions—Ave von Schönfeld and Katharina von Bora—both crouched over the kittens' mother, stroking her fur gently. The 'von' in their names betrays their status, for these are all daughters of minor nobility who were forced into cloisters at a young age and have now made their escape to join the movement in Wittenberg. For an instant, he looks at the mother cat sprawled over the cobbles, another two kittens sucking from its teats. He thinks he has seen the thing wandering the streets these past few months, but one cannot be certain with the number of strays about.

"Herr Doktor! Did you get the pages I sent you?" Elisabeth asks.

A former Premonstratensian nun of Pomeranian origin, Elisabeth was discipled by Bugenhagen, in whose house she now resides. She has taken to the new theology with a fervor exceeding many of his male students, devouring her host's library of books and spending her nights writing poetry. He has seldom witnessed such enthusiasm in the housewives of Wittenberg, whether poor or rich, for the nuns are better educated than their female peers and thus more inclined to independent study. Somewhere along the way, Elisabeth found time to befriend his most brilliant student, Kaspar Cruciger, and their mutual intelligence is soon to be molded into an official marriage of minds. Now she stands before him, a woman of decent looks and superior wit, her eyes expectant and her arms full of squirming gray balls of fluff.

"I did receive them," he assures her. "I don't think we can get it into the first hymn book, but perhaps later this year."

Her countenance immediately droops, and it occurs to him that what is simply one of a hundred projects to him is, for her, the supreme intellectual achievement of her young life, placed into his hands in the hope of validation: "Lord Christ, the Only Son of God," a bold declaration of Christ's Incarnation and all its implications. Though he is no great expert in the ways of women, he senses that he must say something immediately if he is to rally her spirit.

"There will be another printing in Erfurt later this year: a far better one. Your hymn will be published—I'll see to it personally."

"There's no need for that," she replies quietly, struggling to maintain control of the twisting beasts. "I come up with these things after my nightly reading. I don't claim to be a great writer."

"No, it is a fine hymn! Truly, one of the best we have! In fact, I was going to ask you about a particular line you wrote toward the end."

"Oh?" she breathes, her attention now rapt.

"Yes, you said something that struck me. 'Kill us with your goodness.' I assume you meant, 'Kill the old man, enliven the new.'"

"Yes, of course! That's why I wrote in the next line, 'Awaken us with your grace.'"

"I see what you mean, but it is strange to think of the Lord's goodness putting us to death. Not wrong, mind you! You just made me ponder. We are daily showered with God's goodness, but the hand that heals can also wound. It's simply a matter of perspective."

"'He scourges every son he receives,'" she recites. "Forgive me—I was reading the Epistle to the Hebrews this morning." She sets the kittens down and shoos them back toward their mother, then rises to address him again. "Actually, Doktor Luther, I have something to ask you. Well, Kaspar and I have something to ask you: Will you marry us?"

"What? You don't want Pomeranus to marry you?" he inquires, genuinely surprised.

"Herr Bugenhagen has been a dear friend to me and a great teacher, but I think it would break Kaspar's heart if you didn't perform the ceremony. You know how important you are to him."

"The admiration is mutual. Well, if that is what you desire, then of course I will do it. When is the happy event to take place?"

Her face is alight now: as bright as the late morning sun. "Sometime this summer, whenever his parents can visit. It seems so far away. I tell myself to be patient, but I so long to be married to my Kaspar! Speaking of which, you know Käthe is to be married?"

He immediately looks at Katharina von Bora, who has ceased tending the cat and risen to a height slightly less than her friend's. He remembers Katharina well from the time she and several other former nuns spent in the Black Cloister after their dramatic escape from monastic life. They had been living in the territory of Duke Georg of Saxony—a staunch supporter of Rome—and were therefore subject to the penalty of death should they forsake their vows. The consecrated sisters had to be smuggled out and brought to the safety of Wittenberg. Since that momentous arrival, Martin has found Katharina to be a hard worker, intensely dedicated to her friends, but very forthright in speech. He has long hoped she would find a good husband after her family refused to acknowledge her.

"Is that so? To whom?" he inquires.

"Herr Baumgartner, of course," Elisabeth answers for her, smiling broadly. "He is quite in love with her."

Katharina's expression turns to one of horror as she exclaims, "Elisabeth!" and elbows her friend in the ribs. He notes the pink in Katharina's cheeks: clear proof of embarrassment.

"He asked for her hand last Sunday and she said 'yes,'" Elisabeth reports happily, paying no heed to her friend's objection. "He will make all the arrangements with his parents when the semester is over."

Not wanting to be caught up in any long discussion on the matter, he concludes, "Well, that being so, I am delighted for you, Fräulein. I hope you are delighted as well."

"Of course," she replies, lowering her chin slightly. "I count myself very fortunate. After all, I have nothing to offer him."

"Don't say that, Käthe!" Elisabeth orders. "You know he thinks you the most blessed thing on God's earth. What's more, before too long we might be hearing another ringing of wedding bells for Fräulein Schönfeld!"

His gut lurches as he looks at Ave von Schönfeld—not because she is any threat to him, but rather the opposite. From the moment that wagon arrived within the city walls and the Nimbschen sisters descended to meet the hordes of young men, it was Ave who captured more eyes than any other. The most beautiful of the lot, or so he has heard people say time and again. He does not seek to deny it. Her features are entirely pleasing, not unlike the women of fantasy that Cranach creates in his paintings. He also knows from their time together that she is the sweetest of the group: amiable, eager to please, patient, and kind. She may not be the greatest student, but she is content in any situation, and that is a great virtue. Indeed, he cannot remember hearing her complain about anything.

It was not long after her arrival in Wittenberg that his friends began asking the question: "Wouldn't Fräulein von Schönfeld make an excellent Frau Luther?" Brisger was the first to propose it, having observed the lady at close quarters. Bugenhagen was next, remarking on her attentiveness during his sermons, a feat difficult for any woman to achieve. Then there was Frau Cranach, who was certain that Ave's sweetness would "temper the bitterness to which you are sometimes inclined." As more and more friends suggested the match, he noticed the repetition of two words: Ave was always "sweet" and "pretty." Not clever, nor passionate, nor remarkable in any other way, but "sweet" and "pretty." He heard those words so many times, he began to grow suspicious. Why could they think of nothing else to say?

As he looks at her now, he is certainly charmed by her beauty and kindness, but he is uncertain what depths might lie beyond. He cannot deny that she would make him a good wife, or at least make someone a good wife. Many men would find her irresistible, but something within him recoils at the thought, and not just because he has no real intention of marrying at all given the sentence of death pronounced against him. He ought to feel drawn, but he is utterly unmoved. Whatever would need to catch fire within him has not. He thanks God for her beauty but knows it will never be his.

There may be no threat to him, but there is certainly a threat to Ave. One person promoting her virtues was nothing and two was a coincidence, but three meant there was a general rumor circulating. He wonders if Ave is aware of it—if she has any expectations of him. He is not so proud as to suppose she could be pining after him for his own sake, but he knows how these rumors take on a life of their own. *Might the expectation have spread beyond Wittenberg?* He can guess what his enemies will think: he is seeing her in secret, she is granting him favors, she is a whore and an instrument of Satan. No, Ave von Schönfeld must not become the subject of public discussion, for it could destroy her in more ways than one. Worse yet, Elisabeth has now mentioned it directly in front of the woman. *I will have no choice but to address the matter.* His insides are twisted, not from the thrill of love, but because he must endure an awkward conversation.

And all I wanted to do was buy wax, he groans internally. He has no choice: the moment is upon him, and the issue must be addressed. He swallows hard.

"Fräulein von Schönfeld—" he begins but is mercifully cut off.

"I'm going to marry Basilius Axt," Ave informs him.

He feels the shock of this statement ripple through his body, followed immediately by a wave of relief. It seems there is no need for him to have an awkward conversation after all. *Could the weeks of worry be over just like that? Was there never any expectation on her part? Am I free and clear?*

"Why, that's…" he begins, shaking his head and smiling. "That's wonderful news."

Wait. Who is Basilius Axt? he thinks. *I've seen his name on the roll. Medical student? Yes, one of Schurff's pupils. A fine match. Thank God!*

"Yes, I admit I'm rather fond of him," Ave admits, smiling slyly.

"Fond? You've spoken of nothing else for the past week!" says Elisabeth. "Honestly, we're all sick of it."

He senses his chance to escape. He must make his move before they begin speaking of wedding gowns.

"I congratulate you all and wish you well as you enter the covenant of marriage," he concludes. "Now, I really must be off. Forgive me."

"Herr Doktor, wait!" cries Katharina.

He has half turned toward his destination and now suppresses a sigh as he moves to face her.

Katharina stoops to pick up one of the kittens, then approaches him as the other two ladies bend down to pet the mother again. She moves near him, viewing him through hazel eyes, seeming to study his face. Feeling uneasy and annoyed at the delay, he grunts, "What?" Then bidding himself be courteous, he adds more cheerily, "Is something the matter?"

"I think so," she replies solemnly. "It is written in your features. Something is troubling you."

Now he cannot help but sigh. This was the tendency he noticed during her fortnight in his company before she found a home with the Reichenbachs. The other ladies were deferential almost to a fault, afraid to interrupt him or even meet his gaze. Katharina, on the other hand, experienced no such fear. She was respectful, true enough, but she had an annoying tendency of addressing him personally, claiming to know what he was thinking or feeling. What he found particularly unforgivable was that she was usually correct in her assessments. Now he sees she has not changed at all—still forthright, still overly concerned.

"You need not fear. I am well," he assures her.

"You do not look it," she insists. "There is a shadow over you: a fear of things to come."

"It is true that they seek my life to kill me, but that is nothing new."

"That is not what I mean—something else. But it is no business of mine. I just hope you have somewhere to unburden yourself."

His frustration increases with every syllable that escapes her lips. "I assure you I want for nothing."

Her expression is sad, and he can tell she doesn't believe him. This is hardly surprising, as he does not believe himself, but he dares not risk discussing such a personal matter with her. She seems to have a change of mind and holds out the kitten.

"Take it," she charges him.

He looks at the thing with trepidation, its mouth agape as a tiny squeak escapes its lungs.

"I have no special love of cats," he informs her. *And that thing looks like it just crawled out of the Lazy Stream,* he adds for himself.

"There is nothing like a purring kitten to banish anxiety."

"I really don't—"

It is too late. She has thrust the beast into his hands.

"Stroke its fur," she instructs.

Why do you have to be this way? he wonders, but realizing resistance will get him nowhere, he holds the thing against his chest and does as she commands. Immediately, the rhythmic breathing begins. The vibrations echo through his hands as the kitten closes its eyes in pure relaxation. He strokes behind its ears, down its neck, under its chin. Before he knows it, he is relaxing as well. He feels a warmth in his chest, and not just from the kitten's body heat. *This is wonderful,* he thinks. *I should pet a kitten every day.* Even as the thought passes through his mind, he realizes he has fallen into the trap: she was right. *Oh no!* He pulls his eyes away from the kitten and looks back at Katharina, who is smiling and clasping her hands together happily.

"Feel better, don't you?" she states more than asks.

"Maybe, momentarily," he replies, placing the thing back in her arms. "Now if you'll excuse me, I must purchase some wax to seal a letter."

"Take care, Doktor," she bids. "I pray for you daily. We all do."

He nods softly. "Thank you."

Off he goes to buy some wax to seal a letter to send with Joachim Camerarius across the hills and down to Basel, where barring catastrophe or conspiracy it will be placed in the hands of Desiderius Erasmus. If all were right with the world, that would be the end of the matter: Erasmus would release twenty more editions of Jerome, and he would get on with the business of reformation, their duel never to be. Unity would be preserved. One less breach, one less death.

But all is not right with the world.

17 April 1524
Basel, Swiss Confederation

Who would have thought that Erasmus of Rotterdam would end up in Basel? But who would have thought that Basel would become such a thing?

Situated at the crossroads of Europe just north of the Alpine foothills, the city named Basilia by the ancient Romans was a place of little importance until the previous century, when a new printing press arrived from downriver in Mainz. It was a small event by most standards of measure, but one which would cast a great ripple: a veritable shifting of the earth itself, rerouting the waters, taking life from some and giving it to others. Now the flow of the Rhine turns the mills continually, creating the precious paper that will carry ideas to the four corners of the earth. Rags morph into pulp, which becomes the stuff of dreams, translating the thoughts of one mind, one heart, one soul to be shared by countless others. The success of Basel's printers has made it one of the greatest cities Europe, a haven for intellectuals like Erasmus. Always the water flows, pushing out the old and pulling in the new.

Erasmus' host, Johann Froben, is sole owner of his business and four properties around town: the original house on the so-called Dead Alley, which serves as his printing shop; a bookshop just outside the center of town; a garden on Malt Street in which Erasmus has enjoyed many a pleasant hour; and the pair of neighboring houses on Nadelberg. These last have been combined to suit the tastes of Johann, his wife Gertrude, and their three children: Hieronymus, Justina, and young Johann Erasmus. Happily, the properties on Dead Alley and Nadelberg share a courtyard in the rear, which houses a stable and workshop, allowing them all to move back and forth without ever braving the chaos of the streets. It is here that Erasmus exits the white house with its green and red shutters, affectionately known as "Old Faithful." Dressed in his old traveling coat and boots, he meets the morning with something less than enthusiasm.

He takes a quick whiff of the spring air, drawing the air into congested nostrils. Sadly, it is more fragrant with refuse than anything floral. At least the rains have let up for a few days, so the roads should be in good condition. He is making for the city of Besançon in the County of Burgundy in hope of securing patronage, for there is no telling how long the emperor will continue sending Erasmus coin. Once the name Burgundy meant wealth, sophistication, and power. *At least it still means good wine!* He rarely travels in his old age, but this journey should be less taxing than some, and he longs for the relative quiet of the countryside. However, he must first enjoy the hospitality of Christoph von Utenheim, bishop of Basel. The troubles in the city have compelled the bishop to spend an increasing amount of time at his summer home in Porrentruy, where Erasmus will meet him for supper.

He is about to make for the stables when he hears a voice he knows all too well. It belongs to a woman, or at least something resembling a woman.

"Herr Erasmus!"

As he turns to view the housekeeper Margarethe, his mouth twists into a wry smile. She is of old Teutonic stock, her features rounded, shoulders and hips broad, flesh ample, and she delights in nothing so much as teasing him. Today she is clothed in an apron caked in flour, a basket hanging in the crook of her arm.

"What is this braying I hear?" he demands to know.

She takes her stand in front of him, free hand on hip. "There's only one ass in these parts, and it isn't me!" Having pleased herself with this retort, she extends the basket filled with bread, cheese, and fruit. "Take these vitals for your journey."

"You mean victuals," he insists, accepting the gift.

Arms crossed, she leans forward to make a point. "I know what I am, and I know what I mean. Now, be off and leave us in peace!" she concludes with a determined wave of the hand.

How he loves that spark in her eyes! He decides to offer a truce.

"You look exceptionally lovely this morning, Margarita."

Her demeanor changes entirely. She stands an inch or two taller, a mischievous smile on her face. "Yes, my bosoms are particularly ripe," she comments, throwing her shoulders back for greatest effect.

"How felicitous then that I have learned the lesson of Adam and will never take fruit offered me by woman."

With a parting volley of, "You are wicked, sir! Off with you, now!" she leaves him to his preparations.

Still chuckling, Erasmus lets his eyes wander to the other side of the courtyard, where the Froben print house stands, its four stories clinging to the slope of the ground, as so many structures are forced to do in this place of endless undulation. Within those walls, he spent countless hours editing his translation of the New Testament, candles burning low, fingers blistering with the effort. Nearby is a rather shabby construction: the Golden Brook, one of the few public baths that has survived in Basel after the invasion of the French disease. He has begged to have it closed on public health grounds, but the Swiss reserve the right to infect themselves in any way they choose. *A notion of freedom that holds no appeal to me,* he muses. His eyes fasten on the modest bell tower of St. Andreas Chapel, which stands just behind the stables, watching over the row of shops below. *We had best be off. Soon the bells will strike the hour.*

Shaking himself from his torpor, he moves toward the stalls in which six horses are kept, one for his personal use. He will be accompanied this day by two young men in his employ: Hilarius Bertholf, a Fleming whom he picked up in Brussels, and Karl Harst, a minor diplomat in the service of the Duke of Cleves who is finding time to serve as his courier. Frustratingly, it is only Bertholf whom Erasmus finds readying their mounts for departure. The young man has the look of a Burgundian duke of old: long nose, thin lips, and for reasons known only to God, a tightly wound chaperon upon his head.

"How are we doing?" Erasmus asks, setting the basket down on the straw covered dirt.

"All saddled," Bertholf replies, indicating the four horses they will use.

"Good. We have a long journey ahead of us, and I'm already in a poor mood. Where is Karl? Off taking a piss?"

"No, he's passing your notes to Professor Baer, as requested."

The notes in question are Erasmus' latest thoughts upon the matter of free will. This is the ground he has chosen to make his stand against Luther, not so much because it offers him an advantage, but because it will surely provoke strong disagreement. After all, he concurs with Luther that the Church must be reformed. He was calling for the monasteries to be cleansed and the theories of the schoolmen abandoned when his opponent was still studying law at Erfurt. If there is to be a collision, it must be over something of real importance, and preferably a subject where his divergence from Luther will be clear.

Therefore, he has relied on the expertise of his neighbor Ludwig Baer—a professor of theology at the University of Basel with impeccable credentials and friends in the right places—to strengthen any weaknesses in his argument. With every stroke of Baer's pen, Erasmus is moved closer to the moment determined by fate. It is gaining speed now, like a cracking flame consuming the previous year's stubble. All around him, the darkness grows thick.

"What's that?" Bertholf asks, pointing to the basket.

Erasmus tears his thoughts from the coming clash and answers, "Not content to poison us at the dinner table, it seems Margarethe hopes to kill us on the road."

Bertholf smiles, shaking his head. "Why does she vex you so?"

"There is something of the devil about her!" he insists, mostly in jest. "Far easier to let the devil into your house than force him to leave: so she once told me. The one time I ought to have heeded her counsel!"

Their conversation is interrupted by Harst's return. He is a lanky man with a close-trimmed beard and bright green eyes. More importantly, he is practical to the point of utter perfection, never dwelling in the past or dreaming of the future. The present moment is Harst's chief concern, and he will do his duty no matter how ridiculous the request. Such a man Erasmus needs by his side, if not to steady the great ship of his soul, then at least to order his correspondence.

"Ready to depart?" Harsts asks them both.

"If we wait much longer, you will have to carry me in a coffin," Erasmus replies. "My bones grow older by the minute."

"To the graveyard then!" Harst declares, opening the gate for his horse. "Or if we are fortunate, to the bishop's house!"

All is now ready for their departure. They mount their horses—Erasmus with some difficulty—and ride down the alleyway, turning left on Nadelberg and making for the Spalen Gate. The way is level here, the land unmarked by the great struggles of prior ages. Therefore, the old patricians call it home. The inner city wall with its stone arches, timber walkway, and small turrets rises before them. Without delay, they pass through the ancient wood gate and across the moat into the newer portion of the city. Already, Erasmus' thighs are aching.

Suddenly, they come upon a small band of people caught up in some tumult, their voices raised and fists shaking. As he passes at speed, Erasmus just catches sight of a poor Franciscan friar in their midst, frantically clutching his purse as his tormenters cry, "Away with you, you leech! Back to the devil who sent you!" It is a brief flash upon Erasmus' vision, but the harsh words resound like a constant tinnitus in the chasms of his mind.

"This is no town for beggars!" Bertholf calls back, laughing. "He ought to have known better than to wander these streets in the light of day."

Erasmus merely groans. He had a similar experience during his time in Italy, when he was still wearing the garb of a monk: set upon by locals, made to eat the dust. Those with little coin resent the notion that they should give it to others, even those upon God's errands. But the Baselers are under some appalling enchantment now. They lust after blood, bent upon destruction. *This whole city is about to combust*, he grumbles.

The road is mostly clear of carts here, and they quickly arrive at the outer wall with its far more impressive portal. Above the low archway stand a pair of towers, their stones alternating colors of white and red, between which stands a clock with metal hands reflecting the bright light of morning. At the summit, watchmen stand beneath a brightly tiled roof. The four riders pass underneath and enter the land of bakers, innkeepers, and cartwrights just beyond the wall. Next comes the realm of undesirables: prostitutes, beggars, jugglers, and the town executioner. Then at last, they are in open fields, the rows of vines stretching off into the distance.

"Fine weather we're having this morning!" Bertholf exclaims. "We should be there in plenty of time to enjoy your bishop's fine food—that is, if Margarethe's hasn't killed us yet."

"What?" Harst grunts, having missed the earlier repartee.

"Never mind it," Erasmus urges his associate.

He should be focusing on the business of this trip: he is hoping to secure further patronage in Besançon, though not if it makes him beholden. Instead, he is thinking about the notes he left for Baer. *What flaws might he discover?* As they pass over mile after mile of dirt and gravel, the words of the late Pope Adrian VI echo in Erasmus' mind as they were set down in writing, praising his talents and imploring him to defend the faith.

> Can you then refuse to sharpen the weapon of your pen against the madness of these men, whom it is clear that God had already driven out from before his face and manifestly abandoned to a reprobate mind, that they might say and teach and do what is not right? By them the whole church of Christ is thrown into confusion, and countless souls are involved together with them in the guilt of eternal damnation. Arise therefore to bring aid to God's cause, and employ your eminent intellectual gifts to his glory, as you have done down to this day.[22]

Some men could disregard a direct command from the Vicar of Christ, but Erasmus of Rotterdam is not one of them. He knows well enough what Adrian meant: *Either you are with us, or you are*

---

[22] "1324: From Pope Adrian VI," in *Collected Works of Erasmus, Vol 9: The Correspondence of Erasmus – Letters 1252-1355*, ed. James M. Estes, trans. R.A.B. Mynors (Toronto: University of Toronto Press, 1992)

with the reprobates. That is what the letter seemed to say, and if he could perhaps extrapolate further, the Holy Father was testing him to see if he too was a child of iniquity, given over to a reprobate mind and destined for eternal damnation. Pope Adrian was born Adriaan Florensz Boeyens, a Dutchman like himself. He once offered Erasmus a professorship that the younger man turned down.

How much did Adrian know about me? he wonders. *What did he discover about my past?* He sighs heavily, flicking the reins to bid his horse increase the pace.

Since his boyhood, Erasmus has desired freedom above all else, but at every stage, men have attempted to bind him with chains. He has never accepted these bonds willingly. He has fought for the right to study, publish, and speak his mind, striving night and day, sometimes openly and sometimes subversively, refusing to be bound to one location or patron—refusing to be bullied into supporting persons to whom he owes no debt of loyalty.

Thus, he clawed his way out of the pit of anonymity in which the mass of humanity dwells, mud beneath his fingernails, the anguished cries of those left behind reverberating in his ears. He pressed upward, chasing the light, gasping for cleaner air, drawn by the promise of communion. He had heard of a land of green—a place of understanding where he could feel his worth. Climbing, struggling, crawling up that purgatorial mount—for he was damned to go upon his belly—he came at last to his paradise, besting the feat of Sisyphus.

But now that he has reached this second Eden, he finds it a dying land. The tables he dined at are empty. The friends he loved have forsaken him. The flowers have wilted and dropped their petals so all that remains are ugly heads, bald and bent, without glory or honor, scorched by the very sun to which they turned day after day, longing for life. Now he feels the earth tremble beneath him. The ground ruptures and gives way. The hill is collapsing: his whole world is collapsing. He is clinging to the last bit of solid ground, praying that it will survive the remaking of the world, or else he will die upon it.

"There it is!" Harst calls, slicing through his troubled thoughts.

Sure enough, the miles and hours have passed, and before them is the city of Porrentruy, its thatched roofs and half-timbered facades nestled among the green hills. On one of those hills is the bishop's palace.

Within half an hour, Erasmus is sitting in Bishop Christoph's hall, a magnificent room some seventy feet wide and forty deep. Dark marble columns support the arched beams of the ceiling, which is covered in decorative wood panels. The walls are painted with red chevrons and hung with Flemish tapestries, and above the massive hearth is the great sign of the Basel Staff, the symbol of the bishop's power. On the opposite wall are six windows, each stretching nearly from ceiling to floor, and an enormous double door that is open to the outside, letting in the evening breeze.

Bishop Christoph and Erasmus sit just inside the doors on high-backed chairs, while the other ten or so guests of importance are scattered at tables around the room, playing cards and reading. Erasmus glances over at the man quite a bit older than himself, his thin frame mostly hidden beneath his white alb, black cape, and the biretta on his head. On one of the bishop's wrinkled fingers, held in place by a severely arthritic joint, sits the golden ring of his office. The two of them sip wine, staring out at the sky now painted in a stunning display of reds, oranges, and pinks.

"I am glad you could make it, friend," the bishop says, his voice rasping. "There are few enough who dare to visit me here, and I know how your condition worsens with travel."

"What do you mean by my condition?" Erasmus inquires. "Is it that my stomach rejects half the food offered to it, or that my kidneys throw stones with as much relish as the Pharisees of old? My body attacks me wherever I go, but if you had been in the city of late, you would know I am safer here than there. The Germans despise me, and there is a Frenchman in town who has solemnly declared that he will destroy me before the year is out."

"What happened to the 'Great Rotterdamer,' the 'Ornament of the World'?" the older man asks, using two titles the German scholars had previously bestowed upon him.

"All gone, I'm afraid. Quite gone. They are baying for my blood. Did you see what Hutten wrote about me before he succumbed to his pustules?"[23]

"I have no time for such rubbish."

---

[23] Ulrich von Hutten, German knight and Protestant sympathizer, who ended up dying of syphilis.

"Neither do I, but they are burying me under it," Erasmus replies.

The bishop reaches out with a free hand and places it on his. "You are the best of us, Desiderius Erasmus. You must know that. No one can match your wit."

"Who needs wit when any idiot can paint a man with the vilest slanders?"

The light in the bishop's eyes changes, and he withdraws his hand. The look on his face is solemn—even grave. "I know what it is they have required of you, friend—that is, what king and pope have required of you. They do not know what they ask: I can see it in your eyes."

A knot forms in Erasmus' stomach, and he is about to offer a response when they are suddenly interrupted by one of the guests—a tall and richly dressed woman who has evidently tired of cards.

She is Dorothea, wife of the moneylender Jakob Meyer zum Hasen, one of the wealthiest men in Basel. Like Erasmus, Meyer does not belong to the aristocracy, but reached his position through excessive cleverness. Rising to become chief of the moneylender's guild, he took advantage of a change in the city laws that allowed men from non-aristocratic families to serve as mayor. The very next year, he acceded to the office, just as the ink was drying on Erasmus' Greek New Testament. It was 1516. One year they had— one golden moment to enjoy the fruits of their labors before their world was shattered.

Meyer's fall was swift. He was jailed for receiving a pension from the French: a relic of his mercenary past that looked rather like a foreign bribe. He has only just returned to his fine house next to the town hall, and the path to power will be more difficult the second time round, for though Meyer is keen on the New Learning, he does not much care for the new religion. His wife Dorothea is a frequent pilgrim who is rumored to wear a hair shirt beneath her elaborate gowns and has never seen a relic she did not wish to kiss. Today she is wearing a white cap with golden thread, her blue gown cinched at the elbows and wrists. She bows before them, offers a brief greeting to the bishop, then addresses him.

"Herr Erasmus, I am glad you have joined us. The heretics have taken over the city."

Trying too hard, he thinks, noting that her nose is crinkled in disgust. *Your severity does not impress me, nor will it impress the bishop.*

"What is it you would have me do for you?" Erasmus asks, fearing the answer.

"The town council has asked for your opinion on theological matters, have they not?" she inquires.

"They have, but you should know my opinion does not carry as much weight as you might suspect."

She presses on undeterred, gaze intense, hands grasping the folds of her skirt. "They say you have something in hand against these false prophets—something that will expose them for what they are. I beg you to release it!"

Erasmus glances at the man sitting next to him, whose expression clearly indicates he has no desire to get involved. *You are more than capable of handling her, and I am a man of more than seventy in need of rest,* Christoph's eyes seem to say. Groaning internally, Erasmus turns back to address the lady.

"The Holy See and the Emperor are taking this matter in hand."

"They ought to be burning them!" she cries, drawing stares from everyone else in the room. "They say Luther is still alive and freer than you or I, pooping out his vile books, infecting the whole of the Empire. And here in the Confederation, we have heretics breeding left and right, denying the Sacrament and claiming men are free from any law. They ought to be strung up and burned!"

Erasmus clasps his palms together, the frustration burning in his chest. "Frau Meyer, the esteemed Fathers of our Church, when confronted with heresy, did not stoop to means of violence, and little good would it have done them. They defended the truth with their pens."

"Then wield the pen!" she demands. "Save us!"

Perhaps against his better judgment, he stands and looks her square in the eye, breathing steadily, speaking each word with fierce command. "I will wield my pen, but not on behalf of Clement, or Paris, or Louvain.[24] Not even for you, I'm afraid. I will wield it in defense of the God I know, and I doubt it will save anyone, though it may purchase me far more pain."

---

[24] Pope Clement VII was bishop of Rome from 1523-34.

She casts her eyes downward, evidently embarrassed by the force of his response. Timidly, she inquires, "Then is there no hope? Will the whole world burn?"

"That, good lady, is up to God, and who are we to stand against him on the day of his wrath?" he snaps.

When at last she departs and Erasmus returns to his seat, Bishop Christoph chuckles.

"Yes, yes, very humorous," Erasmus grumbles. "Be glad you don't have to deal with this sort of thing day after day."

"You do not have to worry about Frau Meyer."

"She has no sense of the pressure I am under!" he complains bitterly. "One minute of it and that ivory face of hers would crack."

"It is not you who will determine our fates, Erasmus, but men far greater than you or I," Christoph assures him. "Men who wield the sword."

"It is not only the defenders of Rome who fail to realize this," he muses. "For as much as these reformers fret over inane points of doctrine, they take no interest in world affairs, even though these great events determine their success. Were it not for the French attempting to retake Milan and the Turks hoping to seize Hungary, the Emperor would have put a stop to this by now. If Julius had been pope when Luther started making a fuss, the boar would have been turned into bacon: crispy bacon. If Friedrich of Saxony were not an elector, if his cousin had the vote instead of him, if the Golden Bull were written differently, if Duke Charles of Burgundy had produced a male heir! Or imagine if Friedrich had become emperor as the Holy Father wished! All our fortunes are shaped less by the novel workings of the Spirit than by the whims of princes. Luther at least is wise to this fact. He fights to maintain their support. But as for those who claim the name 'Lutheran,' they have no such wisdom. So curious about the spirits, but not a care for the world around them."

The bishop smiles knowingly. "My friend, they are agitating you. Don't allow them to steal your peace."

"It does not follow that if a man steals something from me, I must have allowed it," he objects.

The older man lets out a sigh, staring out at the darkening horizon. "You know how many years I have fought to root out corruption in this diocese, and how I have been opposed at every turn by men who claim tradition, but in fact merely seek a cover for their sin."

"Yes, of course. It is my fight as well."

"That was why I first brought in Œcolampadius. I wanted men of letters around me: men like yourself, unafraid to cut out the cancer. At every turn, the old guard opposed me. They devised the worst slanders against me, as if I were destroying the Church rather than attempting to heal it. Now what do we have instead? Men who do not confine their blades to the cancer, but hack at living flesh without sympathy, putting the body of Christ to death! Yet, I will not allow them to pierce my serenity, for I know their end. Let me simply be faithful to the divine Word. That is enough."

"And what of your reputation? Is that nothing?" Erasmus asks, incredulous.

Bishop Christoph looks at him firmly and speaks with a voice full of purpose. "He who surrendered heaven for my sake will hold me in contempt if I cling unnaturally to the seat of power or cannot bear the insults of men. It is a noble thing to be a bishop of the Church— the noblest thing a man can do in this life, but this life is full of evils. Do not work for the food which perishes, friend."

Now it is his turn to stare into the distance and comment plaintively, "If I can avoid the food that makes me perish, that will be achievement enough."

The sun is low in the western sky, a burning sliver of light in a sky the color of blood. In the distant trees, the starlings have returned from their wanderings, a cacophony every bit as dissonant as that of the theologians. The two friends sit together, final observers of a dying world and parents of a new age more strange and violent than any they could have imagined—so full of fear and unrest that it may kill the ones who gave it life. Erasmus' thoughts race and spin, chasing the end of day, desperately clinging to the warmth that will soon be naught but memory.

He has not surrendered willingly. He has delayed and equivocated until the last possible moment, loath to destroy his options. But the crows are circling—the appointed hour draws near. He has already written two drafts, and he has as good as given his word to the English king that he will print something. From the time Adrian sent that letter—perhaps even from the time he published his New Testament and Luther sent those theses to Archbishop Albert—things were always going to end this way. He only ever had the illusion of choice.

18 April 1524
Wittenberg, Electorate of Saxony

Martin Luther looks down at his tin plate, fork in one hand and knife in the other, ready to consume the single bratwurst that will suffice for his supper. His day has been such a whirlwind, he has only now stopped to attend to the gnawing pain in his stomach. As he cuts into the sausage, the sound of metal scraping against metal offends his ears, sending a shiver down his spine. Then he lifts a bite to his mouth and tastes the salt and spice, closing his eyes in exhaustion more than ecstasy. His stomach will thank him for this deed, but his bowels may not be equally grateful.

He is sitting in a large room on the lowest level of the Black Cloister: one that formerly served as a sleeping chamber for the junior monks. All gray walls and arches, it has now been transformed into a refectory with a pair of long wooden tables and matching benches, one of which bears his weary form as he eats alone. He gazes out a window at the garden to the west. The Augustinians are not particularly known for herbology, and those who lectured at the university were even less horticulturally inclined than their brethren. All that remains of their efforts is a scattering of herbs that should be long dead, but stubbornly return spring after spring, refusing to submit to nature's decree.

Perhaps they cannot admit their tenders have departed, he muses, *or maybe they are hoping to be tended again.*

He will not be the one to lend them life. He is far too busy for such things—too busy, even, for a proper supper. He quickly devours the remaining bites and washes them down with some beer, then rises to confront the remainder of the day. There is a meeting he must attend, even if the very thought of it repulses him.

Looping his leather bag over one shoulder, he makes to exit the building and begin his walk to the Castle Church, but nearly collides with an entering Wolf Seberger, whose arms are full of logs for the evening fires.

"Watch yourself, Doktor!" Wolf exclaims, steadying his load.

"Sorry," he mutters, shuffling aside and thinking to himself, *I did not expect you to be doing what I had requested.* It is safe to say that Wolf keeps his place at the Black Cloister more for sentimental reasons than sterling work: he is not whole in body and would struggle to find employment elsewhere.

"And where are you off to?" Wolf inquires, an air of suspicion in his voice.

"Doktor Jonas requires my presence at a council of war."

Wolf raises one brow. "Oh? And whom are we fighting this evening?"

"Doktor Andreas Bodenstein von Karlstadt," Martin explains ruefully, then mutters, "Like the gnats of summer, he returns with his fellows."

"I thought maybe you were going to say the Pope had come at last!" Wolf exclaims, peeking over the pile of wood. "I wouldn't let them set you alight if it's the last thing I do!"

"If he were in town, this would not be the first you would have heard of it."

"Ha! No one tells me anything around here."

"Your place in the chain of information must be discussed at a later date, for I am expected."

"Well, then, be off," Wolf concludes, making to depart. He yells over his shoulder, "You know what they say, Doktor: better the evil you know!"

"That remains to be seen," he whispers, stepping out into an evening that disagrees with him exceedingly.

There is a chill in the air as Martin walks down Colleges Street—more so than one would expect for mid-April—and he cannot help wondering if the swarming gnats have something to do with it. *Better the evil I know?* He is far more knowledgeable about evil than any man could prefer. He has felt the devil's presence following behind him, a figure dark and immense that sent hot breath down his neck and imbued his thoughts with terror. That is the evil he knows: a prowling menace that seeks to devour him at every turn. Always the sentence of death colors his existence. Always the devil does his work.

Passing the Melanchthon home, he sees Katharina and her daughter, Anna, squatting down in front of the entrance, sorting flowers between two different baskets. Truthfully, the mother is sorting, and the daughter is scattering. The sight of them strikes Martin acutely. He had a plan once. It ought to have worked. They would get Philipp settled with a wife and children. He would be tied to the university, the town, the Elector. All Philipp's needs would be provided for—he would want for nothing else. Whenever the emperor finally got around to killing Martin, Philipp could take up the mantle. It was decided. The plan was perfect: a kind of final testament.

Then when the hour came and Martin was snatched away, another put himself forward. It was not Philipp, but Karlstadt who seized command. How his words worked Philipp's heart like a lump of clay! It provoked a strange fire in the young man, such that even after Martin returned, nothing has been quite the same. Everything seems so fragile—utterly, perilously contingent. And now Philipp has left Wittenberg. *Will he return the same?* But he must put these thoughts aside.

"Good evening, Frau Melanchthon!" Martin calls.

His colleague's wife is a woman in her late twenties, blond hair mostly hidden beneath a white scarf, her face and manners pleasant. She has only two flaws he can discern, if one can call them that. First, she is as likely as her husband to surrender income to every conceivable beggar. Second, her embroidery skills are not matched by any such acumen in the kitchen. A pity, for Philipp must eat.

"Good evening, Doktor Luther!" Katharina calls in return, standing and grabbing her young daughter by the hand.

"Is all well in Philipp's absence?" he asks tentatively.

"Yes, but we miss him terribly," she admits. "Koch takes good care of us, and my mother comes every day. We want for nothing but his company. Still, I rejoice that he can see his family and the place of his birth after so many years. I know how much it means to him."

Her words are a terrible reminder that unlike most of those at the university, Philipp is not a son of Saxony. He has other allegiances: loyalties that may pull him one way or another.

"Very good," he says with a nod. "I am sorry he must be away for so long."

"Don't worry, Herr Doktor. He will be teaching Greek again soon!" Katharina assures him, smiling broadly.

That is not exactly what I meant, Martin thinks, but has no time to correct her. He is afraid to voice his true concern: that Philipp has departed the realm of safety and entered a land of raptors anxious to grasp him in their talons. Shoulders slumped, Martin continues walking west, his thoughts returning to the difficult conversation ahead.

The matter ought to have been settled by now. About a year earlier, Doktor Karlstadt abandoned his teaching duties at the university and his responsibilities as archdeacon of the All Saints' Foundation to pursue life as a small town preacher and peasant farmer, thus angering the Elector, who hates to pay for work not completed. There was a meeting two weeks ago between Karlstadt, Jonas, and Melanchthon at which they hoped to settle things quietly, but negotiations faltered when the parties discovered their versions of events differed, especially regarding Karlstadt's takeover of the pastorate in Orlamünde.

Now there will be a full disciplinary hearing with representatives of the Elector, the theology department, and the law department present. Despite his strenuous objections, Doktor Martin Luther is among those summoned. *This is exactly what Karlstadt wants. It is probably why he refused to give a straight answer at the first meeting,* he groans inwardly. *He longs to fight me man to man, and preferably before a large audience.* Instead, they will all meet in private at the electoral castle. That, at least, is a blessing. *And to think we once stood shoulder to shoulder, we who now spar fist to fist.*

As he passes the inn near the town square, he sees two friends seated at a table outside. One is the court painter Lucas Cranach, the chief source of illustrations for his books, and the other is Johannes Bugenhagen, who the previous year took on primary teaching duties at the city church, relieving Martin of some of the burden he had carried since the death of Simon Heins. The difference in appearance is stark: while Bugenhagen is clothed in a simple black scholar's robe and cap, Cranach wears a richly embroidered scarlet cape over his green coat and matching hose. A gold chain hangs across his chest, a velvet cap with an ostrich plume adorns his head, and a meticulously shaped beard projects from his chin.

"Martin!" Cranach calls, a leg of meat in one hand and a mug of beer in the other. "Come drink with us!"

"Thank you," he replies, "but I am being dragged against my will to meet with Doktor Karlstadt."

"I thought they put an end to that earlier this month," says Bugenhagen, turning to face Martin.

Exasperated, he continued, "It was meant to be a simple question: 'Will you live in Wittenberg and teach at the university or live in Orlamünde and pastor the church?' He cannot do both, but that has not kept him from trying."

"Karlstadt clearly wants nothing to do with the Leucorea, or any university for that matter!" argues Bugenhagen, scowling at the thought of it.

"No, but he wants us to publish his books—rather presumptuous considering he convinced so many students to leave that we almost had to shut the whole thing down," Martin grumbles. "And he has his own printer in Jena now. I've read his pamphlets. All pleasure is a sin. Let go of human attachments. Love God alone: love of others is idolatry. That's what he claims. One can only imagine what his poor wife thinks." *And on top of it all, he has placed a spell on Philipp,* he thinks, but fears to speak the words.

Tiring of the subject, or perhaps hoping to distract him from anger, Cranach implores, "When Doktor Melanchthon returns, you must help me convince him to have his likeness painted!"

"I don't imagine we would have much success. He's a very private person," Martin explains. Again, Philipp's name rings within his mind, forever reverberating like a church bell heard upon a distant hill. To think of Philipp is to think of Karlstadt, and equally to think of Erasmus. "In any case, I must be off. They are waiting on me."

"One last thing," calls Bugenhagen, raising a finger. "I greatly appreciated your recent exposition of the story of Jacob. I've had many favorable comments about it, and I know how much time you devote to these things."

"Thank you," he concludes, "for the kind words, and for your own faithful ministry to the congregation."

Martin makes to walk away, but as usual, Bugenhagen must speak at length.

"I had never quite thought about it that way before: how God condescended to wrestle with him. Is it not strange? Assuming it was God, of course."

"Infinitely strange. Now, if you'll forgive me, I must be going," Martin concludes, his voice strained.

"Go with God, and steer clear of the devil!" Cranach charges him.

With a heavy sigh, Martin takes the remaining steps toward the Castle Church, home of the All Saints' Foundation, pondering Bugenhagen's comments. So desperate was he to extricate himself from conversation, he can only now appreciate the sentiment.

How reluctant he was to take up the preaching office! How it filled him with fear and trembling to know he must speak the very words of God, breathed out by the Spirit, which communicate grace to the faithful and harden the children of wrath! To know that he would be judged for every careless word, and no false deed would go unpunished!

He gave his life to the flock entrusted him by God, and for their protection he stood before a cardinal and an emperor to bear witness to the truth.[25] He descended into hell on their behalf, undergoing the fiercest temptations, enduring the bitter heat of purging fire to translate the Holy Scriptures for them to read.

But even as he was doing this, another proclaimed himself their shepherd: one who thought more of himself than the sheep. He rushed them forward to drink, leaving the weak ones behind. He forced food into their mouths for which they were not prepared, choking them in the process. He gave no thought to their protection and left them vulnerable to wolves.

While Martin suffered for the sheep alone, this other sought the glory, so caught up in visions of theological grandeur that he forgot the most basic task of a shepherd is to strengthen the hands that are weak and bind up the knees that are feeble. Instead, he placed the very body of Christ in hands that could not bear the weight, subjecting the sheep to the fear and trembling that he himself refused. And now Karlstadt seeks in Orlamünde the authority he was ultimately denied in Wittenberg. *He has not gone there to wield a scythe, but a scepter.*

It was so different in the beginning. When Martin arrived at the Leucorea, Karlstadt was among the first to embrace him literally

---

[25] When Martin Luther was first suspected of heresy, he was questioned in Augsburg by Cardinal Thomas Cajetan, who stood as representative for Pope Leo X. Three years later, after his formal excommunication, Luther was called to appear before the Holy Roman Emperor, Charles V, the chief secular authority in the land.

and figuratively. For a while, the two stood side by side, enduring the world's scorn together. Then came a slow drip that built into a torrent: the fierce current of Karlstadt's anger broke through every barrier Martin tried in haste to construct. It overcame all in its path, sweeping even Philipp Melanchthon off toward an inevitable fall. It was all Martin could do to save one of them. Now, he must wrestle with the other.

The tower of the Castle Church looms overhead, and before him stand a pair of oak doors so weathered by years of rain that they have begun to rot at the corners. They are covered in paper notices: jobs sought and offered, official decrees of the Elector, and one scrap that simply reads, "I love Elisa." There are also announcements of upcoming debates at the university, one of which he posted last week. He has added countless others on behalf of himself and his students over the past decade and a half, posting them at both the Castle Church and the parish church of St. Mary's in line with university policy.

Once, seven years earlier, he was informed that a debate could not take place, as he had failed to post notice at the Castle Church. In fact, the announcement had been stolen and printed without his knowledge in Leipzig, Nuremberg, and Basel. That all seems an eternity ago. With a deep breath, he opens the right-hand door and enters the church that is home to the Elector's vast relic collection and an ever-decreasing number of canons still loyal to Rome.

The church has a decent sized nave but lacks the endless chapels one finds in cathedrals. High above, the vaulting frames a series of windows through which the late afternoon sun streams downward. This church used to be full of pilgrims moving slowly from niche to niche, stopping to pray before every severed finger of a saint or fragment of the True Cross. Now the relics are hidden away, the trade in indulgences mercifully ended.

By the door across the nave, his colleagues Justus Jonas and Nikolaus von Amsdorf stand with arms crossed, presumably waiting to be called into the great hall of the Elector's castle, where the meeting is to be held. Amsdorf is the same age as Martin and a colleague in the school of theology, a man of medium build with deep set eyes, a rounded nose, and a prominent jawline covered in a beard, whereas Jonas is a decade younger than them both and a good bit taller than Amsdorf, no trace of hair on his face but a short fall of curls beneath his cap. Beckoning with a hand that seems somehow too large for his body, Jonas draws Martin across the stone tiles, where he forms a circle with the others.

"Good evening," Jonas and Amsdorf offer simultaneously.

"Good evening," Martin mutters without a hint of pleasure, looking squarely at Jonas. "Remind me why I'm here."

The provost squints ever so slightly, signaling his confusion. "You are chair of theology."

"This is an administrative issue, not a theological one," Martin insists, *As I've been arguing since the first time you mentioned it.*

"That remains to be seen," Jonas concludes.

"You're here because Melanchthon already tried to crack the nut and could not do it," Amsdorf states matter-of-factly.

With a roll of the eyes, Jonas stresses, "You're here because the Elector wants you to be, and that is the end of the matter! Just try not to say too much."

"I thought I'd made myself clear," Martin replies. "I don't want to say anything. But why summon me if I am to remain mute?"

Jonas sighs in exasperation. "Look, none of us want to be here. We must make the best of it. I'll buy you both a drink when we're through."

Even as he says this, the door to the hall opens and a middle-aged man in fine clothing sticks his head through and announces, "Gentlemen, we are ready for you." It is Gregor Brück, electoral chancellor and legal councilor for the town. He has been involved in the Karlstadt affair for some time and will serve as the voice of the Elector at the meeting.

Jonas looks at the other two and mutters, "Let's get this over with."

They enter the hall of the Elector's castle, a room fifty feet by a hundred, its dark ribbed vaulting contrasted with white plaster. The lower walls are covered in linenfold paneling and decorated with heraldry. A suit of armor is displayed in each of the four corners of the room, halberd and all. Between the windows on the western wall, an assortment of weapons are mounted, mostly swords but some arquebuses as well.

Seated in one of six faldstools around a single round table is Andreas Bodenstein von Karlstadt, dressed in the simple gray tunic and felt hat of a peasant—but he is no peasant. This has merely been his preferred costume of late as he has sought the inspiration of the Spirit poured out on the common man rather than the type of wisdom one gains from books. He has let his beard grow, which unlike the rest of his blond hair includes a surprising amount of red. He is thoroughly out of place in this hall that is a testament to the martial power of the Elector, but it does not seem to bother him. He is leaning back in the chair, arms and legs crossed, his blue eyes immediately fastening on Martin and a sly smile spreading across his face.

Martin looks into Karlstadt's eyes, searching them desperately. *Where is the man I once knew?* There was a time when those eyes looked upon him with a steady confidence, ready to pass down the teachings for which Martin had come to the university. It was Karlstadt who was the senior then, and he never let Martin forget it. But there was no wrath in Karlstadt's spirit in those days, and when Martin came to see the light of biblical revelation, his colleague's vision became utterly rapt, looking to Martin with the fervor of one upon the brink of something transcendent. Long hours they spent sitting together, blowing the dust off volume after volume, turning the leaves of vellum as if any delay would cost them everything. And Philipp was there too, the three of them forming a triune mind of unquenchable curiosity.

But there is no hint of affection in Karlstadt's gaze now. The cords of communion have been irreversibly snapped, their minds now thoroughly at odds. *How did it all go wrong?*

"Doktor Karlstadt," Jonas mutters in recognition as they approach. When the man responds with a polite nod, Jonas asks, "How is Anna?"

By this he means Anna von Machau, the barely pubescent daughter of a minor nobleman to whom Karlstadt attached himself in wedlock two years ago. He was among the first clerics to take this step, declaring vows of celibacy to be extrabiblical impositions on the conscience. Even if he did intend to marry, Martin does not think he could take on a woman who is essentially a girl. He wonders if Karlstadt sought an aristocratic wife or simply one he could easily control. In any case, they were married sure enough, and she has borne him a son.

"Excellent," Karlstadt informs them. "She is excellent."

When they are all seated, Brück begins speaking, shuffling a series of papers on the table before him. "Doktor Karlstadt, we are called here to discuss the matter of your employment. You are archdeacon of the Foundation of All Saints and professor of theology at the Leucorea, both of which exist under the authority of Elector Friedrich of Saxony. From these, you draw an annual salary in exchange for performing your duties. However, in May of last year, you took up the pastorate of Orlamünde, a benefice of the Foundation of All Saints, without appointing any person to fulfill your duties here in Wittenberg."

Throughout this speech, Karlstadt has been staring at Martin, and it is only when he must answer that he bothers to look at Brück. "There is no rule that says I cannot hold both positions at the same time," he states.

Jonas retorts, "I think you will find that the rule in question is that of human embodiment, which precludes you from being in two places at once."

"It is nowhere written that I must be present," Karlstadt objects.

"But it is written that a substitute must be appointed in your place to teach your classes and serve the Foundation," Jonas insists, leaning upon the table.

"How can I appoint a substitute when you will only refuse any person I suggest?" Karlstadt asks, clearly annoyed. "You ban me from preaching, refuse to print my books—"

"You cannot expect the university to promote your work when you have publicly defamed it, causing no little damage to its reputation and finances!" Jonas states emphatically.

Karlstadt pushes up on the arms of his chair. "But you will not let me print anywhere in the Elector's territories!"

Jonas bristles. "Is that any wonder when you have caused such trouble for the Elector?"

"How have I caused trouble?!" Karlstadt demands to know. "I have always shown him respect!"

Brück holds up a hand for silence, which he miraculously receives. He then begins reading from a page on top of the stack he has formed. "Let us review. In 1515, when the Elector gave you leave to study in Italy, you stayed longer than agreed and failed to appoint anyone to take up your duties. You only returned to Germany when threatened with imprisonment. In 1517, you confirmed a priest to the

Orlamünde parish without the Elector's permission. Then in 1521, you repeatedly introduced religious innovations in violation of the Elector's command, so that the whole territory was threatened with imperial visitation. Do you not recall any of this?" Brück asks, looking directly in Karlstadt's eyes, which are rolling in disgust.

"I could provide you with a good explanation in each case!" Karlstadt insists.

Unbowed, Brück continues reading. "And just this past year, you personally took on the pastorate of Orlamünde without electoral approval."

"I wrote to Duke Johann![26] The congregation requested me specifically!" Here Karlstadt beats a palm upon his chest.

"Yes, but the Elector tells me he never approved it," Brück states calmly, refusing to meet the level of his opponent's tone.

Karlstadt closes his eyes and shakes his head violently. "It was my understanding that he did."

"You are mistaken," Jonas assures him.

Karlstadt sends a piercing glare in Jonas' direction. "You act as if I were a devil, but I have always been at the service of the Elector, the university, the foundation, and the simple Christian folk in my care. Thank God I became a vintner that I might be spared the controversies of the city! And this one has always hated me," Karlstadt concludes, pointing directly at Martin.

That is a lie, Martin thinks. *There was a time when we had a love as strong as brothers, sharing ideas and promoting reform together. It was only when you intruded upon the preaching office that things soured.* He wants to say it. The heat is rising within him, every muscle in his body tensed. He ought to say it, but he must not allow things to descend into a two-man fight.

Fortunately, Amsdorf helpfully responds, "That is not true! Doktor Luther stood up for you when you picked that fight with Eck and got yourself added to the bull. It is only because of him that you were not summoned to Worms and subjected to imperial justice, even as he was."

"You speak as if those were good things—as if he acted selflessly," Karlstadt sneers, still staring at Martin. "In fact, he was thinking only of his own fame."

---

[26] The Elector's nephew.

You have no idea what I have suffered, Martin thinks, desperate to defend himself. *No idea.*

Again, Brück holds up a hand for silence. "Doktor Karlstadt, we are not here to discuss the behavior of Doktor Luther, but your own."

"He told Duke Johann to ban my works!" cries Karlstadt, pointing at Martin angrily.

"Because you attempted to circumvent the ban already in place," Jonas argues. "Must I remind you that Jena falls within the Elector's territory?"

Karlstadt drops his hand and turns to address the others. "Is it not my right as a free Christian man, to speak as I choose and be heard by my brothers and sisters? But you fear my words! You know their power! That is why you all attempt to shut me away."

"We are not shutting you away, Doktor Karlstadt," Brück insists. "We are bidding you fulfill your public duties here."

Karlstadt slumps back in his seat, allowing his palms to rest on the table. With resolve, he announces, "Very well. I shall return. I will fulfill my duties here, and you may appoint whomever you like in Orlamünde."

"You may also give up your positions here and remain there," Brück reminds him.

Which we would all greatly prefer, Martin thinks.

Karlstadt seems to read his mind. "That would suit you all, wouldn't it? No, I will return to this city from which you cast me like a scapegoat to wander in the wilderness alone, the mark of iniquity upon my head. I will take up my rightful place!" he declares, drumming the table with one finger.

"You would give up your pastorate, just like that?" Amsdorf asks with more than a note of disgust. "You would abandon your sheep?"

"What choice do I have?" Karlstadt inquires contemptuously. "You all have forced it on me."

"You are the one who has been claiming all this time that scholarship is worthless and you wish to be a layman and simple peasant," Amsdorf reminds him. "I admit I always found that a bit ridiculous when we all know you to be a man proud of your heritage, fond of fine clothing, and determined to marry well."

Amsdorf's words seem to pierce the most sensitive point in Karlstadt's soul as surely as any of the weapons on the wall. Visibly enraged, he leaps to his feet and bellows, "You insult my marriage?!"

Martin grips the table instinctively, his pulse quickening. It has been a good twenty-five years since he engaged in a true fist fight, unlike his father, who probably still returns from the Mansfeld tavern each night with bruises. Martin can see out of the corner of his eye that Jonas is bracing himself for action as well, but their colleague seems not the slightest bit shaken.

His voice and expression perfectly calm, Amsdorf responds, "I do not mean to insult you or your wife, but there is more than a bit of the ridiculous in your assumption of the peasant role, as demonstrated by the fact that when forced to choose between your sheep and your position, you choose the latter."

Karlstadt scoffs loudly. "I do not expect you to understand, Doktor Amsdorf. You, like Doktor Luther, are tied to the things of this world. Positions mean nothing to me anymore! Fine clothes, fine food—these mean nothing to me! I have let them all go. I live by the Spirit, not the flesh. I take pleasure in nothing but God. I know that all these external things are idols sent to seduce me. It is the inner man that counts. That which comes into a man is nothing." Here he pounds his chest with his hand. "The flesh profits nothing! Let it be done with! I abandon all creation and am united to the Spirit!"

With every syllable Karlstadt utters, Martin's anger increases even as his grip on the table strengthens. It is a wonder the wood does not split. *This is a monkery to outdo the monks!* he rails internally. *It will lead men to eternal ruin!* And despite the warnings he has received from others and those he has given himself, he is compelled by both nature and reason to speak.

"You are in error because you have failed to understand the Scriptures and the power of God!" he cries.

At once, the other four men turn their eyes on him. Amsdorf looks bemused—Jonas dismayed. Brück appears entirely confused. But Karlstadt—the one who gave Martin his doktor's cap in this very building and stood with him in the ordeal at Leipzig—stands amazed, smiling more broadly than one would expect for a man just accused of falsehood.

"Well, then," Karlstadt says softly, shaking his head in wonder. "He speaks!"

Martin has already surrendered the first point to Karlstadt by entering the fray. He must hit him hard.

"To live by the Spirit is not to do away with all things physical," Martin argues, remaining in his seat but leaning forward. "Grace is brought to you from outside, by the Word and sacraments. Those are the physical signs sent to strengthen your faith by their connection to the divine promise. When you deny the flesh of man, you deny the flesh of Christ! When you teach this doctrine of perfection, you place men under a second Law!"

His opponent's expression morphs into a glare. Karlstadt inhales deeply to release the fire inside.

"You accuse me of the Galatian heresy?!" he cries.

Martin grunts. "I think you would make Jews of us all if you had your way."[27]

Karlstadt places his hands in the middle of the table and pulls his weight forward, almost laying himself down to decrease the range from which he will launch his verbal assault. From beneath the brim of his hat, his blue eyes teem like waters tossed in the violent surf.

"You are the one denying the gospel by setting aside the commands of Christ!" Karlstadt howls, his voice rattling with the stress.

There was a time when such a charge would have shaken Martin Luther, especially coming from a brother professor. But now, he feels an inner peace: a certainty purified by years of fire. The words are building within him—drawn from the deepest reaches of his soul to strike the forces of error.

"The gospel and the law are utterly opposed! The law damns us! Only the gospel saves!"

---

[27] The term "Jews" has been used in different ways throughout history. Luther is here referring to Christians who believe they become righteous before God by perfectly following the divine law. Such a group existed in the earliest years of the Church. Sometimes known as the Judaizers, they told fellow Christians that they must follow all the Jewish religious laws to achieve salvation. The Judaizers were strongly criticized by St. Paul in his Epistle to the Galatians.

Karlstadt is quick with a response. "Who is the one who is in Christ but the one who follows his commandments? You leave men in their sins!"

"Gentlemen!" Brück bellows, pounding the table. "We have wandered very far from our purpose. Doktor Karlstadt—"

"Brother Andreas!" Karlstadt snaps, looking back at the seated Brück. "You know I care nothing for these worldly titles!"

The councilor nods wearily. "In line with your choice, we will make arrangements for your return to Wittenberg."

A pause for breath. Karlstadt appears to think for a moment, then replies, "Let me wait until winter semester, for I must finish a few things first."

"Very well," Brück concedes, "but you must nominate someone to cover your classes."

"You will hear from me," Karlstadt assures him. "All of you will hear from me. Especially you, Doktor Luther!"

Here Karlstadt turns on Martin again, breath coming fast, fists clenched. "Do you think I've forgotten what you did? You threw me to the dogs! You saw how the hearts of the people were bound to me, and you had to destroy me. I was laying the foundation here for years before you began teaching! It is only by chance that you were thrust to the fore!"

Here he points at Martin accusingly and continues. "I made you a doktor! But you are too much of a coward to do what needs to be done: that is what I could not see then. You peddle old ideas while I lead the people into the Promised Land! You would send them to wander in the wilderness for forty years because you lack the necessary vision!" He leans forward and speaks the final words softly, menacingly. "I've done things you've never dreamed of, Doktor. I am not too weak in faith to carry the work to its logical end."

Martin follows suit, leaning forward and saying quietly, "I object to the use of the word 'logical' to describe what you're doing. You make your stand, but take heed lest you should fall."

Karlstadt jerks his head back quickly, the breath escaping from his nose—a clear mark of derision.

"You hope to frighten me with talk of God's judgment, but I am not afraid to stand before him!" Karlstadt declares. Pointing at Martin again, he charges, "But you should be afraid, Doktor. You should be! He knows what you are, even as I do!"

The ferocity of Karlstadt's glare, the finger pointed straight at the heart that pounds within Martin's chest—it carries Martin back to the darkest moments of torment as he struggled against the world's censure. *Fraud. You are a fraud.* But he bids himself remember. *I am a son of God.*

Having seen enough, Brück declares, "Doktor Karlstadt, either sit down and cease these insinuations, or I shall have no choice but to surrender you to the Elector's justice."

Karlstadt scowls at Brück, at Martin, at the room entire. Then he surrenders to his fate, sinking into the chair more than sitting, his arms crossed and chest puffing up with each breath. An uneasy truce for one moment in time. "You'll hear from me again," he mutters.

The rest of the meeting is mercifully bland, with Brück lulling them all into apathy with legal recitations. Soon, Martin is walking with Amsdorf back in the direction of the Leucorea buildings, his outward demeanor calm but his spirit trembling.

"There for a minute I thought he might strike you," Martin informs his colleague, kicking a pebble forward, attempting to release the tension.

Amsdorf chuckles. "There for a minute, I thought he might strike you! But it seems he prefers to wrestle with you verbally. I do not think familiarity does you any favors in this case."

"'Better the evil you know' indeed," he mutters, shaking his head.

Placing a hand on his shoulder, Amsdorf asks, "Are you well, Martin? I do hope this terrible business has not brought you low in spirit."

He sighs deeply. "Trials of the spirit are an evil I know better than most, but I assure you, friend, I am well. I meet with Bugenhagen every week, or whenever I need it. There is nothing as healing as absolution for the soul in anguish."

"Well, if it's Erasmus who concerns you, have no fear! You will pulverize him!" Amsdorf declares, slapping him on the back.

"Erasmus..." he whispers, allowing the name to hang in the air. These days, it seems the air is always full of talk of Erasmus.

As the sun sets and the two of them walk together along the dusty road, his mind travels far from the streets of Wittenberg—far even from his own time. He is standing on the bank of an ancient river, staring at a ghostly figure who beckons him to a struggle. It is the story of Jacob on which he has just preached. He sees it before his mind's eye as never before.

There in the unforgiving wilderness, Jacob fought with God as man with man, rolling in the dust from which he was formed, grasping and heaving, flesh uniting with flesh. He struggled through the watches of the night, beating his fists against that unearthly force, colliding with the Ancient of Days. Then a single touch revealed all he was: crippled and helpless before the Almighty. His strength exhausted, his spirit surrendered, he reached out one final time, no longer under his own power, but by some special gift of heaven, and demanded the fulfillment of divine promise: a blessing passed from the hand of God to the heart of man. And there the Lord held him, an impotent creature in the embrace of his Creator, only now Jacob was created anew: "Israel," he that strives with God. That was his new name.

In the last fading rays of the light, Martin wonders, *Am I Jacob? No, am I Israel?*

3 May 1524
Basel, Swiss Confederation

Erasmus of Rotterdam looks with great joy upon the Froben house again. His journey has been long—his thighs and back ache. Not for the first time, he laments his decision to travel on horseback.

The trip was nothing like he hoped. Soon after arriving in Besançon, he fell ill. For most of a week, he lay in bed miserable, fending off visitors and cursing himself for not taking better precautions. He has not secured patronage, and what is even worse, some Lutherans who happened to be in town are now spreading rumors about him. Therefore, the sight of "Old Faithful" does him good, its four stories prepared to greet him with the sounds and smells of something like home. Already, he can hear the voice of Johann Erasmus—the youngest of Froben's offspring—carried out an open window, chiding whoever has had the gall to object to his juvenile business. *Finally, some decent company,* he reasons, *and what is just as important, some food that agrees with my stomach!*

Once the horses are returned to the stables and he is set on the precious earth again, he walks across the courtyard toward the house. Margarethe is waiting by the door, ready to take his cloak. Her smile is devilish, and he can only imagine what insults she is devising, but their skirmish must be postponed. A youth is approaching him in a light blue jacket and hose, a gray cap on his head and satchel slung over his shoulder. His brown hair is disheveled, his face peppered with the pink spots of early adulthood, and a sad attempt at a beard clings to his jawline. Erasmus has seen this young man wandering the streets of Basel before—an errand runner of sorts—but what business could they have with each other?

"Can I help you, boy?" he asks.

"Are you Desiderius Erasmus?" the youth inquires, butchering the pronunciation.

Erasmus grumbled, "If I must be."

Is that a snort he hears escaping from the young man's nose? The expression is clearly one of derision. He watches as the boy reaches into his bag and holds out a pair of sealed letters with soot covered fingers.

"For you," he announces, "from the post."

Erasmus wrinkles his nose and takes the letters carefully, wondering what diseases the young man might be carrying.

"I'll just take my wage then," the boy informs him, dirty palm extended.

Erasmus looks down derisively, examining the cracks and fissures of that filthy skin. He is disinclined to offer anything in exchange for such cheek, but society operates by certain rules that bind even Erasmus of Rotterdam. He therefore reaches into the purse at his waist and retrieves a single coin, dropping it in the youth's hand.

"Thank you," Erasmus mutters, expressing more gratitude than he truly feels.

"Don't you want to know my name?"

He stares at the boy blankly. This conversation has exceeded the limits of necessity. "I suspect you will tell me whether I wish to know or not."

"Sebastian!" he cries. "It's Sebastian. You rich people never care about us, do you?"

I have known poverty you cannot possibly imagine, Erasmus fumes, but instead notes, "You didn't care enough to pronounce my name correctly."

Sebastian's nose wrinkles. "Well, what kind of name is Desiderius? Your parents knew how to curse you, eh?"

In an instant, Erasmus' annoyance flares into rage. *He cannot know,* he tells himself. *He cannot know why that is so offensive. He doesn't know who I am.*

"This discussion is at an end," Erasmus declares, turning on the spot and walking toward the house.

Letters in hand, he tosses his cloak to Margarethe without a word—too angry to engage in their usual nonsense—and makes his way into the ground floor of the house, passing the kitchen and servants' quarters. He is about to ascend the stair when a ball comes bouncing down the steps. Sitting at the top is Johann Erasmus, his shoulder-length brown locks tousled as befits a seven-year-old.

"Erasmius!" he calls up to the boy, using a favorite pet name. "Are you attempting to kill your godfather?"

"I didn't see you!" the boy insists, galloping down to him. "Why were you gone so long?"

"I fell ill."

"Again?! You're always ill!" Johann Erasmus complains.

He smiles at the boy, patting him on the head. "That is what happens when you grow old. Is the rest of your family present?"

"Father is at the shop with Hieronymus and mother went to the market with Justina."

"And they left you in charge?"

"Yes!" he proclaims, stretching to his greatest possible height and smiling broadly. "I'm the lord of this house. You must do as I say!"

"Ah. I was not aware we were under a dictatorship at the moment. Are the barbarians at the gates?"

The boy cocks his head to the side. "You mean the Lutherans?"

It is an unintentional jest, as far as Erasmus can tell, but one that amuses him greatly. He pats the boy on the shoulder.

"The Lutherans are already within the walls, and not only here," Erasmus notes ruefully.

Continuing up the steps, he arrives at the first floor and walks into his study with its windows facing Nadelberg. He sets the letters down on the raised desk and takes a good look at them for the first time. Both bear his name and place of residence on the front. There is no sign of mishandling—a relief, as his correspondence is often read by ten persons between sender and receiver: some are even published without his knowledge. He turns one over and examines the seal, squinting to make it out. *Open or leave aside?* he wonders. If there is some symbol here, he does not recognize it. He will have no choice but to open the thing.

He reaches in the drawer for a pen knife and cuts through the seal rather than tearing it. Unfolding the letter, he discovers that it has been sent to him by Kaspar Hedio, a fellow proponent of the New Learning and preacher of the cathedral in Strasbourg. Despite Erasmus' remonstrations, Hedio is not of one mind with him when it comes to the enforcement of laws in Strasbourg. He has clearly made a move toward Luther, or at least toward those who call themselves Lutherans. Though it is written pleasantly enough, the letter frustrates Erasmus greatly, and he is about to sort it away when he comes across a passage that changes his attitude entirely.

"You are perhaps aware that I am an old school friend of Philipp Melanchthon, having studied with him at Pforzheim. I hear that he and Camerarius are making for our part of the world and hope to meet with you in Basel. Whether they will pay a visit to Strasbourg, I do not know."

Melanchthon coming here? Could it be? he wonders. *What caused him to take leave of Wittenberg? No, surely it doesn't matter. Preparations!*

Letter still in hand, he runs back into the hallway and flies down the stairs calling, "Margarita! Margarita!" His tone is wild—his pulse rushing. *Where in God's name is she?* He looks in the kitchen, the cellar, the dining room: all empty. *Always there when you don't want her, then when you do, she absconds!* In a panic, he races across the hall and past the servants' quarters, arriving at Margarethe's door and pounding it with his fist, in which the letter is still clutched.

"Margarita! By Jesus and all the saints, open this door!"

It swings open, and Margarethe stands before him, her wet hair hanging loose and a stained cloth in her hand.

"Yes?" she asks far more calmly than he feels is warranted. "What is it, Your Highness?"

He is about to answer when he smells something extraordinary, and not in a good way. There is a strong scent of vinegar, but that is not the whole of it. The only proper descriptor is putrid—utterly putrid.

"What on earth is that smell?!" Erasmus asks, placing a hand over his nose and stepping backward.

"I'm dyeing my hair," she informs him without hint of embarrassment. "Don't you ever wonder how my locks stay dark at my age?"

He shrugs. "I assumed you were a witch."

A roll of the eyes and she asks, "What is it, then? You were ready to spit."

"I am having guests for dinner."

"Tonight?"

"Maybe," he says, still covering his nose. "I cannot be certain."

Placing a hand on her hip, she inquires, "And how many guests will I be expected to feed?"

"I'm not certain of that either." This provokes a heavy sigh, so he quickly adds, "But I know what I wish to be served. German food—specifically of Franconia. You must know something good."

She gives him a pointed look. "I'm no more German than you."

"And get some wine from the Palatinate if you can," he continues, ignoring her comment. "It is to be a sumptuous feast, Margarita. We must impress them!" When she merely snorts, he insists, "This is very important to me! I will accept no excuses on your part. Hire more help if need be."

"I trust you'll be paying me extra," she says pointedly.

"Yes, yes. Of course. Now, get you to it!"

The business attended to, he makes his way back to the study, mind still racing. *If Melanchthon is coming here, then this is my chance—that is, if I am ever to persuade him.* He sets Hedio's letter aside and picks up the other one. *He must feel entirely at home. He must know the lengths to which I am prepared to go.* The penknife slashes through wax and paper. He unfolds the letter. *I only hope we—*

And then, in an instant, his thoughts redirect. Philipp Melanchthon is forgotten entirely. He is gripped—petrified by the name on the letter: Servatius Rogerus.

The torment of memory strikes him. He feels it coming in white hot waves made cold as ice upon the skin: tall grass swaying in the wind, a river of crystal blue water, the croaking of storks. Unbearable loneliness. Endless hours of weary work. Sick—so terribly sick. The library, the books, the smell of vellum, the feel of its wrinkles upon his fingers! The dawning of a new world. The discovery of purpose. Heat, longing, shame, grief. Weeping that lasts for the night with no hint of joy in the morning.

It began in Gouda, the town of his youth. His mother and father were dead, their bodies consumed by the plague. He and his brother Pieter had been entrusted to the care of three guardians whose primary concern was to dispose of them as soon as possible. They had worked on the boys for months, twisting their minds to the point of breaking. "You have no choice. It is the only way. What life will you have otherwise?" The boys were illegitimate: non-persons. Only the Church would have mercy on them. Then Pieter gave in to the guardians' demands and agreed to enter a monastery. Only Erasmus was left, and he was standing alone.

"I will not go! You cannot make me! I am a free person!"

He repeated these phrases until there was no breath left in his lungs and his will was utterly crushed. He had no money, no prospects, no hope. His brother had already capitulated. What choice was there for him but to yield? He entered the Augustinian priory of Steyn—accepted the cowl and tonsure. It was always going to end that way, no matter how hard he fought.

He found the cloister unbearable for the first few weeks. It was everything he feared: dull, monotonous, lonely. He was still grieving the deaths of his parents—not that he ever had much of a relationship with his father—and he had a nagging illness that sent him often to the infirmary. Then, when his health began to recover, the monks discovered his intelligence and allowed him more time in the library. Their collection was not equal to the greater houses, but it would do. He read the multitudinous volumes of the Brethren of the Common Life, but it was the smaller collection of ancient Latin works that ignited his mind: Cicero, Livy, Ovid, Terence. He devoured them, sneaking volumes into his room after dark, finding friends within their pages. He was still half miserable, but only half.

He began tutoring fellow monks. Try as he might, he could not inspire in them the same passion for good literature that existed in himself. Then he was assigned a new pupil one year behind himself: Servatius Rogerus. This young man, at least, took a keen interest in all things Greek and Roman. Their lessons were productive and enjoyable. They read Juvenal's *Satires* and made their way through *Eunucus*.[28] What joy to find a kindred spirit after months of despair!

So eager were they to continue their studies that the hours allotted them were insufficient. They began passing notes—finding other times and places to meet. They had no choice but to endure the endless recitation of the canonical hours, but Erasmus was keen to embrace the minimal freedom afforded them. "What would I do without you?" he asked Servatius. "Our time together is my only comfort in this life." For his part, Servatius was equally bound. "I cannot go a day without hearing from you. Write to me—I beg you. Tell me how you are."

The duties of monastic life pulled them further apart, so they arranged to meet in secret. One night, after everyone else had gone to bed, they made their way separately to the library, where they read through *Heauton Timorumenos* line by line, each reciting different parts.[29] They had sneaked in a bottle of wine from the church. There was much laughing and joking. His friend grew weary, and Erasmus bid him, "Lean your head upon my shoulder and rest. I will continue reading." One page, two pages, then Servatius fell asleep.

Erasmus set the book aside and gazed upon his friend's face, which was gently illuminated by the candlelight. He felt the warmth of Servatius's body—watched as he gently breathed in and out. *You are my whole world,* he thought. *My whole world.*

He was amazed how quickly it happened: how hastily desire was born. He felt his flesh respond—he could not deny its signs. Then came the rush of fear. He was very aware of his own breath, the flow of his blood, the beating of his heart. He recoiled in horror at the thoughts that flooded his mind, even as he fanned them like a bellows. He reached out with his free hand—placed it upon Servatius's. Erasmus' pulse was like the drums of war or the churning of the sea in a tempest. Everything within him was awakened, but he took no

---

[28] A play by Terence still performed in the Renaissance era.

[29] *Heauton Timorumenos,* meaning "The Self-Tormenter," is another play by Terence.

further action. He let Servatius sleep until just before Lauds, keeping a silent vigil over his slumber, far too agitated to get any sleep himself.

Days went by. Their lessons continued, but they were not the same. How could a thing that brought Erasmus such pleasure also fill him with so much fear? He could barely admit it to himself. He had felt love for another human being, and it was not warm and freeing, but cold and harsh, like the edge of a knife.

He reconsidered everything he knew about himself. He wondered how he could go on. Every moment was filled with a desperate longing he feared would never be fulfilled. He wrote to "my dearest Servatius" and told him, "You are dearer to me than these eyes, than this soul, than this self." He called him the only hope and solace in his life without whom he had no reason to live. "When you are away, nothing is sweet to me; in your presence I care for nothing else."[30] To his delight and terror, Servatius responded with his own effusions of praise. "Dear Erasmus, the best of me and best of this world, in whose love I hope to find myself always."

Erasmus knew what he was contemplating was a mortal sin, but he felt as if he was being pulled toward it by some unnatural force. This was the most alive he had felt since entering the cloister—perhaps the most alive he had ever felt. He sought the consummation of his desires, even as he feared it.

At last, he could bear it no longer. He asked Servatius to meet him after Vespers under a birch tree at the far end of the grounds: one of their favorite places. The last light was being drained from the sky. As he watched Servatius approach, the knowledge of what he was about to say—of what he hoped to do pressed down on him like a fearful weight. But he would not yield: *I am a free person!* When they were within a single pace of each other, he took a deep breath— summoned up his courage.

"What is it, Brother Erasmus?" Servatius asked. "You said it was urgent."

"It is urgent. Dearest Servatius! I cannot stand it anymore. I cannot live like this. I must know!"

---

[30] "Epistle 7: Erasmus to Servatius" in *The Epistles of Erasmus: From His Earliest Letters to His Fifty-First Year*, trans. Francis Morgan Nichols (London: Longmans, Green, and Co., 1901), 47-8.

"Know what?" Servatius asked, his tone hushed and expectant.

In that moment, Erasmus felt himself standing upon some riverbank, the devil at his back, staring down into the black water. He was a torrent of expectation.

"Do you love me, Servatius?" he whispered. "Truly love me?"

Without hesitation, his friend replied, "Why, of course I do! You know I do."

Blessed elation! Passion began flowing through Erasmus freely. He moved to embrace his dear one, heedless of the risk—heedless of anything but the fire within him. Then with tears in his eyes, he held Servatius's face with both hands, barely able to make out his features. The moment had come for Erasmus to act, and so he did. He pressed his lips against Servatius's, savoring the feeling—the softness. He was filled with unspeakable pleasure. Then suddenly, he was pushed backward and struck across the face, his skin burning with pain. Stumbling, lost and confused! His mind was dizzy, unable to make sense of the strange turn of events. Then Servatius shouted.

"What the hell do you think you're doing?!"

Erasmus's lips were still inflamed from the kiss they had shared, only he was beginning to suspect they did not share it at all. He was reeling—falling without point or purpose, incapable of righting himself. He was about to be dashed upon the rocks.

"How dare you?!" Servatius bellowed.

"I...I..." he stuttered. "I thought it was what you wanted—what we both wanted."

"Have you lost your mind?! I am no sodomite!"

"But you said—"

"We were friends and that is all! How dare you?!"

Then Erasmus began crying for a different reason—shrinking into himself. He was robbed of breath, overcome by sorrow, splintered and broken.

"Who are you?!" Servatius cried. "Do I know you at all?"

"Perhaps you don't," he admitted softly, eyes fixed on the ground. "Perhaps I don't know myself."

"You disgust me! You hear that? You disgust me!"

Stabbing, rooting pain tearing into his flesh and searing his spirit! "Please don't say that," Erasmus begged.

Servatius took a step closer and yelled directly into his face. "Do you know what happens to sodomites, Brother Erasmus?! They are sent to the lowest circle of hell to spend eternity with coals in their mouth and up their ass!"

"Where on earth did you read that?!" he asked, taken aback.

"Beg for mercy, son of iniquity!"

"What? How—"

"You know exactly what I mean: the son of a priest and a whore! No wonder you're so perverted!"

He was bowed down, humiliated, driven from the divine presence. Only a tiny part of him could stand and fight—could cling to the slightest fragment of dignity he still possessed.

"My mother was not a whore!" Erasmus cried. "How could you say such a thing?!"

There was an uncomfortable silence, then Servatius sneered, "Repent, Brother Erasmus, if you can."

Darkness. Emptiness. Another sleepless night, but this time for a different reason. Erasmus begged absence from the first prayers of the following day, but he was due to perform the Scripture reading at Terce. He had no choice but to drag himself there. His spirit still quaking, uncertain of why he was continuing, he stood behind the lectern and opened to the first chapter of St. Paul's Epistle to the Romans. Servatius was present, and Erasmus struggled to ignore him. *Will he tell the prior? Will he tell everyone?!* He was not really taking in the words he was speaking. Then, like a thunderbolt from on high, he read, "For the wrath of God is revealed from heaven against all ungodliness." It seized him in the chest. He became cognizant of his place within the spheres—that he was living and breathing and reciting before the face of God—and to Erasmus that was a fearsome thing.

The words he read heightened his anxiety, lunging at him, grasping him by the throat, pummeling his abdomen. "God gave them over…lust…impurity…" The syllables sliced and penetrated. "They exchanged the truth of God for a lie." He pronounced the words with great effort, and though to anyone watching he might have appeared perfectly at peace, his pulse was quickening, his mind wrestling. "God gave them over to degrading passions." He was remembering the heat, the tightening, the longing. "Men with men committing indecent acts…receiving in their own persons the due penalty of their error." He struggled not to cry.

There it was before him: Those who are unrighteous are rightly condemned by God. He gives them over to a depraved mind. And what is the chief evidence of this? What could only be done by a person who has turned to idolatry?

He breathed in deeply to read the final verses—"Those who practice such things are worthy of death"—then as quickly as possible slammed the book shut with a force greater than intended. It took him by surprise, as if it were not really him closing the book at all. The vibration moved through his hands into his body: he felt the very gate of heaven slamming in his face.

I was born and bred in sin, he shuddered. *I am a crime against nature, and now his wrath is upon me. He has given me over.*

No sooner did he think this, than something within him rebelled. *No! I am a free person! I can change!* But that other voice in his head—chilling, abrasive, unforgiving—taunted him to his core. *Too late! Too late for you. What is done cannot be undone, you filthy, stinking sodomite!*

As Erasmus departed from the lectern, shoulders slumped and head bowed, striving mightily to avoid Servatius' gaze, he convulsed internally, his bowels tormented. Again and again, the word repeated—*Sodomite! Sodomite! Sodomite!*—until he reached his seat and collapsed more than sat. He placed his head in his hands, feeling as if his skull would burst from the pain.

No one seemed to notice his struggle, which was just as well, for he was too thoroughly mortified to discuss it. Great waves of shame washed over him unrelentingly, pulverizing his spirit, wrenching his heart in his chest, making him long for death. *Yes, death! The only possible release from this shame.* They say a man upon the rack will beg for death, and that was exactly how he felt in that hour: as if he were being torn apart, dismembered, stripped of his very flesh.

Well, let me be stripped of it! he thought. *Let it be severed from me, if only I may be free of this shame!*

But he was captured: trapped forever in his flesh. It belonged to him, and he to it, and together they would be plunged into the fires of hell, where annihilation would be a mercy. So visceral was his reaction to this thought that his body shook. It must have been so, for he soon felt a hand on his shoulder that caused him to lurch from his reflections no less than if he had heard the growl of a bear. He looked toward the hand's owner: it was Brother Ansfrid, one of the priory's older residents, his dark eyes full of concern beneath his voluminous gray eyebrows. Were Erasmus in a better frame of mind, he might have read compassion in Ansfrid's gaze.

"Brother Erasmus, are you well?" the old man whispered.

And just like that, something within Erasmus slammed shut. A wall was erected in the space of a breath: a wall that would remain there for decades.

"I am perfectly fine. I am at prayer!" he barked a bit too loudly. "See to yourself!"

The torment was unceasing over the following days. Though Erasmus managed to avoid Servatius' person, he felt him as a torturous presence every waking moment. Sleep was Erasmus' only escape from the shame. He could not abide his own company. When no one was looking, he would strike himself again and again, the pain rippling through his flesh. *I cannot go on like this,* he lamented. *I cannot go on!* Then one morning, while the rest of the monks were at prayer, he walked down to the River Yssel. No longer a peaceful stream, it seemed an abyss of unending darkness. It was his personal Styx, ready to carry him to his eternal destiny.[31]

Glancing around to see that no one was watching, he discarded his shoes and clothing in the tall grass. What he was about to do, he could not do as an Augustinian. He would enter this water the same way he entered the world: naked and helpless, weeping and longing for comfort that he would never experience. He felt the cold air against his bare skin and shook uncontrollably.

I should have done this long ago, he thought. *My father forsook me. God has forsaken me. I will make an end. I will forsake this world.*

He waded into the river, the icy water wrapping him in a chill embrace. Soon he was up to his neck, unable to swim and yet at peace.

It will hurt. It will hurt for a moment, and then it will be over.

---

[31] In ancient Greek mythology, one had to cross the River Styx to enter the underworld of Hades, although versions of the myth differ, and it is sometimes the River Acheron that is said to guard the way.

He took a final breath in—prepared to let himself slip into the eternal current, held by the frozen hand of death, surrendering all control. Then he heard a voice calling to him.

"Brother Erasmus! Brother Erasmus!"

Ignore him, he told himself. *Do it. They cannot stop you now. How could you ever explain this? There is no way out. You must go under.*

"Brother Erasmus! God loves you! He loves you, Brother Erasmus!"

He turned his head toward the speaker. It was old Brother Ansfrid standing amid the grass, yelling into cupped hands. "God loves you, Brother Erasmus! He loves you!"

I cannot commit this act with him screaming that, he thought, *and yet I cannot return.*

"Take my hand," the monk called, extending it from his spot upon the bank. "It will be alright. Everything will be alright. Trust me!"

Erasmus focused on the extended palm: the hand that could either strike or bless. He searched those folds of skin, the wrinkled remnants of youthful vigor stretched over arthritic joints. Somehow that hand seemed to reach inside Erasmus and spark a forgotten membrane of his soul—a single bit of tissue in which the rush of hope still pulsed. There alone was the existence not snuffed out: the bit of Erasmus that still longed to be. He found himself desperate to take that hand, or perhaps to believe that he was a person who could take it. With each breath, the feeling grew, until his spirit was thoroughly roused to act—at least, to be acted upon.

And so, Erasmus returned to the bank by some power known only to God. His fellow monk held him, dripping and naked. He placed the cowl upon Erasmus' body again—led him back to the cloister.

"I do not know what drove you in there, brother," Ansfrid said, "but no one else need know about this. Do not despair! God loves you!"

Erasmus did not truly believe the words escaping Ansfrid's mouth. *I will continue living if I must, but I cannot remain at Steyn. It is impossible. Better to live on the streets than at Steyn!*

Then the prior called Erasmus into his office one day. They sat in chairs opposite each other, and the older man said, "I know what is troubling you, Brother Erasmus."

"You do?" he asked, terrified of what might come next.

"Yes. You are discontent. Your mind is too sharp: your thirst for knowledge too great. A spirit like yours must drink from the fountain of ancient wisdom. It must be nourished by other great minds in the centers of learning."

This was not remotely what Erasmus had expected. All he had known for weeks was darkness. The mere hint of light overwhelmed him.

"The bishop of Cambrai needs a secretary," the prior stated matter-of-factly. "He is traveling to Rome. Much as we would hate to lose you, if it is your desire, I grant you leave to accompany him. Perhaps some time among others like yourself will grant you relief from depression."

"Father," Erasmus stammered. "I do not know what to say! I never thought to have such an opportunity in all my days."

"Then you accept it?"

"Yes, most assuredly."

Finally, Erasmus felt something like hope awaken in his heart. He would be allowed to escape this land—to break free from his past!

"Then go with my blessing, but let me say a word before you do," the prior requested.

"Anything, Father," he replied, genuinely interested.

The prior took a deep breath, the look on his face entirely serious—even grave. "Perhaps you are one of those rare men who can transcend the boundaries of his time and see with the terrible sight of the gods. But there is a price for such sight: a cost exacted over an endless space of moments, leeched day by day from a man's spirit. You would be a seminal person indeed if you could walk such a path and chase after the great mysteries of faith: the wellspring of divine knowledge. Those things are only gained through struggle of the highest order. Are you a second Jacob, Brother Erasmus? Would you suffer it all for the hard blessing? Count the cost before you set out, for some things once done cannot be undone."

Count the cost. How right that man was! Now as Erasmus stands in Froben's house, staring down at Servatius' name in black ink, he feels the accumulated pain of those endless moments, and he understands what his prior meant. Who would have thought then that Servatius would rise to become prior of Steyn? That he would be placed in authority over Desiderius Erasmus? For despite his papal exemptions, Erasmus is still a brother of Steyn, and he must live with the knowledge that his superior knows: that he was there that night under the birch tree. No matter how far he wanders, he cannot escape that terrible bond. He lives every day on edge, knowing that Servatius Rogerus holds the power to destroy him.

At last, he reads the words on the page.

"You have waited too long, Brother Erasmus. You must enter the arena. Write against Luther. Refute his arguments. If you do not, I shall have no choice but to tell His Holiness what kind of man you truly are. No more evasions! For the good of Christendom, and for your own sake, do not delay any longer."

The paper shakes in Erasmus' hand, and suddenly he does something he has not done in years: he weeps.

4 May 1524
Bretten, Electoral Palatinate

Philipp Melanchthon stands just inside the open door to his mother's house, captivated by the sight in front of him. Raindrops fall softly on the cobblestones outside, a soft chorus, each with their own voice. His eyes trace the jamb and lintel, taking in every line and crevice, every warp and splinter, then locking on the wooden threshold. He feels a jolt in his stomach: the memory of fear. *Twenty years. Could it be twenty years?*

He is there again now, in the same location but two decades previous. What did it sound like? First, he heard a struggle: metal clinking against stone, flesh colliding with flesh. A cry of agony. Anxiety surging up his breastbone. Fists pounding on the door. His grandfather moved toward it on feeble legs—pulled it open with shaking hands. A landsknecht entered the house covered in blood, eyes wild with panic, then promptly darted into the kitchen and out the back way.[32] More pounding on the front door. "Open up, Reuter! We know he's in there!" The old man obliged. They pressed their halberds against

---

[32] The *Landsknechte* were German mercenary soldiers of this period known for their service to the Holy Roman Emperors. They took part in the Landshut War of Succession in 1504, to which this story refers.

his chest. Philipp's brother Georg, so tiny then, buried his face in their mother's skirt. On the wood floor below, a trail of red seeping into the fibers, leaving a permanent mark.

There are some things a man never forgets. Philipp was seven years old when Duke Ulrich of Württemberg laid siege to Bretten and he learned the meaning of war. The sound of artillery firing: again, again, again! The sight of men with bandaged wounds, stumbling back into town half-dead. Watching his young friends cry as their fathers were buried in the churchyard. He had heard about death, but in that hour, he knew it as surely as he knew himself: a gaping void of nothingness at the center of his soul.

Then there was the day his father returned from the war to this house—the home of his grandfather, Johann Reuter. When Georg Schwartzerdt passed over that threshold, they could tell something was different: his face ashen, forehead covered in sweat, eyes weary to the point of death. No weapon of war had brought him low, but a poisoned well. For the next four years, he lingered on in pain, groaning and twisting, longing for the beatific vision. Then Philipp's father and grandfather passed in quick succession, and his mother Barbara was left to raise five children alone.

Philipp continues to stare at the door, transfixed by a holy yearning. *I came to Bretten to escape sorrow,* he thinks, *but I will never be free of the past.* He is just as restless as always, struggling to sleep, lamenting the things he could not do—the people he could not save. Twenty years have passed. He never grew as tall as he hoped, and his shoulders never straightened out. He bears the same memories, and now many others have joined them.

"Philipp!" his mother calls, breaking into his thoughts. "I'm going to confession. Walk with me?"

He looks at the woman who bore him, now forty-eight years old and her best years behind her. It was she who held their family together after the cruel theft of their patriarchs, and the struggle has taken a toll. Since he last saw her six years earlier, her hair has gone fully gray, her skin is wrinkled and discolored in places, and she is haggard—rendered gaunt by years of trial.

"Of course," he replies, holding up an arm to which she can cling.

After securing a scarf over her head, she walks with him out into the marketplace, rainwater flowing through the channels between the cobblestones. With each step, they displace the liquid beneath their feet, sending it rushing this way and that. He places his free hand on hers, more an offer of comfort than stability. His mother is not in good health. Her hands are arthritic, she struggles to sleep, and she has constant pain throughout her body. Certain aspects of the physical world seem to overwhelm her: light that is too bright, smells that are too strong. Her new husband has told Philipp that the constant weariness, aches, and difficulty concentrating began about a year earlier. She struggles to read a book or take in what is spoken in the homily. She seems to float through life rather than live it, save for the times her pain flares, when she is splayed on the bed in agony.

"I fear for her," the old man confided. "I fear she walks under the shadow of death."

Her primary solace is her faith. Not the new one—the old one. She goes to Mass daily and confession almost as often. The canons at the collegiate church are like family. She keeps images of the saints in her home and prays before them regularly. When she is in too much pain to walk about, she clutches her beads fiercely, hoping with every "Ave, Maria!" to escape what her life has become. He can sense her weakness as she holds fast to him, and it shakes him to his core: the rock of his childhood faltering at long last.

"You should have told me you were ill," he says softly as they depart the square and make for the church. "I had no idea it was this bad."

"It's no worse than what others are forced to endure," she murmurs, her voice full of the fatigue that colors her every moment.

Philipp turns to face her, halting their progress. He stares deeply into her eyes: the first ones to ever look on him with love. "I wish I could take this pain from you."

"You are a kind soul, Philipp," she says, patting his arm, "but I would not have you suffer on my account. This is the way it is meant to be: the aged suffer, the young flourish."

They begin walking again and he says, "I admit there are days I feel neither young nor flourishing."

"What you need is more sleep. That will set you right."

"No, it is more than that—a strain upon my spirit." Here he pauses again, overcome by a sharp feeling of loss, like a cry sounding from the depths of the sea and echoing across the waves. "I have spent my youth upon immensities, and now I grow old before my time."

She nods silently. "I wish you would consider the offer Heidelberg made you."

Her words break the spell of his yearning, kindling frustration within him. Two days ago, after he had been in Bretten for most of a fortnight, some men arrived from the University of Heidelberg. "Will you forgive us for refusing, on account of your young age, to admit you for the Master of Arts?" they wished to know, hoping to make amends for the past. They had clearly heard of his fame and wished him to teach at the university. They left disappointed.

He sighs and guides her along, making the turn onto Pforzheimer Street.

"I've been over this. We are happy where we are," he reminds her.

"Are you? If I believed that I would hold my tongue, but I see no signs of it in your features. You have changed, son. You are not the same man who left for Saxony."

"Well, of course not. I have a wife and daughter now."

"Whom I have never met! But you must forgive me. I do not mean to pour guilt upon you."

"Only sprinkle it, perhaps," he notes with a smile. His mind is pulled back to Wittenberg and the two females who fill his heart. "I do wish you could meet them. I believe Anna has the Reuter look about her."

"Then she ought to be among her own," his mother states with an air of authority.

He refuses to play along. "She is. She sees her other grandmother nearly every day."

He catches his mother rolling her eyes.

"Son, I do not doubt that those Krapps are fine people, but they cannot do for her what we can," she insists, referring to the family of his wife. "Your father gave all of himself to ensure our position here. Will you deny that to your daughter?"

Tension courses down his neck. There is so much left unsaid. They are talking about Luther, but not talking about him. They are discussing Philipp's convictions—the journey of faith he has undergone—but they cannot speak the words. They must not force a breach.

"She is happy there," he assures her. "We both are happy there."

They take a few steps in silence, the rain falling lightly upon their heads, their shoulders, their hands. He suspects every cobble bears the mark of his young feet.

"I don't see why you had to take a wife at all," his mother suddenly comments, shaking her head. "It is not the way of scholars."

Something fierce awakes inside him, but he strives to answer calmly. "It is becoming quite common in our part of the world."

"I still don't see why you had to do it," she remarks rather ungraciously.

His frustration pushes him into a personal admission. "Because I fell in love—that's why."

She looks at him with wide eyes, clearly taken aback. "Is that all? I thought they coerced you somehow."

"Well, love may be a form of coercion, but it's one I'm willing to bear," he chuckles.

"I do not mean to insult her," his mother replies earnestly. "She must have been the best of women to have tempted you into such an act."

The words are intended to sting, but instead they fill Philipp with pride. "She was—she is. I thank God for her every day. But why did you marry again, mother?"

Her eyes study the cobblestones below, words coming slowly, as if requiring a great exertion of spirit. "I had no purpose when I was alone. My whole life felt empty after you children left. But now I see that God brought him into my life because I needed a caretaker before the end."

There it is again: the shadow of death. He nods solemnly and whispers, "I'm sorry."

"Let us speak of it no more, son," she replies, moving closer to him and patting his arm. "I am proud of you. Whatever I may say or however I might act at times, I assure you, you are my pride and joy, Philipp, despite it all."

At the sound of these words from his mother's lips, Phillip's heart is filled to the brim. Were he a man more prone to such things, he would speak of his great affection for her and the bitter distress he feels that the great loves of his life should tear him in opposite directions. He wants to be with her, but he also wants to be in Wittenberg. He wants to respect the old ways, but his mind and heart have been captured by something sweeter still: the oldest of ways, though it is new every morning. Grace upon grace! The fountain overflowing! He cannot communicate what he feels by any words of man. It is something that must be experienced—this love, this salvation.

So, in that moment when he must speak all he feels, granting rest to his mother in her dying days, he can utter nothing more than, "Thank you." A coward's reply. His impotence is like the schoolmaster's rod, beating him bloody. The shame is acute.

"I am sorry your friend Camerarius has gone," his mother says, mercifully changing the subject. "I've seldom had a more pleasant guest. Where is he headed again?"

"Basel—to see our friends there."

"I hope you did not stay behind on my account. I could have let you go for a few days."

He smiles. "I doubt that, but have no fear: it is not solely on your account that I remain. I was afraid my presence there would complicate things."

"What things?"

"Camerarius is meeting with Erasmus."

"Oh, Philipp!" she exclaims. "If you had told me that I would have insisted you go."

"And now you know why I didn't tell you," he says with a laugh.

"But why shun his company? Would your new friends think badly of you?"

"Other way around, mother. His friends would think badly of him."

Frowning, she diverts her eyes. *She is disappointed,* Philipp thinks. *She fears I am hurting the family reputation.* They move forward slowly.

"He was a good friend to your uncle Reuchlin when he was having that trouble with the Dominicans," his mother notes.

At the mention of his uncle's name, Philipp is filled with sorrow. He looks up at the sky, his mind drawn to a higher sphere. The clouds have parted slightly, and a single beam of light makes its way to the ground.

Father! Call me father!

Philipp's eyes begin to water. He has taken flight to a time in his former existence when he was sent to the home of Johann Reuchlin, the greatest scholar of Hebrew in all Christendom and by happy chance, also his great-uncle. Not truly a man yet, Philipp looked into those ancient eyes: golden, beckoning, full of life. Reuchlin placed a hand on his shoulder.

"It falls to me, as your mother's uncle, to ensure your education. Do you know Latin, boy?"

"Not as well as I should, sir," Philipp replied timidly.

"Simler will be your tutor. You will learn Latin and Greek from him."

"Greek as well?" To his young mind, it seemed an impossible task.

"Yes, for you are to be a scholar! That is what you desire, no?"

"Yes, uncle. Of course, uncle. I want to be like you."

One year later, he stood in Reuchlin's house again. His studies with Simler had gone well. He had already bested many of his elders in his knowledge of ancient languages. Reuchlin placed a doktor's cap on his head.

"One day you will receive your own," the old man promised.

Philipp beamed. His hard work was paying dividends.

"I have something else for you," Reuchlin explained, holding up a finger.

His great-uncle then walked over to a set of shelves in the corner and retrieved a Greek grammar, the cover text laid in gold leaf upon red leather. Philipp accepted it as one might a precious jewel. Robbed of speech, he could do nothing but stare in wonder.

"Open it," Reuchlin instructed.

Philipp pulled back the cover to reveal the title page, upon which Reuchlin's coat of arms was prominently displayed. Some handwriting below explained that it was a gift to "Doktor Philipp Melanchthon of Bretten."

"I translated your name into Greek. Do you like it?" his great-uncle asked.

"I don't know. It seems so strange."

There was a twinkle in the old man's eyes. "One day, Philipp. One day, you will be ready for it."

A year or two later, Philipp attended a banquet at the Pforzheim monastery where he and his young friends performed one of his great-uncle's comedies. At the conclusion, the crowd burst into applause, and Reuchlin rushed forward to meet Philipp, face beaming with pride.

"Philipp Schwartzerdt!" Reuchlin cried, shaking his head in wonder. "Raised from the earth as the men of Athens and a far better Grecian than they.[33] Already a scholar of some renown. Destined to rise higher than your fellows. You are my pride and the pride of this house, but you have become greater than your name. I therefore christen you anew: no longer Schwartzerdt, but Melanchthon is your name. Philippus Melanchthonus! That name will be famous in all Christendom!"

Philipp felt no embarrassment at this loud proclamation in front of his friends, for he had by this point identified so thoroughly with Reuchlin that he could think of no greater good than to be just like him.

"My Philipp," his great-uncle continued softly, "it is an odd chance of fate that you are sprung from the loins of my niece and not myself, but my heart declares you are my son, the very image of myself," Reuchlin said, patting his own chest. "From this day forward, you are a son to me, and I a father to you. Your good will be my good, and I will promote your advancement as long as I live, for I see in you the hope of Germany."

Philipp was overcome with gratitude. "Dearest uncle," he stammered, voice trailing off.

Reuchlin placed a hand behind Philipp's head and pulled their faces close together. There was a keen intensity in his eyes.

"Father! Call me father!" his great-uncle insisted, sounding almost desperate.

Despite his best efforts, Philipp began to cry. Since the passing of his father and grandfather, he had felt an emptiness of the soul that he doubted could ever be filled, but upon hearing Reuchlin's words, he was brimming with joy.

"Father," Philipp whispered. "You know how much I love you. I long to make you proud! But I am young. I have much to learn, and I think others do not see in me what you do."

"Because they are imbeciles!" Reuchlin scoffed. "Most men are imbeciles, but you will best them in the end: mark my words."

---

[33] The ancient Athenians believed that their ancestors had been literally birthed from the soil of Attica.

"If they refuse me a place—"

"Then I will find you another place!" Reuchlin insisted. "When one door closes, I will force another open. You must simply walk through it."

Philipp nodded quickly. "Of course, father. You know I love you. You know how I crave your advice."

A smile broke across Reuchlin's wrinkled face. "Very good, son. Come! Let us sit together, Philippus Melanchthonus, and I will teach you the ways of great men, for that is what you will be. Indeed, that is what you are."

Next came years of disappointment. Philipp was awarded his baccalaureate at Heidelberg but denied further study on account of his age. Reuchlin opened a door for him at Tübingen, where he flourished for a time and befriended Œcolampadius. His professors claimed they had never seen a student of Philipp's quality. He would excel Reuchlin, they predicted—perhaps even the great Erasmus! Still, jealousies abounded, and in time there was no place for Philipp at Tübingen either. His great-uncle put out inquires, but the old universities were in no mood for innovators.

Then at last, an offer from a far corner of the Empire: a new university open to new ideas and passionate about the study of languages. They were looking for a professor of Greek, and Reuchlin bid Philipp enter the service of the Elector of Saxony. He would be just like Abraham, his great-uncle wrote, departing the land of his youth for the land of promise. He spoke of Philipp tenderly. "My work and my consolation." His parting words were biblical in their gravity. "Go, therefore, for a prophet is not honored in his own country."[34]

Therefore, Philipp said farewell to his homeland and made for the Electorate of Saxony. There he found the university in tumult. A theology professor had recently shaken his fist at the gods and provoked a debate over indulgences. Philipp began to hear things he had never heard in all his years of study. Almost immediately, he was won over. His correspondence with Reuchlin grew less frequent, and not only on account of distance. Philipp traveled with Luther and Karlstadt to Leipzig for their debate with Johann Eck. They left having

[34] This translation appears in the following work: Clyde L. Manschreck, *Melanchthon: The Quiet Reformer* (New York: Abingdon, Press, 1958), 42.

admitted that both popes and Church councils can err. Philipp's fellow professors were in danger of excommunication, and he was standing beside them, embracing their theology as they did his.

Another letter from Reuchlin arrived. Philipp's great-uncle had taken a position at the University of Ingolstadt, where Eck was chief theologian. He was living in Eck's house! Eck, their sworn enemy! Eck, who was traveling to Rome to secure a papal bull against Luther! Clearly, Philipp's great-uncle supported the renewal of learning, but not the renewal of the Church. "Whatever you may have said to offend Eck, he is willing to forgive you," Reuchlin wrote. "He offers you a position here. I regret now that I pushed you toward Wittenberg. Come home, my son!"

Philipp replied to his uncle in anguish. He certainly never intended to offend Eck, but he could not abandon his duty to the Elector. It was the will of God that he should remain in Wittenberg. "I must consider what Christ has called me to do more than my own inclinations."[35] Even as he wrote the words, he prayed, *Lord, you know how I love him. Help him to see.* He sent the letter with fear and trembling. At long last, an answer came.

Doktor Melanchthon—

You have betrayed me and cast your lot with heretics. I can have no dealings with you. Do not write to me again. May God have mercy on your soul.

—Johannes Reuchlin

Was it hot or cold as he held that letter in his hands? Morning or evening? Philipp recalls little of the day. All he knows is he was standing in his study alone, note in hand, feeling as if his insides had been ripped from his belly. Falling to his knees, he cried great heaving tears that wrest the breath from his lungs. He was aching, tortured, melting. It was as if his father had died again—as if one of his limbs had been hewn away and his blood was gushing forth in a rapid stream. He cannot remember how long he remained there,

---

[35] Ibid., 53.

folded into a ball, gasping and wailing. It was so unlike him, but he had reached the end of himself. His mind was bound in darkness.

Even as he stands in the present, walking the streets of Bretten with his mother beside him, the wound is still fresh in his breast. Four years have passed since he received that letter and two since Reuchlin died, removing all hope of reconciliation. The Greek dictionary is still on his desk in Wittenberg, but he cannot bring himself to open it. No quantity of years would be enough to fully heal him. An ever-present grief. An absence of belonging. A silent lament that reverberates across the years, denied its fulfillment. A doubt that eats at him in the dark when no one else is there to see.

I can never go home, he thinks. *I cannot even move on. I wait upon God as the watchman waits upon the morning.*

They have made it to the church, his mother still clinging to him tightly, unaware of his troubled thoughts. As Philipp looks at the place where he spent so much of his childhood, he thinks, *How big and grand it seemed in my youth, but now I see it is no different than the thousand other churches in every German town.* The reddish tiles on the roof are turned brown with many winters—the ivory walls have been robbed of their luster. He leans over and kisses his mother on the cheek. "I love you, mother. Shall we go in?"

Her attention has been stolen. She is looking to the left, where a young man stands alone in the rain, staring back at them. He is wearing a brown cloak so plain it seems designed to escape notice, but underneath Philipp can barely make out the dark robe of a scholar. There is something menacing about the way the stranger continues to make eye contact without speaking a word. Philipp's every fiber is on alert.

"Who is that man?" his mother asks. "Do you know him?"

"No. Let's get you inside," he replies, steering her toward the door.

Moments later, Philipp's mother is speaking with a priest beyond the choir screen, and he sits in one of the few chairs at the back of the nave, not far from the font in which he was baptized. He remembers how richly decorated this church was in his youth: painted ceiling, icons in every niche, many relics to display. But war has brought the parish low, and now there are only a few images before which the afternoon visitors can pray, the rest sold off to repair the walls

and help the destitute. The stained-glass windows—prime fodder for
the Duke of Württemberg's cannons—have been replaced by simple,
clear panels.

Karlstadt would be happy, he muses.

It is strange to think that in this place where he was baptized,
he can no longer receive the Sacrament. Bretten is not much of a
reforming town, and word of his theological exploits has reached
them. The provost informed him as soon as he arrived in the vicinity:
as a kindness to his mother, Philipp is permitted to set foot on the
grounds, but no consecrated bread is to pass through his lips. He
feels somewhat lost without its comforts—a kind of famine of the
soul. *This place can never be what it was to me,* Philipp laments. *I
can never truly return.*

Suddenly, a voice behind him asks, "Brother, may I sit beside
you?"

He swings his head round, and to his alarm, it is the same young
man who was staring at him on the street. He has lowered his hood to
reveal a flat cap atop a head that bears no tonsure. His accent belongs
to the South: likely Milan or Venice.

"You may," Philipp concedes.

As the stranger takes a seat, Philipp's mind churns. *A southerner
in Germany seeking me away from home. He must have traveled up for
the diet in Nuremberg, but then why would he be in the Palatinate?*[36]
A moment more, and he makes the connection. *Cardinal Campeggio
is in Heidelberg*, he thinks, recalling the last tidings of the papal legate.
*I just received visitors from Heidelberg. Surely this is no coincidence.
And if he is Campeggio's man, this is not a friendly visit.*

Philipp stares at the ground, head bent and hands folded, rubbing his thumbs one against the other. He will not be the one to start

---

[36] The word diet here refers to an official meeting. Imperial diets were regularly held within the Holy Roman Empire to conduct official business. A main
concern of this particular diet was the enforcement of the Edict of Worms,
which called for Luther and those who taught Lutheran doctrine to be arrested
and turned over to state authorities. Cardinal Lorenzo Campeggio was at various times cardinal-protector of both England and the Holy Roman Empire,
and thus an extremely powerful Church official, perhaps second only to the
Pope. He was sent as Pope Clement VII's official legate to the 1524 Imperial
Diet of Nuremberg.

this conversation, even if it is unavoidable. He thinks of his wife and daughter—his brothers at the university.

Finally, the stranger asks, "Do you know who I am?"

"You are Campeggio's man," he answers without looking up.

"Very astute. I am Frederic Nausea of Trento, secretary to the papal legate. You must know why I've come."

"Yes," Philipp whispers, still refusing to look him in the eye. *Nausea—they named you correctly.*

"Your mother is at confession?"

"Yes."

"I am glad to find she has not abandoned the ancient faith."

He pulls his gaze from the floor tiles and looks into Nausea's dark eyes. The implication is not lost on him: Unlike his mother, Philipp has abandoned that faith. Therefore, Nausea would negate his baptism, cutting him off from salvation, thrusting him out the doors of the church forever.

"I am not opposed to confession," Philipp insists. "I object to the coercion of the conscience in penance. The Church ought to be comforting troubled souls, not placing them back under the Law."

"Is this your own thought, or another's?"

How dare you come to me here! How dare you treat me like a child! Philipp fumes internally.

"I am perfectly capable of thinking for myself in this matter and many others," he assures Nausea.

"Ah yes, the boy wonder!" Nausea exclaims. It is an odd statement coming from a man who appears younger than himself. In an instant, the foreigner's expression morphs into the most solemn of frowns. "Your mother is not well, or do my sources deceive me?"

"She has been better," Philipp replies, wondering how Campeggio received this intelligence.

"Wouldn't you like to be near her? After all, you are the eldest son. It is your responsibility."

Philipp's anger sparks. He clenches his teeth—breathes deeply through his nose. *I must not respond in kind.* But it is a cruel blow that ought not be borne. *You have abandoned your mother. You are a bad son.* Nausea might as well have said those words. One more breath, in and out, and he brings himself under control.

"I have a duty also to my own family and to the gospel," he states calmly but firmly.

Nausea shakes his head. "You have run a long way from home, Philipp—a very long way. Is there not some part of you that longs to return: to be welcomed into open arms?"

"Of course. Who wouldn't want that?"

Leaning in closer, Nausea whispers, "Come home, brother."

"To the Palatinate or to Rome?" he asks, unwilling to play along.

Nausea sits up straight again, circling around for a new attack. "You are young and eager to tread the fearful path. You press against the limits, wishing to know if you are immortal. I understand. I am young too, after all. Every man is owed that time, but sooner or later there comes a moment of decision: we must put aside childish things and follow the path of our fathers. And you had a great father, Philipp. His land is your land, and his faith is your faith."

The mention of his father rekindles Philipp's anger. With no attempt to hide his disdain, he mutters, "You didn't know him."

"I know he was a good Christian."

"And I am not?"

Nausea closes his eyes momentarily in contemplation. Then he places a hand on Philipp's and begs, "Come home, brother. All will be forgiven."

"You think of me as the prodigal brother," Philipp replies, "and perhaps I am, but it seems to me that you are the other brother, embittered that I should receive the lavish grace of our mutual Father."

Sighing deeply, Nausea pulls his hand back and crosses his arms. "Doktor Melanchthon, there is a lack of fear that we call courage and one that we call folly. It seems to me you are in danger of the latter. Despite the gentle correction of many older, wiser men, you pursue heretical ideas and throw away the immense gifts granted you by God, endangering your loved ones and your reputation, to say nothing of your eternal soul." Raising his voice, Nausea demands to know, "What is your purpose, Doktor? What do you wish to be?"

Philipp looks briefly at the few parishioners making their rounds, all of whom are staring at them, though under the weight of his gaze they return to their supplications. He addresses Nausea again.

"I do not know what I wish to be, but I know what I am: a sinner saved by grace. I will not trade that grace for whatever comforts you offer."

"There are different sorts of comfort in this world, some true, some false," his opponent says pointedly.

"It is no false comfort to say that a man is justified by grace alone through faith alone."

Nausea smiles bitterly and shakes his head in disapproval. "Against the wisdom of the ages you will place the ideas of one man."

Philipp grits his teeth. "Why do you assume I received that idea from Luther?"

At the sound of a closing door, both men look toward the choir screen, where Philipp's mother emerges from her conference, hands still clasped in prayer. Perhaps unwilling to give himself away, Nausea stands and releases a final harangue.

"I can see there is no point in continuing along this line, Doktor Melanchthon. I simply ask you to consider this: How sure are you really? It's one thing to say it to me here. It's quite another to say it when your mother is dying alone, bereft of her son in this life and the next. You have already lost friends. The day may come when you are placed under the judgment of the Church and the Emperor. What will become of your wife? Your daughter? All your works will be burnt. Does that mean nothing to you? Does the destruction of your flesh—of all you are—mean nothing to you? Are you certain enough in this teaching when the fruits are only violence and disorder? Are you certain enough to stand before Almighty God and answer for every word you have written—all the souls you have led down this path? Because I think you are scared and lonely, overwhelmed by the pressure, doubting those around you, longing for a safe harbor for your soul. When you are prepared to admit it, the Church will be waiting for you with open arms."

The words penetrate deep into Philipp's soul. No matter how committed he is to the work of reformation, it is not pleasant to imagine the trials that could await him. And yet, there are elements that the secretary has missed: aspects of his belief that have gone unacknowledged. To his mother, he might yield a point, but never to this man.

"You don't know me—not really," Philipp replies. "There is more than what you see."

"Come home, brother. Come home," Nausea whispers, then turns and departs the church through the main door.

Philipp has no time to think about what has been spoken. His mother has already arrived at the back of the nave, her gaze flitting between him and the closing door.

"Is everything alright, son?" she asks, her eyes filled with concern. "You look as if you've just seen the herald of death."

As he looks upon her weary form—the drooping shoulders, the eyes red with exhaustion—he feels an ache that no poultice can allay.

"I'm sorry, mother," he says softly, tears forming in his eyes. "I'm sorry I cannot be what you want me to be."

Few words, but they understand one another. Their eyes are saying what their lips cannot.

"I am tired," she breathes.

They link arms and depart the church. The rain has stopped, but the town remains quiet. Philipp's eyes dart to and fro, seeking out Nausea's form, but like a phantom of the mind, he is no more. They are the only ones on the road. He hears the phrase echoing upon the wind, giving voice to his desires even as it awakens his anger.

Come home.

5 May 1524
Basel, Swiss Confederation

Erasmus of Rotterdam is bent over his wash basin, stomach raging, ears ringing, legs weak. Pungent smells rise from the kitchen below to fill his nostrils: garlic, onions, spice. His insides cramp and contort. He retches, given over to the violent stirrings, but there is nothing left to expel. Did he eat something tainted, or is this the harbinger of a new attack of the stone? All he knows for certain is that he feels horrific.

His body having ceased its convulsions for the moment, he lumbers into his study, collapsing into one of the chairs by the hearth. He is positively burning from the inside out. Breath heavy, eyes closed, he attempts to lure his body into comfort. *Be still. I say, be still!* Now he hears a knock on his door.

"I am unwell," he calls, voice rasping, lungs protesting the act.

"Do you want the turpentine again?" a female voice responds.

He can only manage a grunt, but it is enough to convince Gertrude Froben to enter the room carrying a silver platter, her brown hair swept up in gold netting, the arms of her red gown slit to reveal the white fabric underneath. She is a sight far too fair for the foulness of his state. Reaching his chair, she presents a goblet of Burgundy wine and some oil of turpentine, the latter purchased off a Hansa merchant who was recently in town. Favored by Baltic seamen for purging the bowels, he began using the turpentine at the first sign of indigestion.[37]

"Your remedies," she informs him.

He reaches out weakly, taking the vial of medicine in his shaking hand. He swallows a bit and feels it slide down his throat, singeing as it goes. *Christ!* He winces in pain and Frau Froben offers him the goblet. "Here—drink!" When he has consumed a satisfactory amount, she inquires, "Feeling any better?"

"Worse," he moans, eyes closed in pain. "Much worse. I don't think I can move from this chair."

"Shall I tell your guest to leave then?"

He raises his lids in a flash and demands to know, "What guest?"

"A scholar of some sort—I forget his name—come from Bretten. He is waiting in the small parlor."

Melanchthon! he concludes, blood surging. *He is here!*

"Help me up!" he commands, pressing against an arm of the chair and struggling to raise himself. "Quickly!"

She sets down the platter and takes hold of both his arms, lifting him to his feet. A new surge of nausea radiates through his body. The droning in his ears increases.

No, I must not give in! he thinks. *I must speak with him. This is the best chance I will ever have to turn the tide—to preserve all that I have built.*

"Are you quite certain you are in a condition to receive him?" she asks. "I can tell him to come back—"

"No!" he insists. "He will not be here long. It is now or never."

He nudges her aside and begins striding toward the door, weaving slightly as he goes. He has thought through this conversation so

---

[37] Turpentine is distilled from the resin of pine trees and has legitimate medical uses...if applied topically.

many times. *I will be conciliatory and understanding. I will forgive the faults of the past.* What he has neglected to write for fear of thieves, he will say face-to-face. He has heard of Reuchlin's final days: how he forsook his nephew. *An excellent scholar, Reuchlin, but stubborn to a fault.* Desiderius Erasmus does not abandon friends so rashly. Miraculously, he makes it down the stairs without falling, a hand pressed against his belly. Here the kitchen smells are overwhelming, wafting from the hearth directly into the hall.

He turns to the left and makes his way toward the parlor. *Be strong, legs. I must pry him from Luther's grasp. Everything I have accomplished—all my work. It must be saved! Be strong!* Why should he feel so poor on this day of all days?! The Fates are keen to add embarrassment to his torture. As he enters the foyer, he is met by his young secretary, Karl Harst.

"Herr Erasmus!" Harst cries, grabbing his arm. "Is everything alright? You look as if you ought to be in bed."

"Do not stop me, Karolus!" he responds hoarsely. "That man"— here he points in the direction of the parlor—"is the key to all our efforts. I must convince him to join me, even if it kills me."

Eyes wide, Harst responds, "I had no idea he was so important. Is he to help you with your Greek translation?"

"Precisely. He's the best Greek scholar in Christendom."

"I might have thought you would bestow that title on Melanchthon," the younger man says, brow furrowed.

"Yes, exactly, that's what—" Erasmus drops off his speech, overcome by recognition. It pounds him in the chest, the sensation rippling into his extremities. "Wait. Who exactly is in the parlor?

"Doktor Camerarius," Harst informs him, the blow crushing. "Joachim Camerarius."

Erasmus shakes his head, disgusted at his mistake and disheartened at the loss of a golden opportunity. "Brilliant," he mutters, feeling anything but. He has dragged himself down here for nothing! *Perhaps not for nothing,* he reasons, grasping for any hint of light. *Camerarius is one of Melanchthon's closest friends. There is work yet to be done.*

Erasmus summons up the minimal strength within himself and declares, "I will meet this Camerarius. If I only—" A necessary pause. He feels as if he might retch again.

"Can I help you to a seat?" Harst asks desperately.

"No, no!" he insists after regaining control. "I just imbibed from the fountain of turpentine. I will be well soon enough."

The younger man raises his brows in alarm. "Turpentine? I heard one should never swallow that stuff, be he ever so ill."

"Karolus," Erasmus says pointedly, placing a hand on Harst's shoulder for balance as much as anything, "get out of my way."

Harst obeys him, and within seconds Erasmus is entering the small parlor adorned with his own portrait, sun streaming through the windows, the sounds of the city echoing outdoors. Whitewashed walls reflect the light, awakening the hues of the silk curtains: red and gold flowers playing on a dark background, with trim the color of emeralds. The oak floor is partially covered in a fanciful carpet imported from the Orient. Facing away from him on a small couch opposite the marble-lined hearth sits a man in the black robe and cap of an academic. Taking a deep breath, Erasmus commands himself not to be ill—places a hand on the arm of the couch. After two more hesitant steps, he gets a proper look at Joachim Camerarius, a young man with a dark beard and friendly face. A leather bag sits beside the visitor on the couch, and he holds a sealed letter in his lap. Upon seeing Erasmus, Camerarius stands and removes his cap, bowing low.

"Herr Erasmus—my great teacher!" Camerarius exclaims. Rising again to his full height, he continues, "Ornament of the world! You cannot know what joy it brings me to look upon your face and receive your hospitality! I am quite undone."

"The honor is entirely mine," Erasmus insists, extending his hand. They clasp palms and he adds, "I'm afraid you have caught me at a rather poor moment, as I have been unwell today."

"My sincerest apologies!" Camerarius exclaims. "I had no idea!"

"Please, there is no need to apologize! Perhaps you could just be so good as to pull over that chair," he suggests, pointing to a richly upholstered seat in the corner. "My strength is not what it once was."

Camerarius fetches the chair in question and soon they are sitting beside one another. As he attempts to find a comfortable position, Erasmus recalls the points he hopes to make—considers how to tailor them to his new audience. *I must not fail.*

"Allow me to offer my regrets on behalf of my colleague, Doktor Melanchthon," Camerarius explains. "He longed to see you with all his heart, but he knows how you have been accused by those who wish you ill, and he feared if it became widely known that he visited you, the suspicion and abuse would only increase."

"In that he is likely correct," Erasmus says weakly, a new pang resounding in his stomach, "but please know I would have gladly suffered reproach to meet with him. In fact, I would travel to Wittenberg to speak with him and Luther, were I not old and ill-fit for travel."

"I understand. You must know the great esteem in which they hold you for all your contributions to scholarship."

He smiles wryly. "I suspect that Melanchthon's opinion of me is far better than Luther's. I have not forgotten what Luther said about me to Œcolampadius: I am Moses leading you all to the Promised Land but unfit to enter. That is his assessment of my character, although he has never met me."

Camerarius fidgets slightly in his chair. "I do not know what Doktor Luther might have said to others, but I know for a fact that he was among the first to adopt your New Testament in his lectures on the Holy Scriptures. It was he who drew us all to Wittenberg to introduce the New Learning, along with Herr Spalatin, the Elector's secretary. Do you know Georg Spalatin?"

"We have exchanged letters. He seems a good man and quite learned. But tell me: what is that missive you're cherishing?" Erasmus asks, nodding in the direction of the letter.

Camerarius holds it aloft and says, "I have this directly from the hand of Doktor Luther for you alone to read. I take God as my witness that no other hand has touched it between here and Wittenberg. I kept it always on my person, and now I deliver it to you."

His stomach quivering, Erasmus extends his hand palm upward and receives the letter as one might a pile of gunpowder, for its contents will be equally combustible. *What on earth could he want?* he wonders. *Does he know about my book? I suppose he must.*

"Did he say anything to you when he handed this over?" Erasmus asks.

"Nothing in particular. Just to give it to you in person, or else burn it."

Not promising, he thinks, breaking the seal.

Head aching and insides burning, Erasmus opens the letter and finds three pages, all seemingly written in Luther's own hand. He has seen examples of it before: black letters slightly slanted, flowing one into the next more pleasantly than one would expect for a man so crude. He struggles to make a few of them out, though the general haze over his mind might have something to do with it. He looks up at Camerarius, pointing to the note.

"Do you mind if I read this now?"

"Not at all!" his visitor insists. "I assumed you would."

His gaze returning to the letter, Erasmus braces himself for the onset of nausea, though on account of his illness or Luther's words, he cannot be certain.

"Grace and peace from our Lord Jesus Christ! I have remained silent long enough, dear Herr Erasmus, waiting till you, as the greater and elder, should break the silence, but having waited so long in vain, charity impels me to take up my pen."

He struggles not to roll his eyes and continues reading.

"We perceive that you have not been endued by God with such steadfastness and courage that you can confidently go forward with us to combat this monstrosity—hence we do not expect what is beyond your ability to render. But we have borne your weakness patiently, and highly appreciated your gifts."

Which is to say, 'You are a coward,' he reasons, *as if foolhardiness were true courage.*

"Up till now I have held my pen in check, in spite of your conduct towards me, and have also written to friends, that I would restrain myself till you attacked me openly. For although you were not of us and rejected some of the principal points pertaining to everlasting blessedness, or hypocritically refused to give your opinion on the matter, still I shall not accuse you of obstinacy."

It was your people who attacked me! They have been pummeling me with pamphlets day and night, spreading falsehoods to the far corners of the Empire. I have only defended my honor! he fumes. *For the love of God, what do you expect me to do?!*

> "If I be mediator, I would ask these people to give up assailing you, and permit you, at your advanced age to fall asleep in peace in the Lord. They would do this if they considered your weakness and the magnitude of the question at stake, which is far above your head."

Pleur op![38]

> "I say all this, excellent Herr Erasmus, to prove my earnest wish that the Lord may give you a mind worthy of your great name, and if he delay doing this, I beg of you only to be a spectator of our tragedy, and not unite with our opponents, nor write against me, seeing I shall not publish anything against you."

I am not on their side. I am not on your side. I am on no one's side! he laments.

> "Take my child-like simplicity in good part, and may you prosper in the Lord. Amen."[39]

Erasmus takes a deep breath and sets the letter aside, rubbing his tired eyes. *What on earth am I to do with this? The man could hardly have been more insulting, but I suppose he thinks this an act of mercy.* He looks at Camerarius, who is waiting expectantly. *I must not reveal how offensive I find it—not if I am to have any success,* he reasons.

"Thank you for delivering it, and for your discretion," Erasmus offers. "Would you be willing to take a letter back to Wittenberg on my behalf?"

"Of course. I would be happy to," Camerarius assures him.

Without warning, something strikes the front door of the house. Once, twice, three times! Pounding unrelentingly, colliding

---

[38] Literally, "Get tuberculosis!"

[39] "CII: To Erasmus of Rotterdam, April 1524," Martin Luther, *The Letters of Martin Luther*, Volume 1, trans. Margaret A. Currie (London: MacMillan and Company, 1908), 122-4.

repeatedly, pummeling the thing raw. They both look in the direction of the noise and hear the house's matriarch welcoming a new guest into the foyer.

"Where is he? I must see him at once!" a deep voice grunts in a thick accent, perhaps of Bohemia or Poland.

Frau Froben explains, "He is with another visitor. Can you just wait—"

"No!" the man insists. "I cannot wait! I have already told you that."

Camerarius leans closer to Erasmus and whispers. "Do you know who that is?"

"My guess is the new ambassador of the Polish king, come to request some favor," Erasmus answers just as softly.

"I can wait if needed," Camerarius offers.

Erasmus groans softly, annoyed by the interruption and tortured by his nausea. He would prefer to spend his minimal energy on an appeal to Camerarius. He considers the path to the foyer. *How many steps would it require of me?* His stomach is cramping—he feels wretched. Then the ambassador sticks his head through the door and proclaims, "Herr Erasmus! I am Hieronymus Łaski. You have heard of me, perhaps?"

Frau Froben nudges her way into the room beside him and apologizes to Erasmus. "He said he was desperate, and that you were the only person who could help him."

Erasmus raises a hand to indicate pardon and asks Łaski, "What do you require of me?"

The intruder fumes, face reddening, fists clenched. "The damned Lutherans! I only just arrived in town, and they have stolen my purse! I didn't know where else to turn. You know the members of the town council. Speak for me, or I will be out on the street!"

"Please, Your Excellency," Frau Froben says, "we can offer you hospitality. Our cook has prepared a splendid meal, and we have a spare room next to the library. You may remain here until everything is sorted. We can provide you with some money."

"Many thanks to you, my lady," Łaski says, bowing his head, "and I have no doubt my lord will repay you twice over, but this is a foul injustice. These men must be found and hung in the town square! That is how you deal with thieving heretics!"

Don't ruin it for me, fool! Erasmus thinks, attempting to judge Camerarius's reaction. Thankfully, the Wittenberger looks more amused than enraged.

"I will write to the councilors. We will sort it out," Erasmus says to Łaski, "but I bid you moderate your language around our German guest."

Having previously ignored him entirely, Łaski looks down at Camerarius as if examining a particularly unpleasant beetle.

"If you are from Germany, then tell Luther to stop sending his disciples among us!" Łaski declares.

"Disciples?" Camerarius asks in confusion.

"You know what I mean!" Łaski bellows. "We have had trouble with the Hussites for years now. There's been quite enough of that, thank you!"[40]

"Please, let me show you to your room," the lady begs, the tension in the room clearly putting her to pain.

At length, Łaski gives way to her entreaties and is shown to the upper level. *He may be a good enough man, but he has no sense of timing or courtesy,* Erasmus groans. Turning his attention to Camerarius again, he says, "I am deeply sorry for that interruption and any offense caused."

"I understand, sir," Camerarius assures him. "All is well."

"Because I want you to know that I do not think as Herr Łaski thinks. It is true: I cannot own some of the doctrines you own, for I have not been convinced of them in my own mind. It is not cowardice that holds me back, but the principles I treasure. Luther declares his right to obey his own conscience. I ask for nothing more."

"Of course. You will hear no argument from me on that score," Camerarius assures him, his voice soothing, his eyes kind.

Erasmus takes a deep breath. The time has come. "I am glad we are of one mind, for there is a message I wish you to take back to your fellow professor: something which I insist you hold in the strictest confidence."

"You have my solemn pledge," Camerarius declares, placing a hand on his heart. "Whatever you share, I will guard as a sacred trust."

---

[40] The Hussites were followers of Jan Hus, a fifteenth century Bohemian theologian who anticipated some of Luther's doctrinal positions and was condemned and executed by the Council of Constance in 1415.

"I believe you," he replies, still holding down the nausea, every second a test of his strength. "I sensed you were true from the moment I met you. Therefore, tell this to Doktor Melanchthon: I know he broke with Reuchlin before the end, and the last few years have been a torment for him. I also know he is attempting to support a family on a meager salary, living among people who do not know his true worth. From the first time I read his work, I said, 'This young man is the best of us. He will surpass me.' And he has surpassed me in many ways. He is everything his uncle and I dreamed he would be."

Erasmus pauses for a moment, uncertain of the best way to continue. Camerarius seems receptive enough. *How to convince him without offense?*

"Tell me, Camerarius," he begins. "You know him as well as anyone. Do you think he is happy—truly happy in Wittenberg? Is this how he wants to live out his days, overworked and underpaid, harassed by madmen of the Spirit, warring against the forces of chaos?"

"He has suffered much hardship," Camerarius admits, "but I know he is committed to the cause of the gospel."

"And I am not?" Erasmus asks pointedly, pressing in for a strike.

"You will not hear that from me," the young man insists.

His insides raging and about to combust, Erasmus leans forward in his chair. "Tell me honestly: do you approve of Luther's methods? The way he expresses himself? The forces he has unleashed? Can you support all the decisions he has made?"

"He can certainly be abrasive," Camerarius says quietly, "but what is your purpose in asking these things?"

Erasmus nods. "Only this: The day will soon come, if it has not already, when Melanchthon may have cause to doubt the man he so loyally follows, and then he will doubt everything. When that happens, I will have a place for him here—with me, in Basel. The great work of my life to preserve the ancient writings: it must not die with me! Already, I feel myself spent. The last illness was nearly the death of me. But Melanchthon is a better scholar than I will ever be. He is passionate about the Scriptures, so let us translate them together! He is passionate about theology, so let us offer commentaries on the Fathers! Froben would even publish his *Commonplaces* if he could amend it, for there is much of it that is good Christian teaching. We could give him a fine home, access to manuscripts, the best press in Germany, daily communion with great scholars.[41] He could teach at the university here. They would not be opposed to his views. His friend Œcolampadius is here: they could work together. I would receive him to myself as a son. Everything that is mine, I would give to him, if he would only consent to support me in this work. Since I first learned of his talent, I have known he was the one. Please, tell him all this. Let him know my sincerity."

Camerarius breaths heavily, looking down at the floor with widening eyes. He seems to be considering it all—attempting to arrive at a conclusion. *Perhaps their friendship is too great for him to judge impartially,* Erasmus thinks. Nevertheless, he can sense deep in his bowels that this must be the moment of decision, if only because he is about to be sick. His ears are ringing again. He feels the sweat running down his back.

"And what of his convictions?" Camerarius finally asks. "You have stated that you do not share all of them. It seems to me he will have to abandon them and return to communion with Rome, or else you and Herr Froben will have your own communion broken."

"You are right to ask the question," he says with a nod, "for that is the hour in which we live, but Basel is different. There is a certain degree of toleration here. I have some influence with the town council, and the Emperor has a high opinion of me. As long as Melanchthon does not go about trumpeting his views loudly and inflaming every man's opinion, as some of these French imports do, he will have no real trouble from the authorities: certainly, no more than he will have if he continues to cling to Luther. I am old, and I know which way the wind is blowing. I will die soon, and this city will fall to the Lutherans: it has already begun. He would be in a position to take advantage, and I will be out of the reach of Paris and Louvain, thanks be to God."

"That makes sense," Camerarius concedes, "though I am not entirely convinced it would work, and perhaps you will not fault me if I prefer to keep my friend nearer myself."

---

[41] The modern nation-state of Germany did not exist at this time. Though Basel was part of the Swiss Confederation, Erasmus tended to refer to it in his letters as part of "Germany," thinking of a general German-speaking region.

Erasmus locks eyes with him, willing his words into the young man's soul. "But surely you believe that is his decision to make."

A smile, and the Camerarius answers, "Yes, of course. I know enough of his character to believe he will receive your offer in the generous way you intend it, though I cannot imagine he would ever break with Luther, be the circumstances ever so difficult."

"Perhaps not," Erasmus admits. "You must not speak of this to another soul. If it should become widely known—"

"Please, sir!" Camerarius begs, seemingly pained. "Please do not think of me like you do the others. I know we live in evil days, but I am true to my word. I would rather die than betray your trust!"

He breathes deeply, bidding his trembling spirit be still. "Very good. I believe you. Now, if you will excuse me, I must go. I am unwell."

"Of course, Herr Erasmus. Thank you for everything."

"Come back tomorrow, and I will give you the letter to take to Doktor Luther."

They rise to their feet, and Erasmus is struck by vertigo. Camerarius seems to sense it, reaching out to steady him, but Erasmus grasps his hand and says, "Safe travels, brother. Thank you so much for coming."

"I will tell him what you said. You have my word," the younger man assures him, then with a gleam in his eyes, he adds, "But you know, you could always move to Wittenberg."

Erasmus groans once again, whether from the suggestion or his condition, he himself is uncertain.

"Many have mentioned it, and I will tell you what I tell them: I will stay with this Church until I find a better one."

"Fair enough," Camerarius concludes.

As Erasmus stumbles out into the passage, making directly for his bed chamber, he nearly runs into Margarethe, who has emerged from the kitchen with a smile on her face, eyes expectant.

"So how many will it be for supper then?" she asks. "Everything is prepared."

He shakes his head dejectedly. "The supper is canceled. Give it all to the Polish gentleman."

Margarethe's expression morphs from smile, to frown, to deathly glare. Making to ascend the stairs before she can cause him bodily harm, Erasmus hears her calling after him, no doubt shaking her fist in indignation. "You'll pay for this, sir! You'll pay!"

He has no strength remaining for a retort. He spends the whole evening in bed, never far from the basin. Still, he feels he has done well. He has planted a seed and can only hope it will grow and flower.

As the fluids pour out of him and he twists and turns in misery, he thinks upon Camerarius's final words. *Abandon the Church? How could I?*

Outside is the dark: a barren wilderness stretching into eternity. No comfort does it afford, but the dust rises and chokes. The blistering earth sears the flesh. To walk there is to walk alone against the world, the flesh, and the devil, toiling under the wrathful eye of God—to do battle endlessly, limbs weary, chest heaving, spirit beaten. But no saint will come to aid you, and there is no holy water left to dull the pain or rest upon one's burning tongue.

There he would be forced to tread, a pilgrim in a desolate land, gazing back at the light with dreadful longing. There Learning goes to die and Culture breathes its last, and there too Erasmus would linger and decay, until men forgot that he was once something. For the shackles of the light are less stringent by far than the choking dust and the scorching heat. The devil gave up heaven to have his freedom in hell, but Desiderius Erasmus is no such fool. *I cannot hope to struggle alone,* he thinks. *Not without the consolations of the Church.* But there is something else inside his head. An echo—no, a whisper. *You are already alone.*

27 May 1524
A Forest, Landgraviate of Hesse

Philipp Melanchthon stares ahead at a rapidly approaching crossroads. He had seemed to be on the right course, but now another path juts aside, lending doubt to his previous judgment. Struggling to keep his horse in line—for he has never been truly comfortable in a saddle—he looks down the endless corridor directly before him, a thick forest of beech trees on either side blocking much of the sunlight. The other path leads downhill, past an assortment of scraggly pines and off to God only knows where.

I don't like this, he thinks, a sense of foreboding brushing him like a chill wind upon the neck.

He whistles for the horse to stop. When this has no measurable effect, he tugs hard on the reins, and the animal rears abruptly, almost sending him toppling. His traveling companions—Joachim Camerarius and William Nesen—have been following close behind and are forced to cease their own progress.

"What are you doing?" Nesen asks, pulling his horse round in front of Melanchthon's.

"I wasn't sure which path to take," Philipp explains, sending a judgmental glance at the leaf-covered ground, as if it were at fault for the horse's behavior.

They were meant to take the road to Fulda, but the spring rains have flooded it to the point of impassibility. They have therefore changed course at great cost, winding their way through the Hessian forest. Tracing the roots of the hills, they have lengthened their journey precisely when Philipp feels he cannot go another day without seeing his family. Worst of all, they have entered territory unknown, relying on the direction of strangers, praying to avoid the watchful eye of any who might wish them ill.

Camerarius pulls up next to them both. "It's the right path. We continue north and then to the east. Let's keep moving."

"I couldn't see the sun properly," Philipp feels a need to explain. "The trees are so thick here."

"Come. No more prevaricating," Nesen concludes, whipping his horse round and continuing along the path.

Camerarius hangs back, looking at Philipp knowingly. "Are you alright, friend?"

Sighing deeply, Philipp sends his horse into motion with a click of his tongue, leaving Camerarius to follow. He does not think it the best time to go down that particular road. It has been more than a fortnight since Camerarius returned to Bretten and told of his visit to Basel. Philipp was pleased to hear that Œcolampadius is doing well and somewhat alarmed by the reports of Farel's behavior, but it was naturally the tale of Camerarius' meeting with Erasmus that held Philipp rapt. Two weeks of contemplation, and he can still barely make sense of it. He had expected Erasmus would have much to say about the possible clash with Luther and feared how the Great

Rotterdammer would react to his colleague's letter. But it seems he does not know Erasmus as well as he thought, for the old man was primarily inclined to talk about him: Philipp Melanchthon.

What is he to make of the offer? *Could it possibly be sincere? Would Desiderius Erasmus, who has made a great show of staying out of the arena, descend into it for my sake? Would the man who has done so much to protect his reputation be willing to risk it for the chance to work together?* It seems too good to be true. Could it be a bluff: an attempt to pull Philipp away from Luther when they are poised on the brink of war? Is Erasmus truly so flexible, so dedicated to letters rather than theology, that he could overlook their differences in an hour when no one else seems inclined to do the same? The whole matter puzzles Philipp exceedingly.

Onward they press down the woodland path, hooves pounding the scattered leaves and twigs, their eyes and ears vigilant for movement in the trees. Although they have suffered no harassment in their travels, Philipp could be subject to the Edict of Worms: the imperial decree condemning those who promote Lutheran doctrines. Any official in the Empire has not only the right but the duty to apprehend such persons and subject them to imperial justice. Beyond that, there are committed defenders of the papacy who see no need for formal judicial procedures before hanging a man by the neck.

He attempts to distract himself by recalling the tales of Siegfried that he whispers to his daughter Anna as she drifts off to sleep: a hero wandering through a wood much like this one, slaying an evil dragon, bathing in its magical blood. He remembers her smell as he kissed her brow, her blond curls so like her mother's—the vision of utter peace as she passed into the land of dreams. Perhaps she sees him now, weary and aching, longing to reach his own precious bride. But Siegfried was not invulnerable, and neither is he.

They come upon a small clearing at the bottom of a hill with much of its rocky face exposed. The dark gray of the stone contrasts with the bright green moss that is conquering the hill bit by bit. Beams of light dance upon the forest floor as the branches above sway in the gentle wind. Thoroughly parched, they consume the final remnants of water in their bottles.

"I can have a look around—see if there is a creek nearby," Nesen offers.

That is when Philipp hears it: the distant sound of a blaring horn. Now there are dogs barking in chorus, and close behind come the voices of men. He looks at his fellow travelers and sees in their eyes the same fear that grasps him in its clutches. "What do we do?" he mouths to Camerarius, but there is doubt in his friend's eyes. *Flee, hide, or stand?* Philipp wonders. They are remarkably unarmed for such a journey, carrying only the most basic of blades with which they have no special skill. *Flee, hide, or stand?* His heart beats with such force that he can feel the blood pulsing through his neck, the vibrations resounding in his ears.

Suddenly, an entire family of boar—a mother and six piglets— race across the path in front of them, squealing as they go. Close behind come hounds, salivating in pursuit. It is too late to hide or even flee. By instinct, the three men move their horses close to one another, their backs to the rocky incline. Now the horns are sounding again and a whole company of men pours into the clearing, pulling up quickly to avoid a collision. They are hunters, as evidenced by their tall boots, brimmed caps, horns, and crossbows. Now three knights arrive behind them, no longer in simple green and brown attire, but red and blue outfits with puffed sleeves and braies, plates of armor covering their chests and brilliantly plumed hats on their heads. Each carries an arquebus at the ready.

Philipp's thoughts race faster than the hounds. *Who are they? Hunters might not be bad, but whom do they serve? Will we be their next kill? Lord, deliver us!*

One of the men whistles for the dogs, who begin to circle Philipp, Nesen, and Camerarius, barking and growling. A particularly bold one nips at the front hooves of Philipp's horse and is subsequently kicked hard in the face, sending the dog hurtling backward. Thwarted of their prize, the hounds seem determined to eat the three strangers instead. But something else captures their attention—the crowd of riders parts. Into the middle of the circle rides a herald, a coat of arms emblazoned on his robes: stars on a field of black, two gold lions and one red, then in the center a fourth lion with white and red stripes against a field of blue. *Hesse,* Philipp thinks. *Landgrave Philipp.* Then a gut-wrenching conclusion: *Not a friend.*

No sooner does he think it than an excellently dressed young man enters the circle on a tall, white horse. His coat is richly embroidered in black and gold, and he wears a grand chain over his high-collared shirt. Philipp takes in the man's prominent nose and ears, a jaw as sharp and unyielding as the rocky crevices behind them, and hazel eyes that seem to pierce his own. Just above the pale lips is a thin, black mustache. Most of all, Philipp is struck by this man's height, which seems to exceed any of his fellows.

"You!" the young man cries, pointing at all three of them. "You have lost me my boar!"

Philipp's intestines twist, and he laments internally. *Am I really going to die because of a pig?!*

"Who is it that accuses us?" Camerarius demands to know.

The young man lets out a savage chuckle. Riding closer, he declares, "I am Landgrave Philipp of Hesse, rightful lord of this wood! You pass through it only according to my pleasure."

Camerarius and Nesen both look at Philipp, their eyes wide and anxious, for the Landgrave sides with the Emperor. He will have no compunctions about enforcing the Edict of Worms. Philipp knows the potential penalties well enough. *Arrest and then hanging, or burning, or beheading? Perhaps all three in turn.* His muscles stiffen at the thought of it. *Our best hope is anonymity, but how long can we hope to maintain it?* The answer is swift in coming.

"I have heard that a group of scholars was traveling this way— scholars from Wittenberg," the Landgrave explains, his every word causing Philipp's bowels to wrench. "And here I find you in the middle of the forest, scholars by the look of it. You were taking the road to Fulda, but it was flooded. You asked for direction and were told to ride north into my domain. Have I guessed correctly?"

In this moment, as his earthly existence seems very much in doubt, Philipp Melanchthon thinks not of the mother he has so recently kissed farewell, nor of Luther and their work together, but his beloved Katharina, whom he has not seen since the middle of April. What were the last words he spoke to her? He took her in his arms, held her close, and whispered to her, "I wish you could come with me. I will miss you with everything I am." Then she kissed him on that early April morning, the dew still on the grass, the pink rays of the sun breaking over the Elbe. He didn't know then, though somewhere in his heart he might have feared, that he was kissing her for the last time: that she could not come with him because he was entering eternity, and he would miss her in heaven until death reunites them.

"What is it you want with us?" Camerarius asks.

As if reciting the next line in a play Philipp has already read, the Landgrave inquires, "Which one of you is Philipp Melanchthon?"

I must not beg, Philipp tells himself. *That must not be my story.*

He reaches into his reserves of strength—looks the Landgrave squarely in the eye—and answers, "I am."

His heart exceedingly heavy, Philipp makes to dismount and bow himself before authority, but now comes a line he had not seen in the script.

"Please, stay on your horse! I merely wish to speak with you."

Uncertain what to make of this declaration, Philipp does as the Landgrave requests, his hands clinging so tightly to the reins, it is a wonder they do not cut into his flesh. *Perhaps he does not mean to arrest me. Perhaps there is a way out after all.*

With this tiny speck of hope within his breast, he explains, "I am Doktor Philipp Melanchthon of the University of Wittenberg, and I am not afraid. Ask me whatever you like, and I will answer truthfully."

Now the Landgrave is laughing: a bad sign. "Are you so brave?" he asks, or rather accuses, pulling his horse directly next to Philipp's. "Don't you know that I could turn you over to Campeggio? Oh, how it would please him! I am on my way to Heidelberg to meet with him and the princes. We only stopped to enjoy some sport. Perhaps I should bring you along. Think how the Pope and the Emperor would favor me!"

What to say in response? *I must be strong. I must not falter.* Philipp decides the simplest answer is best. "You must do what you believe to be right."

Then the Landgrave reaches out a hand, and to Philipp's immense surprise, places it on his shoulder in a kindly manner.

"Have no fear, Philipp Melanchthon! I have decided something, you see. I met your Luther at Worms. He was most impressive."

"Ah, yes. I remember," Philipp says, and in his memory Martin's summary of the man's character reverberates: *Massive philanderer.*

"I hope you do not think my heart hard or my mind closed," the Landgrave continues, pulling his horse round. "You have read the works of Erasmus, have you not?"

"Yes, of course," Philipp replies automatically, shocked that this is to be their subject of discussion.

"He says a good Christian prince is duty bound to care for his people as a father would his children: to rule with justice and foster wisdom. Most of all, he stresses the importance of good education. I think you believe in this as well, Doktor."

Again, Philipp responds simply, "Yes," still attempting to regain his emotional bearings.

"My parents failed to educate me properly. I seek to be a good Christian: to rule my people with fairness and equity. But what am I to make of you theologians? The things you speak of dizzy my mind so that I hardly know which way is up! I am a practical man in search of practical solutions."

"Forgive me, Your Excellency, but I am uncertain of your aim," Philipp admits, wondering how he can be expected to carry on pleasant conversation under the circumstances.

The Landgrave smiles, his lips twisting in a somewhat unsettling manner. "They say you are the cleverest man in Germany. I want you to write me a summary of the Christian religion for my further study. Send it to Marburg, and I will review it. The teachers here are all great bores. I beg you, write me something of interest."

That is all?! he thinks. Without hesitation, he replies, "Of course. I would be only too happy to oblige."

"Good," the young ruler concludes. "Now, as for you and your fellows, you are free to go in peace, but I expect you to keep your word to me: you will send me what I have requested."

"Yes, you have my solemn pledge!" Philipp insists.

"Be off then, Doktor Melanchthon!" the Landgrave cries with a flick of the hand and a broad smile on his face. "Run home to your books!"

In a flurry, the Landgrave's whole company moves as one back into the depths of the forest, disappearing behind the endless tangle of green. The moment of peril has evidently passed. Philipp glances at Nesen and Camerarius, who look as stunned as he feels.

"We'd best continue," Camerarius says softly, as if afraid someone will overhear. "May the Lord spare us from future excitements."

He receives a pair of nods in reply, and the three of them continue around the northern edge of the hills, Philipp's heart still pounding from their fearsome encounter. No words pass between them, as if speaking of what has occurred might curse their good fortune. *But is it merely good fortune?* After all, they might have taken the road to Fulda, not knowing it was flooded, or perhaps the rains could have been fewer that spring, leaving the road dry. They could have stopped for water earlier. The Landgrave could have been less desperate for meat. Indeed, they could have opted for the breakaway path just minutes before the encounter. Any of these possibilities would have kept them from encountering Landgrave Philipp of Hesse.

God must have wished it to happen, he concludes. *He wanted me to speak with the Landgrave. But does it bode ill?*

Still in need of water, they are delighted to come upon a stream cutting quietly through the trees. There is a small clearing near its bank—the only trees that survive have had their bark stripped by deer, which have left their hoof prints in the mud. There is no bridge, but it should not be difficult to ford. The three travelers dismount and allow their horses to drink while stooping to refill their bottles. As he crouches by the moving water, Philipp remains on alert, scanning both banks for signs of movement. He can hardly believe he is not in custody...or worse. Flee, hide, or stand has become his way of life. As he lowers his bottle to capture the flow and then raises it to drink, he is joined by Camerarius.

"I was afraid they were going to arrest you, and then what would I have told your wife?" his friend remarks softly, the tension still evident in his voice.

"Marry better the second time," Philipp immediately responds, sealing the bottle once again.

This prompts a bout of nervous laughter from them both, the fear lessening for the space of a breath. Then the shadow falls again, and Philipp is caught upon the sharp edge of a memory.

"I could see her face, Joachim," he explains, voice catching in his throat. "I said I was not afraid, but I was terrified."

Camerarius grips his arm in brotherly affection. "You did well, exactly as you should have done. But tell me, friend: how do you feel now?"

Philipp considers for a moment. *I feel torn at the seams and ripped asunder. I am desperate to cling to every breath. I don't know whom to trust, and I wonder why God seems so distant. What does he intend for me? Will it be fire without or fire within?* At length, he responds, "I just want to get home as soon as possible."

"That's fair," his friend says, nodding. "You have suffered much these past few years and usually in silence." All speech ceases for a moment. Camerarius looks over at Nesen, who is relieving himself next to a tree, then addresses Philipp again, his voice low. "I wonder if you should accept Erasmus' offer."

"You mean run away?" Philipp asks, slightly offended.

Camerarius shakes his head. "I mean start anew. Grant stability to your family. You have given so much to the work of reformation already. No one could fault you for stepping back. It would not be cowardice."

How to explain? In his mind, Philipp Melanchthon delves into every nook and cranny of his being, seeking nuggets of purpose and splinters of belief. He considers the events of the past few years, turning them this way and that, examining them from every angle in the glow of hindsight. He is not sure he can express it properly, but he will try.

"I was called to Wittenberg, Joachim. I heard and saw things that I was certain could only be of God. All my life, I had longed to see him renew his works in our days. I had known the fearsome silence and yearned for its breaking: that the Spirit would pour forth as it did at the first. I longed for it, and yet it terrified me. I thought I found it in Wittenberg. Even that winter, when everything seemed to spiral, I listened to the new prophets. I wanted to believe that the gospel would sweep all before it, but it seems it was not God's will. I was a fool, Joachim! A dreadful fool. I allowed myself to be carried away. I remember sitting at our dining table, my spirit completely sapped, and telling Katharina, 'I cannot do it. I've failed. I need to leave. I need a new start.' I will never forget what she said to me. 'I will follow you anywhere, Philipp—through the very gates of hell—but I still believe. The Word has not failed. God called you here, and until he calls you elsewhere, I think you should stay. By God's grace, we can endure it.' How I needed that wisdom! I could not have survived those dark days without her. And now, I think of her words. Until God calls me somewhere else, I must remain where I am."

"It is hard to argue with that," Camerarius concedes, "and what is more, I should hate to be parted from you."

Their conversation is broken by a quickly approaching Nesen, who calls to them, "Look! Over there on the ridge!"

Philipp's eyes move in the direction that Nesen is pointing. To the right is an incline covered in a dense thicket of green, and overhead three birds are circling, their cries ascending to the heavens. Their feathers are blacker than night, their voices a series of rasping croaks issuing, it seems, from the foul belly of the underworld. They move around each other, weaving concentrically as if performing the dance of death.

"What kind of omen is this?" Nesen asks. "They seem to be doing a victory dance of some sort, or am I mistaken?"

Having devoted himself to the study of astrology and the reading of signs, Philipp Melanchthon is in no doubt as to the meaning, but he hesitates to reveal it. Instead, he says, "Crows are often seen as messengers from another world and bringers of transformation. They signal that great change is in store."

"Change," Nesen mutters breathlessly. "But for better or for worse?"

Camerarius looks at Philipp knowingly. They have read the same stories and studied the same texts. He will know as well as Philipp that three crows moving in a circle can only mean one thing, and the look on his face seems to say, *You have to tell him.* Philipp sighs and forces himself to answer.

"It is an ill fate that we should come upon them here, or rather that they should come upon us, for crows are the heralds of death. The meaning is thus: very soon, one of the three of us will die."

Nesen's face seems to droop precipitously. "What? Just like that?"

"It is not a guarantee," Camerarius suggests. "Perhaps the devil is playing with us, hoping to strike fear in our hearts and distract us from God's work."

"Let us hope so," Nesen concludes.

Philipp looks back at the crows still caught in a sinister dance, their cries grating his mind. He stands hypnotized by the sight, swept up in the cascading narrative of events—the portents of doom. It is written in the heavens, and now he reads it in the lower sphere. A thought rises within him like the twisting and tumbling birds.

What a fearsome thing it is to be held in the hands of God.

Summer

23 June 1524
Basel, Swiss Confederation

Erasmus of Rotterdam sits at the grand table in the Froben dining room, a beaker of wine in one hand and a freshly printed pamphlet in the other. It is the Eve of St. John the Baptist, a day for warding off evil spirits and seeking divine protection. Soon the entire household will be making for the marketplace to witness the lighting of the bonfire. He is all for banishing the devil but wishes it could be done at a more sensible hour. It is well past supper, and he would prefer to retire from his day's labor, but it must be night, they say: the darkness must descend before they release the light.

On the opposite wall is a painting of the Rape of Persephone by someone in Holbein's workshop. In it, an implausibly muscular Hades arises from a crack in the earth to seize the daughter of Zeus and drag her into the depths, there to spend the remainder of her days as Queen of the Underworld. There is something unsettling about the way he wraps his hardened arms around her soft, ivory body, teeth clenched and will unalterable, while Persephone's eyes are wide in dismay, clinging to their final glimpse of the light. He remembers hearing the tale as a boy and fearing that at any moment, a fissure would open, and he too would be captured in the grip of some god or demon, pulled into a cathartic abyss. It is an odd subject to feature in a dining room: he has said as much to Froben on more than one occasion.

He takes a long drink and glances down at the pamphlet in his hand. Published anonymously, it carries the heavy stink of Guillame Farel, and a more slanderous work Erasmus can hardly imagine. *Here*

is a demon for the modern age: not a god, but a man of flesh and blood
whom no magic herb can chase away. He made it through the first few
pages, a lie in every paragraph, but found it hindered his digestion.
Now he sits sipping the fruit of Burgundy and pondering what he
has read. Harst and Bertholf have already gone out and are no doubt
spending half their wages on food and drink. He ought to be celebrating as well—he has just survived another bout with the stone—but he
is hardly in the right mood.

   Johann Froben enters the room dressed in a dark coat with fur
lining: too warm for the evening by far, but it will make an impression.
For the past quarter hour, sounds of commotion have been raining
down from the upper levels of the house, and Erasmus suspects this
is why his friend looks harried and out of breath.

   "We're having a bit of trouble with Justina," Froben explains,
referring to his thirteen-year-old daughter. "She discovered a new
sore on her face and is afraid to be seen with it."

   "What does she think anyone will see in this darkness?" Erasmus
inquires.

   Froben shrugs in resignation. He then notices the pamphlet and
demands to know, "What is that?"

   "This?" Erasmus responds, raising it for display. "It is the latest
production of our friend Phallicus."[1]

   Froben smiles mischievously. "Phallicus? You mean Farel?"

   "Well, I thought it was the least I could do to Latinize his name.
He is said to be a great scholar, after all."

   "I doubt he'll see it as a compliment."

   "On the contrary, if I know the man at all, he will take it as high
praise."

   As Froben laughs, his son Hieronymus, a young man who could
not be more precisely the image of his forebear, enters the room,
selects an orange from a bowl on the table and inquires, "Why must
you have a daughter, father?"

   The smile on Froben's face disappears. "What now?"

   "She cannot find her brooch!" Hieronymus complains,
tossing and catching the fruit with his right hand. "She only thinks
of showing off!"

---

[1] It means what you think it means.

Even as he makes this declaration, Froben's younger son, Johann Erasmus, runs into the dining chamber, clutching bundles of St. John's wort in his arms.[2]

"How much longer?" the youngster complains. "We're going to miss it!"

"Come here, boy," Erasmus instructs. His godson happily joins him at the table, laying down the yellow flowers and sitting in Erasmus' lap. "There is something you must learn about women: they cannot be rushed."

"But she's not a woman! She's a girl—a stinking girl!" the boy whines in a way only a little brother could.

Erasmus pats him on the head. In truth, they have all grown weary of Justina's moods. The young lady is locked in an ongoing conflict with her mother, their skirmishes coming sometimes thrice daily. The men of the house have taken to ducking for cover, praying they are not caught in the crossfire.

Pointing to the pamphlet, Froben says, "You shouldn't read that, you know. It will only infuriate you."

"Not this time," Erasmus explains. "This might be the evidence I need to convince the town council to banish him."

"I thought he had set off for Zürich to join Zwingli," says Hieronymus. "Is he not one of their number?"

"He is a devil of hell, that's what he is," Erasmus concludes, "and he has returned like the plague to torture us. He is staying with Œcolampadius."

Froben shakes his head and mutters, "Johannes ought to know better. He seemed a man of sense when he was working for me."

Erasmus looks at the painting across the room: the captured woman being torn from her people and dragged into the depths. "Nothing is at it seems," he whispers.

Now their discourse is interrupted by the sound of Frau Froben bellowing up the stairs. "Justina! Justina, get down here now!"

"I can't go out like this!" the girl shrieks, the heat of her voice sufficient to curdle milk. "It's impossible!"

---

[2] St. John's wort is one of several herbs that were traditionally harvested on the Eve of St. John the Baptist's feast day. They were believed to help ward off evil forces, black magic, and the like.

With a look of exhaustion in his eyes, Froben directs the men into the hallway, where they find Gertrude with both hands pressed against her temples, her eyes bulging and breath coming heavily. Froben places a hand on her shoulder.

"She was so sweet as a girl," Gertrude whispers. "So sweet! But this thing that lives among us now: I can't, husband. I just can't."

"If she wants to stay, dear, let her stay," Froben says, kissing her forehead softly. "I will speak with her later."

This settles the matter, and soon they are all walking into the night air, cutting past the shops in the alleyway, then turning left onto Schneider Street. Here the St. Andreas Plaza is full of vendors selling herbs for the festival, pies, cheeses, painted fans, noodles, cut flowers, and oranges. A whole pig is roasted over an open flame, smoke wafting to the sky, illuminated in the flickering light. Now they turn right on Town Hall Street, crossing over the River Birsig through which the city's waste is carried to the Rhine. It is buried under the marketplace but emerges just to their left, and combined with the smell of the fish stalls, it causes Erasmus' stomach to lurch.

Finally, they arrive in the center of the city: the market square thronging with activity. It is packed with human life, the only open spaces left for jugglers, tricksters, and the mound of logs itself. They are pressed against the crowd, unable to move, with more people pushing behind them. The light of the sun is fading, and soon Erasmus will be trapped here in the dark with half the city's population. *Why did I agree to come?* he wonders. There is chanting and singing, dancing and imbibing. There are drums banging with the force of cannon.

"Lift me up! I cannot see!" demands Johann Erasmus.

The boy's father raises him with some effort, for he is no longer a little thing. A drunkard steps on the hem of Frau Froben's dress, and she cries, "Stay back! I've just had this cleaned!" Desperate for a way out, Erasmus looks to the right, down past two of the merchant's houses to a tavern called The Swan. There he can just make out patrons sitting at wooden tables, remarkably undisturbed.

"I need a drink. I'll meet you back at the house," he shouts to the Frobens.

"But you can't leave now!" Johann Erasmus moans. "It's almost time for them to light the fire!"

The boy's father, however, is more understanding and offers a nod of acknowledgment.

Erasmus forces his way through the sea of bodies, moving with the flow of the current. The heat of summer, the smell of beer, the cacophony all around—they make their claims upon him. Fire breathers and painted men, strings of sausages hanging from poles, a man grasping a woman's buttocks and a babe wailing for her teat. Still the drums bang. His senses are beaten bloody, shocked to the point of numbness. Finally, he arrives beneath the painted sign with its great white bird. Before him are six tables and accompanying benches, but only one is full and the crowd is keeping back from it. A man stands on top of the table, gesticulating and holding court, and as Erasmus makes out his features in the fading light, he realizes why few have dared to tread close.

"Popery and superstition—that's all it is!" cries Guillame Farel. "Why do you look to this fire for salvation when you ought to be looking to Christ?!"

A newcomer to the German lands, Farel can only address them in Latin, so the passersby look at him bewildered, perhaps concluding he has had too much to drink. For the first time in his life, Erasmus regrets knowing the language of Virgil.

"The Scriptures forbid us to make images and worship them!" Farel shouts. "They forbid anything in worship not ordained by God! Why then do you cling to herbs and light fires when you ought to be reading your Bible and going to Church?! This city is ripe for the judgment of God!"

Sitting below him are Johannes Œcolampadius, Conrad Pellicanus, and surprisingly Michael Bentinus, an employee of Froben who until recently Erasmus would have considered a man of good sense. *Can you ever truly know a man?* he wonders. So impassioned is Farel, he stomps his foot in exclamation, shaking the mugs of beer and causing the liquid to slop on the table.

"Why do you while away your days when the wrath of God is fulminating?!" the Frenchman cries. "The way to hell is paved with the gold you waste on conjurer's tricks!"

"Shut up, or you'll be tinder for the fire!" someone yells in the local tongue.

No drink is worth this, Erasmus decides, but as he starts walking away, the voice of Conrad Pellicanus calls out to him.

"Erasmus! Oh, dear Erasmus: you are a fine sight for weary eyes!"

He turns around slowly, wondering why he agreed to come at all. They are all looking at him now: Pellicanus, Œcolampadius, Bentinus, and probably even Farel, though Erasmus refuses to meet his gaze. Instead, he focuses on Pellicanus, the Franciscan friar and expert in biblical languages. *Here is a man I once thought serious.* He stares at the monk's brown habit and wonders how long he will continue to wear it, for Pellicanus like so many is drifting ever closer to Luther, or at least away from Rome. *How can he stand to fellowship with that fool of a slanderer?! And to think I once loaned him my manuscripts!* Sadly, a response will be necessary.

"Your eyes cannot be as weary as mine, for I see little of you in this darkness," Erasmus responds.

"Come!" Pellicanus calls, beckoning with his hand. "Have a drink with us!"

He would be willing to sit with Pellicanus. He could even tolerate Œcolampadius. But how can he sit with the man who has been maligning him to every person who will listen, or at least every person who can understand Latin?

"Thank you, but I must seek a better view," he begs.

Farel dismounts from the table directly in front of Erasmus, a sneer on his face. Evidently intent on making his presence known, the Frenchman steps closer—so close, in fact, that Erasmus becomes uncomfortable, but he must not back off or be seen to shrink from the fight. He stands his ground as the far younger man stares at him, creeping ever closer. He feels like prey being sized up by a beast, only the beast in this case is about to be smacked on the nose.

Then cries of delight rise from the crowd. A surge of heat and burst of light! Erasmus glances in the direction of the bonfire that has just been lit, sparks ascending to the heavens, crowd thoroughly enraptured. The drums are beaten and the church bells ring. As one, the people sing together, cursing the devils of the night. Erasmus looks upon his adversary again, now clearly visible. The nose is exceptionally Gallic—the beard without a trace of gray. The scholar's robes are a good bit too big, perhaps purchased off another man. The eyes are pools of inky black in which the light of the fire plays, lending them an unnatural fierceness.

"Erasmus of Rotterdam," Farel begins. "How I have longed to meet you in the flesh and see that you are only a man! Such praise they heap upon you, it is a wonder you do not suffocate!"

No, he thinks. *I will not be drawn. If we must do this, it will be on my terms.*

"I have nothing much to say to you, Monsieur," Erasmus replies, his words clipped. "I know you denounce me to everyone you meet as 'Balaam.'[3] You borrowed that from Du Blet, though why he thought it an appropriate title, I have no idea. I have never accepted money to write against Luther, nor, I might add, did Balaam accept money to curse Israel."

Erasmus feels the truth of these words in his bones, for as he stares into Farel's crazed eyes, he longs to counter the menace they represent. *I am right to oppose Luther in print. Surely, I am. The fault for this lies at his door.*

Farel snorts derisively. "Whether you have accepted money, I know not, but I should be surprised to see you write against anyone if it costs you a meal at some great man's table. You declare yourself as unyielding as Terminus, but you have no beliefs and no god but your stomach!"

Erasmus feels the heat rippling on his skin as his pulse keeps time with the drums. The crowd must have their show, but his audience is only Pellicanus, Bentinus, and Œcolampadius, who by the look of things are dreading this exchange. It grants him confidence.

"Let me ask you this: why do you think it wrong to invoke the saints?" he inquires. "Is it because it is never expressly mentioned in Scripture?"

"That's right," Farel replies.

"So where in Scripture does it say to invoke the Holy Spirit?"

Another snort. "He is God. Therefore, it is right to invoke him."

I have you, Erasmus thinks. *I have you in my grasp.*

---

[3] Balaam is a somewhat obscure figure in the Old Testament: a foreigner who became caught up in the Israelite conquest of Canaan. Bribed to curse the Israelites, Balaam ended up prophesying on behalf of the true God instead, somewhat lessening the effect of Farel's intended insult. Of course, most people know Balaam as the man who was forced to converse with an ass, a comparison that Erasmus might have found more pleasing under the circumstances.

"Now, understand I am speaking for the sake of argument," he continues, "for I fully endorse the invocation of the Spirit. Nevertheless, by your own standard, I charge you to demonstrate its validity from Scripture alone."

Farel chuckles savagely, looking back at his companions with eyes full of glee.

"Why do you laugh?" Erasmus demands to know.

"Because it amuses me—you, trying to catch me out!" Farel retorts. "But if you insist, there is the passage in John's first epistle."

"I beg you to tell me which passage you mean, remembering of course that I only argue to make a point."

"'The three are one.' That is what it says."

He shakes his head. "That is not what it says. The passage reads, 'For there are three that testify: the Spirit and the water and the blood, and the three are in agreement.'"[4]

There is a momentary flash in Farel's eyes, as if for the space of a breath he realizes he has made a mistake. He recovers swiftly and attempts to flick away the argument like a biting fly. "'One,' 'in agreement': same difference."

"I beg you to see it is not the same difference, for the passage is not speaking about an equality of nature, but an equality of witness. It is not even certain that John is speaking of the Trinity." When Farel snorts yet again, he insists, "No, do not scoff! That part about the Father, the Word, and the Spirit does not appear in any of the ancient manuscripts. It was not quoted by the Fathers. Unless you have another passage to offer, I submit that you have not demonstrated the point."

Farel is beginning to lose control. Hands on hips, he charges, "This is ridiculous! You protest in vain to glorify yourself!"

A killing blow, Erasmus thinks. *I have bested you.* He moves so close to Farel that he can smell the beer on his breath. Erasmus locks eyes with him, raising a finger of rebuke, his speech measured and deliberate.

"Listen to me, young man: I am wise to your ways. I know it was you who wrote those libelous pamphlets about me and had them printed by Welshans. I know you told Thomas Grey that I have the

---

[4] 1 John 5:8.

right ideas but am too much of a coward to defend them, despite
your claim that I have no beliefs at all. Do not pretend to know my
mind, Monsieur!"

"You have no proof of any of this," Farel replies quickly—desperately.

"I know everything that happens in this town. Do you think you
are the only one who listens to gossip? I have three times as many
people ready to surrender gossip to me, for they find me far more
tolerable! I know you have pledged that you will not rest until you
have destroyed my reputation. You have devoted yourself to it every
day, though I have not written against you. In all my years, I have
never come across a more habitual liar! You slander me in every
canton and province!"

Farel takes a step back, glancing at his fellows for support, but
they are mute, their expressions testifying to their dismay. Therefore,
Farel turns back to him and cries, "Oh, give it up! You are played out.
Do you think you can stand against the tide and force back the waters?
God alone holds them in the hollow of his hands! Our moment is
come, and yours is passed. Declare yourself for us or retire from the
stage!"

Erasmus breathes deeply, embracing the heat, allowing it to flow
through him. He concentrates his energies in aging muscles, summoning the powers of his intellect to meet the moment.

"I have one or two cards left to play, even if I am being pulled
under by the current," he assures his opponent. "You misjudge me,
Monsieur. What you call 'courage' is mere vainglory, but there is
a courage that gets out of bed: that swims out into an uncertain
world, subject to the tide of fortune, struggling against the currents
of change, seeking a safe harbor for the soul. That is the pilgrim way.
You may try if you wish to walk upon the waves, but I must face my
going under. We will see who is left standing in the end."

Farel spits on the ground to signal his disgust, but Erasmus is
entirely satisfied with his performance. He moves around Farel and
begins walking away from the scene, having accomplished his desire.
Then he hears Œcolampadius cry, "Herr Erasmus!"

Sighing deeply, he waits for his former colleague to reach
his position. The noise from the crowd is like a constant pressure
on his head, and he longs to be free of it. Erasmus looks upon
Œcolampadius—a man of forty-three with a pointed nose, dark

beard, and brown eyes—and is gripped by a sense of loss. Here is a brilliant scholar, a man with whom he worked side-by-side, and a potential heir to his work. From the same region as the younger Melanchthon, Œcolampadius is like his friend in many respects. But were Erasmus being honest, it was never Œcolampadius whom he wanted to carry on the work: it was always Melanchthon. Not that it matters, for Œcolampadius favored first Luther and now Zwingli, to the point that Erasmus has had to beg him not to mention their prior friendship in print.

"Herr Erasmus!" Œcolampadius calls again, out of breath. "I am sorry about that just now. He was carried away by the moment."

"Why do you keep company with that fool?" he demands to know. "You know as well as I do: he is a villain with no self-control."

The younger man's eyes focus on some distant object as he shakes his head. "I have spoken with him. Pellicanus has spoken with him."

"Well, unless you told him to go about slandering me from post to pillar, I'd say your efforts have been rather fruitless."

Now Œcolampadius looks directly into Erasmus' eyes and insists, "He is passionate. God makes use of passionate men."

"What is a passionate man but one who has no control over his emotions and actions?" he objects. "I would think that a better tool for the devil."

A nod and a deep sigh from Œcolampadius. "I will speak to him again. We will sort this out."

"It is too late," Erasmus informs him. "I have spoken with the councilors. We are putting an end to this. They will banish him for libel. He must find another audience for his invectives."

There is a pained look on Œcolampadius' face. His mouth is slightly agape.

"Erasmus," he breathes, unable to continue.

"I always thought you were an honorable man, Œcolampadius. Are you still an honorable man?"

The younger man nods swiftly. "I trust the Lord has made me so."

"Then have the courage to take on the wolves, or I will not be the last sheep bitten and bleeding. Now, if you will pardon me, I am off to the cathedral to pray."

"It doesn't have to be like this, Erasmus!" Œcolampadius insists. "We can reach an accord! After all, we are sons of the same Father!"

Erasmus offers no response but keeps walking, leaving the crowd behind, passing between the elaborate Town Hall and St. Martin's Church, where Œcolampadius is pastor. The clamor mercifully reduced, he walks by the buildings of the University of Basel standing as sentinels upon the River Rhine, managing the descent as best he can in the dark. Rome is a city of seven hills—Basel, seven hundred.

I will not heal the wound lightly, he thinks. *There is no point in pretending we can reach an accord when we both know full well what Farel is doing.* A few steps further, and he grouses, "Same Father, indeed! What do you know of my father?"

He has come to it now: Basel Minster. Here is the seat of his friend Christoph, who after the feast of Peter and Paul will be heading back to his manor in the country to wait out the summer heat. The twin towers of the red stone cathedral are mostly cloaked in darkness, and he can see nothing of the colorful tile work, but the windows shine with an ethereal glow from the candles inside. He stands for a moment simply staring at it.

Where is he? Where is our father?

The words echo in Erasmus' head like a chant in a grotto. He inhales quickly, overcome by emotion. He remembers the response of his mother to that simple question. They were standing in their tiny kitchen. He was eight years old, or perhaps nine.

"I've told you, schat. He has his own family. You cannot know him."

"What makes them better than us?" Erasmus protested, his young mind unable to grasp the matter.

His mother looked at him with mournful eyes, her blond hair hidden beneath a simple scarf.

"You must promise me not to go looking for him. Do you understand?" she asked.

"But—"

"No 'but's! I don't want you looking for him, and I don't want Pieter looking for him," she insisted, referring to his older brother.

"But how can I not know my father?!"

No answers were granted, so he spent his days running along the streets of Gouda, past the wheels of cheese laid out on cloth. Within his breast were questions that tore at his young heart: *Who is my father? Who am I?* Always the equivocations from his mother—always the denials. She was called Margaretha Rutgers, but he had been given no surname. The children in the street would label him a bastard and her a whore. There was little work for a shamed woman. It was only the generosity of the Church that allowed them to eat.

"See how good the Church is to us, schat!" his mother would tell him. "Father Gerard is so gracious!"

Indeed, everyone in town set great store by Father Gerard. He had a sharpness of mind beyond that of most priests, but to Erasmus, he was primarily the man who handed out sweets and asked after his welfare. Already the recipient of so much unkindness at a young age, Erasmus was naturally drawn to the one man who treated him like a full human being capable of worthwhile thoughts. He assisted Father Gerard with chores and was even allowed access to the priest's small library of books. It was Father Gerard who directed the education of Erasmus and his brother, Pieter. The priest was always prepared to answer any question Erasmus might have—always happy to provide a listening ear. When Erasmus admitted one day that he wished he knew his father, the priest said to him, "You must not doubt your worth. God is your Father, and his love for you is great."

So swift was his progress in the faith and so keen was his mind, it was decided Erasmus would be confirmed on the same day as Pieter despite his young age. They knelt beside each other at the rail, their eyes wide as Father Gerard anointed them with the sacred chrism. They listened as he extolled them in Latin, and Erasmus felt a rush of joy as Father Gerard laid a hand on his head, proclaiming him sealed with the Holy Spirit.

Only one more sacrament was necessary to mark Erasmus' full participation in the family of God: his first Communion. Perhaps this would be just the thing to fill his emptiness. Denied an identity, he would take the name of Christ. He had never been this ready for a thing in his young life. Erasmus stood next to his mother and brother during the Mass, longing for the moment when he would walk forward and receive the body of Christ—not the blood, for he was no priest. As he watched Father Gerard elevate the host, Erasmus was overcome by emotion. Tears filled his eyes, blurring the candle flames. The moment had come.

Clothed in a simple tunic worn at the edges, shoes full of holes and hair unkempt, he walked up the central aisle of the church, eyes focused on Father Gerard. He felt a strange longing—an ache in the pit of his stomach. Even in that most sacred hour, he was desperate to know his father. The promises of God seemed distant in comparison to the pain he suffered in the here and now. He had to know! *You cannot know him, schat.* That was what his mother had said. *He has his own family.*

Erasmus was halfway up the aisle, watching as the other congregants received the consecrated bread on their tongues. He remembered what someone once said to him after watching the priest teach him how to use a slingshot. *He shows such concern for you, as if you were his own son.* Erasmus' heart began to beat faster. He was caught up in a whirlwind of thought. *As if you were his own son...* He was cut to the quick, scarcely able to comprehend it, even as he reached the altar.

Erasmus knelt beside Pieter—prepared himself to receive. His eyes were locked on Father Gerard as the priest offered the bread to each congregant in turn. *His nose is just like mine,* Erasmus thought. *His eyes are the same color as mine.* The truth was pummeling him like an avalanche: *The other family is the congregation. A priest is bound by celibacy.* This explained his mother's warning. A silent wail issued from the deepest reaches of Erasmus' being, for he knew nothing of canon law, but he understood the bond of blood. He knew when things were not as they should be.

Father Gerard smiled down at him and spoke the words in Latin: "The body of Christ, given for you." Erasmus stared in wonder at the priest's blue eyes, captured by a powerful desire he could not explain: a need to be known and accepted. He accepted the morsel on his tongue, gazing upon Father Gerard, caught up in something like the ecstasy of the saints. He whispered a single word: a question and a plea.

"Vader!"

He spoke not in Latin, but Dutch. If he were merely referring to Gerard's priestly title, he would have used the Latin as he always did, but this was different: a personal claim. Father Gerard sensed it immediately. The look on the priest's face changed from one of serene pride to a strained frown of concern. For just a moment, he paused rather than moving down the line and looked upon Erasmus. The priest's lower lip was trembling almost imperceptibly, but the boy noticed it.

Then a hardening: an unwillingness to be moved. Father Gerard set his face like flint and repeated in Latin, "The body of Christ." Then he moved to the next person.

For days, Erasmus spoke of it to no one. He had tasted from the tree of knowledge, but it had not granted him the peace he sought. Instead, he felt angry—far angrier than a boy ought to be. He was filled with wrathful indignation. He had been taken for a fool! This whole time, he had thought Father Gerard wanted a part in his life, but it turned out the opposite was true: he wanted no part of Erasmus the bastard. How many times had they spoken together? Every time was a lie, for every time Father Gerard chose not to inform Erasmus that he was his father of the flesh.

Eventually, Erasmus' mother realized he was acting strangely. "Why don't you go to see Father Gerard anymore?" So, Erasmus confessed that he knew the truth and watched as she was overcome by tears. "I'm sorry, schat. What could I have done?"

"You could have told me the truth!"

"And risk his position? Don't you know he provides for us? He is the only reason we aren't on the street!"

These arguments had little effect on Erasmus. He still saw the world in simple contradictions, and all he knew was that he wanted a father: a real father. Then one day, his mother convinced Father Gerard to speak with him. Erasmus was led into the same tiny chamber he had visited many times before, with all the priest's books sitting in perfect rows upon wooden shelves. How beautiful they were! Erasmus sat in a simple chair opposite Father Gerard, their knees no more than three feet apart.

Staring into his matching eyes, the priest said, "You are a remarkable boy, Erasmus. I've always thought so."

"Because I know and Pieter doesn't?"

"No. Because of who you are."

He could see that his father was trying: attempting to make things right. But it was no good. There was too much left undone.

"You don't have to say those things just to make me feel good," Erasmus replied quietly.

"I understand why you feel that I've failed you—"

"You have failed me," he stated with authority, not hesitating to interrupt the man whom he so respected only a week earlier.

"Erasmus," the priest said softly, falling silent and then regaining his voice. "There was no other way."

"Because the Church says so?"

"Because I have a duty to God."

Erasmus shook his head, overcome by confusion and anger. "Don't you care about us?"

"Of course, I do! I have always cared for you. Surely your mother explained this to you?"

"She told me you give us money. You try to look after us."

"What more would you have me do?"

"Why can't we live together like a real family?" Erasmus inquired, daring to speak his deepest desire.

"I have two families, Erasmus," the priest explained, attempting to remain calm but clearly becoming emotional. "The Church is my family as well, and I made a commitment to serve it above all else."

"Then why did you sleep with mother?!" he cried in anger. "Why did you make us at all?!"

His father was taken aback. He stammered but could not make an end of it.

"Do you love her?" Erasmus demanded to know.

Here an answer was quicker in coming. "Yes. Yes, of course I do."

"Then why did you become a priest?"

"It was complicated. I don't expect you to understand."

"No!" Erasmus shouted, his sense of justice offended. "Don't treat me like a fool!"

Perhaps because he did not know what else to do, the priest fell back upon an appeal to authority. "You would raise your voice to me?"

"Why shouldn't I? You don't want to be my father. You don't want us."

"That's not true," his father objected, clearly pained.

"Then why did you do it?"

Father Gerard sighed, looking down at the floor. "I had no other choice."

"I don't believe you. I think you're lying to me!"

The priest's gaze met him again, and Erasmus saw a vulnerability there—a weakness that repulsed him.

"If that is what you believe, then I cannot change your mind," Father Gerard conceded, "but I promise you, I am not ashamed to be your father."

"Then why not tell everyone you're my father?"

"Erasmus—"

"You're a liar!" he cried, despairing in his situation, knowing that he would never have his desire. "You're a liar, and I hate you!"

Father Gerard nodded softly. "That is your right. Were I in your place, I might feel the same way."

There were tears in Erasmus' young eyes, and he did not know where to go—where to run from the anger and shame. "Tell me," he whispered.

"Tell you what, child?"

"Tell me I am your son."

By this point, Father Gerard was crying as well. He nodded and spoke slowly, with great depth of feeling. "You are my son."

And in that moment, though he was still a boy, Erasmus experienced a certainty for which many men long. Made bold by anger, he looked his father in those eyes so like his own: the eyes that beckoned and rejected him at the same time, looking on him in love, but not in love. Eyes that called into question all he was.

Erasmus spoke emphatically. "No, I'm not."

Later that evening, he was in the kitchen again, helping his mother knead bread. She risked raising the subject of his conversation with Father Gerard, but there were few details Erasmus was willing to surrender. Finally, his mother charged him, "You must not tell anyone, schat. It's very important that you keep it a secret."

"I know, I know. I'm not a child."

"Oh, but you are, schat, even if you bear the world's weight on your shoulders."

"I know how to keep a secret," he assured her. "Isn't that what men do? Keep secrets? Not tell anyone what they're thinking? I can be a man."

His mother looked upon him with sad eyes. "You are old before your time. It grieves me."

Yes, it is all coming back to Erasmus here in this distant land, beneath the towers of Basel's cathedral, on a night so short but somehow darker than all others. He is captured by the memories, wallowing in the pain, stretched unto the breaking point. He can see it all in his old age just as he saw it in boyhood, for no amount of time can blunt the force of his father's rejection. He has refused to take the name 'Gerritz'—refused even to associate himself with Gouda. Whether Desiderius Erasmus or Erasmus Rotterdamus, these are names of his creation and an identity all his own. It ought to fill him with pride, but he could hardly be emptier. As the distant sounds of revelry fill the night air, he knows one thing for certain: he has no father.

10 July 1524
Wittenberg, Electorate of Saxony

Ache. Terrible ache!

That is what Philipp Melanchthon feels as he stands upon the tile floor of St. Mary's Church, surrounded by men of the congregation. It is the Lord's Day, and he has come to be among the Lord's people, but it feels as if only his body is present. His mind is far away—in a barren land where the dead still walk, abandoned by the living. Were it not for the eternal yammering of his back and the ache in his feet from standing at length on stone, his thoughts might abandon his body entirely. But as always, it is the pain that draws him back and ties him to the earth.

Yet, the pain in his soles is nothing compared to that within. The memory of his own mortality is etched on him like the scars of war in crevices carved deeper with each human parting. After his encounter with Landgrave Philipp of Hesse, he had longed for nothing more than a swift return to Wittenberg: to hold his wife and daughter in his arms and cover them with kisses, swearing his eternal love. That joyous reunion was not to be. As soon as he crossed the threshold, he found his wife weeping. He dropped his satchel and ran to her, holding her face in his hands—wiping her tears with his fingers.

"What is it, my love? What's wrong?"

He had never seen such sorrow in her beautiful eyes: not even in the dark days three years earlier.

Breathing deeply to calm herself, Katharina told him, "It's our brother Hans," then was struck by another wave of sorrow.

She meant Johannes Schwertfeger, the Professor of Jurisprudence at the Leucorea who had recently married Katharina's sister, Anna. Smart and amiable, Hans had quickly become a central part of the Krapp family—Philipp's kin as surely as those with whom he was raised. They could hardly imagine themselves without dear Hans. Thus, Philipp had waited in agony, his mind tortured by the possibilities her statement unleashed.

"What's happened to him?" he asked. "Käthe, what's happened?"

"He fell ill," she sniffled. "It was so fast. One day, he helped me carry things back from the market. The next they had to call for Herr Bugenhagen." Another pause to cry, and then she spoke the words that confirmed his fears. "He's dead, Philipp. He's gone."

What a blow to receive upon returning home! His letter to Landgrave Philipp, his efforts to improve education, his involvement in the Karlstadt affair, his reply to Erasmus: everything had to be put on hold to attend to the needs of the family. He wondered if he might have read the sign of the crows wrong. Were they warning him not that he, Camerarius, or Nesen would die, but that the death of a loved one had already occurred? Much as he had striven to learn the science of astrology, he knew it merely grants warnings, not faultless predictions.

Any doubts he may have had about the birds' odd dance were cast aside three days later when he learned that William Nesen had drowned in a boating accident, compounding both his pain and his fears. One moment he mourns the loss of two vibrant young lives; the next he worries who else will join them in the hereafter. It is the year of the Great Conjunction, and he has heard the dire predictions for years: a flood of such ferocity that it will remake the world. Much as he attempts to cling to joy, he finds he can only lament.

Therefore, as Philipp Melanchthon stands at attention in the center of the nave, watching Martin Luther mount the stairs of the pulpit, he finds himself utterly distracted by grief. About ten feet in front of him, his wife Katharina is sitting with their two-year-old daughter, Anna, asleep in her lap. To their right is Katharina's mother of the same name, and to the left is his sister-in-law also named Anna, so recently widowed. Looking at them stokes the burning ache in Philipp's heart, prodding it into full conflagration. The loss of a loved one is always difficult, but the elder Anna's grief has been particularly deep. "It feels like half my soul has been torn away, and I am bleeding profusely." That is what she said to him in an unguarded moment. Hans was advancing at the university. They had great hopes of a house full of children. Why would the Lord snatch him away just when they had found an earthly joy that so many never experience?

Martin has reached the lectern, opened the Bible, and laid out his notes. His text today will be from the eighth chapter of the Gospel of Mark. The temperature is sweltering, and several of the women are fanning themselves. Philipp feels drops of sweat running down his back and wishes for all the world that he could remove his scholar's cloak. High above, Martin's eyes briefly scan the crowd, then he begins to preach, his voice carrying free and clear to the far corners of the hall.

"I fear the time will come when we will hear much less of the gospel for which we have hungered. Consider what it says in the eighth chapter of the prophet Amos, the eleventh verse: 'Behold, days are coming when I will send a famine upon the land, not of bread or water, but of hearing the words of the Lord.' It would be the greatest plague on earth to take away this Word of God which we have had."[5]

He ought to be paying attention, but Philipp's eyes are drawn to his sister-in-law, whose head is now bent and her shoulders moving up and down. He can hear her breath coming in and out in gasps—a kind of grunting in her throat. Clearly, she is given over to tears. Suddenly, she rises to her feet and walks quickly toward the north portal. To do so, she must pass directly beneath the pulpit, and for an instant Martin is distracted and looks down in concern. Indeed, every eye in the place is on Anna Schwertfeger as she flies out the door and into the yard where the cemetery is located. A cascade of whispers moves through the congregation.

Regaining his composure, Martin continues. "As I was saying, God throws the faithful into want, dangers, et cetera, so that it appears as if all things will perish. But he does this in order to test their faith."

---

[5] This is based upon the following text: Luther, Martin. "*Predigt am 7 Sonntag nach Trinitas*," in *Doktor Martin Luthers Werke, Band 15 – Kristliche Gessamtausgabe, Weimar Ausgabe* (Weimar: Hermann Böhlaus Nachfolger, 1899), 649. Translation: "Sermon upon the 7th Sunday after Trinity," in *Doctor Martin Luther's Works*, Vol. 15, Weimar edition.

Half the congregation remains caught up in Anna's brisk and emotional exit. Philipp's eyes jump to his wife Katharina, who still holds their sleeping daughter in her arms. She looks back at him desperately, motioning with her head in the direction of the door and mouthing the words, *Go to her.* Nodding in acknowledgment, he attempts to extricate himself from the clump of men as quietly as possible, stepping on Nikolaus von Amsdorf's toes in the process. After a whispered plea for his colleague's pardon, Philipp too walks beneath Martin's gaze and reaches the north portal, throwing open the door and stepping out into a wet morning.

He passes beneath the carved figures of Peter and Paul that stand above the door and walks across the gravel path. The air is terribly hot, and the sun is shining between the clouds, but a light drizzle falls from heaven to earth, rising as steam off the hot ground. Before him, rows of headstones sit in the green grass and a single oak tree stands at the center of the cemetery, which is walled on three sides. One of the graves is more freshly cut, and it is before this marker that Anna kneels, dressed in the plainest of brown gowns, a translucent veil covering her face. This is the way she has chosen to express her grief outwardly. Although the Krapps are traditionally tailors and prominent in the town, they can no longer afford the black fabric favored for this purpose by royalty. As drizzle softly falls on her, Anna Schwertfeger weeps, her tears falling onto the burial place of her late husband.

Placing his cap on his head, Philipp walks a few steps closer, treading on the wet grass. It is quiet on the surrounding streets, for nearly everyone is inside listening to Martin. They are, at least for the moment, blessedly alone.

What should I say? he wonders. *What comfort can I possibly offer her?*

Evidently sensing his presence, Anna attempts to stifle her tears and says, "Forgive me. I'm sure they all think I've gone mad."

"Hardly!" Philipp assures her. "Most of us know the pain of losing someone we love. I too have suffered that grief. No one thinks it strange."

She lifts her veil to converse more properly. Her eyes, so like his wife's, appear red and fatigued. "Of course. You lost your father."

"I do not claim it is the same as losing a spouse. That is a pain I hope never to know." He thinks of his Katharina, on account of whose love he was made part of the Krapp family. He thinks of what he felt in the Hessian forest—how it continues to agonize him weeks after the fact. His gaze directed squarely at the ground, he remarks, "Perhaps I fear more that my wife will experience that pain—indeed, that she will experience it soon."

He dares to raise his eyes and look into Anna's. They are staring at him with a fierce intensity of grief: a kind of visual moan. It is as if she is hanging by a thread over the icy waters of death, desperate for someone to draw her back to the land of the living. *She is not really looking at me,* he thinks. *She is seeking the face of God.*

He kneels on the grass beside her, and they both stare at the name 'Johannes Schwertfeger' cut into gray stone. The dates that bound his earthly existence are there for all to read, but they capture nothing of Hans' intelligence, vivaciousness, or faithfulness to those he loved. They cannot record the way he looked at Anna on their wedding day or the pride he felt when Jonas gave him a doktor's cap. Hans is in a place of ultimate fulfillment, but those who loved him are left empty, safeguarding the broken shards of who he was.

He risks a dangerous inquiry. "Tell me, is it getting any better? Are you sleeping more soundly?"

Anna sniffs again, still staring at her late husband's name. "I wish I could tell everyone I am doing better. Perhaps then the questions would stop, or at least come more slowly. I appreciate them and I hate them: the questions." Now she turns to look at him, eyes moist. "I swear, Philipp, just now, when I was sitting in there, I felt such terrible grief, it was as if I was robbed of breath—as if something were pressing on my chest." Here she places a hand over her heart to emphasize the point. "I started to weep. I couldn't stop it. I'm sure you heard me along with everyone else."

"It's alright, Anna," he says with a gentle firmness. "You must trust me: it's alright."

She nods sadly. "I felt a desperate longing to come here—to be as near him as possible. I know his soul is in heaven, of course." Here she pauses and looks at the ground, as if ashamed. "Though if I were to dare a bit of honesty, I find nearly everything doubtful at the moment."

"That's normal. After my father died, I felt as if my whole world had been destroyed. Of course, he had been sick for some time, but the finality of it still, as you put it, robbed me of breath."

"Were you with him at the end?" she asks, her voice full of concern.

"Yes. Georg and I were recalled from school. I remember it was dark in his room: there was only the light of the candles." Now he finds himself tearing up and is forced into a brief pause before continuing. "He was lying in his bed in a simple white tunic that seemed to devour him—he was so gaunt by that point. He beckoned me with one finger. I knelt by the bedside and held his hand. I remember being so frightened, afraid even to look at him in that condition. He was always the ultimate proof of strength, my father, and the ultimate proof of goodness. He pulled me close—he could only really whisper—and said to me, 'Philipp, I have seen many changes in my life, but greater changes are coming.'"

"Did he truly?!" Anna exclaims, her eyes wide. "Well, that was a prophecy and no mistake!"

"All I knew was that I was about to lose my father forever, and I did. Our priest said it was a blessing that his suffering was over, but I was eleven years old: I wanted my father. And I lost my grandfather Reuter that month as well."

"I'm so sorry, Philipp," she whispers, shaking her head. "That must have been horrific."

Now it is only the sunshine that rains down on them. Philipp raises his face and closes his eyes, soaking in the warmth from on high. He thinks of all that has happened since he arrived in Wittenberg—everything that God has asked him to bear.

"I have lost some that I love to death and others to estrangement," he explains, eyes still closed. "In some ways the former is worse, and in some ways the latter." Here he thinks not only of his father and grandfather, but Reuchlin and Karlstadt. Will the cord of communion with Erasmus of Rotterdam also be broken? The bonds of love with the dead remain while the bonds with the living are destroyed.

"Hans was such a kind soul," Anna laments, shaking her head in disbelief. "It seems unnatural that he should be taken away now, without any warning. I had no chance to prepare myself—to realize what was happening. I went to bed one night a wife, the next a widow. I've been so sick with grief, Philipp." Her eyes seem to bore into him, begging for relief. "Why has God done this to me? To us all?"

With all he is, he longs to give her an answer—anything that might salve this soul inflamed by grief—but the truth is veiled from his brilliant mind. There is a thick darkness before him, beyond which the pure light of God's glory shines with a burning intensity beyond that of the sun. His frail humanity cannot withstand the heat of that flame. He is not even sure he wants to know the God beyond human comprehension. The darkness is a gift: he must believe this. The Lord Almighty has set the line upon the world as surely as he has laid its foundations. "Thus far you may come, but no farther."[6] That is his decree for man as surely as the seas.

"I wish I could tell you, Anna, but I don't know," he admits softly. "It is as the Scripture reads: 'The secret things belong to the Lord our God, but the things revealed belong to us and to our sons forever.'"[7]

"All those years of study but no answers." Her tone is equal parts bitterness and commiseration.

"Yes, but that's the thing about studying the divine: you will as soon discover what you can't know as what you can."

Anna holds out a finger and traces the letters on the headstone, her breath catching and spouting. He watches as she plants a hand on the top of the stone and rests her forehead upon it, eyes closed, new tears running down her cheeks.

"So cruel! So abominably cruel!" she cries, her tone voracious. Raising her head and looking at him again, she speaks out of the desperation within her. "I will admit it: I've been angry—angrier than I've ever felt in my life. Yes, there is sadness, but I feel anger just as often."

"To whom or what is your anger directed?" he asks, feeling he already knows the answer.

"To God, Philipp! To God!" Almost panting, she looks down, her eyes darting back and forth. "I know we must praise him in all things, but how can I?" She locks her gaze on him and clenches her teeth. "This didn't have to happen! If he is sovereign, he could have prevented it!"

She is losing control, overcome by grief. He thinks it best not to echo her emotion, but to speak calmly and soothe the fibers of her being.

---

[6] Job 38:11.

[7] Deuteronomy 29:29.

"Sadly, when our first ancestors sinned, the world fell under the sway of evil, and we must taste the bitterness of death: the mortification of all we are."

"Yes, but it didn't have to be this way, surely," she continues, her voice less caustic than before. "God could have created a world where there was never any sin. He could have made it so Eve never took the apple or Lucifer never fell! He could have spared us all of this. Why didn't he? Is our suffering nothing to him?!"

It is a question Philipp has asked himself many times. As Anna succumbs to a new bout of tears, his gaze wanders to the nearby wall, where an image of Christ as Judge of the World is displayed. The Son of God sits enthroned, gripping a rod of iron that proceeds from his mouth. There is nothing remotely comforting about this vision of Christ, but a savage fierceness not unlike a rabid dog. *Think of the cross,* Philipp instructs himself. *Think of Christ stretched out, drawing the world to himself in love.*

He takes a deep breath and says, "I can assure you of one thing, at least: suffering means something to the one who suffered on the cross."

Anna dries her eyes and nods her head. "Truly spoken. I know what I'm saying is terrible, Philipp."

"No, these are questions we all must ask."

Will it do to make some personal admission? He does not have the ability, or perhaps the desire, that some people have of discussing his most intimate feelings. It seems to him an obscene thing to drop such details casually into correspondence or share them with strangers. Of course, Anna is family, but he has not trusted her with everything. He can tolerate disclosures from others. He would not call it a weakness in them. Yet, he does not know what to do with the thoughts that plague him. He is afraid to reveal them to another and wish them immediately unsaid. Few people, he thinks, could understand him, and fewer still would want to understand. Even so, he senses he must meet her in the open if he is to grant her the consolation she so desperately needs. Therefore, he speaks with feeling, trusting himself to the one he calls sister.

"Sometimes I simply wonder why life must be so fearful. Here we stand at a joyous moment in history, when the pure teaching of the gospel is restored, and you would think that God would clear every obstacle in its path. You would think we would see the Spirit working as never before, forming love in the hearts of men. But instead, what do we have? Opposition on all sides. Frustration at every turn. I go to bed each night with a knot in my stomach, worried that I am failing to protect those dearest to me. The righteous are imprisoned and burned. The wicked prosper in their halls of gold. Anna, if I could tell you why all of this is the case—why we must walk the path of fear and not peace—then I would be as wise as men seem to believe. But I am searching for answers, just like you. I believe that the Lord is good—that we will see his goodness even in our days, even on this cursed ground. But I am waiting, same as you. I am waiting in fear and trembling."

She lifts her chin and inhales sharply, then closes her eyes and releases the air. Looking at him again, she pats his hand and says, "Thank you. Thank you for those words, Philipp. It means so much to know that I am not alone."

"That is just the thing: we feel alone and ashamed when we ask these questions, but in truth it is part of what joins us to all humanity."

"But I love God!" she declares, shaking her head in confusion, or perhaps disgust. "How can I be so angry with him if I love him so?"

"Well, whom do you fight with the most?"

"I assume you mean verbally."

Philipp chuckles. "Of course. I've never seen you take a swing at someone."

"Then I suppose I've fought most with my family," she explains, shrugging her shoulders.

He attempts to tread carefully. "Knowing the Krapps as I do—"

"You are a Krapp, silly!" she objects, a smile finally emerging on her face.

"—that does not surprise me. But I would also stake my life on the fact that it is a loving family, and that you too love them—love us—with all your heart."

"Oh, yes! More than anything!"

"Then you see that anger and love are not always opposed. You must care about something for it to have the power to anger you."

She smiles again. "How very wise you are, Doktor Melanchthon, and how fortunate that our Katharina was able to pull you from your books long enough to catch your eye."

"The books are plotting their revenge," he assures her, and the two of them share a brief burst of laughter. It is healing: exactly what is needed for their weary souls.

Now Philipp hears his daughter's voice crying, "Papa! Papa!" He turns to see her emerging from the north portal of the church holding her mother's hand. As he watches young Anna walk toward him, her blond curls dancing in the wind, her body clothed in a beautiful white dress crafted by her mother, he is filled with a pride he never knew until this little girl arrived: this miraculous gift from heaven, which has destroyed and exceeded his expectations. She smiles widely, her blue eyes sparkling.

"She woke up," Katharina explains. "The first words out of her mouth were, 'Tante? Where Tante?'"

"Oh, dear one!" Tante Anna responds. "Come here!"

Katharina lets go of their daughter's hand, and the little girl runs into the outstretched arms of her namesake, where she is squeezed tightly and covered in kisses. When they finally part, young Anna turns to her father and gifts him a smile that somehow banishes and ignites his anxiety simultaneously. He is filled with the hope still left in the world, even as he hears an echo in his mind.

What will become of your wife? Your daughter? the voice of Nausea taunts. *Does that mean nothing to you?* Philipp remembers what happened when his own father was taken away: the unending void of his presence, year after painful year.

"Papa!" young Anna cries. "Papa, up!"

With a firm act of will, he bids the shadow depart. He will not allow it to sully this golden moment. He takes hold of his daughter's waist with both hands and raises her to the heavens, standing to his full height. She lets out a giggle of glee, even as her mother warns, "Careful, Philipp!" He lowers young Anna again, holding her tightly in his arms, rubbing noses with her.

This is all I am working for, he thinks. *This is all I am.*

Then the moment passes. She begins tugging his hair, his lower lip, his beard—anything to provoke a reaction. She laughs in delight even as he says, "Let papa go! You're hurting me."

"Just let her run," Katharina instructs. "She is bored of staying in one place."

With great care, he sets her feet upon the earth, and she is off like a shot, running between the rows of stones, arms waving happily, her dress flowing with the wind, seemingly without a care in the world. She is a thing of pure joy: a spirit of the sun bringing life to the place of the dead. The contrast strikes Philipp like an arrow to the chest. *All life is fragile. Everything is uncertain.* One illness and she will make her descent beneath the grass and dirt, joining those who have gone before. *What a miracle is life! How it rests upon the edge of a knife!*

Katharina grasps his hand. "We made a good one, didn't we?"

"Yes," he says, watching as the older Anna chases after her niece. "Yes, we did."

Stepping in front of him, Katharina looks deeply into his eyes. *You are so beautiful,* he thinks. *How on earth did I end up with you?*

"I'm sorry about Nesen," she whispers. "I'm sorry for all of it."

"I just fear what is coming next," he admits. "If Karlstadt returns, if Erasmus stands against us, if the Edict is enforced and Luther is burned…" He struggles to continue. "How will we pay for it all, Käthe? Some things cost a Guilder, and some cost all our peace of mind."

She sighs softly and nods her head. "If you tell me you want to go to Basel, I accept it. I will follow you wherever you go. You have done so much here. You have given it your all."

He pulls her close, kissing her forehead. Then as they watch their daughter succumb to her aunt's tickles, he says, "The fear would follow us to Basel. It would follow us wherever we choose to go. Fear is the common state of all living things."

As he stands there with his wife, feeling the warmth of her embrace, he imagines himself upon some great height, standing as it were at the cliff's edge. There the wind is constant from east and west, north and south, and he is caught between them, pushed to within an inch of his life—a single breath from the plunge. He looks down into the abyss, a darkness that surrenders no hint of its contents. He feels both drawn and repulsed. There is nothing solid to which he can cling but the cliff face below him, and even that is buffeted and slowly faltering, surrendering pebble by pebble to the punishing force of the wind. He can feel the rush inside him, the muting of inhibition, the voice calling to him, *Jump!* No, he will not jump, but he may well be pushed.

22 August 1524
Jena, Electorate of Saxony

Martin Luther lies on a feather mattress in his rented room, mind consumed with the events of the day. Rising at the break of dawn, he preached for an hour and a half, expending himself in body and mind. He had hoped to gain some rest before preaching again tomorrow, but the day has unleashed a surprise: he will be forced to debate with Karlstadt.

In this private room at the Black Bear Inn, the latest temporary home on his preaching tour, the only light comes from a window to his left. The few belongings he has with him are laid on the floor next to a simple wooden desk. An off-colored mirror, wash basin, green tiled stove—he ignores them all. He is thinking of another day five years earlier, when he and Karlstadt were visiting Leipzig for their debate with Johann Eck. Karlstadt entered the lists first, and it went badly. Then it was his turn to spar, and despite his outwardly bold demeanor, he was gripped by uncertainty and felt very much as if he would be sick.

You are better than Karlstadt, Melanchthon had whispered in his ear. *Don't be afraid.*

In the present, he holds a silver gulden aloft in his right hand, flipping it over time and again, nervous energy flowing through him.[8] On one side, Elector Friedrich of Saxony is seen in profile holding the great sword of state. On the other, Dukes Georg and Johann face one another, lending no hint of the religious strife that has afflicted their great family. Martin continues turning the coin, fidgeting as much as considering. He thinks of the hall in the Elector's palace, the walls covered in weapons, the disdain with which Karlstadt unleashed his prediction of divine judgment.

I am not afraid to stand before him, but you should be, Doktor! You should be!

---

[8] A gulden (short for *Guldengroschen*) was a common coin in German-speaking lands at this time, though its value and construction varied by region.

Sighing, he slips the gulden into the purse at his waist and sits upright on the edge of the bed. Feeling a sudden throb, he rubs near the spot on his right thigh where a blade pierced him all those years ago, shortly before his encounter with the lightning bolt. It still hurts from time to time: a constant reminder of how close he came to death. He doubts there is any man with a keener sense of his own mortality than he, Martin Luther.

I must get up, he thinks. *I must face him.*

Since their meeting in Wittenberg, Karlstadt has spiraled further into mysticism and obfuscation. Despite pledging to return to his duties at the Leucorea and All Saints' Foundation, he has remained in his pastorate at Orlamünde. Here in Jena, he has published numerous pamphlets of late, each seemingly more radical than the next. The attacks on all things physical have reached their natural conclusion: Karlstadt is telling his congregants that the Lord's body and blood are not present in the Sacrament.[9] At least one man has been advised to take multiple wives, for if Abraham did it, why shouldn't he? A lawyer by training, Karlstadt can only see law in Scripture, failing to distinguish it from gospel. This is the ultimate affront: a betrayal of the movement they started.

Martin stretches his aching legs and rises from the bed. Glancing in the mirror, he attempts to straighten his hair, but it has a will of its own. There is an increasing pressure in his bowels—the drum of his heart is pounding. *Breathe. Let it pass,* he bids himself. This is something his brother Jakob taught him for dealing with the tension. He has found it necessary to employ it increasingly. *Softly. Breathe. Breathe.* He repeats the commands as he stares into the mirror, willing himself to endure the scourge of anxiety and emerge triumphant.

He knows what you are, even as I do!

That was how Karlstadt taunted him, pretending to take the measure of his soul. His fellow professor always assumed a greater deal of familiarity than truly existed between them. Though similar in age and education, they are utterly opposed in temper. Karlstadt has allied himself with the radical preacher Thomas Müntzer, who has conquered the nearby city of Allstedt with his heretical teachings and

---

[9] When this word is capitalized, it signifies the Sacrament of the Altar, also known as the Lord's Supper, the Eucharist, or Communion.

calls for revolution. Poor, illiterate peasants are taking the madman at his word, believing their plowshares can conquer swords. Müntzer sends them to their deaths while Karlstadt offers friendship. He has even heard a rumor that Karlstadt is joining Müntzer in denying children the sacrament of baptism, but it seems too absurd to be true. What cannot be denied is the link between the two: acquainted for years, Karlstadt and Müntzer have been exchanging letters of late, bidding each other remain firm in the Lord.

It is not the Lord who compels you, but the devil, he thinks. *You know how to destroy things, but what are you building for the sheep when you bid them cast away the consolations granted by God: confession, baptism, the body and blood of Christ, the Church itself?! You call for insurrection against divinely ordained governors. You are leading your sheep to slaughter. May the Lord make you cease from tending them!*

This is why he has entered the heart of Karlstadt's domain—the region of Thuringia—to preach in its churches: he must combat bad teaching with good. His last stop will be Orlamünde, the parish 'Brother Andreas' has claimed for himself, but Karlstadt evidently cannot wait for a confrontation.

Earlier in the day, Martin had risen in the pulpit of St. Michael's Church in Jena to condemn the radical spirit of Allstedt, scanning the faces of the congregants to judge their reactions to his words. Sitting with his head down throughout the sermon was a man in a gray peasant's tunic and matching felt hat, the same costume Karlstadt wore at their last meeting. Then when Martin returned to the inn to partake in a simple meal of leek soup, rye bread, and beer, Karlstadt's brother-in-law, Doktor Gerhard Westerburg, approached to request a meeting.

Whatever Martin's former colleague has to say, it evidently could not have been uttered in the church that morning. Instead, they will converse here in the Black Bear Inn at Karlstadt's express request, where the audience will be mostly travelers from foreign lands.

Suddenly, a painful surge in his bowels. "No, no!" he moans. "Not here! Not now!" There is a pot in the corner, but it may not suffice for what ails him. Two flights of stairs and a hallway: those are what he must overcome as quickly as possible.

Cursing his terrible digestion, he races out the door and toward the first flight of stairs but is forced to pause. Turning the corner on his ascent is a young merchant: his brightly colored silk sleeves, velvet cap, and overstuffed purse reveal him as such. The man makes eye contact with Martin, his expression somewhat quizzical. *He is going to ask after my identity. I have no time for this.* Martin moves to the right, attempting to pass where there is truly no room. The merchant extends a hand to stop him.

"Are you who I think you are?" he asks with the sound of Augsburg in his voice.

A Fugger man?[10] Martin wonders, but his curiosity is very much overcome by the burning rush inside him. Reasoning that the shortest answer will end things quickest, he replies, "No."

"Oh, but you are!" the man exclaims. "You are Martin Luther!"

"Ah, well, in that case, yes."

The merchant looks as if he is about to set off on some long speech, so Martin has no choice but to speak first. "Forgive me, I must go—now!"

The pain is too great. He will never make it to the latrine. Without explanation, Martin turns on the spot and runs back up the stairs, flying through the door to his room and slamming it behind him. *The pot! Where is the pot?!* No, he has lunged toward the wrong corner of the room! It is on the other side! Turning again, he trips and crashes onto the wooden floorboards with a groan. Then comes the instantaneous release. He cannot stop it. He is completely helpless against his own body.

You think you are something, Martin Luther, but you are lying in your own shit, a voice in his head accuses. *You're a piece of shit bound for hell!*

The onset of terror, sharp and grating, like a rush of acid! As shame swells within him, he grasps his left wrist with his right hand, feeling his own skin and bone. Repeating words he has spoken many times before, he declares, "I was marked in baptism. I am flesh of Christ's flesh. He has claimed me for his own. He promised!" With these words, the crisis seems to fade. He can sense the shame lifting from his form, his fibers relaxing.

---

[10] Jakob Fugger II was a banker, merchant, and entrepreneur located in the city of Augsburg. His financial operation was at the time the most powerful in Europe, and he had many employees who carried out his business far and wide.

Embarrassed but triumphant, he rises from the floor and begins the unpleasant process of cleaning, his nose fighting against the smell. He can date the beginning of these digestive attacks to the year he received the bull from Leo.[11] Even as his mind was filled with anxiety and his spirit brought low, his bowels began to torment him as never before. He would either be stopped up to the point of excruciating pain or forced through hours of bloody purgation. While things are not as bad as they once were, he still suffers attacks. It can happen at any time but becomes particularly violent whenever he faces a major test of some sort. Three different physicians have failed to define the problem, but he suspects it is the devil's hand upon him.

With no time to wash his braies before Karlstadt arrives, he puts on his clean pair and leaves the messed ones for later. It seems this day will force him to deal with both literal and figurative excrement. As he makes his way into the hall again and descends the stairs, he suddenly remembers something that was said to him only a few months earlier.

There is a shadow over you: a fear of things to come.

Much as he hates to admit it, those words were true. The Allstedters have burned the Marian chapel in Mallerbach and Müntzer is now telling his congregants they need neither sacraments nor Scripture. There are wars and rumors of wars boring into his soul. No one can know what it is like to be him—to bear the weight of this angst. *Will it break me?* He recalls Erasmus' complaint, delivered by Camerarius: "Do you honestly think the gospel will be restored by perverted creatures like these? Are men like this to be the pillars of a renascent church?"[12] He feels those words in his bones as he makes the turn onto the next flight of steps.

His own congregants remain mired in sin: theft, fornication, gossip, debauchery. They ought to be eating solid food by now, but he must nurse them on milk, never progressing to the greater things.[13]

---

[11] The bull *Exsurge Domine* ("Arise, O Lord") was sent to Luther by Pope Leo X in 1520 and called on him to recant his teachings or suffer excommunication.

[12] "Epistle 1445: To Martin Luther" in *The Correspondence of Erasmus, Vol. 10 – Letters 1356 to 1534*, trans. R.A.B. Mynors and Alexander Dalzell (Toronto: University of Toronto Press, 1992), 256.

[13] Reference to Hebrews 5:12-14.

How desperate he is for the help of capable men! Therefore, the final lines of Erasmus' letter pressed the brand of doubt into his flesh: "I found Joachim most congenial. It was a pity there was no opportunity to meet Melanchthon."[14] He fears there was more intended in those words than was plainly expressed. *What will this clash cost me?* Never has he seen men driven so mad by words, and he fears the ones he and Erasmus must exchange. Karlstadt is like a broad sword swung wide, caught up in its own momentum, but Erasmus is like the blades of the Orient, swift and quiet, advancing and retreating in the blink of an eye. *One foe at a time...*

Finally, he reaches the ground floor and enters the common room. Here there are three simple tables with matching benches, a small bar staffed by the middle-aged innkeeper, and two pairs of men playing cards on empty barrels. The double doors facing the street are open to accept patrons, but the shutters are closed on the window to the right. There is a young man sitting cross-legged in one corner playing a mournful tune on his flute. A group of men are tossing dice on the wood floor, and somewhere out in the alley others are surely bowling. He elects to sit at the only empty table.

Now the owner, Nikolaus Börner, approaches holding a towel in one hand and three dirtied glasses in the other. "Doktor Luther," he says, "what will you be having?"

"Just beer, thank you," Martin replies, then as the innkeeper turns to depart, he places a hand on Börner's arm and warns, "I may need more than one before this is done."

Smirking, the innkeeper departs to undertake his charge, and at precisely this moment, Karlstadt enters the room accompanied by his brother-in-law Westerburg and Martin Reinhard, the pastor of St. Michael's Church. Looking upon his old colleague again, Luther feels a pang in his gut that travels up his breastbone. Spotting him, the men remove their caps, and Reinhard makes to join him while Karlstadt and Westerburg walk toward the bar.

"Good afternoon, Herr Doktor!" Reinhard greets him, setting a leather case on the table and unfolding it to reveal sheets of paper and writing instruments. "We thank you for accommodating us on short notice."

---

[14] "Epistle 1445: To Martin Luther".

Martin merely grunts in reply. Reinhard is his former student as well as Karlstadt's. Martin can still see the sores of youth on the younger man's clean-shaven face as he takes the seat opposite. *Why are you getting yourself involved in this?* Martin wonders, but instead asks, "Are you intending to prepare your pamphlet while we speak?"

"What pamphlet?" Reinhard asks innocently enough, pulling a jar of ink out of his coat pocket and setting it on the table.

"Whatever you are going to write about this conversation."

Reinhard leans back slightly. "I assure you, Herr Luther, whatever I write will be the absolute truth, with nothing omitted or added."

As Martin watches Reinhard unscrew the lid and dip a pen in the black contents, he mutters, "What a relief!"

Karlstadt joins them with a mug of beer in hand, setting it in front of Reinhard. Westerburg, for his part, is still chatting with the innkeeper at the bar.

"You do not drink?" Martin asks his former colleague.

"No, I need my mind sharp," Karlstadt replies, pounding his temple with the pad of his finger.

With a nod of acknowledgment, Martin motions toward a place directly across the table. Taking his seat, Karlstadt inquires, "How shall we begin?"

Another rush of anxiety strikes Martin. Underneath the table, he grips his knee. *How has it come to this?* But he remembers Melanchthon's words: *You are better than Karlstadt. Don't be afraid.* He breathes in deeply, wanting to believe it.

"You requested the meeting," Martin reminds his opponent.

Karlstadt places a hand over his heart, closes his eyes, and bows his head in a seeming mockery of respect. Then he speaks, eyes open wide.

"Herr Doktor, I pray you won't take offense at my appealing to you here, but I was compelled to do so. In your sermon, you included me in that group of 'riotous murdering spirits,' as you choose to call them. Whoever throws me in the same pot as them is a liar!" When Martin begins to shake his head, Karlstadt objects, "Yes, I know you were thinking of me because you spoke about errors in the Sacrament—you attacked me too strongly! Truly, no one has written about the Lord's Supper more in line with the apostles than I have. I deny that I have a murdering spirit or, as you claimed today, the same spirit that exists in Allstedt. Müntzer and I have nothing in common when it comes to the Sacrament!"

Martin had been at great pains not to mention Karlstadt's name during the morning sermon, so this accusation annoys. Nevertheless, he senses it is time to make his views fully known.

"Herr Doktor, you can't prove that I was talking about you," he insists, "but since you assume I was striking in your direction, then be struck in the name of God. It saddens me to see the people so misled. Therefore, I preached against this riotous spirit today and I will do it again."

Karlstadt shakes his head angrily, his beard swaying. "I maintain what I said, and what's more, I will prove from Scripture that you are preaching the gospel improperly. You have done me real violence by putting me in the same pot with 'the murdering spirit'! I object before everyone here. I have nothing to do with those who preach armed rebellion!"

These final words are spoken at great volume, and Karlstadt lifts himself off the bench slightly. The men playing dice glance in the direction of the noise, but their eyes quickly return to the game.

When Karlstadt is settled again, Martin assures him, "That is not necessary. I read the letter you sent to Müntzer. I know you are opposed to armed rebellion." *Although you do little to discourage it and in effect aid the rebels,* he adds in his own mind.

"Then why did you say I have the same murdering spirit that exists in Allstedt?" Karlstadt gripes, arms crossed. "A spirit that smashes images and attacks the Sacrament?"

"I never named you."

"But it was obvious from the context, for I have also criticized the misuse of the Sacrament." Karlstadt pauses for a moment, leaning forward for emphasis. His blue eyes lock with Martin's, fire meeting fire. "Look, since you call yourself a Christian—if I am in error, you should have pulled me aside and instructed me like a brother before stabbing me publicly! You like to preach about love, but what kind of love is that?"

Reinhard's pen is scribbling furiously, and it grates on the fabric of Martin's person. This language of betrayal is ridiculous. After all, he has not changed his opinion: it is Karlstadt who has changed. And as for pulling him aside, how many times was Karlstadt warned by those at the university and in the Elector's court? *Perhaps he is losing his memory along with his good sense.* Rather than debating previous encounters endlessly, Martin chooses to call out the harshest comment Karlstadt has made: the implication that he, Martin Luther, has betrayed the gospel.

"Since we are speaking of how brothers ought to behave toward one another, you claim I am preaching 'another gospel.' If I have done so, I am unaware of it," Martin asserts.

"Oh, I can prove from your theology of the Sacrament whether you are preaching a true Christ or one of your own invention! Is it a theology of the cross or a theology of glory?"

Karlstadt smiles wryly, no doubt thinking himself clever. After all, it was Martin who first contrasted the theologian of glory with the theologian of the cross: the former exalting in his own human reason, the latter submitting himself to the revealed mystery of God.

"If you can prove it, then write about it freely," Martin challenges, tapping the table with his finger. "Be bold. Bring it to light."

"Believe me, I'd love to!" Karlstadt cries, granting a clear flash of his teeth. "I am no coward as you suppose. But I know you will not spare me in a public debate, so I will not spare you either! I know how you hold the people under your sway."

Martin shakes his head. "No one is threatening you. Come forward freely and do your deeds in the light."

"I want to come into that light. Either I will suffer public disgrace, or the truth of God will be revealed. I will gladly take all the shame upon myself so that God is glorified!"

Here is a man who pretends to be a martyr, yet he has never stood where I have stood, Martin thinks. *He has never felt himself a dead man or offered up his body for the sheep.*

"You say your doctrine is from God, but let's examine the fruit," Martin suggests. "You smashed all the images in Wittenberg—"

"I didn't do that alone!" Karlstadt objects, the blaze in his eyes catching wind and sparking. "I had the support of the council and even some of your friends. It was only after you returned that they allowed me to hang alone. I appeal to their testimony."

The implication is not lost on Martin: *Melanchthon supported me.* That is what Karlstadt really means. *You protected him and fed me to the wolves because you could not bear to lose your familiar.*

But he is not really yours. He will break from you some day: mark my words! This hits very near the point of Martin's fears, though it is not a desertion to Karlstadt that most worries him.

"I wouldn't recommend that," Martin concludes, keeping his worries to himself. "Things are less in your favor than you suppose."

"Nor are things as much in your favor as you suppose. I am comforted at least to know that I have the truth. On Judgment Day, God will reveal all. Everything that is hidden will come into the light. Then we will see who is right: you or me."

Reinhard is writing furiously now, returning to the well with reckless abandon, creating ink streaks on the page.

Again, Martin addresses Karlstadt. "You always seek judgment, but I long for mercy."

"Why would I not seek God's judgment? He is no respecter of persons. The small and the great he treats as equal in worth. But look what kind of judgment you offer: you bind me up and strike me!"

"When did I strike you?" Martin objects.

"When you wrote, printed, and preached against me!" yells Karlstadt, pounding his fist on the table. "You had my books seized from the press. I was forbidden to write—forbidden to preach. If I could have spoken as freely as you, you would have seen what my spirit can do! You've never shown me a place where I erred. You simply use force. You should have come along in private with one or two brothers, like our Lord commands."

"I did," he insists, galled at any suggestion to the contrary.

"Ha! If you did what you claim, then may God disgrace me before everyone here!"

"Wait and it will happen."

"You lie!"

"No, I did come to you as Scripture commands."

"With whom?"

"With Melanchthon and Pomeranus."

"Oh really? Where?"

"In your own room!" Martin insists, shaking his head in disbelief. "How can you not remember this?"

"That's not true! You may have met with me, but you didn't provide me with any examples of error," Karlstadt claims rather improbably.

"We brought you the official note from the university listing the articles where we believed you to be mistaken."

"No. That was never shown to me."

Martin shakes his head again, uncertain whether Karlstadt has truly lost his mind or is so utterly defeated that he can only spout falsities. "Whenever I provide you with evidence, you just call me a liar," he objects.

"If that is so, then may the devil tear me limb from limb before you all!" Karlstadt proclaims solemnly, looking around at everyone in the room. "But you never gave it to me."

Sensing there is nothing more to be gained from this line of argument, Martin pauses for a moment and stares into Karlstadt's enraged eyes, thinking back over the course of their relationship. He sees him in their first meeting at the Castle Church, when Karlstadt was the rising star of the university. He sees Karlstadt awarding him the title of Doktor of Theology and whispering in his ear, *Do well, brother*. Then he sees a moment with no particular date, but real nonetheless: the moment he eclipsed Karlstadt. He sees Karlstadt attempting to take on Eck in the Leipzig debate and collapsing under the repeated battering of argument. He sees the moment they bid farewell before Martin's departure for the imperial diet at Worms, when he had worked so hard to protect Karlstadt from being summoned as well, only to have his colleague say, *Oh, that I could join you!* And he sees Karlstadt as he is now, sitting with crossed arms, a phantom fled from home and driven wild in the wasteland but still desperate to feel his worth.

"Oh, Doktor," Martin says, lamenting all that could have been, "I know you of old."

Karlstadt scoffs. "And I you, far more than you imagine!"

"I know you are an arrogant boaster who goes around puffed up, begging everyone to praise him."

"I think you are the boaster seeking his own honor, not me."

"I remember your behavior at Leipzig. I reproved you there when you were so eager to have the glory."

"No, no!" Karlstadt cries, his words full of bile. "That is not how it went at all! Eck challenged me, not you. I spoke first because it was not known if you would even be able to speak. Why must you always present things as if you are the saint and I the devil so that you can

SUMMER

induce the people to hate me? What was your sermon today but an attempt to do just that?"

Their dialogue is reaching a crisis point. Martin attempts to remain calm.

"As I said earlier, I preached against this spirit today and will continue to do so in spite of any resistance I might receive."

Karlstadt pounds the table again, then shakes a finger in Martin's face. "Very well, then do it! But you'll see what I have to say about it."

"Go ahead!" he replies, pushing the finger away. "If you have something to say, then write it without fear."

"I certainly will do it without fear."

"Write against me publicly. Enough of this secrecy."

"If I had known you were so eager for me to do so, I would have done it long ago!" Karlstadt declares, leaning so heavily on the wood table that the boards groan.

"Very well. Do it. What are you waiting for?"

"I will!"

"I'll even give you a gulden for it."

"A gulden?" Karlstadt asks, confusion temporarily lessening his furor.

"Yes. I'm not a scoundrel."

"Very well, give it to me," Karlstadt replies with a snort. "I accept your challenge."

Here is a new moment in their history together: the point when the last threads of friendship are severed. Martin's heart is heavy but very much prepared for whatever invective Karlstadt might devise. He reaches into his purse and pulls out the coin he examined earlier, holding it up for Reinhard to observe. Then with a flick of the wrist, he sends it scuttering across the table toward Karlstadt. This simplest of actions seems to be laden with meaning, as if the rumbling of the coin were the very breaking of the earth.

"Take it," Martin instructs his former colleague. "Attack me with boldness now. Hold nothing back!"

Karlstadt smirks, having achieved what he set out to do. He takes the coin in hand and stands to his full height, waving it for everyone in the room to see. "Dear brothers, I want you to see this. It is Doktor Luther's pledge that I have the right to publish against him. You are witnesses of the fact."

"That's not necessary," Martin mutters, once again appalled at the man's need to draw attention to himself.

"What did you say?" Westerburg calls from his place at the bar, but Karlstadt has already retaken his seat on the bench and begins bending the coin with two fingers, marking it as a sign of their pledge. Then placing the gulden in his pocket, Karlstadt extends his right hand in an apparent attempt at good will. There is even a smile on his face.

"Here, take my hand on it," Karlstadt requests.

Feeling very much that he would rather not do so, Martin says, "If you insist."

He grasps Karlstadt's extended palm, noting as he does so that it bears fewer callouses than one would expect for a working peasant. There is something slightly endearing in Karlstadt's smile: a final remnant of the fellowship they once shared. Despite the many trials that have led them to this point, there is a part of Martin that still hopes for reconciliation. Without fully realizing what he is doing, he smiles slightly in return. But no sooner does he allow himself this brief reminiscence then a shadow seems to fall over Karlstadt's demeanor. He tugs on Martin's arm, pulling him across the table with real force so that their faces nearly touch. Then with his free hand, Karlstadt snaps his fingers next to Martin's right ear, causing him to flinch. This seems to lend Karlstadt a real sense of pleasure as he leans forward to whisper in the other ear.

"You are dead to me, Doktor," Karlstadt declares too softly for the others to hear. "You mean nothing to me."

Immediately, Karlstadt releases his grip and Martin pulls himself back to his own side of the table, his spirit deeply troubled by what he has just heard. His former colleague acts as if the moment never happened, rising to his feet and patting Reinhard on the shoulder.

"Come. Let us leave," Karlstadt declares cheerily, leaving the younger man to begin packing his things. "Gerhard, we're leaving!" he calls to his brother-in-law, who quickly downs the rest of his beer and moves to join them.

Unwilling to let Karlstadt have the last word, Martin raises his glass and declares, "A toast to you, Herr Doktor, for so you will always be, whatever you would have men believe."

Karlstadt stops mid-stride and turns slowly to face him. "And I beg you again, Herr Doktor, not to block me from printing or continue this persecution of me, my family, and my livelihood. I will earn an honest living by the plow as the generations of peasants before me. I do not exalt myself like some men."

"Why would I try to prevent you writing? You have my gulden. I told you not to spare me. The fiercer your attack, the better. And I have no intention of harming your livelihood or your family."

"We are in agreement, then. I pray that I will not fail you in your desire."

With that, Andreas Bodenstein von Karlstadt makes his exit with Westerburg at his side and Reinhard and his papers trailing behind. Feeling as if he has been lifted by some giant and shaken to within an inch of his life, Martin sits staring at nothing in particular, fearing he will be attacked by his bowels again. He thinks to himself, *I have lost a friend: a friend I evidently never had.* A double loss. A piercing blow.

22 August 1524
Basel, Swiss Confederation

Desiderius Erasmus stands at an east-facing window in Johann Froben's library, looking out over the brown rooftops of Basel turned gray in the final light of day. In the courtyard below are the animal pens and stables, and beyond is the old Froben house, now the Froben print shop. Immediately to the right is the house of Doktor Ludwig Baer, professor of theology at the University of Basel and provost at the collegiate monastery of St. Peter—but Baer is not at home. Instead, he is seated at the great oak desk in the center of the library, working by the light of the twin hearths on the northern side of the chamber. The southern wall is covered with shelves displaying a great horde of human achievement: every book Froben has printed, those printed by his old partner Amerbach before him, and a few hundred volumes useful for reference or simple pleasure. Croesus himself was none so rich, and Baer has left his fingerprints on every inch of the horde.

Erasmus tears his gaze from the window and glances over at the diminutive Baer, who is bent over a copy of the 1516 Greek New Testament, one hand on his wrinkled forehead and the other pressed against the pages. He mouths the words as he reads, leaning back and forth in turn, the rhythm hypnotic. To the professor's right is a stack of handwritten pages that make up Erasmus' work *On Free Will.* Baer has been absorbing it line by line, allowing it to seep into his membranes, as if by the smallest flicker of a nerve he might distinguish any mistakes or weaknesses.

"Friend, I have never seen a man read with such fervor as you display now, unless he be a Jew at his prayers," Erasmus comments.

"A great deal depends on this," Baer responds in a deep voice, neither looking up nor breaking rhythm. The first time Erasmus heard that rumbling voice issue from Baer's petite frame, it was rather a shock, but now he cannot imagine the man with the aquiline nose and pointed brows speaking in any other manner.

"Perhaps. Or perhaps not. I am not so arrogant as to suppose that I alone can change things. I have written nothing in those pages that has not been written before and by more skilled theologians."

"Theology is one area in which we should hate to read anything new," Baer concludes, pushing the Bible to the left and taking up the manuscript again.

The implication is not lost on Erasmus: *Novelty in theology is the very definition of heresy, and they will burn you for that.* The mere thought of it stiffens Erasmus' muscles. He has heard no serious threat that he will be brought up on heresy charges—not yet. *Not yet is different from not ever,* he reasons. *Indeed, the difference between those two things could hold the universe entire.*

Attempting to put such things out of his mind, Erasmus walks toward the desk, his leather shoes brushing a Persian rug dyed in colors of lapis lazuli, a sea of blue more perfect than any he has seen in nature. He looks over Baer's shoulder and asks, "Which part are you reading now?"

Baer points at the following words:

"Who will be able to bring himself to love God with all his heart when He created hell seething with eternal torments in order to punish his own misdeeds in his victims as though he took delight in human torments? For that is how most people will interpret them."[15]

Having reviewed the passage, Erasmus looks at Baer and asks, "What is the problem with that?"

---

[15] Erasmus of Rotterdam, *De Libero Arbitrio* ("On Free Will") in *Luther and Erasmus: Free Will and Salvation*, trans. and ed. E. Gordon Rupp (Philadelphia: The Westminster Press, 1969), 41.

"You wished me to point out anything Luther might seize on, did you not?"

He sighs. "I believe my precise words were, 'You are more in favor in Paris and can help me avoid their censure.' Only after that did I mention Luther."[16]

"Do you want my suggestions or not?" Baer asks, arms crossed in annoyance.

Erasmus sighs again, this time deeper. "Very well."

Again, the deep voice proceeds from Baer's throat, as hypnotic as his gesticulations. "Your argument here is based on the idea that a God who damns men or takes delight in human sufferings is hard to love."

"Yes," he repeats. "I ask you again, what is the problem with that?"

"He may say we owe God love because he created us and for no other reason."

Erasmus scoffs. "That is not what Scripture says. 'We love because he first loved us.'[17] How does he display his love in such a manner and why would anyone respond in love? If a man has no true choice whether he does good or evil, then it is God who chooses the good or evil for him. How can such a man be rightly condemned? It defies any sense of justice devised by man or revealed in Scripture."

Baer nods softly, straightening the stack of papers. "I understand. In fact, I share your opinion. But does man ever have a right to deny love to God regardless of what he does?"

"What are you suggesting?" he inquires. "Do you imagine that God is the Creator not only of good, but evil? Do you imagine a God of monstrous appetites, who feeds upon human souls with devilish glee? For there would be no difference between the devil and the divine in this world of Luther's creation: no difference except in name."

Baer rubs his face with his hands, as if straining to rub out the sagging folds, then crosses his arms again. "Why did our forefathers

---

[16] The University of Paris, as one of the chief centers of theological study in Western Christendom, was often looked to as a kind of referee for theological disputes. For example, the scholars there passed a judgment on the 1519 Leipzig debate between Luther/Karlstadt and Johann Eck. The university was generally known to be very conservative.

[17] 1 John 4:19.

in the faith fear the coming of the glory cloud? We must admit, there is something terrifying and altogether unfamiliar about the divine. When Joshua saw the angel of the Lord, standing in the darkness with his sword drawn, he knew not whether he was the Savior of Israel or a servant of the enemy. Yet, I agree with you that this view of man's nature promoted by Luther goes too far. I do not object to your argument on a personal level, but I warn you as a matter of logic: it does not follow that if God exists, he must be good."

"He must be if he is the God of Abraham, Isaac, and Jacob!" Erasmus snaps, having grown angrier with each syllable rolling off Baer's sonorous tongue. "Does the revelation of God count for nothing?"

Baer takes up his quill to write again, but first points it in Erasmus' direction and declares, "I remind you: it was you who told me to hold nothing back. 'You must be savage with me, for Luther will be savage.' That is what you said."

Erasmus groans, cursing his situation internally. "I did say that. You are correct."

"Then I bid you let me finish my work, unless you have changed your mind about this whole enterprise."

"No," he replies softly. "No, it is far too late for that."

With a quick nod of the head, Baer returns to his work, and Erasmus walks back to the window. The sky has turned three shades darker in his brief absence. This is no surprise: he could feel the shifting of the air in his bones earlier that day. The clouds are grown heavy and must relinquish their burden. He watches as the first drops hit the sill, portents of the deluge to come. He hears Baer's pen scratching away behind him, making yet another correction. Will there be anything left to send to Luther when he is done?

Now the pace of the rain quickens. It is falling with firm intent upon the stones far below. The bells of St. Andreas ring out the hour: eight in the evening, the last remnants of daylight hidden behind the storm clouds. He thinks of the accusation leveled against him by Duke Georg of Saxony, brother of the Elector Friedrich, in a letter two months earlier.

"How much easier it would have been to extinguish a fire that just then was breaking into flame, instead of trying to put it out now when it has grown into such a vast conflagration! The blame for this, to speak my mind freely, falls in the first place on you."[18]

Oh, how he had longed to write to the duke in return and say, 'It is your fault, Your Excellency, for failing to control your relatives. That is why the Lutherans succeed.' But he was not free to speak thus. It has been all he can do to avoid falling into either extreme: the prejudices of the Scotists,[19] who oppose the study of good letters, or the hatreds of the radicals, who now sound as if they will tear down not only images, but society itself.

How often he has imagined himself navigating upon dark waves through a narrow strait, with the biting dogs of Scylla on one side and the whirlpool of Charybdis on the other. Odysseus had striven only to avoid the wrath of one extreme, but he has increasingly found himself battered from both sides no matter what he does. The pass has narrowed since the former days—shrunk to the point of non-existence. He has felt the crush of iron jaws upon his flesh even as he has been pulled inexorably into the swirling abyss. He no longer has much hope of saving what he loves but simply longs to escape whatever he hates most.

Alas that this should be man's fate, he laments. *Not a steady climb up the salvific mount, but a despairing flight from the darkest terrors of the soul, driven further and further into the wilderness until at last one's will is utterly spent.*

So trapped is he within these thoughts, he does not notice that Baer has ceased scrawling and turned to address him.

"What is troubling you, friend?" the professor asks as Erasmus continues staring out the window.

Above the distant river, a flash of light in the clouds. A great rumble as of some giant provoking a drum. He remembers the storms that formed over the fields of his childhood: gray rain falling upon waves of gold through which the silver canals cut their course, drawing the water back to the sea. He breathes deeply.

---

[18] "1448: From Duke George of Saxony" in *Collected Works of Erasmus, Vol 10: The Correspondence of Erasmus – Letters 1356-1534,* ed. James M. Estes, trans. R.A.B. Mynors and Alexander Dalzell (Toronto: University of Toronto Press, 1992), 261.

[19] Erasmus tended to use the term Scotists to refer not only to followers of the philosopher Duns Scotus, but to any academics who adhered stubbornly to the traditions of medieval scholasticism.

"A storm is coming, Baer. The clouds have been gathering for years. Now they are lit with an unearthly flame, and we will feel their scorching wrath. What of man will be granted mercy when the thunder rings out over Christendom and the lightning is driven to earth by the god of war? The whole of Europe is now the Field of Mars, and he has placed his brand upon the human heart."

"You speak of things primordial, which have been from the beginning and create new beginnings," the professor says softly.

"I speak of my fear, which is better known to me than anything of this earth."

"What kindles this terror within you?"

And then, across the infinite space of Erasmus' mind, a flash not of light, but darkness. The heat upon his lips—pain scorching the skin of his face. *You disgust me!* The despair of rejection, both human and divine. *Repent, Erasmus, if you can.* He must give some answer, surely, but not that one. He turns to face the professor again, spirit trembling. *Can I trust him?* he wonders. *Can I really trust him?* It is a tremendous risk to grant unchanging words to an ever-changing human being. Nevertheless, he must shoulder the risk: a small one, but a risk nonetheless. He will surrender another of his fears.

"Baer, was I wrong?" Erasmus asks. "I sought to kindle a love for peace in the hearts of men, but they hearken only to the call of Mars. All this time, I have been at war with a god. I have been struggling against a power, a force far greater than myself."

"Man can be reformed," Baer insists. "I have seen it with my own eyes. Look at everything we have accomplished! Men are filled with knowledge as never before, but it will take time, Erasmus—it will take time for that knowledge to blossom and flourish. Do not lose hope. It is our fate to welcome these things only from afar."

He looks out the window again. Another clap of thunder—another streak of ghostly light.

"How can I believe in this God of despair?" Erasmus asks himself more than Baer. "The lightning strikes where it wills. Nature knows nothing of compassion. Is that how we should think of the one who is Father of us all? No, I cannot believe it! That is a pagan god: it is the Fates at their spinning wheel. It is not the God who became man, nor the God who hung on a cross. Did he come merely to drive men to despair? Can we honestly call that good news?"

Baer answers him quietly. "'For just as the lightning comes from the east and flashes even to the west, so will the coming of the Son of Man be.' Wrath to the unrighteous, grace to the righteous. To every man will come his deserts. That is what Scripture teaches: the righteous will inherit the earth, and the unrighteous will be damned. There is no man damned who did not damn himself. You are right to defend the goodness of God against these new Stoics." He pauses briefly, then evidently feels a need to drive the point home. "You are right! Be certain of that! The Church is fortunate to have you at such a time as this."

With this declaration, Baer turns back to his work, pressing nib to paper, and Erasmus is left once again to his thoughts. The heavens are fully opened now: the Birsig will burst its banks, and the refuse of the city will pour into the streets. *Thank God the Frobens live uphill! But going out will be a misery.* Those who set store by such things say the fountains of the deep may soon break forth again. It is written in the stars, or at least men selling books have claimed so. *I will not be bound by the stars.*

No, Desiderius Erasmus will not give way to fear, though it should rise within him like the rushing waters, threatening to pull him under. There is hope, or there is nothing. God is good, or there is nothing. He is free, or there is nothing. The mind cannot comprehend nothing. If it tried, it would collapse upon itself, crushed under the weight of its own existence. The one who turns inward cannot move outward toward humanity. The one who despairs cannot possibly move toward God.

The idea he holds—the radical idea—is that grace is granted to all but rejected by many. We are given great gifts, and we squander them. We could have peace, but we delight in war. We are granted the supreme revelation, and we cannot be bothered to read it correctly. We take our stand on falsehood rather than the truth. The way is narrow that leads to Christ, and only the most Christlike walk upon it, or only those who walk upon it become Christlike.

He believes there is no Christianity apart from the pursuit of Christ. He believes all truth is sacred, but none more so than

that revealed directly by God. He believes that education can
improve society, and that the final consolations of heaven do not
negate the need to reverse the effects of sin here and now. He takes
the teachings of Jesus seriously. He believes that ambiguities in
Scripture can be harmonized by viewing them through the lens of
the central ethic and teaching brought by the incarnate Son of God.
He believes there is nothing that would not be made better if it
became more like Christ or the stainless world he created. And so
he prays with whispers of the soul, joining his spirit to that of the
prophet.

Lord, I have heard the report about You and I fear.
O Lord, revive Your work in the midst of the years,
In the midst of the years make it known;
In wrath remember mercy.[20]

And then, at a stroke, his thoughts return to the present.

"I'm afraid that's all from me tonight," Baer concludes, rising
from his seat. "Same time tomorrow?"

"Yes," Erasmus replies softly, mind thoroughly distracted.

Baer approaches and places a hand on his back: an amiable gesture. "I admire you, friend. This cannot have been easy."

"What I have suffered in writing it will be nothing compared to
what I suffer when it is read," he concludes.

"Escaping Scylla, you will plunge headfirst into Charybdis."

"That is the fear, yes."

Baer laughs—a sound not so different from the thunder. "They
have forced you to write a book on free will. Forgive me, but there is
humor in that."

The worst of the storm has passed. All that remains is the fall
of water returning to the earth whence it came. Rising to the surface, forming new streams, reaching confluence, passing into the sea.
Boiling and steaming, ascending to the heavens, stored up in clouds
before it falls to earth again. He looks Baer in the eye.

"I have sought at every turn to escape the shackles thrust upon
me by men, but my very success has doomed me in this regard. A man
known to all is not permitted silence. I cannot be what I was once,
shunning the controversies that bind others, forging my own path.

---

[20] Habakkuk 3:2.

The man who is known to all belongs to all. Fame is the end of freedom."

23 August 1524
Orlamünde, Electorate of Saxony

On and on the wheels turn, drawing Martin Luther toward the appointed hour. He sits in an open wagon with the two companions who have accompanied him on his tour of Thuringia: his old prior and current housemate, Eberhard Brisger, and the Elector's court preacher, Wolfgang Stein. A pair of horses, either gray with white spots or white with gray spots—he cannot be certain—pull the cart along, each bump in the road increasing the pain in his back and neck. A young man named Lukas holds the reins, whistling softly to himself, evidently free of the cares that haunt his elders.

Laying on the floor of the wagon is a crucifix that formerly adorned the altar of the parish church in Kahla. Martin passes over it with his eyes, examining every inch. Constructed of wood overlaid with silver, it is now heavily dented, the figure of Christ smashed beyond recognition. Yesterday, as he climbed the stairs to address the congregation, he nearly tripped over the thing. No accident, surely. The people of Kahla, so loyal to Karlstadt, left it as a warning. *This is what we do to images. This is what we will do to you if you touch the Lord's anointed.* Leave it to Karlstadt's disciples to be so offended by the cross that they would make it a stumbling block for him. He will take it home for repairs.

Now the wheels pull him irresistibly toward Orlamünde, the final stop on his journey. The town councilors, all members of Karlstadt's congregation, have sent him a letter reciting their complaints and naming him a heretic. With many insults they sought to pummel him, but the charge that he denies the gospel has dealt his spirit the greatest blow. They seem particularly indignant that he has warned the Saxon princes about the brewing insurrection. Alas, he must meet these accusers, and the signs are all bad. He does not feel it safe to spend the night in Orlamünde. Even the light of day cannot fully banish the drone of anxiety within him, like the constant buzz of the hornets' swarm. The very air seems poisoned in this part of the world, not only by Karlstadt, but by Thomas Müntzer.

After the arson at the Marian chapel, Müntzer fled Allstedt in the middle of the night, leaving his wife and child behind and calling his erstwhile supporters 'Judases.' *How very unlike a man,* Martin thinks, *failing to protect his own, denying responsibility, placing all the burden on the sheep.* Before his ignominious departure, Müntzer wrote to Karlstadt and asked him to join a seditious league to make war against the princes. Despite his public denials, Karlstadt is siding with the insurrectionists, if only by neglecting to properly condemn them. He hands men flaming words and expects them not to catch fire. Yes, the air is thick with violent intent, and soon the rivers may run red. Nevertheless, Martin Luther must go to Orlamünde.

"Why are you two still wearing habits?" Stein asks, breaking into his thoughts. "What are you hoping to prove?"

Martin shakes his head slightly, attempting to regain his mental bearings. Brisger quickly offers a response.

"There is a time for everything under heaven, but it is not yet the time for that."

A man as full of spirit as his red hair suggests, Stein is undefeated. "When will it be the time? The birds have flown and yet you cling to the nest. Move on! Get yourselves wives!"

Martin rolls his eyes. "Have you been speaking with Argula? She sings the same tune."[21]

Stein chuckles. "The scourge of Ingolstadt?! No, but I admire her spirit. Is she sending you a wife in the post?"

"Certainly not. I've had far too many as it is. I thought I had disposed of them all, but it seems there is one bird, as you say, struggling to leave the nest."

Here he thinks of Fräulein Katharina von Bora, to whom Hieronymus Baumgartner has made a pledge of marriage. Their union was expected by end of summer, but Baumgartner has gone home to Nuremberg, neglecting to send Katharina a single letter in his absence. Martin was informed of this shortly before leaving Wittenberg, not

---

[21] Argula von Grumbach was a Bavarian woman of high standing who became an early advocate of the Lutheran Reformation and took on the University of Ingolstadt for what she believed were its unbiblical teachings and actions.

by Katharina herself, but by her host family the Reichenbachs, who are finding it increasingly difficult to feed an extra person.

Perplexity written on his freckled face, Stein commands Brisger, "Interpret!"

"Doktor Luther helps all kinds of people," his former prior replies with a shrug. "The nuns write to him from their cloisters begging for assistance. Several of them stayed with us. It must have been a year ago now. I never thought to have women in the Black Cloister, but they were pleasant guests. We didn't have to clean or cook, did we, Martin?"

"We weren't doing much of that before they came," he admits. "I barely have time to eat, let alone cook."

"Well, I was sad when they left, but I wish them well," Brisger concludes. "I found them very amiable. Of course, the Doktor would keep aloof. It is his way."

"I did nothing of the sort!" Martin objects.

"You'll never get a wife that way!" Stein declares, ignoring Martin's protestation.

Why on earth should I take a wife when I am likely to die? he wonders, but it is not the right moment for such a dark admission. Instead, Martin says, "I could have a wife tomorrow if I wanted one. In fact, I could have had one twenty years ago. My father was desperate for me to marry Anna Reinicke. Our families grew up together. She was a pretty girl, kind, respectable. Her father was a smelter, same as mine. I could have practiced the law in town and set up a household with her. Instead, I went to the monastery, and she married my good friend Nikolaus. Now they have four boys. Sometimes I laugh: I think that I could be sitting at a desk in Mansfeld poring over legal texts, with four sons and a respectable wife. Instead, I'm sitting in this wagon with the two of you."

Here he gives a pointed look to Stein, as if to say, *Let that be the end of your questions.* The preacher either fails to interpret or elects for willful ignorance.

"Am I to understand, then, that you do not want a wife?" Stein inquires.

"Not for him a respectable life, nor it seems a respectable wife," Brisger quips with a twinkle in his eye.

"Well, perhaps he should find an unrespectable one, and fast!" Stein argues. "He looks as gloomy as any man I've ever met. Has he been unwell? You would tell me if he were unwell?!"

"He is as well as he is ever likely to be," Brisger answers. "He has the melancholy temperament, without a doubt, though sometimes I think there is as much yellow bile in him as black."[22]

His frustration reaching a boiling point, Martin insists, "It is not that simple! What I have experienced—it is best not to speak of it. I thank God that neither of you have had to walk where I have walked. I would not wish it on any man."

They fall silent. The only sounds are Lukas' whistling and the crunching of gravel beneath wheels. In the quiet, Martin's mind churns. *Too much bile? That does not begin to describe it.* He was taken captive: driven from all human communion. For most of a year, he was held in the Wartburg Castle—shut away and stopped up, desperate for news, worried about his friends. The sun lost its warmth and the world its colors. There, at his most vulnerable, the accusing voice was loudest. His work and his sheep came under attack. He had never felt so utterly alone.[23]

At his Patmos,[24] that mighty fortress in which he was exiled, he realized just how uncertain it all was: that he was not marching triumphantly to the hilltop but hanging by a thread over a dreadful abyss, suspended in horror, staring down into the all-encompassing dark, one breath from a collision that would utterly destroy him. Then the thread snapped, severing him from his former existence,

---

[22] The medical theory of the four humors, developed especially by Hippocrates and Galen, was dominant in Western medicine until the widespread acceptance of the germ theory of disease in the nineteenth century. Bodily ailments were thought to be caused by an imbalance in the four humors: blood, yellow bile, black bile, and phlegm. Yellow bile was associated with the element of fire and could cause decisiveness, ambition, or aggression. Black bile was associated with the earth and could make a person fearful, sickly, or slothful.

[23] Following his appearance at the imperial Diet of Worms in 1521, Martin Luther was allowed to return to Wittenberg under an order of safe conduct. Following that, he could be arrested anywhere in the Holy Roman Empire and put to death. However, Elector Friedrich of Saxony was sympathetic to Luther's cause and arranged to hide him in the Wartburg Castle. Luther lived there for most of a year before returning to Wittenberg without the Elector's permission.

[24] Patmos was the island to which St. John the Apostle was exiled for his adherence to the Christian faith. Luther symbolically referred to his own place of exile as such.

and he fell into the unnamed caverns, away from the light of the sun, descending beneath the piles of the dead—the awesome weight of human civilization. Below the mountains' roots, past the hidden fountains, and into the very underworld he came. What he saw there, he cannot relate by any words of human speech.

He perished every day. He was scorched with heat, left naked and freezing before the pummeling wind. He fed upon sorrow and became one with despair. He was pierced with a thousand blades: torn open within the fissures of the deep, for he who rends the heavens rent him. And out of that deep, he cried to heaven. He waited helplessly, longing for absolution. How long he was there, he cannot say. He knows there are deeper caverns still—wells of grief from which he has not yet been forced to drink—for he heard the unearthly cries like a shiver in his bones: deep calling out to deep.

Beneath them all, from the lowest part of hell, came a voice as weak as a dying breath and as strong as the tremors of the earth: *My God! My God! Why have you forsaken me?* Had the Lord not raised him up to walk again in the land of the living, he would have been annihilated—of that he is certain. The memory of that place hangs upon him, coloring every moment. Might he be forced to return? He knows not, but he fears it.

They continue to wind their way along the western bank of the Saale until Lukas finally says, "There it is up on the hill: the old castle!"

Sure enough, the former seat of the Counts of Orlamünde sits perched on a tree-covered ridge. Just to the left is the tower of St. Mary's Church, and further still in that direction the town itself can be seen, the brown roofs of houses barely visible above the trees.

"Up we go!" Lukas calls over his shoulder. "Hang on: the road is not good here."

These words prove all too true. Only fifty feet into the ascent, Martin feels ill. By the time they join up with Castle Street at the end of a long row of houses, he counts it a miracle that the bread he ate earlier is still inside him. Suddenly, Lukas pulls the wagon to a halt, jostling the contents of Martin's already surging stomach. The driver turns in his seat to address the three of them. "How do you wish to proceed?"

"Let me go speak with the mayor," Stein suggests. "I will attract less attention."

In too much discomfort to argue, Martin waves Stein on to the task. The preacher walks quickly, avoiding the scattered piles of horse dung, until the road curves and he is out of sight. A few minutes pass, and Martin decides a beer might do his stomach good.

"I'm going to look for the tavern," he informs Brisger. "Do you want a drink?"

"No, I don't think I could stand it," his friend replies, "and if your condition is anything like mine, I would caution against it."

"There are few disorders of the body that cannot be improved with beer," Martin insists, hopping to the ground and making his way down the street in the same direction as Stein.

A few of the people he passes stop and stare, perhaps recognizing him from prints they have seen. His skin tingles as he looks into their eyes, for those glassy orbs seem to hold violent intent. Peasants in the fields, filled with anger over years of ill treatment, have been filtering into the towns to listen to Karlstadt and Müntzer preach. Martin fears they are falling victim to the twisted aims of others. So great is his concern, he has almost forgotten about his possible duel with Erasmus and how discouraged it is making Melanchthon. *One tragedy at a time, Martin. It must wait. He must keep.*

At last, he reaches an establishment where beer is being sold from an open window. He pays for his drink and stands in the street imbibing. As he does so, he notices more townspeople crawling out of their dwellings, staggering quietly into the light of day. First a few, then a dozen emerge from nearby alleys and the next door down, all staring at him oddly. They are moving closer now, their eyes threatening, but none of them saying a word. It is exceedingly odd, as if he were a dying beast and they the carrion fowl.

The tension in his bowels gives birth to a question. *How quickly could I get back to the wagon?*

The scene is broken by the reappearance of Wolfgang Stein, this time at the head of a party of a dozen or so men. From their clothing, Martin gathers they all work at decent trades. One wears a chain indicating he is mayor. Martin abandons his drink and walks out to meet them, taking care not to stumble on the loose cobbles. As he does so, the lurkers find places to hide, their eyes still transfixed by the unfolding drama.

"The mayor of Orlamünde, Herr Vogel, and the rest of the town council," Stein announces, stepping to the side.

Stand firm, Martin bids himself. *You are in the right.*

The mayor approaches him, removing his green cap to reveal a head of gray hair. "Highly learned and favored Doktor Luther, I bid you welcome to the town and parish of Orlamünde!"

Remembering the harsh words in their letter, Martin responds, "There is no need for that. I know well enough why I am here." He will not pretend as if all is right with the world when it clearly is not.

"You do not remove your cap?" the mayor asks, frowning at the offense.

"You have insulted me in no uncertain terms and cast me out of the Church."

Herr Vogel chuckles softly, then inquires, "Tell me, Herr Doktor, do you intend to preach today?"

"No. I would not feel safe doing so. I wish to address the letter you sent here in the open," he insists, unwilling to be cornered physically or verbally.

"That is just as well, for we prefer to hold our meetings in the open air. It promotes an equality between persons."

Oh, spare me this act! he thinks. *You are so equal that Karlstadt is making all the decisions, rendering your council impotent.*

Surely, that will not do. Martin responds instead, "If you say so. Now, as for this letter you sent—the one where you reprimand me for calling Doktor Karlstadt a false teacher—it is only because you have been exposed to this false teaching for so long that you fail to see it for what it is. To deny the sacraments is heresy, for they are the ordained means of God's grace."

"No one here denies the sacraments!" a member of the council objects, even as his fellows cry out, "Liar!" and "Papist!"

"Friends!" the mayor pleads. "We are all open minded here. If we have erred, then let Doktor Luther instruct us in a Christian manner, but he must humbly and willingly accept instruction as well."

A humble people would never have sent me that letter—not with that wording, he grouses.

"Be honest, now: did you even write those words?" Martin asks the assembled councilors. "Was it not Doktor Karlstadt who put them into your minds? Was it not he who pressed seal to paper? He has been forcing himself on you from the beginning."

The mayor responds in deep annoyance. "We called him to this pastorate, thank you! Everything was done properly. And as for the letter, Brother Andreas didn't write a word of it."

He scoffs. "Perhaps not with his own hand, but he planted the thoughts in your brains."

"You must think we're stupid!" one of the councilors objects, a short man with a great brown beard and a cloth tied round his neck. "We have plenty of men here who can read and write."

"That is a good bit different from grasping the intricacies of Scripture and having a proper knowledge of the Fathers," he insists.

"We don't need your Fathers!" the same man proclaims, evidently granting him ownership of Gregory, Augustine, and Hilary. "Any man with the Spirit is as wise as they!"

"Doktor Karlstadt taught you this?" he asks. He has noticed Karlstadt moving in that direction, deemphasizing the importance of Scripture in favor of a new work of the Spirit—telling young men they don't need an education. The so-called prophets who plagued Wittenberg during Martin's time at the Wartburg Castle made a conquest of his former colleague in that regard. "If so, he has misled you most severely," he assures them.

This prompts a rising chorus of insults: "Slanderer! Back stabber! Hell hound!"

Their cries seem to light a fire under the mayor, who declares, "We know how you have mistreated that man of God, slandering him to the Elector! You are a lying wolf: a viper in league with the devil!"

"Is this how you address a brother in Christ?" Martin asks, his outer demeanor calm, but his mind furiously calculating the number of steps back to the wagon. As the townspeople cry, "You are no brother of ours!" and "Did not Christ speak to the Pharisees thus?", he looks to Stein, who is standing with his mouth slightly ajar in disbelief. Discretely, Martin signals with his hand for the preacher to return the way they came. This message at least Stein interprets correctly.

When the noise dies down a bit, he addresses the crowd again. "Setting aside your assumption that you have the same wisdom as Christ when he addressed the Pharisees, I will call you my brothers and sisters, for I have some hope yet for your souls, be they ever so badly deceived. You have been led down the wrong path by your shepherd, but do not fear: soon you will have a new shepherd who will lead you in the way of truth."

"Are you calling us ignorant?!" one of the councilors snaps, and Martin notes that his fists are clenched.

He shakes his head. "You are confused. Take images, for example: you say they ought to be destroyed because they can be misused, but then you might as well kill all your women and dump all your wine, because those can be misused as well."

"Yes, but God created those things, and he didn't create the images," says the man with the cloth round his neck.

"Anything can become an idol if you make it one, and most anything can be a gift of God if you allow it to be," he explains, truly annoyed at how poorly they have been taught.

"No, no!" another man cries. "It's like Jesus said: the bride must come to the bridegroom completely naked, emptied of all earthly things that would weigh her down—pure and holy. That is why we must break and destroy every image, so we can be completely free of created things."

There it is again: Karlstadt's assault on the things of this earth, he grouses.

"Where to begin?" Martin inquires. "First, our Lord never said that. Second, created things are not evil! Truly, this is a pernicious doctrine!"

"A what?" someone asks.

"It's evil, that's what it is!" he cries, driven to anger. "There is nothing wrong with created things, nor is there anything wrong with a man bedding his wife, regardless of how much clothing she wears."

Now a bulging hulk of a man steps forward—a laborer of some sort judging from his lack of any apparel but a shirt and hose. He looks as if he could break Martin with his bare hands.

"I've had it with your slandering Brother Andreas!" this man cries in a deep voice. "Say farewell, heretic!"

The laborer stoops down, removes one of the loose cobbles, and rises again, hurling it in Martin's direction. He ducks by instinct and the thing flies over his head and through the window of the tavern, crashing into a stack of earthenware mugs. His heart beating fiercely, Martin rises to his full height and stares at the man, who is visibly seething. In the space of a breath, he passes from thinking, *I could have just been killed!* to realizing, *I am about to be killed.* He has time for only one retort, and then he must fly.

"And here I was going to suggest you should just read my books," Martin mutters, feeling none of the ease this statement suggests.

The veneer of civility as shattered as the mugs, several of the councilors and townspeople begin stooping down, attempting to pry stones free from the pavement. Martin does not wait to judge their success but turns on the spot and runs toward the wagon, his breath puffing with every stride. His work at the university, the reforms of the churches, any further hope he has of joy in this life: they all hang on his ability to make contact with the wagon before a stone makes contact with his head. He hears one land somewhere close to him and strives to increase the pace.

"Go in a thousand devils' name!" someone shouts. "You are damned to hell, Luther! Damned to hell!"

Then in an instant, his foot catches a rut. He is hurtling forward, his weight pulled by the force of the ground. With the curses of the Orlamünders ringing in his ears, he lands face first in a pile of excrement. As unpleasant and embarrassing as this is, it is nothing compared to the sound of death approaching behind him. The tension is sharp within his muscles. He is gripped by panic, fierce and hot. They are catching up with him, weapons in hand.

He raises himself on shaking arms, hands pressing into shit, and lifts his frame from the earth. Wiping the stuff from his eyes, he begins running again, praying his feet will find solid ground, latching onto the first sight of the wagon. He feels something strike his left heel: perhaps a stone, perhaps some other projectile. He hobbles for just a moment and then tells himself, *No, you must place your full weight upon it! You have no choice.*

So, he presses on, certain that he is bleeding. *Almost there! Almost there!* He strives to outrun his terror as much as the crowd. Finally, he reaches the side of the cart, where Brisger and Stein pull him up and lay him on the floor of the wagon.

"Drive, Lukas!" Stein commands.

"But—" the young man begins, leading all three men to cry, "Drive!" in unison.

As the horses are spurred into motion and the wheels begin turning, Martin sits up and looks back to see at least a dozen men approaching quickly, some with stones in hand, shouting all kinds of insults and obscenities. Another cobble is thrown but falls well short of the wagon, and as the horses power their way down the broken road, the cries become more distant.

When at last they are out of danger, Brisger inquires, "Where is your cap, Doktor?"

He places a hand on his head and realizes it is missing. "I must have lost it when I fell," he mutters.

"At least you didn't lose your head!" Stein concludes. "I thought it might all be over for us."

Martin reaches down and removes his left shoe. There is an ugly looking cut along his heel bone, but nothing more serious: a great relief. Brisger hands him a cloth to clean himself. He accepts it with shaking hands, the full extent of the experience only just hitting him. Suddenly, he begins weeping uncontrollably, his spirit overcome by it all.

"Here!" says Brisger, handing him another cloth to wipe the tears.

"I beg your pardon," Martin requests, the moment passing. "It all caught up with me. Those eyes! They had death in their eyes!"

He looks up at Stein, who has a sly smile on his face.

"What is it?" Martin demands to know, offended by the apparent insensitivity.

"You could have married the Reinicke girl," the preacher observes, laughing and shaking his head.

29 August 1524
Wittenberg, Electorate of Saxony

Philipp Melanchthon scurries about the ground floor of his home preparing for an august gathering. He has already secured some ivy from the garden in the back. Now he steals a wooden spoon from the kitchen and makes his way into the small parlor with dark panel walls. *Two, four, six, eight,* he counts the places to sit: the couch can hold two, then the four chairs normally used for dining, and two pupils can sit on the chest. He sets the spoon on a simple wood mantle above the modest hearth and quickly twists the ivy into something approximating a ring, depositing it next to the spoon. He arranges the seats in a circular pattern just as his student boarders come galloping down the stairs, talking loudly amongst themselves.

Now Veit Winsheim, Theodor Fabricius, Erasmus Sarcerius, and Georg Sabinus all enter the room in quick succession, each clad in a student's robe with books in hand. They are part of a study group known as the Akademia in honor of the famed school of Athens. He, Doktor Philipp Melanchthon, is their always enthusiastic but sometimes weary leader, or as he is known among them, the scholarch. There are eight members including himself—nine when Doktor Camerarius is able to join, but tonight it will be left to Philipp to lead them all through a portion of Plutarch's *Lives*.

"Is everything ready?" Fabricius asks, a native of Cleve with a red beard and curly hair to match.

"Yes," Philipp assures him. "The others should be here soon." He then says to the oldest and tallest among them, "Veit, it is your turn to procure the sacred flame. They know you'll be coming."

The very mention of it brings a smile to Winsheim's face. Bowing low, he proclaims, "I shall procure it with all haste!" and departs both the room and the house.

"Where is he going?" inquires Georg Sabinus. The youngest at only fifteen years of age, Sabinus is something of a boy wonder, even as Philipp himself once was. Though he cannot yet grow a beard, he is among the greatest Latin poets Philipp has ever met, and that is saying something. Sabinus has only just started boarding in the "Poor House" for the upcoming winter semester, and this will be his first Akademia gathering.

"At the ancient Akademia, when night had fallen over Athens, the students would visit the altars of the city with torches, then run with flames in hand up the hill to the altar of Prometheus. They would carry the fire to that sacred hill of Athena, goddess of wisdom," Philipp explains.

"Yes, but where is Veit going?" Sabinus asks again.

"To the Elster Gate, of course," Fabricius explains with more than a hint of condescension. "Don't you know what happened there? Doktor Melanchthon and Doktor Luther burned the canon law and Pope Leo's bull!"

Sabinus sneers. "The place where they burn the rubbish? That's nothing special."

"Did you not hear what I just told you?" Fabricius chides, literally looking down on the younger man.

"Go easy on him, Theodor. This is his first meeting," Philipp instructs. "Georg, if you're going to be part of the Akademia, you will need a healthy imagination to sustain the illusion," he explains to Sabinus, pointing to his head.

Suddenly, there are sounds of a struggle in the hall. Philipp hears the household servant, Famulus Koch, grunting in frustration.

"What are you doing in here, stupid thing?!" Koch cries amid the sounds of pounding against the walls and floor. Philipp runs into the hall just in time to see Koch lifting the family goat with all four of her legs flailing.

"Apologies, Master Philipp!" Koch calls to him. "She got inside again. Don't know whose fault it was this time."

"Ah," he replies, realizing he forgot to latch the door upon returning with the ivy. "Just put her back in the pen. Thank you."

The goat continues kicking and squealing as Koch maneuvers her out the back way. Cursing himself for his idiocy, Philipp turns around to see the final members of the group—Christoph Lasius, Lucas Edenberger, and Veit Dietrich—walking through the front door. He moves to return to the parlor but is met by his wife Katharina coming down the stairs, her plaits let down at end of day.

"Philipp, can I speak with you for a moment?" she asks, stopping just short of the floor and grasping the railing.

"Is this what you were wanting to talk to me about this morning?" he inquires, faintly recalling a missed conversation just before he rushed off to his first lecture.

"Yes. I thought perhaps now would be a better time. I've put Anna to bed, and—"

"Is it going to take a while? Because I have Akademia this evening."

She scrunches her nose. "The noisy ones?"

"That's a bit harsh," he concludes. *Though not inaccurate.*

Clearly perturbed, Katharina huffed, "Well I was hoping to sleep. I'm quite exhausted. Philipp."

"Herr Doktor, it's time!" comes the voice of Edenberger from down the hall.

"Thank you, I shall be there momentarily!" Philipp calls back.

When she has his full attention again, Katharina asks, "What's that?"

"The arrival of the sacred flame from the Elster Gate."

"The slaughter ground?" she remarks, scrunching her nose again. "That place smells of the devil."

Now it is his turn to huff deeply and state with mock sincerity, "My dear, I must beg you not to insult the home of the sacred flame."

"I take it then you do not have time to talk?"

"Not at the moment, sadly. After the meeting—it won't take more than an hour or two."

She scoffs. "That's what you always say."

A bit surprised by her attitude, which seems far more negative than usual, he stutters "Käthe, I—" But then from his right come the cries of, "Professor! Professor, it is time!" The young men are lining up by the open front door. Looking back at Katharina, he says softly, "I must go."

He can see the pain in his wife's eyes: she looks as if she is on the verge of tears. "Fine, then go," she concludes, "but sometimes, Philipp, I think you don't care how I feel."

Sensing the danger of her words, he objects, "What?! No, we can't leave it like that!"

But it is too late. She is already lifting her skirt and ascending the stairs.

"Try not to burn the house down," she calls back over her shoulder.

Troubling! Yes, very troubling! His partner in life—the flesh of his flesh—doubts his affection. *Well, not my affection exactly. My respect? Or is it simply my attentiveness?* He recalls Martin's words: *I dare say your wife sees the trouble.* But Katharina is not one to complain about much of anything, hence the shock of her comments. She loves the students as much as he does. Normally, she brings them all food and drink, laughing at their little games, but not tonight. *Why?*

She complained of weariness. He thinks back over the past few weeks and realizes she has often made comments to that effect: "I am tired," "I must lie down," etc. He thought it nothing more than what any mother of a young child experiences, particularly when grieving the death of a loved one and attempting to provide for a husband who insists on working all hours of the day and night. Perhaps because he is so exhausted, he has failed to appreciate her exhaustion.

Could she be ill? No, surely, she would tell him if she were. *But maybe that is why she wishes to speak with me.* Now a deep pang—a trembling within his breast. *My love, my life, my precious one!* There is no time to feel it: the sacred flame is come. He must set these thoughts aside for the moment. There are seven young men desperate for his attention.

In strides Veit Winsheim holding a flaming taper in his right hand, the look on his face gleeful. The remaining members of the Akademia stand three to a side, clapping in rhythm and chanting, "Sacred flame! Sacred flame!" Winsheim strides between them, displaying his candle as one might a monstrance, and enters the parlor, moving with purpose toward the hearth.

As the rest of the young men crowd in and claim their seats, Winsheim proclaims, "I bring the sacred fire from its source at the Elster Gate, where burned the bull of Antichrist and the second law of the Church's captivity! Come, sacred fire, and gladden the hearth of learning!" He then bends low and touches flame to logs, setting them alight. This is followed by a great round of applause, so much so that Philipp fears for the slumber of the other members of the household.

As the cheering gives way to laughing and discussion, Philipp retrieves the ivy crown from the mantle, still shaken by his wife's words. *You must set it aside for the moment,* he bids himself, breathing deeply. Holding the crown in both hands, he announces, "Gentlemen, before we begin, it is incumbent upon me to bestow this laurel on one who has shown exceptional scholarship of late."

Every man in the room leans forward or cranes his neck to get a proper view. There is anticipation written on their faces: the hope of praise from their leader. He continues.

"I am pleased to announce that the winner of this honor for the week is a young man who, though enduring much hardship in his youth and only learning to read when he was as old as Sabinus here, is now mastering the Hebrew language, to say nothing of the brilliant questions I am told he asks in the theology lectures of Doktor Amsdorf and Doktor Luther. Yes, gentlemen, I bestow the laurel upon Herr Theodor Fabricius!"

The decision meets with the approval of all. Fabricius is a kind soul, and his achievements are remarkable considering his late start and lack of resources. As Philipp places the makeshift crown upon his pile of red curls, Fabricius looks at him with great fervor and says, "Thank you, Herr Professor. I am greatly honored."

Philipp nods in acknowledgment. "As well you should be. We do not give out laurels to just anyone here, even if Herr Edenberger did manage to snag one last week. Wear it with dignity, friend!"

As the excitement among them continues, Philipp takes the seat nearest the hearth, but not before retrieving the wooden spoon from the mantle—or as it will be known this evening, the scepter.

"Brothers of the Akademia, as scholarch of this esteemed institution, I call the meeting to order!" Philipp proclaims. His words are met by a great pounding of boots on the wood floor and a collision of palms with knees. When the noise dies down, Philipp asks, "What business have we this fine eve?"

Winsheim is the first to speak. In his second year boarding with the Melanchthons and participating in the group, he has the seniority. "Oh, revered scholarch, upon whom we all gaze with loving hearts, we have with us an esteemed pupil of the late Petrus Mosellanus who wishes to join our gathering."

He refers to Erasmus Sarcerius, whom Philipp knows well as the young man has been boarding at the "Poor House" since arriving in Wittenberg.

"I suspect he can speak for himself," says Philipp.

"Not until bidden, scholarch, for he is not yet one of our number," Winsheim insists. "You must grant him the scepter to loose his tongue."

This is certainly a rule of their gatherings, but not one Philipp has always taken to enforcing. Sensing that a bit more ceremony could rouse their spirits further, he replies, "Right you are," then looking at Sarcerius, says, "Oh, newcomer from the great city of Leipzig—"

"Blessed location of Eck's dismemberment!" Edenberger interrupts, drawing a few grunts of approval.

Philipp sighs and continues. "I extend to you the scepter of good letters and bid you speak with the wisdom of the immortal gods. And now," he proclaims, pointing the spoon in Sarcerius' direction, "orate!"

The young man nods silently. His is a quiet spirit less accustomed to the exclamations of those at the Leucorea, but in time, Philipp senses, he will find it in himself to be raucous.

"Greatest thanks, august one. My name is Erasmus Sarcerius. I hail from the Rhineland."

"And I hail you, brother of the same motherland," proclaims Lasius, "and perhaps the scholarch will also greet you thus."

Philipp nods. "You know in what love I hold my mother Rhine, but remember gentlemen," he says, pointing the spoon at each of them in a sweeping motion, "when we come together, we are Greeks and Romans and nothing else."

This provokes cries of, "Hear, hear!" and, "Yes, scholarch! Wise scholarch!"

"Continue, brother Sarcerius," Philipp urges.

A man of slight build and deep-set eyes, Sarcerius pauses for a moment—seemingly to summon his courage—then explains, "I have journeyed to the Lecuorea and now the Akademia to join in the pursuit of the New Learning and good letters, thus bringing light to the study of theology, my chief love."

Philipp nods heartily. "I say he has spoken well. What say you all?"

"So say we all!" the brothers chant in unison, once again stomping their feet on the floor.

Philipp looks again at the newcomer, who seems heartened by the cries of approval. "Brother Sarcerius, welcome to the Akademia." Another round of cheering erupts, then Philipp asks, "Is there any more business?"

Now the young Sabinus seizes the floor. "Oh, revered scholarch, with your permission, I should like to recite a poem I have composed."

Philipp hears a muffled groan coming from the direction of Edenberger's seat. Sabinus' tendency to recite lengthy works has not won him great admiration among the older members of the Akademia, one or two of whom expressed opposition to the inclusion of a fifteen-year-old. Philipp well remembers the rejection he faced at that age, not least from the University of Heidelberg. He can perhaps understand the jealousy and frustration at seeing a young man succeed with such apparent ease, but he also knows that one ought not fault a lad for possessing intelligence as long as he wears it well. He therefore ignores the groaning and tells Sabinus, "I bid you recite it mellifluously. We wait upon your voice as the simple farmer awaits the rain."

The poem is indeed long. One or two of the brothers appear to be drifting into slumber at various points, whereas Philipp is captured by the beauty of the young man's Latin. *Remarkable in one so young,* he thinks. *He will have his pick of professorships. I wonder if we could keep him here? Probably not.* When at last the recitation comes to an end and Sabinus retakes his seat, Philipp asks, "Is there any other business?"

"O scholarch, will you be lecturing on theology come winter semester?" Veit Dietrich asks. A Nuremberger by birth and breeding, Dietrich is passionate about theology, which likely explains the question.

Philipp demurs. "No, for our most excellent Elector has paid me only to teach Greek."

"But does not Professor Luther wish you to teach theology?" Dietrich inquires, grinning slyly.

You devil. He told you to ask that question, Philipp thinks. After all, Dietrich is undoubtedly one of Luther's favorite pupils, and the admiration is entirely mutual. If his fellow professor was going to plant a question, this would be his chosen instrument. Philipp doesn't truly mind, but he decides to call Dietrich out for humor's sake if nothing else.

"Professor Luther is not the scholarch here, young man. He is but a rumor to our ears."

"But surely—

"Do I sense your loyalties wavering?"

Dietrich's expression changes to one of shock as he places a hand over his heart. "Not at all, scholarch! You know I bleed only for you, scholarch."

Philipp smiles. "That is music to my ears. Very good. I absolve you. Any other business?"

"But you must teach theology, scholarch!" Fabricius interjects, belaboring the point. "You are the best teacher we have!"

"First, that is nonsense," Philipp insists. "Second, we have already put this business to rest. You are out of order, brother."

"But—"

"Do you wish to continue wearing the laurel crown?" Philipp asks pointedly.

"You mean the ivy crown?" Fabricius inquires with a devilish grin.

"Do you wish to wear it?!"

"Yes, scholarch," Fabricius promises, nodding his head with such fervor that he must place a hand on the crown to keep it in place. "Of course, scholarch."

"Then I bid you cease this relentless harping."

Fabricius breaks into a smile again, and evidently unable to stop himself, prods, "Have I annoyed you, scholarch?"

That's it, Philipp decides. *You will now become an example for the others.*

"I am above annoyance, as you well know," he assures Fabricius, "but I nevertheless impose upon you the rule of silence."

"What?!" the young man cries in mock outrage. "No!"

The rest of the students begin pounding their fists on whatever hard surface they can find, chanting, "Silence! Silence! Silence!" Fabricius opens his mouth to protest, but bound by the unflinching hand of the law, remains mute.

"Now, is there any other business?" Philipp asks. "Otherwise, we should move on to our reading of Plutarch."

"Please, scholarch—with your leave, scholarch," Lasius requests.

Philipp extends the scepter. "Speak."

"What will happen to Doktor Karlstadt, scholarch?" Lasius asks. "Is he banished from Saxony forever?"

They are meant to be studying the great authors of ancient days, but instead they are once again discussing university politics. Philipp narrows his eyes into a glare and complains, "You are not playing by the rules of the game."

"I too would like to know," adds Winsheim.

"And I!" proclaims Dietrich.

Philipp looks around the room. "Do you all wish to know?"

Seven heads nod in the affirmative.

"Very well. I see there is no point avoiding it," he concedes. "As most of you are aware, Doktor Karlstadt has never cared much for the Elector's good opinion. Well, now he has lost it completely. Rumor has it he has fled to Bavaria, or perhaps beyond. I do not expect we shall see him anytime soon."

"Did he really say Doktor Luther has thrown the gospel under the bench?" inquires Edenberger.[25]

"I was not there, but I believe he did," Philipp replies cautiously.

---

[25] The equivalent idiom today would be that something was thrown "under the bus."

Edenberger shakes his head in something like disgust. "How changed he has become! Scholarch, doesn't it make you wonder?"

"Wonder what?"

"Well, can we really trust anyone?"

Philipp looks from one pair of eyes to the next. Here are young men wanting to believe, having come from far and wide to join something bigger than themselves. They have not only paid tuition: they have placed their faith in a message. The days are long gone when a man would enter the Leucorea simply to learn a heap of facts. They have chosen to associate themselves with the work of reform. Eager to trust, they are particularly vulnerable to the failures of others. Philipp decides he must answer them honestly, tempering their admirable faith with a word of warning.

"Totally trust? Perhaps not. But then again, what do any of us know without the slightest hint of doubt? Such faith is only rightly placed in God."

"But the Church," says young Sabinus breathlessly. "Can we trust the Church?"

Of course, this would be the question. It is the eternal inquiry: the one that lit the sacred flame.

"You can trust that the gates of Hades will not prevail against it," Philipp concludes. "Let that be enough for this evening."

An hour later, the young men have departed to their own rooms, and Philipp is pouring himself a glass of wine as part of his nightly ritual. It is sometime after ten: later than he prefers given that he must wake at two the next morning. As he climbs the stairs for one last trip to his study, it is their conversation about Karlstadt that consumes him. After all, Philipp trusted the Church: he trusted Andreas Bodenstein von Karlstadt. In the excitement of the hour, he was caught up and carried along. He wanted to believe that the Spirit was working. He wanted to believe it all, but his hopes were disappointed. Martin is always telling him that the goodness of the Church is an article of faith and must be accepted as such based on God's promise. *Truer words have never been spoken,* he thinks.

It amazes and repulses him, the way these thoughts hang on: the number of times he is forced to put them down. Why after all this time does his grief hold such power?

He was young. Brilliant, yes, but fragile. He was insufficiently broken—insufficiently befriended. He has taken in sorrow like a sponge and sat in it for two years, festering and rotting, wallowing and putrefying, desperately seeking release.

Every time he reasons himself free, the grief bites anew. Every time he imagines he has learnt his lesson, it forces him to endure another. He is still longing, still aching, still lamenting those experiences and the decisions he made. Time is meant to heal wounds, but his, it seems, were never properly mended, and now they are thick and crusted, inflamed and diseased, sinking into his bones and marrow, becoming one with his core. He is wasted within an inch of his life by all that he has lost. Despite his incomparable blessings, he is never more than half a thought away from darkness—far more empty than full.

He thinks, *My heart is a leaking vessel that can never be filled, but cries out unceasingly, seeking some reply.*

As he sets his goblet down on the desk, the candlelight falls upon his red leather volume of Greek grammar. There it sits innocently enough, a blessed object now cursed by the pain of estrangement. He is drawn to it as a sailor to the siren song. Perhaps if he opens it one more time—if he sees those elegant letters etched on paper again—it will all begin to make sense: the confusion he feels, the way it left him disoriented and reeling, grasping for something more solid than that which he thought as firm as stone.

He reaches out in trepidation, spirit quivering, prepared to be struck by a sight that will pierce him through. He turns back the cover and glances at the note left by Johannes Reuchlin proclaiming the love between them: the bond of a father and his son. Then, in an instant, he slams the thing shut. No, it can never be for him the comfort that it once was. He pinches his eyes closed and breathes deeply, the holy yearning flowing through his veins like molten metal—the eternal desire for communion. He whispers to himself in the solitary darkness.

"What is this flame that burns so brightly? It enlightens and consumes. What is the destiny that calls to man? It builds and destroys. Upon the stone it has its foundation, in the kilns of the deep. It calls to me. But who would suffer his own destruction to be remade by those hands?"

With a sigh, he turns to leave, but out of the corner of his eye, he sees something else: a scrap of parchment briefly illumined. *I did not leave that there.* He takes a closer look under full light and realizes it is a cutting saved from the bin and left for him to find. Normally, he has a strict rule against reading correspondence just before slumber, knowing how it tends to put his mind off the business of sleep, but the message is in his wife's hand. He leans forward and takes in the unmistakable message: "I am with child."

His whole being is seized by her words, for he realizes this is what she has been meaning to tell him all day—perhaps even for several days. Too busy with his own affairs, he has failed to listen to her voice and note the changes in her body. "I am tired," "I must lie down," et cetera. The uncharacteristic outburst of emotion: "You don't know how I feel!" All at once, it makes sense. It is exactly like when she was pregnant with Anna. He missed it, she gave up trying to tell him, she left a note.

Immediately, he departs the study, candle in hand, and climbs the stairs to the second floor. Here their bed chamber sits just beside Anna's. He places a hand on the knob, stopping for a moment, listening for any signs of movement. Might his Katharina still be awake? Will there be a chance to discuss this, or must he endure the hours of waiting until morning, knowing all the while that he has failed her? He places his palm flat against the wood of the door, touching his ear to it, attempting to quiet his breath. *My love—oh, my love!* Hearing nothing, he blows out the candle in disappointment and opens the door as quietly as possible.

A faint hint of moonlight comes through a single window on the far wall. He can just make out the form of her body in sleep. In his haste, he has come in still wearing his robe, cap, and shoes. Setting the candle on the floor, he removes all three as quietly as possible and lays down on his side of the small bed they share. The thing creaks terribly as he adjusts himself for sleep that is unlikely to come. He can feel the warmth emanating from Katharina's body as she lies beside him. *Should I wake her? No, she is so tired.* He resigns himself to staring up at the wood beams above, which are little more than a gray and black haze to his eyes.

Then she whispers. "Philipp?"

"Yes!" he replies, softly but urgently. "Are you awake?"

Katharina rolls over to face him. He does the same, meeting her in the middle of the straw mattress.

"Did you see the note I left you?" she asks.

"Yes," he replies, shame striking him again. "I'm so sorry. You've been trying to tell me for a long time, haven't you?"

She takes his hand in hers. He can only just make out the features of her face. "It's alright. I probably should have waited, but I couldn't keep the secret any longer. I was excited to tell you."

"Then you're not angry with me?"

"No," she assures him, determination in her voice. "I was a bit angry when the men kept banging. I was afraid they were going to wake Anna. But angry with you? No, not really. I cannot be angry with you long."

He exhales deeply, receiving the grace from her hand, his tension releasing. The fear dissipates just enough to allow him to savor the joy: God is giving them a second child. True, he has no idea how they will afford to put food in another mouth. They will have to rely on Koch even more for assistance around the house. Their difficulties will increase, but so will their joys. If only the child arrives healthy, if only Katharina remains healthy. He thinks of Erasmus' offer: a safer and happier life for all of them. The thought of it demands his attention, but he refuses to entertain it. *I cannot leave this place. My children will be raised here. Everything we love is here.*

"How do you feel?" he asks, realizing this is the appropriate question.

She breathes in deeply. "Exhausted, exhilarated, terrified, full of gas." With this last comment she laughs softly.

"I feel all those things except the gas." After another moment of contemplation, he concludes, "Well, this is wonderful news. I wish I could be a bit less terrified by it."

"I know. Do you think it will be a boy this time?"

He assures her, "It doesn't matter." Then wanting to drive the point home, he repeats, "It doesn't matter if it is a boy or a girl."

"You said that last time, but I know you want a son who can follow you into the university. You are a teacher at heart, and you want most of all to teach your own son. I want that too."

Here he speaks his deepest truth. "I want to see you and any children of mine healthy and happy. That is what I want."

Katharina shuffles slightly, nudging closer to him. "So here we go again, then?"

He kisses her softly and says, "I love you."

To his eminent delight, she replies, "I love you too, my Philipp."

Autumn

1 September 1524
Basel, Swiss Confederation

Desiderius Erasmus walks upon a gravel path in Froben's garden on Malt Street, driven less by the movements of the earth than those of men upon it. He threads his way through a corridor of boxwood trees pruned to conical perfection, then passes a plot of herbs drawing life from the sunlight that daily diminishes. Here are Frau Froben's prized rose bushes—there an apple tree that Johann Erasmus insists is his and his alone. The sounds of the city are distant here by the wall. He can almost imagine that he is the only man left on earth, a prospect both terrifying and exhilarating.

This is no ordinary day. He has birthed another child of parchment and ink, and seldom has the labor been so punishing. He felt himself torn with each new push, pulled toward an outcome not of his making. Worst of all, his suffering has only begun, for now the child is sprung forth into an unkind world, and for as long as it remains there, he will fear for it. This is what the release of *On Free Will* means to him: he has stood by his principles even as men have sought to bring him down. His enemies may yet accomplish that feat, tearing the remnants of his freedom from clenched fists. His is a stand no less bold than that of Luther at Worms, though it will get nothing like the applause. How often he has thought of Diogenes, wandering the streets of Athens, searching for a true man.

If there be any man true, he does not turn the wheel of the world, Erasmus muses. *The shocks I feel are not of his making. The very thing that propels a man perverts him.*

Now, as he walks past a bed of poppies in second bloom, he is approached by Lieven Algoet, recently returned from doing Erasmus' bidding in England. Algoet is a man of Ghent some thirty years old, whose education Erasmus has overseen since his youth. It was in Louvain that Algoet first entered his service, and though they speak the same language by birth, they share this in common: they are truly citizens of Rome and prefer the language of Cicero.

"Livinus!" Erasmus exclaims, looking the scrawny man over and thinking, *The English diet agrees with you even less than it does with me.*

"My liege!" Algoet responds with a wide grin, gripping both his shoulders, slapping him on the back. "I've just come from admiring piles of your newest work. It will be in all the shops by afternoon."

Stomach tightening, he asks, "Did Froben set aside the ones I asked for?"

"Yes, a tremendous stack," replies the younger man, shaking his head in wonder. "Will anyone actually be paying for it?"

"Three are going to Rome—Giberti, Aleandro, Hezius."[1]

"You're sending Aleandro a book? You ought to send him a bomb."[2]

This draws a chuckle. "The world would be a happier place, but it seems, on occasion, Minerva must teach the swine."[3]

"Fair," Algoet assents with a nod of the head.

He proceeds through the list of recipients. "Three to Saxony, naturally: one for the Duke, one for the Elector, one for Melanchthon."

Algoet looks at him, brow furrowed, head cocked slightly to the side. "You're not sending one to Luther?"

"No need. Everything I write ends up on his desk of its own accord. But I am quite keen to get one to Melanchthon, along with my note."

---

[1] All three were officials in the papal curia at the time.

[2] Gunpowder was widely used in Europe by this time and incorporated into various devices for explosive purposes, though the term 'bomb' is a later addition to the English language.

[3] A common idiom at the time was, "The sow teaches Minerva," meaning an unintelligent or foolish person was teaching (or supposing to teach) someone intelligent or wise. The phrase is here reversed to imply that a truly superior person is teaching a truly inferior person.

"Will you send one to Farel?"

"Ha!" Erasmus cries so loudly that a sparrow deserts a nearby shrub. "You made the offer of gunpowder. Is it still good?"

"Afraid I'm all out at the moment," Algoet replies with a wink.

"Pity. At least I managed to convince the town council to banish him. He is off to Burgundy now to terrorize them." Then for a moment he pauses, considering the ramifications of this statement. "Oh, *Godverdomme!* He's going to poison my wine!"

Algoet ignores his lament and inquires, "What of the other copies?"

"For the English, and that is where you come in, friend," Erasmus explains, pointing a finger squarely in the middle of Algoet's chest. "I know you have just returned, but would you mind revisiting the sodden isle?"

"The weather was quite good when I was there last," Algoet assures him.

"Well, well. The Lord still works miracles. Do you accept my commission? I must get a copy to King Henry. The whole thing was his idea."

Now it is Algoet's turn to scoff. "May the good Lord bless him!" he declares facetiously. "He clearly has a great concern for your health."

Erasmus presses on with his instructions. "And you must deliver my letters: Wolsey, Warham, Tunstall, Fisher, More, Bere—"[4]

"I think Bere might be dead," Algoet notes.

"Is he really? I've heard nothing of it."

"He was gravely ill. They were preparing him a place next to Arthur."[5]

"Well, take it to Glastonbury, nonetheless," he says with wave of the hand. "Hopefully he will be alive to read it. If not, pay your respects and mine."

"Very well, my liege," Algoet replies, bowing his head.

---

[4] The Bishop of York, Archbishop of Canterbury, Bishop of London, Bishop of Winchester, Speaker of the House of Commons, and Abbot of Glastonbury, respectively.

[5] The Abbey of Glastonbury traditionally claimed to be the burial place of King Arthur.

"Make haste before the crossing grows dangerous. The Channel is wretched too late in the year."

"Yes, my liege."

Now Erasmus takes the younger man's face in his hands and looks into his eyes, which have the same fervor they possessed in former days. There was no beard then, nor any need for it, for Algoet had not yet acquired the distinctive marks of the pox. Looking upon the scars mostly covered by brown-red hair, he thinks of how close he came to losing his Livinus. With the world at war and the crossing never certain, he wonders, *Will I ever see this face again?*

"Be careful, Livinus," he urges him. "You have come close enough to death already."

"It is you I worry about," Algoet replies softly. "How many troubles you carry! Would that I could take them from you!"

"This task, at least, is yours for the taking," he surmises. "Now, get you gone. When the water grows cold and the ill winds blow, you will catch a fever long before you drown."

The younger man walks backward slowly, declaring as he does so, "Even so, the die is cast! There can be no turning back."

Thus goes Lieven Algoet to call upon a king, while Erasmus is left in the city of printers, waiting upon a dread fate. Just down this road is the St. Albanteich, its waters continuously turned by the city mills. Within one of those buildings, great wooden hammers are pounding in turn. Pulp is being shaped into sheets which will be hung to dry. Upon some of those pages, his own words will be stamped in ink—upon others, those of Martin Luther. *What will the wild boar make of my book?* The swine sometimes teaches Minerva, but this he also knows about all things porcine: it is in their nature to revel in mud.

And what of Philipp Melanchthon? *Did Camerarius pass on my message?* His letter to Philipp is longest of all those he is sending out, and it caused him the most trouble in composition. So many words he wrote, attempting to defend himself and make the young man see reason. There are those who would tell him to save his breath: *He has made his choice. Let that be that.* He does not know why he must keep trying when all hope seems to have faded. Perhaps it is because Melanchthon is no pig and will not take kindly to being covered in Luther's waste.

Onward Erasmus of Rotterdam treads, pondering great events. Here is a path through a sunlit garden, springing into color as much as life, nourished and fed by the sun and the rain. Here is the smell of new blooms, the gentle hum of bees, the soft brushing of his shoes upon gravel. It is a balm for his soul: a safe haven amid the rising tide of war.

But he is not walking upon this path. No, he is somewhere else entirely: the same path, but drained of color. Darker, colder, with sharper edges producing a thousand corners behind which wild beasts crouch, ready to spring, their mouths dripping, teeth gnashing, tongues wagging—so eager to devour. He hears the cawing of the crow as surely as if it had entered his ears. From the tips of his toes to the skin of his scalp, the fear ripples and flows, up and down, up and down.

How could this terrible place be bonded to the one he loves? How does he walk in one world and also the other? Is the darkness the work of the devil who means to frighten him off the path, or is it the light that deceives? He knows not. He walks in fear and trembling.

4 September 1524
Wittenberg, Electorate of Saxony

Martin Luther sits at a small desk in the sacristy of St. Mary's Church, running his finger along the outline of its frame. The evening Mass has ended, and the congregants are departing. It was not his job to act as celebrant: that duty was performed by Bugenhagen, and it is upon this friend and brother that he now waits, hidden from others. Before him is a copy of the holy Scriptures that he has read countless times, sometimes thumbing the pages with a barely contained fury to search out the truths therein, and at others absorbing the words with measured intent, allowing them to caress his soul with divine comfort. It is that consolation he now seeks, for even as Bugenhagen spoke the words commanded by Christ, he had a vision of the future that terrified him.

In his head, he hears the taunting voice of Erasmus. *I told you it would happen. I warned you. What have you done, Luther?!*

He turns in his chair to face the rest of the room, rubbing his temples with his hands, skin pressing against skin. The screws are tightening—the fever heightening. He allows his gaze to wander about the sacristy, taking in the features of this place where he has engaged in so many bouts with the devil, he expects to see scorch marks on the floor. Oak cabinets are set against three of the walls, their insides packed with vestments, candles, censers, prayer books, chalices—everything necessary to serve the congregation. In the middle of the room is a large table used for preparations, and on the northern wall two windows let in the waning light. Here, concealed from the prying eyes of the world, he finds both his weakness and his strength.

His eyes focus on a painting on the wall opposite. There he sees Christ as the Good Shepherd, humbly dressed and carrying a rescued lamb upon his shoulders. It is the last thing he looks at before departing to preach—a reminder of the task God has set before him—and today it seems filled with a powerful urgency. The Good Shepherd would rather sacrifice his life than surrender the sheep to the wolves, while the hired hand abandons them in the hour of hardship. He never sought to abandon his sheep, but he was snatched from them for a time. How quickly the wolves began to circle, snarling and gritting their teeth! It took everything he had to fight his way back to them. Even now the wolves are scratching at the door: he can hear their ghastly howls, and it casts a chill over his person. Within his breast burns a fierce desire to protect his own.

Is there anything in this life as fearsome as being a shepherd? he wonders.

Now the door on the right opens and Johannes Bugenhagen enters the room still clothed in the vestments of his office: a gray chasuble draped over a white alb and gold-fringed stole. A taller man than Martin, he bears himself with a general sense of contentment that pairs well with his academic spirit. Setting the empty Communion vessels on the table, Bugenhagen moves to the cabinet on the opposite wall, failing to realize he is not alone.

Martin clears his throat and utters, "Hans."

Bugenhagen swings round, his brown eyes locking onto Martin's. "Ah! I didn't know you were in here. Are you hiding?"

He exhales deeply. "Would it be so wrong of me to do so?"

"I should think not," Bugenhagen replies, stepping closer and leaning against the table. "The older I get, the more often I wish to be alone." This is hardly a surprising comment given that Bugenhagen's wife Walpurga has recently given birth.

Martin hesitates, conscious of the breath escaping his lungs, slowly, purposefully. "It is the silence I treasure, but I am always alone."

In an instant, a change upon the Pomeranian's face. Martin can guess easily enough what Bugenhagen is thinking: *This is going to be one of those discussions.* The sentiment exudes from his friend despite any efforts to disguise it. Martin feels a twinge of guilt as he thinks of Walpurga waiting for her husband, a crying babe in her arms. But however annoyed Bugenhagen might be, he seems to sense the turmoil in Martin's soul. His expression softens. He is ready to give of himself.

"Is something troubling you?" Bugenhagen inquires. "More than usual?"

"Are they waiting for you?" Martin asks in turn.

"Eventually, but I can spare some time."

"Then remain as you are for the present," he instructs, seeking to converse with him as confessor rather than colleague.

Bugenhagen understands immediately and responds, "Very well." In the work of a moment, he pulls another chair from the corner and moves it so the two of them can face each other at short distance, even as they have a hundred times before. Settling into the seat and folding his hands, Bugenhagen asks, "How have you been, brother?"

"Poorly, I'm afraid," Martin begins. "That is, in most things I am well."

His voice trails off. He struggles to give order to his spinning thoughts.

Bugenhagen prompts him, "But in other things?"

Now Martin enjoys a moment of clarity: he realizes what lies at the heart of his troubles. It is a fearsome thought—a dread notion. He must speak it.

"I fear I have lost something of the joy of my salvation," he whispers.

His confessor leans back slightly, adjusting his position. "It grieves me to hear it. Tell me, brother, have you been praying?"

"Yes, often—desperately."

"All your disciplines you keep?"

"I attend always to the Word. I am never without the Sacrament."

"And have you been angry?" Bugenhagen asks more pointedly.

A cut close to the bone. He looks at his feet and whispers, "Yes."

"Is it Doktor Karlstadt who creates this anger in you or something else?"

Close to the mark again, but it is not the heart of his concern.

"I met him in Thuringia, twice," he mutters. "It did not go well."

"He is preaching and publishing against you. I can't imagine that is easy."

"No," he says pointedly, looking Bugenhagen in the eye.

"You were friends."

"I don't know if I would say that."

"Then what were you? Colleagues? Brothers? Adversaries?"

"I don't know," he admits with a sigh. "When it comes to Doktor Karlstadt, I feel I don't know anything anymore."

His confessor nods but says nothing, again adjusting position. It seems he is stalling for time to think. Finally, Bugenhagen asks, "Have you been controlling your temper?"

Here is a question Martin never enjoys. It is a fault of his from his youth: his mother allowed him no doubt on that score. A switch on the wrist. A tugging on the ear. *Go to your room, boy! Don't come out until you are fit to face the world!* He has striven to conquer his moods, but at times they conquer him.

"I confess I have not always done so," Martin admits. "The devil always has his snares."

Again, his confessor simply nods, declining to press further. "I hear Erasmus is likely to write against you. Does that trouble you?"

He snorts. "Yes, though perhaps not for the reasons people think. I never placed much faith in him."

"But that is quite something, is it not?"

The question is innocent enough, but he guesses at the meaning: *When it hits you, it will strike with the force of an avalanche.* "It is and it isn't," he concludes.

"If you say so. Is there anything else bothering you?"

Here they come to it. He thinks back to the moment, just minutes earlier, when he watched Bugenhagen elevate the host. Within his mind, he saw a vision of the world to come. He felt the fracturing of communion like the tremors of the earth: a new threat as real as any from Rome. He saw it, and he was terrified.

At last, he gives voice to his fear. "They say Zwingli is of the same opinion as Karlstadt—perhaps even Œcolampadius agrees with them."

"In what way?" Bugenhagen asks, lowering his brow.

"They are teaching that the Lord is not in the Sacrament."

His confessor's eyes seem to bulge. "Are they truly?"

"It seems so. I cannot think of anything more injurious to the Christian than to tell him that Christ does not really give himself to us in the Sacrament. If we are not flesh of his flesh, if he does not give himself to us fully..." He cannot finish. The thought is too disturbing.

"Perhaps you have misunderstood Zwingli," his confessor offers.

Martin chuckles softly, his face breaking into a pained smile.

"Oh, that it were so! But I think not. This is the new opinion: the rejection of all things physical. I saw it first in Karlstadt, and now it spreads like a cancer. God no longer meets us here on earth. He leaves us to reason our way along with minds of dirt and dust: to endure trials and temptations without succor. If I thought for a moment that the Christian life was like that, I would fall into despair."

"And what do they make of the phrase, 'This is my body'?" Bugenhagen asks.

This single spark, so innocently offered, falls upon the tinder within Martin, eating away at fuel that is readily prepared. It is bursting into flame! He struggles to direct its energy. His flesh is searing—his sinews breaking apart. He is weary of holding it in! Now his thoughts rush forth like a fiery torrent.

"Tell me, if it is not Christ's body, and if the covenant is not sealed in his blood, then what are we standing on but a hill of sand? We are still in our sins! I remember the first time I lifted the bread to heaven and spoke the words, 'This is my body,'" he explains, making the motion. "I was filled with dread, overcome by something beyond my ability to comprehend. The hands that shaped the mountains were pressing down upon me! The Almighty God who set the stars alight—he was made flesh, and his flesh was given for man, and his flesh was in my hands! 'This is my body, given for you.' Sunk in the mire of my sin, I felt it like a flaming iron upon my soul and longed to flee from the face of God. But by faith, I now feel it the most

comforting thing in the world to rest in the divine embrace. They
would sacrifice that upon the altar of human reason!" He pauses for
a moment, overcome by a strange mix of anger and sorrow. "Forgive
me. I need not convince you, but the more I think of it, the more it
enrages me."

He ceases speaking, his breath coming heavily. Having received
this deluge of words as patiently as any man could, Bugenhagen
attempts to redirect Martin's thoughts.

"Perhaps they can be reasoned with," Bugenhagen says in a deep
voice like a trickling stream. "Œcolampadius is a good man and a
great scholar. I would not lose faith in him yet."

"We are physical creatures, Johannes," Martin insists, shaking
his head. "Whatever we do, we do in the body. In our flesh we work
the works of God, and it is our flesh we defile when we sin."

"And have you experienced any temptations of the flesh?"

Now it is Martin who is taken aback. He was proceeding along a
clear line, but this question, connected weakly to the previous matter
at hand, knocks him off course. He is forced to repeat the question in
his mind. *Have I experienced any temptations of the flesh?* Quickly,
he arrives at an answer, stating, "Yes," without hesitation. When the
color seems to drain from his confessor, he adds, "I don't know why
you should have that look on your face."

Bugenhagen opens his mouth to speak but appears unable to do
so. He blinks rapidly, struggling to adjust to the revelation. "Forgive
me, but I can't help but feel a bit concerned. You always told me you
had fewer difficulties in that area."

Again, he can read his confessor's thoughts: *You bastard! How
could you?! You've sunk us all!*

Suppressing a laugh, Martin assures him, "You mistake me. I
have not committed fornication, nor am I filled to the brim with
lust. What I mean is that I experience my flesh more fully than ever,"
he explains, pressing a hand to his chest. "I feel a yearning within
my bowels."

"A yearning? What do you mean?" Bugenhagen inquires, evidently afraid he will speak of his movements again.

Martin closes his eyes and concentrates on each part of his
body in turn. *What do I feel?* He moves from his feet up the legs,
considering his chest and arms, investigating the tension in his neck

and head. The hairs of his head demand his attention—his skin and muscles will have their say, but he cannot describe it with any words of man.

"If I knew what I meant, I would tell you," he concludes softly. "Whatever you may have been led to believe, I assure you, I am not made of stone. I am crafted of human flesh and subject to fear like any man. I suffer and decay. I am a creature of desires, both righteous and unrighteous, and were you to place me in fire, I would burn. I may yet have the chance to prove it."

Looking as if he will cry, Bugenhagen whispers, "Martin, perhaps it is time."

"Time for what?"

"To put off the cowl for good. I think the people are ready. What's more, I think you are ready."

The words strike him squarely in the heart. A surge of memory fills his being: The lightning bolt. The final supper with his friends. Receiving the tonsure. He is laying face down on the floor, surrendering his being to God. He is one in an endless line of brothers. The bread in his hands. The terror in his chest. Shame. Burning shame! Lashing his back again, again, again—attempting to beat out his flesh. Knees pressing against stone, level after level. Staupitz speaking to him beneath the pear tree. *Staupitz! How could you?!* The breaking light. The breach. He feels the power of each moment that has composed his existence as a brother of Saint Augustine. As a woman seized with labor pains, his entire being is overwhelmed, unable to handle the sensations thrown its way, thoroughly surrendered to the wrenching spasm that is memory.

"You speak of it as if it were a simple thing," Martin replies softly, keenly aware of the sound of his voice, a weak thing upon the air.

Bugenhagen nods. "I know very well that it is not—not for any man, and especially not for you. But I know your struggles, brother. Do not attempt to face them alone."

Tears are running down Martin's cheeks. He is powerless to stop them. "The devil is sifting me like wheat, but I have this assurance: that Christ himself is praying for me, and one day my accuser will be thrown down."

"Amen," his confessor says with real determination. "That is the consolation you need. That is the joy of your salvation."

He shakes his head. "It is not so simple. The Spirit of God is both a consoling force and a consuming fire. Many years, I have wrestled with him: my suffering and my salvation. But this yearning is something new in me. I cannot account for it."

Bugenhagen rises from his seat and places a hand on Martin's shoulder. "Think about what I have said. And as for the Sacrament, the Lord does give himself to you, Martin. He has granted you grace, and he will do so again: grace upon grace. Have that assurance."

Now Bugenhagen places a hand on Martin's head—the warmth of human connection passing through his scalp into the extremities of his form—and speaks the blessed words: "Having heard your confession, I forgive you of your sins in the name of Jesus Christ. Go and sin no more."

By the power of this word, Martin stands and says, "Thank you, brother. I have kept you too long."

"The church is empty now. Stay and pray if you wish," Bugenhagen offers.

Releasing his friend to the noisy house, Martin makes his way into the choir of the church. The congregants have indeed departed—the place is grown dark. It is numbingly quiet, but he is not alone. His thoughts begin to spiral as he looks at the altar table still covered in white cloth, a silver crucifix seated upon it. There are distant voices: some coming from the market square outside, and some within his own head. The echoes of the past are beating upon the door of his mind, demanding entrance to his thoughts. He stands behind the table, resting his hands upon it. He closes his eyes and breathes, in and out, in and out.

He is no longer in Wittenberg, but Erfurt, in an hour long past, when he stood behind a similar table in St. Augustine's Church. There, for the first time, he would celebrate the Sacrament of the Altar as a priest of the Church of Jesus Christ. The work of years had reached its completion. His whole family was there: he could see them standing in the congregation. Hans Ludher[6] was among them, having made peace with his son's choice. More than made peace, he had embraced it wholeheartedly, traveling down from Mansfeld with a host of fellows in tow, showcasing the family's position in

---

[6] This was the original spelling of the family surname.

society, celebrating a new form of achievement. Hans' friends had convinced him to give his firstborn son to God, even as the saints of old. All was well.

And yet, Martin felt the trembling—the uncertainty. Nothing was how he had imagined it. Whatever peace he had been longing for was not there in the church. Something dark was pressing down on him, draining the moment of its color.

You are just nervous, he told himself. *Speak the words. Everyone is waiting.*

He lifted his hands and began to recite the liturgy, shaping the tone of his voice, allowing the music to flow through him. He had done little but practice this for the previous month. Another rush of fear! He attempted to push it away, imagining himself joined to a millennium and a half of saints: men who stood before the bread and wine even as he, offering the same prayers, seeking the same blessing. But as Martin continued to chant, the rhythm flowing through his veins, he was struck by a sharp sense of fraudulency. He was not one of those saints. He never could be.

Whom are you trying to fool? You can fool the people, your brothers, your prior, but you cannot fool God!

He refused to give in, speeding up the words, moving closer to the moment of truth, wishing it over and done with. He clung to the familiarity, rejoicing that it was not he who had to devise a prayer to the Almighty in that most sacred hour. His voice broke as he recited, "We humbly beseech you, then, most gracious Father, through Jesus, your Son, our Lord, to accept and bless these holy sacrificial gifts that we offer to you for your holy Catholic Church."

Who do you think you are talking to? a voice within him accused. *It is not the vaulting you address, but the righteous one of heaven. Who are you, Martin Ludher? Who are you?! In sin your mother conceived you. In sin you live and breathe!*

By this point, his pulse was racing, the sweat releasing from his pores, and yet he continued. He was certain everyone could see what he suffered: could hear in his halting tones the sin which condemned him. Their eyes threatened to crush him, so he attempted to focus on the task at hand, clinging to the sight of the bread of heaven offered to men. From his throat poured the words of institution granted by Christ: "Take and eat, all of you. This is my body."

His hands shook as he held the host aloft. His lips quivered, and his tongue stuck in place. Before his mind's eye, the face of God gazed upon him, not in love, but the fierce heat of wrath. He was struck by a vision of majesty—driven deep within himself. Like the blinding light of the sun was the presence of the holy one, and he longed to run: to flee from this thing that horrified him, digging deep within the earth of his soul, begging the rocks to fall upon him. Like a man before the gallows, he shrank and fell, his spirit buckling. He held the flesh of Christ within his sin-stained hands, receiving not grace but guilt, condemning himself with every word.

I cannot do this, he thought. *I cannot do it! I am damned!* A single word gripped his consciousness: *Flee!*

In a panic, Martin turned to address the prior standing proudly behind him, the body of Christ still in his own trembling hands.

"Lord prior!"

"Yes?"

"I am filled with terror. I must depart the altar."

The old man's features twisted, then froze in great annoyance.

"Get on with it!" he commanded. "Quick, now!"

"But—"

The prior slapped him on the back. "Quickly!"

His fear momentarily overcome by embarrassment, Martin muddled his way through the rest of the service, still oppressed by a sense that he, Martin Ludher, was the worst of sinners: a wretch counterfeiting as a saint. How could he stand between the people and God? He was a man of unclean lips serving a people of unclean lips! Even as he entered the sacristy afterward, exchanging one set of vestments for another, he felt the tension boiling beneath the surface of his thoughts, bubbling up in violent spurts, causing any hope to evaporate.

He attended a dinner held in his honor, which helped to improve his mood. His siblings had always known how to bring him cheer, particularly his brother Jakob. He was almost free of his immediate worry when he noticed Hans Ludher sitting with his arms crossed, notably mute, wearing a grimace rather than a smile. *I must speak with him,* Martin thought. He had not done so all day, and he longed to know that somehow, despite it all, he had made his father proud. When Hans rose from the table, Martin followed at a distance, departing the refectory and entering the cloister. There, amid the carefully manicured roses bushes, he watched in disgust as his father relieved himself. Knowing how hard Brother Gerhard had worked to encourage the beautiful blooms, it seemed an obscene thing for his father to choose such a location.

"You come here to watch me piss, boy?" Hans asked, his back still to Martin.

Uncertain how to respond, he waited as his father secured his belt and climbed the few steps to the covered walkway. A master smelter, Hans Ludher was clothed in a coat lined with fur, a sign of his increasing wealth. The son of peasant farmers, Hans had pulled his way up with blackened hands to become a master of others, and Martin was reminded of his words: *We bet everything on you!* Years of toil and sweat. Years of disappointments and the recent loss of two sons. Martin longed in that moment to know that the sacrifice was worth it: that despite their earlier quarrels, his father had found worth in the vocation pressed upon Martin by God.

"Father," he whispered.

"I suppose I must call you 'father' now," Hans remarked.

There was something dismissive in the way Hans spoke these words. It seemed more insult than compliment.

"I am still your son," Martin replied.

"Oh, are you?" Hans scoffed, moving close to him. "I thought sons were meant to honor their fathers."

The smoldering embers of Martin's anxiety were fanned into dancing life by his father's words. Again, the panic set in: he was overcome by shame. Hans Ludher had clearly never made peace with Martin's decision. He had been putting on a show for others while harboring bitterness in his heart. Martin had come to him for words of comfort, a son longing to hear from his father that everything would be alright. Instead, he was being ambushed.

"I thought..." Martin sputtered, unable to finish.

"Now, you tell me, because you're the one who reads all the books," his father sneered. "What is the fourth commandment?"

I must not weep. I must not let him see my pain, Martin charged himself.

When he did not answer immediately, Hans cried, "Tell me!" His eyes were lit with a fearsome glow.

Martin swallowed hard and recited, "'You shall honor your father and mother.'"

"That's still one of the commandments, eh?"

The words came harshly, like blows to chest. Martin reached deep for a response. "Father, you must believe me: I meant no disrespect by doing this."

Then his father slapped him on the face. The heat of it rippled through Martin's skin. Hans Ludher was breathing heavily—almost growling.

"Stop lying to yourself!" his father cried, shaking with rage. "You did this to spite me, and you know it!"

"That's not true!"

"I gave you everything, and all I ever asked in return was that you do this one thing! Take up a trade, marry, breed—do what men do. Oh, but it wasn't enough for you! You had to be better than us!"

His father spit on the floor trod by generations of brothers, making his opinion abundantly clear. *I must not weep*, Martin reminded himself. *I must not let him win.*

"You don't understand," Martin replied quietly, "but you have never understood me."

"Ah, right. The thunderstorm—the lightning bolt. You had no choice. You had to do it. Everyone has a choice, boy!" Hans bellowed, grasping onto Martin's habit and pushing him back against the wall. "How do you know it wasn't a ghost you saw that night?!" he yelled into his face, the smell of beer filling Martin's nostrils. "How do you know it wasn't the devil?"

Silence fell. Nothing moved but the air in and out of their lungs. They were locked in the throes of strife, spirits colliding as like against like.

"Father," Martin whispered, seeing in those eyes the reflection of his own. "I wish—"

"What?!" Hans screamed, pushing harder against his chest. "What now?!"

"I wish I could make you see how much I respect you—how much I wish to honor you."

Another slap fell, this one harder than the first. Much as he longed to exchange blow for blow, Martin knew he must not.

"Is that why you've turned yourself into a gelding?" Hans demanded to know. "To honor me?! I see you there shaking and whimpering, shitting your pants and blubbering like a girl. Thank God he gave me one son at least who's not afraid to be a man! I can never bring the other two back!"

"Please," Martin begged, no longer able to contain the tears. "Please, father! This is the most important day of my life."

Hans Ludher scoffed and responded, "I hope not, son. I hope not."

The vision ceases. He is back in St. Mary's Church, no longer Ludher, but Luther: the freed one.[7] He is free from the wrath of God—free even from the wrath of his earthly father. By one thing only does he remain bound. *It is time*, he tells himself. Returning to the Black Cloister with great intent, he enters the privacy of his bed chamber. There, with tears in his eyes, he removes the black cloth of the Order of Saint Augustine for the last time. He will be what God declares him to be: a free man.

30 September 1524
Wittenberg, Electorate of Saxony

It is early evening in the New College building of the Leucorea, where Philipp Melanchthon stands in an empty lecture hall, the last of his students having departed. He has been tutoring since six in the morning, stopping only once to eat some bread. Weary in body and soul, he gathers his books from the lectern and places them in his shoulder bag, only to notice something that has been concealed there all day. It is Erasmus' treatise *On Free Will*, which arrived at his threshold a week earlier and was devoured in one night's insomnia.

He retrieves the thin brown volume and opens the front cover to reveal a letter from the book's author: a message intended only for him. Page after page, the ink flows in the unmistakable hand of the greatest scholar in Christendom. As a boy in Latin school, Philipp could hardly have dreamed of receiving such a thing: no cursory missive sent out of obligation, but a long and winding discourse.

---

[7] The name Luther is derived from the Greek name *Eleutherius*, which is itself a cognate of the Greek word *eleutheros* (ἐλεύθερος), meaning "free."

He has read it over at least five times, always looking for some new insight—a further glimpse into the man's thoughts.

> One of my friends wrote and told me that you would have come here too, had you not been afraid you would rouse ill feeling which would make me unpopular. My dear Melanchthon, I could easily have met that ill feeling with contempt.[8]

The whole thing speaks of genuine regard. "Your gifts have always inspired me with respect and affection."[9] There is also a host of complaints, some of which seem beneath Erasmus' dignity: an outpouring of negative commentary about Zwingli, Farel, Œcolampadius, and Capito, but also clear frustration with Aleandro and the other hardliners in Rome. Philipp is willing to overlook this excess of lamentation given the attacks Erasmus has suffered from all sides. "Relying on your good nature, my dear Philipp, I have poured all this into your sympathetic ear. I know that as an honorable man you will see that it does not get out into the wrong hands."[10]

He is opening his heart to me. He is making me his confidante, he thinks. *Perhaps it is true: he wants me to succeed him.*

Near the end, a piece of news that gives him pause: Cardinal Campeggio has sent someone to speak with Erasmus. *Nausea must have gone to Basel after speaking with me,* he reasons. Their conversation was not limited to the weather. Nausea has asked Erasmus if he, Philipp Melanchthon, would be willing to move to another location. Of course, this was the same thing Nausea pressed upon him in person. With characteristic modesty, Erasmus reports, "I replied that I wished a man of your gifts might be free from these disputes, but that I had no hope of your undertaking a recantation."[11]

---

[8] "1496: To Philippus Melanchthon," in *Collected Works of Erasmus, Vol 10: The Correspondence of Erasmus – Letters 1356-1534,* ed. James M. Estes, trans. R.A.B. Mynors and Alexander Dalzell (Toronto: University of Toronto Press, 1992), 378.

[9] Ibid., 379.

[10] Ibid., 386.

[11] Ibid., 386.

Was that meant as a compliment? he wonders. Conversing with Erasmus is like conversing with the Delphic oracle.[12]

As for the book itself, it is more gracious than Philipp expected, treating Luther as an intellectual equal. "Dare Erasmus attack Luther like the fly the elephant?"[13] That is what he asks, claiming for himself the lesser position. In fact, Erasmus has behaved so reasonably, it might convince Martin to temper any possible response. That is Philipp's sincere hope. In a time when few men can be trusted, Desiderius Erasmus has shown himself at least mostly true. They can disagree on matters of doctrine, but they need not bite and devour one another. For months, Philipp has worried about what it would mean for Erasmus to publicly condemn them. Now he hopes to never find out.

There is a knock at the door. Bag slung over his shoulder, he walks over and opens it to find Martin Luther standing there in a scholar's robe and cap. Given his colleague's novel adoption of this dress, Philipp finds himself squinting slightly, feeling as if his eyes deceive him. But it is indeed Doktor Luther clothed in the same academic attire as himself, though with a significant advantage in height, Martin seems to wear it with greater authority. Suddenly, Philipp realizes he is still holding Erasmus' book. He quickly stuffs the small volume in the bag, not wishing to cause offense. There is a surge of fear up his breastbone, which he attempts to suppress.

"Come have a beer with me," Martin commands, nodding his head in the direction of the stairs that lead down to the student tavern.

"I'm afraid I'm absolutely exhausted," Philipp explains, certain that another social interaction will be his undoing.

"Why do you think I asked you? Come! I haven't spoken with you properly in at least two weeks."

There is something desperate in Martin's eyes—a yearning that cannot safely be denied. With a sigh, Philipp shuts the door behind

---

[12] The oracle of Delphi was a famous seer in ancient Greece frequently sought out for prophecies. The oracle typically responded in riddles so vague that they either tricked the recipient into making the wrong choice or could be interpreted as predicting any outcome.

[13] Erasmus of Rotterdam, *De Libero Arbitrio* ("On Free Will") in *Luther and Erasmus: Free Will and Salvation*, trans. and ed. E. Gordon Rupp (Philadelphia: The Westminster Press, 1969), 34-5.

them both. It is not that he seeks to avoid Martin, but he has been trying somewhat unsuccessfully to spend more time alone with his family. *I will make this as quick as I can,* he tells himself as they begin to walk down the passage.

"How is Katharina?" Martin asks.

"Better. She is over the worst of her nausea, I think."

"Oh, is she sick?"

Philipp pauses mid-stride, and his colleague follows suit. He realizes he has not told Martin about Katharina's condition.

"We are expecting another child," he says matter-of-factly.

"Ah, forgive me," Martin says. "Did you mention it before?"

"No, we haven't told many people."

Martin smiles and pats him on the back. "Much happiness to you and your wife. How fortunate that I instigated the match!"

"That is not how I remember it," Philipp says quietly as they resume walking. "In fact, it was I who asked her to marry me."

"You would never have noticed her if it weren't for me, constantly trapped in your study," Martin crows. "That's two children now who owe their existence to me!"

He chooses to ignore this heavily exaggerated comment, saying instead, "We had the babe's horoscope read recently. Apparently, it will be a boy."

Something like a snort escapes Martin's nose as they descend the steps to the lower floor.

"What is it then?" Philipp asks. "You clearly disapprove."

"You set too much store by the stars when you ought to confess the sovereignty of God," Martin asserts.

Philipp has heard this complaint before, and he cannot account for it. Every scholar of the natural sciences has respect for the astrological method. The sun governs the times and the seasons. The moon governs the tides. *Why then is it so hard to believe that the stars have some purpose of their own?*

"The two are not in conflict," Philipp explains. "Scripture tells us that God created the stars as guiding lights. They declare his glory day by day. Even so, they speak to us now, warning of evils and calling us to repentance."

Martin shakes his head. "But who can interpret their speech? These prophecies are either so vague as to be of no use at all, or they predict things which never come to pass. That is the very definition of false prophecy."

Philipp takes a deep breath. It is he who devoted much study to this topic at university, not Martin. *Whose opinion is more likely to be correct?* He feels a need to defend himself as much as the discipline. "They do not declare what will come to pass. They warn of what might come to pass if we ignore them. We are not bound by the stars but called by them to a higher purpose."

Again, Martin shakes his head. "It still seems like a load of shit to me."

They have reached the bottom of the stairs. Philipp stands in place, staring at his colleague, the heat rising within him. *Do you not care what I think?* he wonders. *Have you no faith in my conclusions?* Inhaling deeply, he pushes these questions aside and asks another. "Is that how you perceive the highest science? The thing that was dear to my father? He was a pious man who would never have countenanced anything that violated Scripture."

"No man thinks he violates Scripture, as the papists are ever reminding me," Martin responds with a roll of the eyes.

You're not hearing me! Philipp screams inside. *You're not really listening!*

Annoyance reaching a crisis point, Philipp blurts, "Why must you be so—sometimes you are just so…"

They halt their progress, Philipp grasping for words with clenched fists.

"Yes. Finish your thought," Martin prods.

Quickly looking down the passage to ensure no one else is listening, Philipp cries, "Difficult!"

His fellow professor smiles broadly, evidently amused by the outburst of emotion. "Is that all? I thought you were going to accuse me of something far worse."

This is not a joke to me, Philipp thinks, *but I must not be harsh. After all, I am exhausted. That must be why I feel this way.* "This has not been a good conversation," he concludes simply, marching in the direction of the tavern.

"Do not fear the stars, Philip," Martin instructs, walking beside him. "Fear the one who holds true power over you, body and soul, in life and in death."

"Of course, I do," he grunts. "You know I do."

"Yes," says Martin, placing a hand on the doorknob and looking him in the eye, "but none of us are perfect."

With that, the door is swung open, revealing a large chamber with a low ceiling held up by wood beams. The room is packed with students and professors, some sitting at the few tables provided but most simply standing about, drinks in hand. On the far wall is the bar, behind which are shelves full of all kinds of drinking vessels—glass, pewter, and clay—arranged according to their kind.

"Excuse us," Martin begs, weaving his way through the mass of bodies.

Philipp follows him, the sound of boisterous laughter and the smells of sweat and beer pressing in on all sides. "Pardon me!" he calls, uncertain if anyone can hear him above the din. He looks down at a floor that he suspects is incredibly dirty, for his soles seem affixed with every step. The room is dark, the only window partially blocked by the shelves. Candles on each table flicker as the air is tossed to and fro by the movements of men. They have reached the bar.

"Bert!" Martin calls loudly, pounding the wooden counter. "We are in desperate need!"

The man in question turns to face them, back slightly bent, head bald, skin wrinkled. His eyes peer from behind rounded spectacles, and a beard hangs from his chin.

"Good doctors!" he greets them, his voice racked by age. "New ones here for winter term. Thirsty lot!"

"Can we just have the usual?" Martin requests, leaning over the counter and speaking again at high volume.

"Tell it to Fräulein Hilda," the bartender instructs, pointing to a long-haired, black and gray striped cat perched on the far end of the counter. "She's the help."

Philipp looks at the creature licking its paw, eyelids low, oblivious to the rest of the room. "I wasn't aware that your mouser was taking orders now," he says.

"What?" Bert asks, hand to ear.

"It's just, I'm not accustomed to speaking with cats," he explains.

"You're going to have to speak up, son," the bartender replies, shaking his head.

Frustration increasing, Philipp leans forward and yells into the man's face, "Cats don't talk!"

First, the old man chuckles, then proceeds to full-throated laughter, then positively guffaws, slapping his leg in glee.

"Well, of course she doesn't talk! That doesn't mean she's not listening. But look—Doktor Luther has made a friend!"

Philipp glances to the right and sees Martin clutching the cat in his arms and scratching its head. Fräulein Hilda is laying on her back like a babe, paws bent inward, eyes closed in exultation. It is the first time Philipp has seen Martin take any interest in a cat, let alone hold one.

"What are you doing?" he asks, rather absurdly as it occurs to him.

"What are you doing?" Martin inquires in turn.

"You are petting the cat."

Martin shrugs his shoulders. "It's relaxing."

Before Philipp has a chance to question him further, his fellow professor nods to indicate that Philipp ought to turn around. When he does, he finds one of his Akademia members, Erasmus Sarcerius, standing there with a book clasped in his hands, eyes locked on Martin.

"Sarcerius!" Philipp says in greeting. "Can we help you?"

"Yes, Herr Doktor," Sarcerius replies, voice slightly halting. "I was just wondering, if it's not too much trouble, what you both think of Erasmus' newest work." Here he raises the book, alerting them to its existence.

You are quite bold to ask that, Philipp thinks. He is not even sure Martin and Sarcerius have met, let alone discussed issues of substance. Now Sarcerius asks them to comment on the most controversial issue of the day and one of a considerably personal nature. Before either he or Martin can answer, Bert says, "Here they are, professors," pushing a mug of beer and goblet of wine across the counter. Martin releases Fräulein Hilda and takes up the beer while Philipp accepts the wine and responds to his student's question.

"I would rather know your opinion, Sarcerius. Do you think it a fair argument?"

Sarcerius looks around nervously, glancing at Luther, who seems far more interested in his drink than the matter at hand.

"I suppose I should say…" begins the young man, pausing to consider. "It is a good book." The statement seems more question than assertion.

"You need not fear to speak your mind," Philipp assures him. "Personally, I thought it was in the proper spirit of academic discourse. Doktor Camerarius felt the same. It's such an important topic. I'm glad to see it debated by two men I respect."

There is a snort from the end of the counter where Martin is standing. Philipp turns to see his colleague, mug still in hand, smiling and shaking his head in amusement.

"What about you, Doktor Luther?" Sarcerius dares to ask. "How do you find this new book?"

Martin nods, still grinning. "It is a glorious book, and he is a glorious theologian."

He's playing with him, Philipp realizes. Not surprising given the nature of the young man's questions, but he very much hopes that Sarcerius will realize it.

Sadly, the student replies instead, "Really?! That is high praise coming from you!"

Philipp places a hand on Sarcerius' shoulder. "I think you will find it is not praise at all, but derision."

"How's that?" Sarcerius inquires, lowering his brows in confusion.

"For brother Martin, there are only two kinds of theologians: men of glory and men of the cross," Philipp explains.

"Ah," Sarcerius mutters, looking rather embarrassed. "And Erasmus is the former?"

Martin swallows the last of his beer and pounds the mug on the counter. "Erasmus is an eel that no man can grasp. But since you press me, yes, there are few theologians as drunk upon their own glory as that man. At least Eck is in the pocket of the Antichrist, but Erasmus belongs to no one—he believes nothing. I cannot abide that."

The young man turns to Philipp and whispers, "That seems rather harsh. Is Doktor Luther always like this?"

Patting him on the shoulder, Philipp concludes, "I know I speak for Doktor Luther and all the professors when I say we are delighted to have you here, Sarcerius, and we look forward to seeing what you will contribute to our lively academic debate." Here he casts a glare in Martin's direction, but they have lost his colleague's attention.

"Thank you, Herr Doktor," Sacerius concludes. "Enjoy your wine."

When the young man has departed, Philipp turns to Martin, whose eyes are scanning the room furiously. "Every once in a while, you might keep your thoughts to yourself," he grouses.

Martin ignores his suggestion and asks, "Have you seen Glatz?"

"Kaspar Glatz?" he asks in confusion, realizing halfway through that this is the only Glatz his colleague could possibly mean.

"I'm supposed to meet him here. He has something he wants to ask me. I demanded that he tell me then and there, but he was very secretive."

"That's intriguing," Philipp responds. *And that's something I've never said about Glatz before,* he adds for himself.

A professor in the theology department, Glatz is a close colleague of Martin's, but not the greatest favorite at the university. The students dislike him for dutifully reporting every minor violation of the rules, while the professors dislike him for refusing to buy anyone a beer. Fortunate, then, that he is departing to replace Karlstadt in the pastorate of Orlamünde.

"Have you actually read Erasmus' book?" Philipp asks, refusing to abandon the earlier subject.

"Of course, I've read it," Martin insists, tossing Bert a coin. "Even for him, it was vapid. No real scriptural argument. A lot of talk about how things make him feel, and naturally he asserts that asserting things is wrong."

"I thought he made a few good points, though I certainly disagreed with his conclusion. I agree that he is a better translator than exegete."

Martin is looking around the room again, muttering, "Where are you, Glatz?"

"We need to talk about your response," Philipp states. "Not that I doubt your ability to write it, but this concerns us all. If you don't want me as an editor, at least talk to Justus."

Even as Philipp says this, Kaspar Glatz makes his appearance, expression utterly serious—even grave. He is a thin man with equally thin brown hair and beard, somewhere between Philipp and Martin in age.

"Kaspar!" Martin cries. Turning to the bartender, he holds up a pair of fingers and says, "Two more, Bert."

"I don't need to drink," Glatz insists, raising a hand. "I've come to speak with you about the Bora girl."

Philipp's mind immediately sets to work. *Bora? He must mean Katharina von Bora.* Philipp has seen her around town. She may even have been at the party he and Katharina threw around Christmas time. *One of the Nimbschen sisters. Wasn't she married? No, perhaps she is only betrothed.*

"What business do you have with her? I don't know her as well as her hosts," Martin replies.

"They said you were in charge of distributing them," says Glatz, speaking of the women almost as if they were products to be sold. Glatz is prone to these odd turns of phrase.

Martin frowns. "I helped them find places to stay if that is what you mean. The husbands they have mostly found on their own. They were generally eager to wed, and there is no shortage of men in this town with the same desire."

"And yet the Bora girl isn't married," notes Glatz. "They say Baumgartner has cast her aside. No surprise there. He's a Nuremberger: proud lot. His parents will have talked him out of it when he returned home."

"I fail to see how this is your affair," says Martin, accepting a new mug from Bert. "And in case it's relevant, she is not a girl. She's about as old as Philipp here."

"All the more reason for her to wed as quickly as possible," Glatz concludes. "I'll tell you why it's my affair. I've spoken with her several times now. She has some very admirable qualities: intelligent, serious, hospitable. An ideal pastor's wife, I should think. A bit forward, but that will fade once she is happily settled into married life."

"What makes you think that?" Philipp asks.

Glatz leans in close and explains, "The females have tremendous sexual appetites, Herr Doktor. They cannot help themselves."

Philipp glances at Martin, who is laughing so hard, he spits out his beer.

"I don't see what is so funny," Glatz snaps, glaring at Martin. "I've come here to tell you I wish to marry her, and I am happy to provide for her needs: all her needs. Is that so wrong of me?"

Philipp sighs and mutters, "Well, this is an odd discussion," staring at his wine in embarrassment.

Martin places a hand on Glatz's shoulder. "I hear what you are saying, brother. You wish to marry Fräulein von Bora. She is already spoken for, but if the young man fails in his duty, then I am certain she can be yours. I already had it in mind to write to Baumgartner. I shall do so posthaste and see what reply he has to offer. It is possible that the Lord will open that door to you. To marry a minister of the Word of such high character as yourself—she could only count herself fortunate. But we will see what the Lord's will is in this matter."

"Thank you for that," Glatz concludes. "And thank you for offering a good word to the Elector for me. I depart for Orlamünde tomorrow. I hope you will pray for me."

He will need more than prayer! Philipp muses.

When Glatz has finally departed, Philipp says, "He leaves for Orlamünde. I hope you gifted him an arquebus."

"He'll be fine," Martin assures him. "There will be others there to help him."

"We're talking about the town that chased you away with stones, right?"

Martin drains the last of his drink and tosses Bert another coin. "We must not fail to preach the gospel, Philipp, even if we must put our own lives on the line. This gospel will spread to the ends of the earth, and we will preach it not only in our Jerusalem, but in Judea and Samaria, in Bavaria and the Rhineland, and to the very halls of power in Rome, before kings and emperors! We must train faithful men and place them in as many churches as possible, for when the Word is rightly preached, then we will see the work of revival. That is the true evidence of the Spirit."

"And what about Erasmus?" Philipp asks pointedly, still annoyed at Martin's lack of concern.

"He will keep," his colleague concludes. "He will keep."

With that, Martin Luther begins making his way around the room, shaking hands and greeting new arrivals. As Philipp stands leaning on the counter, savoring the last of his drink and licking his mental wounds, Fräulein Hilda rubs her cheek against him. Such an offer of friendship even he cannot ignore. He reaches out and strokes the cat's back, then looks again at Martin holding court in the middle of the room: the center of attention wherever he goes, never without something to say. His colleague's fame is a burden—a weight few could ever bear. Yet, Martin seems at times to relish it, as if it were his strange destiny, and the world were truly set in motion by the movements of his pen. Almost, Philipp can believe it, but he is not sure he wants to do so.

What is the strange fire that resides in him? he wonders. *Is it also in me?*

31 October 1524
Wittenberg, Electorate of Saxony

Martin Luther sits cross legged, leaning back against the pear tree in front of the Black Cloister, tossing pebbles at a stray brick lying some fifteen feet away. The brick was a gift, but he knows not from whom: he found it nestled conspicuously among the browning blades of grass, at precisely the distance from the wall one would expect if it had been tossed from the road.

What message did the giver intend? Did he hope by the slimmest of chances to send it through one of the windows in a feat of godlike strength—and not just any window, but the one at which Martin Luther would happen to be standing, readied by fate to receive the killing blow? Or was it some child showing off for a friend, or a drunk uncertain which way was north? He cannot know for certain, but it reminds him that there are people in the world who wish him ill—that the duration of his life is not his to determine.

In any case, the brick makes a good target for his own sport. He is done lecturing for the day, and tomorrow will be the feast of All Saints: no classes, no meetings, no business of any kind. The pear tree supports his weary form, the ground beneath it covered in the rotting remnants of the year's harvest. He reaches into the pile of small stones on his right and retrieves another, sending it flying in the direction of the brick. A hit! The satisfying sound of rock against rock. He cannot think why he is doing this except that it seems to aid his tired thoughts.

What a loathsome little book! he fumes. *Is this the best you can do, Erasmus? The great scholar! The prince of letters!*

He read the thing hastily—once, twice, three times. A month has passed and still it grates. A load of exegetical nonsense remarkable only for its brevity. A repetition of every sad line uttered from the days of Pelagius to the present. *How can you call yourself an Augustinian?!* he bellows internally, offended that they should ever have held the same allegiance.

Philipp saw only reasonableness and courtesy in Erasmus' book, but he senses the contempt in the Dutchman's heart. "Dare Erasmus attack Luther like the fly the elephant?"[14] That is mockery and no mistake: the reader is meant to think that the roles are reversed. Since when is Erasmus hesitant to thrust the sword of sarcasm or sink his barbs into another man's flesh? It is what the man is: he cannot help himself. He must mock. He must deride.

"It is lawful to speak the truth; it is not expedient to speak the truth to everybody at every time and in every way."[15]

Which is to say, we shouldn't tell people things that might force them to repent of their pride, Martin thinks.

"What would be the point of such an exhortation, to turn and come, if those who are in question have no such power in themselves?"[16]

The very purpose of the Law: to reveal sin for what it is.

"Would it not be like saying to one bound in chains which he would not break: 'Bestir yourself and come and follow me.'?"[17]

No, that is what you are doing, Erasmus. You tell dead men to come out of their graves.

The more Martin thinks about it, the more his anger increases and the greater the force with which he flings the pebbles. They are all missing now—veering wildly to the left and right. Reaching for the last stone in the pile, he chooses instead to throw it as far as he can,

---

[14] Erasmus of Rotterdam, *De Libero Arbitrio* ("On Free Will") in *Luther and Erasmus: Free Will and Salvation*, trans. and ed. E. Gordon Rupp (Philadelphia: The Westminster Press, 1969), 35.

[15] Ibid., 41.

[16] Ibid., 55.

[17] Ibid., 55.

releasing it with a grunt that seems to express what he truly feels about Desiderius Erasmus. Seven years to the day since he steeled himself and sent those theses to Archbishop Albert, and here he is again, fighting the same battle, only this time at least he is making progress toward the heart of the whole dispute. Always one to skirt around an issue and avoid committing, Erasmus has chosen to address the key point of difference between them. For that, at least, Martin owes a grudging respect, though he suspects Erasmus was put up to it by the highest bidder.

What power of heaven must shake the earth for you to wrestle with the true and living God? he wonders.

Now Wolf Seberger and Eberhard Brisger come walking out of the Black Cloister—or limping in Wolf's case, for he has a clubfoot—moving down the gravel path in his direction. Martin waves to them and calls out, "Good evening!"

"Good evening, brother!" Brisger replies. For his part, Wolf dutifully nods his head.

"Off for some supper?" he asks.

"Well, what choice do we have? There's nothing inside!" Wolf complains, gesturing with his thumb back in the direction of the dormitory.

"I would have thought that was your responsibility," Martin responds, annoyed at the implication that he has anything to do with their empty stomachs.

"It would be, if someone had given me the coin for it," Wolf protests.

The two men stop just in front of him, and Martin quickly realizes he forgot to give Wolf the money in question. Embarrassed, he reaches for his purse, but Brisger assures him, "No need, Martin. I've given him some." Sensing an imminent objection, Brisger adds, "I know it's your week. Just get the next one."

Martin nods in appreciation. Somewhere in his sermon and lecture preparations, work on the new hymn book, efforts at correspondence, meetings about Church organization, writing of a response to Karlstadt—somewhere, a few things have gotten lost. Luckily, his housemate is gracious.

"I absolve you, Doktor," Wolf states dramatically, making the sign of the cross. "You know old Wolf won't hold a grudge."

"I know no such thing," Martin says with a smile, for Wolf is as much his sparring partner as his assistant. He would allow no real harm to come to Martin—would lay down his life at the slightest provocation—but he does have something of the devil about him when it suits him.

"Come have a beer with us," Wolf offers, evidently respecting their truce for the moment.

"No, thank you," he replies. "I'd rather be alone for a while, if you don't mind."

"I will pray for you, Martin," Brisger concludes, then adds as a seeming afterthought, "Have you heard anything from Staupitz? He still hasn't replied to my letters."

The words seize Martin cruelly. Of course, their old superior Johann von Staupitz was already on his mind: the sight of the pear tree ensured that. But his annoyance with Erasmus had pushed those thoughts to the side and granted him a moment of freedom from a painful subject. Now it strikes him again out of nowhere, seizing dominion over his emotions. The name Staupitz—such a simple thing, a mere sounding of the throat, a flicking of the tongue—overcomes him with its force.

"Martin?" Brisger asks tentatively. "Should I not have said anything?"

"I hear nothing from him—only things about him," Martin answers, feeling more grief than he expresses.

"We'll be back in an hour or three," Wolf says, and with that the two men depart through the gate, leaving Martin to deal with the pain they have unleashed.

He leans his head back against the tree—shuts the doors of his eyes against the onslaught of the world. Then, an image is conjured before his mind both by and against his will: a day well over a decade ago when he was caught in the throes of despair, unable to confess enough sins to achieve inner peace or read enough books of theology to answer the questions that burrowed through his flesh. Staupitz called him outside—met him beneath this very tree. Staupitz who was ever his mentor, confessor, and second father. Staupitz who put him on the path, pulling him out of depression time after time, assuring him there was a reason to live.

"You are turned in on yourself, Martin," the older man warned, using a phrase he always favored. "Submit yourself to the will of God, and you will find release from this turmoil in your soul."

"What would you have me do?" Martin asked.

"Become a Doktor of Theology. Become chair of the department!" Staupitz urged him. As usual, the solution of distraction: more time studying Scripture, less time pondering immensities too heavy for him to bear. But for Martin, the two things always went together.

"And what good would come of it?" It was a rather disrespectful reply, but one he could not help giving.

Staupitz moved toward him, placing his hands on Martin's shoulders.

"We will do this together, you and I," his superior pledged. "We will restore the Augustinians. We will call the Church back to itself."

Now Martin's thoughts turn to another day most of a decade later in the city of Augsburg. He had been summoned there to answer to Cardinal Thomas Cajetan for his alarming new doctrines: teachings that seemed to Martin little more than the natural out-working of everything Staupitz had given him. Cajetan's inquisition was complete—Martin's transfer to Rome for further interrogation was imminent.

Staupitz called him outside once again, this time to a dark alley behind the Golden Hall of the Fuggers. Clothed in their Augustinian habits, hoods lifted for greater privacy, Staupitz said to him, "I can no longer protect you, Brother Martin. Cajetan made it clear to me: you will be declared a heretic."

Crushing words! They appeared to cause Staupitz terrible pain. Never one to succumb to emotion, his superior pinched his eyes shut, brow furrowed, breathing deeply. Martin could sense what Staupitz was thinking. *This is not what I wanted for you. This is so different from what I foresaw.*

"Father," Martin whispered, trembling inside. "Father, what must I do?"

Staupitz opened his eyes again. "It is no longer for me to command you. I will give us both the only help I can, though it seems to me a thing as foul as hell itself."

Then Staupitz placed his hand on Martin's head as he had so many times in absolution, only this would be something very different: something previously unthinkable.

"Brother Martin, I release you from the vows you made before God to the Order of St. Augustine," Staupitz uttered, gaze intense. "May God protect and preserve you, for I cannot."

Martin was robbed of breath—struck to the depth of his soul. He had never requested to be released, and yet it had happened. In that moment, he saw what the decision cost Johann von Staupitz. He watched it pass across the muscles of his superior's face like a wave upon the sea, stymieing the older man's breath. He feared that Staupitz had not only released him from the order, but also severed their relationship.

"This is not what I want!" he objected. "We can still do this! We can reform the order. We can call the Church back to itself. Please!" he begged rather pathetically—desperately. "This is not what I want."

Staupitz's expression grew stern: a bitterness revealed itself in his countenance. "When I told you to surrender—to release yourself—this is not what I meant. What you have been doing this past year is the opposite of that. You will break the Church, not restore it! How can you stand before the whole world and say, 'You are wrong. I am right.'?"

As if the very devil of hell had put the words in Staupitz's mouth! *What makes you think you know better? How can you be so certain when so many stand against you?* Doubt threatened to overcome Martin. Such a ghastly heat in his breast! He reached for the only answer he could find.

"But it is not the whole world. There are others who are with us—in time, you will see how many."

"'Us'?" Staupitz asked, tone incredulous. "Speak no longer of 'us.'"

"What do you mean?" Martin inquired, terrified to know the answer. "Are you forsaking my friendship entirely? Are you leaving me?!"

"No, Martin," replied Staupitz, shaking his head. "You have left me."

Oh, how that memory tortures Martin Luther! Six years of attempts to restore something of what they had, desperate and angry, living in hope and fear. Forever, the words of Staupitz echo in his mind like the bells of St. Mary's, only shrill and harsh to the ear, like a humming that never stops. When the time came to stand, Staupitz abjured, submitting himself to the Pope rather than God. Now the old champion of Augustine has forsaken the Augustinians entirely, accepting a place as abbot of St. Peter's Abbey in Salzburg, living out the remainder of his days in wealth and comfort, abandoning Martin to struggle alone. The betrayal stings with a biting ferocity.

"Martin!"

This voice is sounding in the present. Opening his eyes, striving to adjust his thoughts to the waking world, Martin Luther looks toward the gate, where Justus Jonas is entering. His friend and fellow professor approaches and asks, "What are you doing under there?"

"Thinking," he mutters.

Jonas frowns in confusion. "Wouldn't you be better off thinking in your study? It's getting cold!"

Is it cold? he wonders. He has spent so many years in brutal chill that it hardly affects him anymore, but as he takes a moment to examine his senses, he finds it is true: the air bears the unmistakable mark of autumn. Not frigid, but cold enough to send a man indoors.

"What news do you have for me?" Martin asks. "For surely you would not come out in such God forsaken weather unless it was a matter of urgency."

"Not a matter of urgency yet, but it may well be," a frowning Jonas explains, pulling his scholar's robe tighter around himself. "There is likely to be war."

That is not news, he muses, rising to his feet. *The whole of history is wars and rumors of wars.* He keeps the thought to himself and requests, "Come inside with me."

The two men walk stride for stride toward the dormitory entrance, passing under the lintel honoring Augustine and into the foyer. There, they wipe off their shoes and Martin retrieves a candle from a sconce on the wall. As they climb the stairs, he asks, "Is it Francis' crossing of the Alps that causes you to say this?[18] Or are the Turks marching to Buda?"

---

[18] King Francis I of France crossed the Alps around this time to invade northern Italy while avoiding Savoy. This was part of the ongoing war between the royal Houses of Valois and Habsburg, which culminated in the Battle of Pavia.

"Neither. Well, perhaps both, but that is not the point," Jonas replies as they exit on the second floor and begin walking down the passage. "I speak of the peasant uprising. Have you heard about this?"

He shrugs his shoulders. "The peasants are always unhappy, and one can hardly blame them. But where is the trouble this time?"

"In Swabia, east of the Black Forest."

As they move into the darkened Aula, Martin pauses for thought. *Swabia, east of the Black Forest.* He quickly makes a connection and declares, "Well, that's no surprise. They all wear tied shoes down there.[19] You remember the note they left me in Worms?"

In the waning light, he can just see the annoyance on Jonas' face as his friend says, "This is different, Martin. They claim to hold evangelical principles. They say the Lord in heaven has freed them from the bondage of their earthly lords."

For the first time in their conversation, Martin is filled with fear: real fear, trickling down his back, filling him from bottom to top, turning his thoughts rapidly from one mode to another. He remembers where he has heard those words before, and all at once, he feels equally vindicated and enraged.

"Müntzer," he whispers. "It's Müntzer, isn't it? I knew it!"

Having released this verbal flourish, he turns and slams his palm against the wall, not hard enough to cause damage, but with plenty of force to get the point across. He continues walking at pace into the smaller lecture hall, heading for his study, with Jonas trailing desperately behind.

"I have not heard that Müntzer is involved, and I would caution you from implicating him without cause!" his colleague warns.

"We have every cause to implicate him! He has been preaching insurrection for months, and now he is on the loose, wandering the countryside. How much do you want to bet that he made his way into the South?"

"Perhaps you are right," Jonas concedes, "but we've both met Müntzer. He did not strike me as a great leader of men."

---

[19] The *Bundschuh* movement (meaning "bound shoes," referring to the tie shoes that peasants typically wore) had been active in this part of the Holy Roman Empire for over two decades, with varying degrees of organization.

"He doesn't have to be great. He must simply be loud," Martin concludes, reaching the door to the tower. "Even the devil couldn't get that man to shut his mouth!" Placing his hand on the knob, he takes a moment to breathe, thinking through the ramifications of this news. He swings his head round to look at Jonas, whose features are lit by the orange glow of the candle. "You spoke earlier of open war. Has blood been shed?"

"Some, yes," Jonas replies, nodding. "These rebellions tend to be put down quickly. I am not suggesting it is any threat to us here."

"It is very much a threat to us here!" Martin insists, swinging the door open and walking through it. "They are preaching the same things in Thuringia, and that is too close for comfort."

The two of them enter the study and Martin walks over to his desk to begin lighting the candles. He feels the slight heat of flame passing from wick to wick. It seems to lend him a strange energy.

"What do you mean preaching the same—" Jonas begins to ask, then stops himself. Apparently grasping Martin's meaning, he says pointedly, "I told you, this isn't about Müntzer."

All four wicks inflamed, Martin sets the candle he has been carrying in a free holder and sits in his chair. The streams that have been carving their way through his mind for the past several months are reaching an unhappy confluence: colliding, shifting, melding one into another to create an irrepressible flow.

"What you must understand, Justus, is that certain ideas have a devilish power," he explains, attempting to steady his voice against the onslaught occurring within him. "When I was still a babe, I was taught that the earth was filled with spirits. Some live in the forest, some in the water. Some mean well, and some harm. Well, I am a grown man now, and I find myself troubled on all sides by spirits, boasting of visions and calling men to arms! They would throw off every form of earthly chain: the duties they owe each other, the governors who rule over them, the very bodies in which they live and move and have their being. They were here in Wittenberg: you remember as well as I do. They took over Allstedt. They very nearly made a conquest of Thuringia. I was there, Justus. I saw it."

"Now, stop right there!" Jonas charges, pointing a finger accusingly. "If you are about to say that Karlstadt is behind this, I must object in the strongest terms! There is no evidence of that, be he the most annoying man on earth."

Martin sighs deeply. *How do I make him understand?* His gaze traverses the room, taking in the shelves of books, the scraps of parchment wadded up and cast aside, the piles of papers on the floor, the filthy window—and then he sees it there on the floor, leaning against the shelves, the light of the candles reflected upon its silver face. There is the crucifix of Kahla, bent and broken. He points at it, and Jonas turns to look.

"What is that?" his colleague inquires.

Martin rises from the chair, crosses the room, takes the thing in both hands. Turning to display it to Jonas, he concludes, "This, Justus, is a declaration of war. It was left for me the day after my meeting with Karlstadt—the day before I was run out of Orlamünde in a storm of rocks. Doktor Karlstadt will swear up and down that he has no part with Müntzer and would never do anything violent. 'Andreas Bodenstein has been overthrown and driven out by Martin Luther.' That is what he is claiming to anyone who will listen. You know as well as I do: I did not drive him out, Justus. You were in all the same meetings. The Elector banished him because he is a public menace, even as Müntzer is a public menace. Men who smash the image of our Lord will not hesitate to smash a skull!"

Jonas' expression is solemn. He looks down at the mangled crucifix, touching it lightly with his fingers.

"Forgive me, Justus," Martin requests. "I do not mean to frighten you. After all, the Lord is in control. Whatever he declares will come to pass." With these words, the anxious flow diminishes, and he feels himself able—just barely—to stand against the current.

As he sets the object back in its place, Jonas says, "This Feast of All Saints makes me think of those we have lost. So many dead already. I fear that others will join them."

Taking his seat again, Martin is unexpectedly filled with a deep sense of grief, not for the loss of his friendship with Staupitz, but something else entirely. It strikes him as a flood in the gut and begins to fill him, bottom to top, pressing upon his lungs. At length, the words begin spilling out of him. He is helpless to stem the tide. It issues from him, burning as it goes, then soothing like water upon molten rock, the passion releasing like a holy steam.

"Shortly after I entered the monastery in Erfurt, the plague came to Mansfeld and remained for some time. My brother Thomas was taken first, then my brother Heinrich. Their passing destroyed whatever serenity I had gained in those early days of monastic fervor, but this was as nothing compared to what was suffered by my parents. Great was my father's despair in those days! In the space of two years, he had been robbed not only of his present, but also his future.

I remember praying to God, crying out, 'Lord, why did you take them? You called me away from the family home, and now my brothers sleep the sleep of death. Only Jakob is left to maintain the name, and who knows if he will survive? Why did you take them, Lord? Why?!' I was filled with anger such that I thought I hated God rather than loved him. But eventually I realized I had been asking the wrong question. Man has always feared the turning of fate's wheel. Was it not our Lord who said that one man would be taken and the other left in the field? We focus on the wrong thing: we ask why people die, not why they live.

Did the Lord send me to Erfurt to avoid the plague? Why was my sister born still and not I? Why was there a surgeon on hand when I was bleeding to death? Why did the thunderbolt hit the ground beside me rather than my own head? Why was I spared from pestilence and war? I know not. Perhaps these things have natural explanations. Perhaps there is a reason one child dies and another lives, but at a certain point one begins to wonder how it could be that my life—this infinitely fragile, fearfully imperiled thing—should be preserved despite it all. I can know nothing of the hidden purposes of the Almighty One: this God who wraps himself in darkness and sends forth his lightnings throughout the earth. I can only know him as he is revealed in his son, suffering on the cross, crucified for me! That is the truth with which I am called to deal. The rest is darkness. The rest is silence."

Jonas moves forward—places a hand on his shoulder. "I cannot comprehend it, Martin. I cannot comprehend the burden you bear."

"You help me bear it," he whispers, placing a hand on Jonas' back in turn, eyes growing moist. "You all help me bear it, but Justus—" His voice breaks—he shakes his head. "Amsdorf is gone to Magdeburg, Glatz to Orlamünde, Karlstadt is lost to us entirely, and Staupitz…" He must stop again. He is crying softly. "Sometimes, Justus, I feel so alone." This admission fills him with angst, even as it reveals the anxiety he already felt.

"You are not alone," Jonas insists, lowering his frame to meet Martin. "I am here. Bugenhagen is here. Melanchthon is here."

Martin turns his face and looks into Jonas' blue eyes—so full of life, so wise. *I must speak my fear,* Martin thinks, and so he says, "Philipp has had an offer to head the new school in Nuremberg. He and his family are practically impoverished, yet they give prodigally to anyone who asks. Campeggio threatened him. He has every reason to go."

"He is not going to leave us," Jonas assures him. "He told me so. He will refuse them."

Martin shakes his head. "They may persuade him in the end. I would never consider a matter closed with him. He is always eager to please others." He pauses for another moment of reflection, looking back at the crucifix. "Has God led us all this way only to fail now? When I see the evils of this world, I am threatened with despair. The taunts of the devil feel stronger."

Jonas closes his eyes and recites, "'I would have despaired unless I had believed that I would see the goodness of the Lord in the land of the living.'[20] And we will see that goodness, Martin. We will see it in our day."

Martin Luther nods his head, thinking of all he has lost, and all he may yet be called to sacrifice.

"I can feel the devil pressing down on me even now. 'Silence Martin! What suffering you heap upon your family and your flock! What fissures you cleave in the Church of Jesus Christ! Why lower the ax of division on a tree as fine as this?' But his words are all for naught, for I have seen the rotting of branch and trunk: it must be purified. And there is a fire inside of me, Justus! The very word of God burns within my breast, and I declare with the prophet Jeremiah, I have grown weary of holding it in!"[21]

---

[20] Psalm 27:13.
[21] Jeremiah 20:9.

5 December 1524
Basel, Swiss Confederation

Desiderius Erasmus stands outside the west front of Basel's cathedral, the great doors of the Gallus portal shut before him. It is unusually cold for the feast of Saint Nicholas: a light snow falls from the gray clouds high above. He pulls his fur coat close against his body, shivering involuntarily from the onslaught of the air. He would depart, but his gaze is transfixed on a rose window high above, its flowered panes radiating from a center in which Christ is portrayed in stained glass. There is the Savior at the center of the cosmos, the spheres in motion at his command. Comfort, certainty, peace—all are expressed in the sign of blessing he lends to those below.

But all is not as it seems. Framing the outside of the rose window is the great wheel of Fortuna. Here are figures solely human, some ascending and others descending, all caught in the machinations of fate. At the summit of the wheel sits a king in his pomp, resting precariously upon the curved edge, the slightest turn to the right or left threatening to bring him down. Here human lives are subject to the twisting movements of chance—plagues of body and earth, upheavals both real and imagined. Some are looking up, bent upon ambition, longing for their moment at the peak, while others can see only the abyss of poverty into which they will be driven regardless of what ambitions they hold.

The message is simple: Trust not in capricious Fortuna but the unchanging Ancient of Days. Move to Christ who is the center. And yet, Erasmus hears the words of Scripture echoing in his mind. "The Lord kills and makes alive; He brings down to Sheol and raises up."[22] *Who then ought a man to fear? Who truly sends him into the abyss?*

Buffeted as Erasmus is by the whims of fortune, he has reached his position through suffering and sacrifice. His power is minimal beyond expression, and yet it cannot be denied that his choices, his actions were necessary to create the existence he attempts to enjoy. *Is my suffering all for naught? Is there no purpose to anything?* Such thoughts could drive a man mad.

---

[22] 1 Samuel 2:6.

At last, he can bear the cold no longer. He shuffles through the thin layer of fresh snow toward the other side of the cathedral, where Bishop Christoph resides in his court for the sacred seasons. The yard is packed with stalls, some selling sweets for the children and others the ubiquitous sausages that infect his nostrils with their scent. Now he passes something more pleasant: a table covered in evergreen boughs. A vender calls to him in the German tongue. "Äste! Äste zu verkaufen!" Erasmus gathers that the man wishes to sell him greenery, though he struggles to make sense of the accent, so different from the regions to the north.

He is about to make his break from the yard when he is tempted by a great steaming cauldron of wine in which float stars of anise, cinnamon bark, orange slices, and whole cloves. This smell is like something of heaven itself, waging war upon the chill, banishing the gray from his heart. He is drawn to its depths, bending over the mixture, breathing in the glorious spices with closed eyes, allowing the warmth to envelop him. He can smell his mother's kitchen, a space so humble that it hardly warranted the name. He would fight his brother Pieter for a chance to try the soup first, pushing the older boy out of the way. *Stop it, schat!* his mother would cry, striking Erasmus' hand with the spoon. *Don't be wicked!*

"Zwei Pfennige!"

This last phrase comes very much from the present. Erasmus looks up from the steaming brew into the eyes of its creator, whose brow is furrowed in annoyance.

"Ein Getränk kostet zwei Pfennige," the man repeats.

Thinking of his meeting with Christoph, Erasmus holds up two fingers to indicate his desired amount. The man sets to work ladling the liquid into a pair of wooden mugs while Erasmus retrieves the necessary coins from his purse. Once the exchange is complete, he departs for the bishop's court, his wrinkled hands now pleasantly warmed.

He arrives at the covered doorway to the residence next to a small group of children, all bundled against the cold. One of them is carrying a sack in which they are likely storing the food and coins pried from their victims.

"What are you doing here?" a particularly obnoxious boy asks him, nose wrinkled in a kind of sneer.

"I have come to speak with my friend," he replies.

"Are those for us?" a young girl asks, pointing to the mugs.

Why on earth would they be for you? he wonders.

Tiring of the conversation, Erasmus knocks on the door with his foot, then answers brusquely, "They are for my friend and me. They are not for children. Do you have any other questions?"

"Just one," the boy says. "Why are you so grumpy?"

A curse upon those who raised you, he concludes.

Fortunately, the door opens, and he is admitted without having to listen to the children sing all three of the carols they have prepared. As he climbs the stairs to the upper floor, striving not to spill the liquid, he considers how happy he is to be free of the endless questions of youngsters. Of course, he has Johann Erasmus. He would endure any degree of annoyance from his godson, whom he loves like a son of the flesh, but random children hold no appeal. *Perhaps it is just as well I was sent to the priory.*

He comes to a medium sized chamber composed entirely of wood, from floorboards to wall panels to ceiling beams and carved columns. The only exception is the gray stone hearth, where a pleasant fire is burning. Upon the walls are images of bishops past: St. Pantalus, Waldo of Reichenau, and Burchard. All brought the see of Basel through difficult hours, but none faced the challenges of the episcopal throne's current occupant. Seated before the blaze is the bishop in question—old Christoph von Utenheim—who stares silently into the flames, his countenance downcast, slumped into a plush high-back chair.

"Excellent friend, I brought you some of the local drink," Erasmus informs him.

The bishop cranes his neck to look upon his visitor, lips breaking into a tired smile.

"Glühwein," Christoph says softly, the word seeming to roll off his tongue. "I have known it since I was a boy." He gazes back into the crackling flames, muttering, "That was a very long time ago."

Erasmus takes the matching seat next to the bishop, handing over one mug and savoring the contents of the other. The blend of spices invigorates his senses. He can almost forget the recent peasant rebellion to the north, the war between the Emperor and the king of France, and the outbreak of plague in Venice that has spoiled his travel plans. Yes, he can set aside the fearsome things of earth and imagine himself, for one moment, in a garden of pure serenity.

"Have you heard anything in response from Luther?" the bishop asks.

Instantly, his mood is ruined. There will be no peace for Erasmus: not as long as he draws breath.

"Nothing," he mutters.

"Ah," Christoph replies, chin falling slightly. "Well, perhaps you worried yourself needlessly."

He sighs and shakes his head. "On the contrary, I am more worried now than ever. I do not know the man personally, it's true, but I gather he cannot simply let a thing go. Normally, yes, he would rush a reply to the press and have it in every corner of Germany by sundown. I would receive my slap in the face and endure it, accepting the congratulations of all his opponents. But the silence means he is doing something different—planning something worse than before."

"Should different necessarily be worse? Maybe he has realized the superiority of your argument."

Here Erasmus scoffs loudly: perhaps too much so for the old bishop's comfort judging by his bulging eyes. "Don't make me laugh, Christoph! We will see a host of spotless leopards before Martin Luther admits he is wrong about anything."

There is a long pause. They both sit sipping, their thoughts fermenting. Since the release of his book, Erasmus of Rotterdam has been praised in numerous quarters, and the complaints from the Lutherans have been fewer than expected, though Œcolampadius wasted no time recording his objections. Erasmus has played his hand well, favoring moderation, avoiding unnecessary polemicizing, leaving open the door for compromise yet clinging to the principles of the Church and his own heart. So, why does he feel this chill in his bones: one wholly unrelated to the snow outside? Why does he sense that amid all this doing of right, he has done something wrong? Never satisfied, never secure. He drinks the last of the wine and sets the empty mug on the floor.

"And what of your friend, Melanchthon?" Bishop Christoph asks.

Erasmus sighs again, holding his chin in his hand, closing his eyes in frustration. "I wish I could call him my friend, but I fear not."

"Has he responded to your offer?"

The bishop is one of only three people who know the details of Erasmus' conversation with Camerarius, the others being Johann Froben and Karl Harst. Three persons is three more than he would prefer to hold such information, and he would not have trusted it to them if he did not also trust them with his life.

"No," he answers, "but I did not expect that he would. My correspondence is always read by others, as he knows full well, so it would be too dangerous to discuss the matter unless he was fully determined to come. I am content to bide my time. Unlike Luther, I do my work slowly. I plant a seed and allow it to grow."

He thinks back to the letter he received from Philipp in response to his own. "As for your diatribe on the freedom of the will, it had a very mild reception here," the younger scholar had written. "Your moderate attitude gave great satisfaction, though you do slip in a barbed remark now and again. But Luther is not so irascible that he can swallow nothing." Oh, how he wants to believe it! But he suspects Philipp is fooling himself, for the young man lauded Luther throughout as nothing less than the second coming of the Lord. That gave Erasmus pause, but something else brought him comfort: "Anything you write to me I shall keep absolutely to myself. I would rather die than commit a breach of confidence. And I do want you to be sure of this: that I have the deepest respect and affection for you."[23]

"You were in rather a hurry with the release of your New Testament," the bishop notes, a twinkle in his eye.

Verdomme! Erasmus has been caught with his mind wandering. *Respond, quickly!*

"That was only because the Spanish are thieving bastards!" he insists.[24] Regaining his calm, he notes, "Philipp says he is pleased with my diatribe, and that is something. He may come round in the end. It will depend on events. So much depends on events."

---

[23] Epistle 1500 – "From Philippus Melanchthon" in *The Correspondence of Erasmus: Vol. 10 – Letters 1356 to 1534*, trans. Mynors and Dalzell (Toronto: University of Toronto Press, 1992), pg. 390-2.

[24] Erasmus was in a race with a Spanish team led by Cardinal Francisco Jiménez de Cisneros to be the first to release a complete Greek version of the New Testament in Western Europe.

The bishop shakes his head incredulously. "I don't see why you should risk so much for that young man when you already have the schoolmen begging for your blood."

"Because he is one of a kind, Christoph. He is far more brilliant than either of us."

"But surely there are others—"

"If there were, I would have asked them, but there are not," Erasmus explains, annoyed that he must make such an obvious point. "Wittenberg has no idea what a treasure it holds. It will be a better world if Melanchthon is the one who triumphs there, and an even better one if we can get him away from them entirely. In any case, Philipp is from good kin, even if he has forgotten it. He has a better knowledge of the world than all these hotheads running around."

Here Erasmus thinks of a recent visitor to Basel: Andreas Bodenstein von Karlstadt, former colleague and now sworn enemy of Martin Luther. They say he is moving from town to town and only stopped in Basel to have his pamphlets printed. No doubt he infected several others with his radicalism. Erasmus saw him once in the street and had half a mind to spit in his face.

Christoph laughs merrily. "Oh, to be of good kin! To have the right father!"

Now, Karlstadt is forgotten. Erasmus stares into the flames, suddenly captured by the memory of his own father: the man who could not or would not acknowledge him. *To think that there are those who take pride in their progenitors! To think that this thing that no man can control should raise others up even as it has brought me down!* "I wouldn't know," he mumbles, his eyes downcast, his spirit stung.

The bishop reaches over and places a hand on Erasmus' arm, regaining his attention. In Christoph's eyes, he sees the compassion of a true shepherd of Christ's flock.

"Forgive me, friend," Christoph whispers. "I did not mean to deride you."

"I know," he assures him, patting the bishop's shoulder. "I am old now. I have heard it all, and I know when a man means to insult me." He moves quickly to change the subject. "Before I came in, I was admiring your wheel of fortune."

"A fine piece of craftsmanship," the bishop says with a nod.

"Sometimes I feel myself floating over the mass of men, rising to the heights of heaven, reaping the benefits of all I have sown. Other times, I feel caught upon a wheel of spikes, driven into the ground, unable to rise by any power I possess."

"Do you ever think how your life might have been different—how all our lives would have been different—had the wheel turned ever so slightly in the opposite direction?" Christoph asks thoughtfully.

"Different how?" Erasmus inquires, unconvinced that this will be a helpful topic of discussion.

His friend pauses to consider, then ventures, "Would you have married?"

What an inquiry! Of course, Erasmus has wondered about such things from time to time, but never seriously. Certainly, no one has asked him this question.

"If I wasn't in holy orders?" he asks for clarification.

"Yes, of course."

Erasmus breathes deeply, considering how to answer without divulging more than he wishes to reveal. Is he, Erasmus of Rotterdam, the type of person who could marry anyone? Certainly, he has met women whose beauty enticed him, though he can't say it has happened all that recently. However, he never built such a connection with any of them that he would have wished to enter the married estate, which in any case is as much about money as anything else. Of course, there was the episode with Servatius: a clear lust of youth that he avoids considering out of regard for his digestion. *What does that have to do with marriage?* He doesn't know. His thoughts are drifting this way and that. He chooses to provide a bland answer.

"The reason I am in holy orders would have ensured I never made a good match."

"Let's say Fortuna had lent you some coin," the bishop prods, unwilling to let him escape so easily.

Erasmus lowers his chin and gives his friend a look of perturbation. "This is a dangerous game, Christoph."

"Of course. That's the fun of it! I am old. I need amusement."

Erasmus slumps back in his chair, hands folded against his chest. *How safe am I really?* he wonders. *Can I trust him?* To every person in his acquaintance, he has mentally assigned a category of sorts: *Tell this to one, but not another. Reveal this to that group but withhold the other thing.* Given the rate at which his private comments tend to become public, it is the only way he has survived with his reputation mostly intact. Up to this point, he has placed Bishop Christoph fairly near the center of his confidence. *Ought I to move him even further inside? What are the potential dangers?* He is running out of time—he must decide. His gut tenses. He speaks.

"If you had asked me this question some time ago, I would have told you that women are pleasing to the eyes and tempting to the loins, but they do nothing for a mind such as mine. I would have said that, and it would have been quite unfair, but it would have reflected my experience, because in those days I had never met a woman with the education necessary to be any kind of match for me."

He pauses, spirit agitated, tongue struggling to give voice to what he feels. *Why am I saying these things?* He is afraid to go on, but Christoph once again nudges him gently: "And what happened?"

He nods and dares to continue. "I was staying in London, renting rooms from the Augustinians there. It was an awful city full of disease, without proper wine, smelling all the time of fish and dung. But then I would walk down Walbrook Street until I came to a place that smelled of sweet spices, where the shops were filled with blooms and freshest fruit, and everything seemed alive with color. And there I would come to The Barge: the home of my friend, Thomas More. There I found light and happiness—a family such as I had never known, living together in love and mutual respect, reading and playing, debating every topic under the sun over the most glorious suppers. Into my ears poured a stream of Latin refreshing and invigorating. There were shelves full of books, glorious to the touch! All the children were being trained in them: the boys and the girls as well. Thomas and I would sit up talking into the darkest hours of the night, but they never seemed dark when there was a fire and a friend at hand. He always made sure to have a bottle of something that would please me. I would share in the family meals and feel myself, for once in my life, home—yes, truly home."

As he ends this description, his voice grows quiet. He has reached something deep within himself, and it feels inherently dangerous. Most dangerous of all, he is on the verge of tears. It takes him by surprise, so rare is the occurrence. *Control yourself,* he thinks.

"A beautiful story," the bishop comments, evidently failing to note his distress, "but I do not grasp the connection. Is my age catching up with me again?"

Erasmus breathes in again—deeply, deliberately. His lips part. He shares.

"I will make the connection. More has a daughter, Margaret. Even then, as a girl, she could converse with me in both Latin and Greek. A mind as bright as her father's confined in the body of a female. I had never witnessed such a thing before, because I had never met another woman who received such education. In the years since, she has grown into a true scholar. Just this autumn, she published an English translation of one of my works. The style of her letters is superior to most of my correspondents, her questions precise, her wit the equal—no, superior to most scholars! I never receive a letter from her that I do not read with great pleasure. I admit the thought has crossed my mind: if I had met a woman like that when I was a young man, with whom I could share in the converse of educated minds, a true partner in my work, then perhaps…"

Painful! So painful these words, unwillingly surrendered. Christoph is looking at him with eyes of compassion, nodding along, lending confidence to his statements, tempting him to share too freely! Erasmus is held down by embarrassment, scared to look ridiculous, or perhaps scared that his friend will not understand. *Just say it,* he urges himself. *You are already committed. He has surely put it together.*

"Yes, I would have married Margaret," he admits. "I would have married her and rejoiced in my good fortune. But that's the very thing: I never could have married her, because had I not entered the priory, I would have been the uneducated one struggling to string together a sentence of Greek. She would have felt impoverished in mind by that match, even as I would feel similarly impoverished by any other match I could make. So, it is a point of no consequence. In the end, no matter which way the wheel turns, it turns against Erasmus."

He completes the tale with a sense of urgency, gesticulating with passion. He must stop if for no other reason than to regain his breath.

Bishop Christoph leans toward him, eyes mischievous. "Friend, have you had unholy thoughts about her?"

Well, now you have ruined it! he thinks. *As I feared, you have turned me into a pervert. I should never have told you!*

"I knew I should not have answered your question," Erasmus declares, his tone hiding the full extent of his anger. "Margaret is very happily married, and I am very happily unmarried. I am easily old enough to be her father. I don't even know what she looks like fully grown. It is her mind I admire: that is all."

"I should think that might be the most dangerous thing in your case," the bishop states, but perhaps sensing the disturbance his comments have caused, he leans back in his chair and adds with a nod, "but I take your point and will cease to be a pest."

"Thank you," Erasmus replies quietly. "Let us speak of it no more."

They sit in silence, each staring ahead, but inside Erasmus' mind, the words are pouring forth at a steady pace. *I am no pervert! I have done nothing wrong. Why would he suggest that? Why did I tell him anything? It is in the past now. It is past! I have changed. I am not that man anymore.* And suddenly he realizes he is no longer thinking about Christoph or Margaret, but things more distant: wounds that have never healed. He is thinking of Servatius.

A half hour later, Erasmus departs the residence with a heavy heart, his thoughts positively black. He fumes against Luther, Farel, the breakdown of social order. *How many men have stomped upon me? How many times have I been forced to endure the cruelness of human nature?* Yet, he continues striving, believing in the goodness that still exists in the world, hoping that one day it will be a kinder place. He wades through snow that is now twice as thick upon the ground. *Cold! Bitterly cold!* He can see his breath spewing forth, dancing in the wind.

Then, as he turns the corner to make for the Froben house, a dark figure springs into his path, sending a shock through his body and causing him to lurch backward. Before his face is a bearded man with deep black skin, a pair of ram's horns protruding from his head. The man is screaming—no, growling! He is flailing his arms about. It seems to Erasmus a vision of the devil, and he is filled with terror, his form grown rigid.

Then, in the space of another breath, he recalls what day it is: the feast of St. Nicholas. He remembers that he is in Basel, and in Basel,

St. Nicholas' arrival is preceded by that of a supposed mountain spirit come to chastise the bad children. As his mind adjusts to the new reality, he sees that the horns are tied on with string, the black skin is made so by soot, and the beard is composed of horsehair. It is all an act meant to amuse the children nearby. The muscles once frozen are now tensed and inflamed, for Erasmus is no longer filled with terror, but rage.

"What in God's name do you think you're doing?!" he bellows into the cold air.

"I am come to collect you," the man replies, lowering his voice for effect. "I know what you've done! I know what you are! You are bad!"

A small crowd has gathered around them. People are laughing and clapping their hands in enjoyment, but Erasmus sees nothing remotely funny about the situation. He is cut to the quick by shame—it burns with the intensity of a rabid beast.

"You have no right to treat me like this, even for sport—even on this day!" he bellows.

"I have every right to take what is mine!" the man responds, licking his lips savagely, moving a step closer.

"How fortunate of you to have a body impervious to cold! Do you think we enjoy the sight of your bare skin, covered in soot though it is?" Erasmus asks.

"I feel no cold," the man insists. "I come from the place of eternal fire—the place where you are going!" Then he comes even closer, lips twisted into a cruel smile, and utters, "I know who you are, Erasmus."

It is only then that it occurs to Erasmus that the man addressed him in Latin from the beginning. This is no common person off the street. It is someone educated: someone who knows him by name. In his heart, Erasmus is terrified of discovery—that somehow this man knows all that he is.

"Out of my way!" Erasmus cries, pushing the pretender aside.

There are gasps and loud complaints in the local tongue. Erasmus has ruined the show, but he does not care, for he is shaken—yes, utterly pummeled from head to toe. Too long! It is taking far too long to reach the safety of his home. He pushes past the shops, paying no heed to anything but his troubled thoughts. *The wheel is turning. The past is coming back round.* He presses on, longing for release.

Winter

24 December 1524
Wittenberg, Electorate of Saxony

It is Christmas Eve in Wittenberg, and Philipp Melanchthon is entering the cold with his wife and their daughter Anna. They are making for the market to purchase items for the twelve days of celebration that will begin tomorrow morning. Katharina is more than halfway through her pregnancy, as is abundantly clear from the daily expansion of her belly. Anna moves as fast as her little legs can take her toward the center of town, wearing a new mantle gifted by her grandmother. It is all her parents can do to keep up with her.

"Oh, the horses!" Katharina exclaims. "The horses have left their marks." She calls ahead frantically, "Anna, mind your feet! Your pretty shoes!"

Katharina need not have wasted her breath, for the young one floats as a fairy upon the night air, her seemingly random steps as sure as the mountain goat's. She is overtaken by the delights of the season, flittering toward the glow like the moths of summer. Her big, twinkling eyes, her grin stretching from ear to ear defy anyone on earth to steal her joy.

They arrive at the market square, a flaming beacon illuminating this darkest eve. It is filled with bustling stalls, some selling roasted nuts, others trinkets carved from pine, still others brilliantly colored ribbons and baskets woven with care. Such a wealth of candles! Their tiny orange lights dance upon the cool breeze. Everywhere, sprigs of holly and spruce, rosemary and fir. Only an hour remains until the

Christmas Eve service, and the Wittenbergers are making their final purchases of food and gifts.

"Mama! Papa! Lights!" Anna exclaims.

"Yes, very pretty," Katharina agrees, echoing her enthusiasm.

"Pretty," Anna repeats, smiling in delight. "Pretty!"

As they cross the Lazy Brook and walk upon the cobblestones, they are met by one of the young Cranach daughters, also named Anna.

"Hello, little Anna!" the Cranach girl says in greeting, taking the young one's hand. "Papa is buying sweets for us all. Come and see!"

Their Anna is only too happy to follow her namesake, leaving Philipp and Katharina standing alone before the booths of wares.

As he turns toward his wife, prepared to make some speech about the things they must purchase, he is struck dumb by a vision of rapture. The fires have illuminated Katharina's face, turning her loose strands of hair into things of shining gold. The blood rushes to warm her skin, casting a pink blush across her cheeks. In her irises, the light is reflected—she looks positively angelic. The Virgin herself could not have been more beautiful when she bore the Christ child. *All that is missing is her halo.* He stares at her, suddenly beckoned by memories.

"What is it?" she asks.

"Just thinking," he replies, smiling helplessly.

Katharina nods and begins examining some carved wooden spoons. As she does so, Philipp's thoughts carry him to a time not so long ago, but a world away.

It was the summer of 1520, and he was still reeling from his break with Reuchlin. Not only that, but they had learned that Johann Eck was riding north, papal bull in hand, to threaten Martin with excommunication unless he recanted. Each day was a misery of emotion such as Philipp had not known since the deaths of his father and grandfather. He threw himself into his work, filling every free moment with study, falling asleep on the floor of the university library, pushing himself past the brink of his physical endurance. His colleagues noted the changes in his behavior and began voicing their concerns. Karlstadt took to sending him remedies of questionable origin, always accompanied by a note reading, "A secret brew of my homeland," or some such thing. None of them seemed to improve Philipp's condition.

Martin declared Philipp must marry for the sake of his health, but Philipp knew well enough what was truly happening: his friend was struck by guilt. It was not an absence of female companionship that had brought Philipp low, but the constant stress of being at the center of the debate tearing Christendom apart. His books had been his only consolation since the debate in Leipzig—since Reuchlin disowned him. *I ought to buy myself more tomes rather than taking a wife who will attempt to tear me from my studies,* he concluded, for he had never felt a particular passion for any woman, and he sensed the feeling was mutual. Why take the risk when he was content enough in academia? *I can bear to live without a wife, but I cannot live without literature.*

Everyone accepted this explanation—everyone but Martin. Unable to pin Philipp down for an extended interlude, he resorted to nagging him whenever they passed each other on the way to various duties.

"Get yourself a wife," Martin commanded him.

"You get yourself a wife," Philipp replied.

"I'm a friar."

"I'm a professor."

"That doesn't preclude you."

"Yes, it does. Save your breath."

The next day, Martin made another attempt.

"Get yourself a wife," he charged.

"We've been over this," Philipp grumbled.

"You are in desperate need. You're halfway in the grave!"

"Then I should hate to pull any woman down with me."

Later that day, Martin adopted a different strategy.

"As head of the department, I must insist—"

"I'm not in your department," Philipp reminded him.

Philipp began taking paths twice as long to avoid meeting his colleague, but Martin was wise to his actions and accosted him as he arrived for a lecture, standing in the doorway, refusing to let him pass.

"Philipp, I'm not joking," Martin assured him.

"Neither am I," he replied firmly. "Now move!"

By this point, Philipp had grown properly angry with Martin. *You are on the brink of excommunication, and you still find time to nag me to death!* Then a dark thought. *Is he trying to make sure I'm cared for after he is gone?* He felt a rush of sympathy, and therefore granted Martin a proper conversation the following day.

"It's pride, you know," Martin accused. "That's all it is: this business about not taking a wife."

"How so?"

"You are afraid what others will think of you."

"Which others?"

"Others in our community."

"In Wittenberg?"

"No, in the universities. Because it is not the historic custom for men in your position to take a wife, you fear to take one and be seen as absurd."

"False!" Philipp insisted. After all, if he were afraid of being seen as absurd, he would never have come to Wittenberg.

Martin ventured another guess. "You're afraid of Reuchlin?"

"Wrong again."

"Your mother?"

"For God's sake! Is it so hard for you to believe that I simply don't wish to marry? That I prefer to focus on my work?"

His colleague gave him a pointed look. "It is very hard for me to believe."

"Well, I'm not lying."

"You don't know your own mind."

"And you do? Just leave me alone!"

Philipp ought to have been more considerate: the man was living under the shadow of death. But he could not help himself! *What right does Martin have to command me? He has no respect for my opinion!*

Fortunately, Martin visited him the next day after lectures were complete and offered a truce: "I will never tell you to marry again, and you will stop acting so morose." Philipp heartily agreed, and the conversation moved on to happier topics.

"Come with me to dinner tonight," Martin offered.

"At the inn? I doubt that will aid your digestion."

"No, at the Krapps."

"Who?" Philipp asked, mind spinning furiously, attempting to pair the name with a face.

"K-r-a-p-p-s. You've been at Greek so long, you forget your native tongue."

He rolled his eyes. "You know what I mean! I'm not familiar with them."

"Old woman with grown children. Father used to be the mayor before he passed on."

"Ah, yes," Philipp replied, nodding in recognition. "I've heard of them—probably seen the mother around, but never spoken to her. And why are you expecting this woman to cook for us?"

"She's the one who made the offer. It's the least we can do to honor her table: make her see she still matters to the town."

"Well, tonight is no good," he insisted. "I have lectures to prepare."

"Prepare them another time," Martin responded automatically.

Growing frustrated, Philipp inquired, "Was I even invited? Or do you have the right to invite anyone to anything in this town?"

"Frau Krapp mentioned you specifically. She is very keen to meet you."

"She may meet me any day, but this evening is no good, as I said."

This caused his colleague to grunt loudly, the annoyance clearly going both ways.

"So, you would further crush the spirit of an old woman with little left to live for?" Martin inquired, or rather asserted.

"You just said she has children, and she can't be that destitute if she means to feed us," he replied calmly—logically.

"So, you force me to go alone? Honestly, Philipp! Is it better to give your love to books or your neighbor?"

"That's a rather harsh way of putting it," Philipp responded, brow furrowed.

Martin folded his arms and stated characteristically, "I call the thing what it is."

"Fine!" Philipp conceded, throwing up his hands. "If you're going to be like that, I'll come, but not for your sake. I don't want that poor woman subjected to you in this mood without someone to aid her."

"Very good!" Martin declared, smiling broadly. "Come by the cloister at seven and we shall make for the Krapps."

Two hours later and very much against his will, Philipp arrived at the Black Cloister. Inquiring at the door, he was informed that,

"Doktor Luther is in the lavatory in the back." He therefore passed the monks' sleeping quarters and exited into the rear courtyard, where he found the lavatory in question and knocked on the door.

When there was no immediate answer, he knocked again and called, "Martin? Martin, are you in there?"

The eventual reply consisted of a groan decipherable only by the Spirit.

"Dear God! What's wrong?" Philipp asked.

"There's so much, Philipp!" came the pained reply. "So much shit!"

"Ah," Philipp replied, very much wishing to avoid any further discussion of the matter. "I'll leave you for a moment then."

But Martin was undeterred. "It's a bog! My bowels, Philipp! My bowels!"

"Do you need a physician?" Philipp asked. Then hearing another gut-wrenching cry of pain, he amended the question. "Or perhaps an exorcism?"

"You laugh while I'm being torn to pieces! That is not Christian!" his colleague asserted.

Philipp sighed deeply, nodding his head, still struck by the absurdity of conversing through the lavatory door. "Forgive me. You have my sympathy, but I fear I must deny you my ears if you plan to give any more descriptions."

"No! Listen to me: I can't go tonight."

"What?!" Philipp cried, sensing the imminent danger of an awkward social situation. "No, you must! You'll be over this soon."

"I've been at it all afternoon, Philipp. I'm cracked and bleeding. It's no good. You must go to the Krapps. Make my apologies to them."

"Are you certain it's really that bad?" he felt a need to ask.

This was followed by more groaning from Martin and the exclamation, "Mary, Mother of God!"

"Alright, perhaps it is that bad," Philipp conceded. "I will make apologies for both of us. We can go another time."

"No, you cannot let her down like that, Philipp!"

Offended at the implication, he replied, "Well, it wouldn't just be me letting her down, would it? And unless Frau Krapp is truly hard hearted—"

"Just go, damn it!"

By this point thinking that Martin was getting what he deserved from his bowels, he replied, "There's no need to curse."

Then came a brief silence. Philipp wondered if Martin might be experiencing regrets.

"Forgive me," his friend finally said. "My bowels—"

"No, please! I've heard enough about that. Listen, Martin, you know I'm no good by myself in these situations. I don't have your easy manner with strangers."

"You will go, and you will charm them, and that will be that!" Martin ordered. "Play the man. Don't be afraid!"

Philipp sighed again. "Are you really going to make me do this?"

"Be a good Christian, Philipp."

Perturbed that his character was once again being called into question, Philipp concluded, "Very well, but remember that I am only going under protest, so if I bore the poor lady and her family, and my students don't receive a lecture tomorrow, you are to blame on both counts!"

"Yes, yes. Your complaints are noted. Now go!"

Chiding himself for giving in to Martin, Philipp made his way west along Colleges Street and came to the market square. The Krapp home was just beyond, past the town hall and next to the print shops. Feeling he ought not arrive empty handed, Philipp purchased a small bunch of flowers from one of the vendors and arrived before the three-story, half-timbered home with his gift in hand. Before he could so much as knock on the door, it swung open to reveal Frau Katharina Krapp, the middle-aged wife of the late mayor, who immediately wrapped him in an embrace, gathering him up in the many layers of fabric adorning her person.

"Herr Professor, you've made it!" she declared excitedly. "We have been looking forward to this all week!"

How have you been looking forward to this all week if you only knew I was coming today? he wondered, gently extracting himself from her clutches.

"Doktor Luther could not make it. He is unwell," Philipp informed her, handing over the flowers.

"Oh, that's alright!" she responded, showing a remarkable lack of concern for his friend's condition. "Come! The food is ready!" As they entered the house, she sniffed the blooms and announced, "These are the sweetest smelling flowers I have received in many years, and so beautiful! Truly, you have a fine eye, professor! So thoughtful."

The Krapps came from a line of tailors, and their house was full of beautiful hangings on the windows and walls. As they entered the small dining room, Philipp noted the red cloth laid over the table: an expensive piece of fabric and likely one of the most valuable things the family owned. Resting upon it were numerous dishes of food: a feast to equal anything set out at Christmas. He felt utterly unworthy of it.

The lady of the house began introducing her family members, who were all standing ready to be seated. "My son Hieronymus, head of the business, my other son Christoph, and my daughters Anna and Barbara." She continued, introducing Hieronymus' wife and children, commenting on the loss of her other sons at a young age, reminiscing about her late husband. The children then began introducing themselves, doing their utmost to make Philipp feel welcome. He struggled to keep track of it all and felt lost in the swirl of verbal activity, but there was something about it that also set him at ease, as if he had somehow known them all for years.

He took the seat offered him and placed his hands in the water bowl, attempting to work off the ink stains of the day. Making little progress, he eventually gave up and looked for a cloth. Suddenly, one appeared before his face. He accepted it from the outstretched hand and offered a quick, "Thank you," his eyes still looking in annoyance at the dark smudges that plagued his fingers. He wiped vigorously, but again without success. Defeated, he offered the cloth back to the one who gave it. Then something happened which Philipp did not expect or intend.

He looked first at the hand: not rough as he had supposed, but elegant, as if it were made for holding lilies and pearls. The fingers were slender, the color only slightly darker than ivory. It was a distinctly feminine hand, and not one that had seen much hard labor.

His eyes traveled up the sleeve of the gown—a beautiful brown fabric—then moved to take in the rest of this woman. He made a great effort not to stare at her chest, the outline of which was just visible under layers of fabric. He preferred to continue upward in any case. His gaze next met her neck, upon which hung a slender gold chain bearing a small garnet stone: again, elegant without being ostentatious.

Then Philipp looked upon her face, and from that moment he was a lost man. He took in her lips, her nose, her cheekbones, her forehead upon which hung the hint of blond curls peeking out from under her veil. All was in perfect symmetry. The coloring, the texture—Cranach himself could produce nothing better. Then he mounted the courage to gaze into her eyes: deep pools of blue that sparkled in the candlelight. He was drawn into their depths, for though he might have expected them to be haughty, they had a kindness about them.

Philipp thought to himself, *This is the most beautiful woman I have ever seen.*

Immediately, his stomach lurched. His muscles tensed. He felt the anxiety closing in, for he realized this woman must be very close in age to himself, she was from a respectable Wittenberg family, and there was no wedding band on her finger. These observations raced through his mind, and before he knew it something was borne in him beyond his ability to control: longing.

If his books could talk, they would have been screaming in horror. For the first time in Philipp's twenty-three years on earth, their hold on his attention was not entirely secure. But were they really in so much danger?

I know nothing of this woman's character, Philipp told himself.

Oh, but he wanted to know her! Though he ought to have been filled with joy, Philipp found he was not. Instead, his fear was rising, for he was the one in greatest danger, not the books. He had looked, but he could not touch. He desired, but he surely could not have. The very beauty that first drew him was now sending him hurtling into despair, headfirst and about to be dashed upon the rocks. A thought that had plagued many a desperate man before him now tortured Philipp Melanchthon.

She would never be interested in me, he moaned internally.

He had worked for years to overcome his feelings of inadequacy on account of his minimal height, misshapen back, crooked nose, and most recently his balding head. He had taught himself to live for the praise of his intellect: to chase after learning and not ladies, for Knowledge is a more forgiving mistress. In her good graces, he had flourished and mostly forgotten the aspects of his appearance that were less pleasing to society. But now, having seen this woman, having allowed himself to imagine for a single moment what it might be like to take hold of that hand—to love her and be loved by her—he was courting disaster.

Then, to his shock, she spoke to him, cutting through his anxious thoughts.

"Doktor Melanchthon, it is a great honor to meet you."

It was his turn to offer a word of greeting, but Philipp found his tongue struggling to leap into action. At length, he attempted to say, "The honor is mine. What is your name?" But it was no good: the words caught in his throat. *No! No, no, no!* He thought he had conquered his stammer years earlier, but it had returned at the worst possible moment! He tripped and fell over the syllables. He sounded like a complete idiot. Then he watched the beautiful face across from him transform from a welcoming smile into a confused frown.

"Herr Doktor—are you well?" she asked innocently enough.

"I beg your pardon," he managed to say. "Sometimes I stam… stammer. See, I've done it again."

"Oh, that's alright! My brother used to stammer too. In fact, he still does on occasion."

These words did little to decrease Philipp's embarrassment.

"I am Katharina," she offered, smiling broadly. "I was in the kitchen earlier when Mama was introducing everyone."

Philipp nodded but could no longer bring himself to speak.

They carried on with the meal, each dish more delicious than the last. Philipp observed the family's interactions, noting the absolute ease in their communication: an openness he had never experienced with his own family. They inquired after his interests, attentive and eager to learn. *Why are you all being so kind to me?* he wondered. At one point, he looked across the table at Katharina, only to find her staring back at him. She quickly looked down at her soup. Fearing he had offended her, Philipp did the same.

When the supper was finally over and everyone began cleaning up, he was surprised to see Katharina walk over, point at the deserted chair next to him, and ask, "Do you mind if I sit here?"

"No," he replied automatically, his throat suddenly dry.

She took the seat, straightening out the folds of her gown, placing her hands in her lap.

"Doktor Melanchthon, I know you are an expert in Latin and Greek," she said.

Philipp reached quickly for a reply that would not seem proud. "I would hope so, after all the years they spent training me." Then he heard his own words, and they sounded awful. *Idiot!*

"Do you know of the poet Ovid?" she asked.

Thank God! A subject I know well! he thought.

"Of course!" Philipp replied. "I first read the *Metamorphoses* when I was still a boy. The quality of Ovid's Latin is without compare among his generation."

"How marvelous!" Katharina responded, then added, "I cannot read him, naturally. I only know our German tongue, though I can at least read that fairly well."

An impulse seized Philipp. *This is your chance!* But another voice in his head said, *Have you lost your mind? She will never agree to it.* He chose to ignore the second voice.

"Would you like me to come over once a week and go through the *Metamorphoses* with you?" he asked. "I could explain the story and help you understand some of the Latin. Free of charge, of course, and only if you wish it."

To his pleasant surprise, she agreed, and one week later, he returned to the Krapp house, book in hand, and began explaining to her the intricacies of Ovid's work. Another week, and he was back again, learning more about her, becoming more comfortable with the family. When they were apart, he found himself thinking about Katharina often: during his lectures, when he was at Mass, even when he struggled to sleep. He would count down the hours until he could see her again.

The more he came to know her, the more he wondered why she had not already been snapped up by any one of the hundreds of eager young men in town. True, her family had been forced to do with less since their patriarch's demise, but they still had a good name. Perhaps Katharina had been quite literally overlooked on account of her height, which was no greater than his own. *What of it? I like a woman I can look in the eye.* Only a fool would allow himself to be bothered by such things.

He wouldn't have thought her inner beauty could surpass that of her outer form, but such was the case. Her qualities were those of the immortal gods! She would sit listening to him drone on and on about Ovid, granting him the gift of her gaze, speaking to him kindly and never judging. He noticed she was like this with everyone, though he dearly wished to believe the looks she gave him were slightly unique. She was generous to all, full of compassion, quick with a smile, and willing to laugh at his jokes.

How on earth is she not already married? She was certainly not an old maid, but how could such goodness make it even twenty-three years without finding its echo in another soul? *It is almost as if...* No, he dared not think it! Such conceit! Still, it almost made him wonder if God had kept her as she was for this moment in time: had been saving her for him. *What a preposterous notion!* He chided himself for thinking it. *I am utterly unworthy of her goodness.*

He soon realized he could not live this way. *Be honest, Philipp: You do not want to be her friend. You want to be her husband.* This admission, even made secretly, terrified him.

Then a new thought seized him. *Did Martin arrange it all on purpose?* He thought back to that night: the truce, the invitation, Martin's sudden ill health that forced Philipp to go alone. *Was he working with Frau Krapp? Did they intend for me to meet Katharina under such circumstances, knowing I would fall for her immediately?* An absurd idea, but one that gave him hope, for if it were true, then the Krapps already approved of him joining the family. Perhaps even Katharina approved of him. *I must ask Martin,* he realized, but in the days following, he found his colleague just as absent as he once was present.

By this point, Philipp was staying up late each night, preparing a gift that would make his desires known: a translation of part of the *Metamorphoses* into German. He would have it printed for Katharina and present it to her at their next meeting. Then on the last page, he would write in his own hand the thing that terrified him—his abounding love for her—and she would choose to accept or reject him.

On the appointed day, he stood outside the Krapp house, gift tucked under his arm, heart filled with equal parts yearning and terror. He glanced down at the freshly printed pamphlet. As soon as he placed it in Katharina's hands, he would have the answer to the question that had hung over him for the past month and a half. In one form it was, *Do you feel for me what I feel for you?* But that failed to reach the deepest level of his fears. For that, he needed another question: *Do you accept me—no, do you love me as I am?*

Philipp longed for an answer but feared to jump off the cliff and discover he lacked the power of flight. For the past few weeks, he had existed in a state of suspended hope. He had been granted the gift of her company but longed for a deeper form of communion: one he could never have unless he took the risk and asked the question. Yet, for as long as that question remained unasked, he could cling at least to the uncertainty, for uncertainty is a kind of hope. There are some lies so pleasant that none would want their true character revealed, but only by daring would he have any chance to gain his greatest desire: a true union of souls in love.

He continued staring at the house, fixed to the spot, unable to go in. *In an hour, it could all be over: the hoping, the imagining,* he thought. Perhaps it was better to remain in his uncertainty than risk the death of his hope. But if he loved her—yes, if he truly loved her—he had to make the leap. He had to bet everything and risk its loss. Only by doing so could he enjoy a life that can only be gained through a kind of death.

"Who among us has the strength to disbelieve a pleasant lie?" he whispered. With this final thought, he moved toward the door and took the iron knocker in hand, beating it on the wood panels one, two, three times.

Soon, he was seated across from Katharina in the parlor, holding out the pamphlet for her to take. She was clothed in a beautiful white dress with blue trim that matched her eyes.

"A gift for you," he explained, trying not to stammer.

She took it with a smile, protesting, "Truly, Herr Doktor, you didn't have to buy me anything."

He did not respond. His insides were clenched with anxiety, which he bounced his legs to release. *Please, Lord. Please, let this go well. I know I am unworthy of her, but please let this go well.*

"Oh!" she exclaimed, viewing the title page. "The *Metamorphoses.*"

"Not just the *Metamorphoses,*" he informed her. "The *Metamorphoses* in German."

She looked up at him, shock written on her face. Having succeeded in impressing her, Philipp felt the slightest surge of confidence.

"I translated it for you," he explained. "Well, not the whole thing—just the first three books. But if you like it, I would be happy to translate more for you and have it printed so wherever you go, you may carry Ovid with you and read it for yourself."

Katharina glanced down at the small book, stunned, flipping through the pages slowly—almost with hesitation. He noted that she was not smiling, and his confidence evaporated faster than the dew of summer.

"I can't believe you did this," she whispered, her features wrinkled in concern.

"Well, I did, and it's yours to keep," he uttered, clinging to a final shred of hope. "It's the only one of its kind."

Then it happened. She placed a hand over her mouth and broke into tears.

Oh no! What have I done?! he wailed internally. *How could it have gone so wrong?!*

"Fräulein! Oh, Fräulein Krapp, forgive me!" Philipp begged, leaning forward to indicate concern, but fearing to touch her. "Have I caused you pain?"

Her eyes met his, filled with—grief, fear, sadness? Philipp could hardly say.

"It is I who must ask your forgiveness," Katharina insisted. "I have allowed you to proceed under a mistaken impression."

Oh no! he thought. *Oh, please God, no!*

"What is that?" Philipp asked quietly, terrified of what might come next.

Her shoulders drooped. "I don't actually care for Ovid."

It took a moment for the words to sink in, and even then Philipp could barely comprehend them.

"What?" he finally asked incredulously.

"It's all a bit weighty for me," she explained. "I prefer the German tales: the *Nibelungenlied* and such."

He shook his head in confusion. "Then why did you tell me you wanted to learn about Ovid? Didn't you say that?" *I am not going insane! Am I going insane?* he wondered.

"I mentioned Ovid because I knew it would make you happy," Katharina said softly, unable to meet his gaze. "That is, I hoped it would."

The weight of realization hit Philipp like a hail of stones. He rubbed his face with his hands. "All this time, I've been boring you. Why didn't you tell me?"

"At first, I was afraid to correct you, and then—"

"Then it took on a life of its own. I see."

I must seem a total ass, he thinks. *How blind I've been! Time after time, lecturing her.* Then the white-hot burn of panic. *The last page! Dear God, she must not read the last page!*

"I'm so sorry, Doktor Melanchthon," she continued. "I never meant for it to go this far—for you to go to this much trouble. I just—"

"It's fine," he interrupted. "If you don't want the book, I can give it to one of my students who might have a use for it." The very thought of his gift of love being passed on to a first-year Latin student who would undoubtedly spill beer on it within a week distressed Philipp, but then again, whom did he love? *Did I even know her?* He stretched out his hand and instructed, "Give it back, and I shall trouble you no more."

This was an unkind reply that Philipp regretted immediately. The shame inside him was great. *She must not read the last page,* he thought. *She must not know how I feel—how I felt.*

"I would like to keep it if you don't mind," she responded, clutching it to her chest. "It's such a wonderful gift."

Well, I'm doomed, Philipp concluded, nodding in consent to her request. He stared at the floor, hands clenched, longing to flee—to run away and never see her again.

"You must think such awful things about me now," Katharina whispered.

"No, I understand. I allowed my enthusiasm to carry me away. I thought—I don't know. It doesn't matter now."

"I enjoyed our times together so much. I would look forward to them every week. I could have told you, but then I feared our lessons would be over, and I would never have a chance to speak with you again."

He was too distracted to fully hear what she was saying. *Philipp, how could you have been such a fool?!*

"I like the German tales too," he insisted. "I am not so high and mighty that I disdain the land of my birth." But then he thought, *Why am I bothering to defend myself? It's over.*

"I never thought that you disdained it!" she assured him, her voice kind but her tone desperate. "I was just so nervous. I picked something I thought would interest you. Everyone knows you are the most learned man in Wittenberg—perhaps even in Germany. I was certain I would bore you. I haven't studied at great universities or written works that leave men in awe. I had just enough courage to ask you to discuss a subject I thought you would enjoy. Once it started, I never wanted it to end. I didn't come to love Ovid, but I…"

As her voice trailed off, Philipp brought himself to look at her properly. Her eyes were wide—her face flushed. *Does she mean what I think she means?* No, he would not make that mistake again! *But she said it or was about to say it. She was about to say that she has come to love me!* Those words, offered so sweetly, were a bellows fanning the flame of hope within him. Philipp's blood was rushing—his senses heightened.

"Well, as I said, I enjoyed our lessons," Katharina concluded, staring down at the book. "I still don't want them to end, but I understand they must. I cannot rely upon your forbearance any longer."

Make the leap! Philipp urged himself. *You must make the leap!*

"Do you mean to say that you simply wanted to spend time with me? Just the two of us?" he asked, and he found as he did so that it was only his fear that had overcome him: that he never ceased loving her, even in rejection, and that the love was now blossoming into something glorious.

"Yes, I couldn't think how else to do it," she explained, shaking her head in embarrassment. "You must think me a great fool—as dim as a rock. All this time, I actually thought…"

"Thought what?" he asked, attempting not to sound too desperate, though he could not be more eager to hear the next words out of her mouth.

And then their eyes met again, hers still moist and full of sadness, his searching out the depths of her soul, awakened by the possibility of union.

"I thought that perhaps you cared for me," she whispered. "God only knows what you must think of me, Doktor Melanthchon! Such a foolish notion to think—" A momentary pause, and then she regained her strength. "To think that you would ever be interested in someone like me. Forgive me."

Ecstasy! Pure ecstasy! Philipp smiled and shook his head at the strange chances of life. He was overflowing with joy, but poor Katharina was still wallowing in misery, so he quickly reached out, bridging the distance between them, and flipped the book to the final page. He pointed at it with intense purpose and begged her, "Read it, please!"

She seemed hesitant at first, but finally acquiesced. As her eyes passed over the words he had scrawled out in ink, declaring his affection for her, realization slowly dawned on Katharina's face. She gasped softly. A smile! Yes, the joy that had filled Philipp was now overflowing into her heart as well. She reached the end and looked up at him, mouth slightly agape, shaking her head in disbelief. Her eyes seemed to latch onto his with an almost unearthly power.

"Can this be true?" she breathed.

"That is the truth of what I feel," he replied, nodding determinedly.

"I can hardly believe it," she said, looking back down at the page. "I don't recognize myself in your words."

Now! Philipp urged himself. *Do it now! Ask her!*

"It's true, I swear it," he pledged. "I never thought I would be in this position. I was ready to spend the rest of my life with my books, but now all I can think about is spending it with you."

Philipp's heart was pounding. He was very aware of his breath: aware of every sensation and inch of his flesh. His fear had lifted completely. He was more empowered than he had ever been in his life.

"Doktor—" Katharina began.

"No!" Philipp cried. "Please call me by my Christian name: the one granted me by my father."

Melanchthon was the name Reuchlin gave him. The name of his birth, the one with which he was baptized, the one with which he stood before God: that was what he wished to hear from the lips of the woman he loved.

"Are you sure?" she asked. "I mean no disrespect."

"It would be so sweet."

She smiled broadly and nodded. "Philipp, thank you for this precious gift. It means everything to me." Then she paused, her expression more serious, and added, "You mean everything to me."

He felt himself drawn inexorably. Before he fully realized what was happening, he was kneeling before her—taking her hand in his. He felt as if he was no longer chained to his own existence. Surely, he was living someone else's life! But the body was his, the mind was his, and still she was there before him, holding his heart in her hands. He felt compelled to say the words. Never had he so desired to speak.

"Dearest Katharina, whom I love with all my heart, will you consent to be my wife? Will you take this man, who it seems is very blind, who is small and weak, and who in the face of your beauty becomes a stammering wreck? Will you take this man who writes treatises by the dozen but could never produce the beauty that you work with your hands? Will you have me for as long as we live, vowing our devotion before the face of God? For I would be faithful to you until the end."

To his eternal delight, she replied, "Yes! Yes, of course, I will marry you! Nothing would make me happier, Philipp!" Then she leaned forward to embrace him, and he felt for the first time the infinite goodness of holding his Katharina in his arms.

Ten minutes later, Philipp approached Frau Krapp to make his intention known.

"You know we have experienced hard times since her father passed," the matriarch explained. "She does not come with much of a dowry."

"I don't care," Philipp responded. "Truly, I do not care."

Frau Krapp smiled broadly and declared, "Then name the date and she is yours, and much good may she do you! Welcome to our family!"

Before he knew it, Philipp was swept up in a hug. The Krapp children came pouring into the room, joining in a collective embrace. There was much happy shrieking, and while it still felt odd to Philipp, it was a good kind of odd: the kind he could live with quite happily for the rest of his days.

There was only one whisp of cloud to sully the sunshine that rained down upon him. *Martin will be insufferable,* he thought, laughing to himself. It was a cross he was willing to bear. *Let him think he has done it all. It will do him good, and I know the truth.*

Three months later, they were wed in St. Mary's Church, and soon after that, he and Martin gathered up the books of canon law and burnt them along with the papal bull, their students and fellow professors joining in the act. It was a moment of great fear, but Philipp had the strength to face it, for he had found the one his soul loved. Nevertheless, their first months of marriage were difficult. As he had feared, his books began gathering more dust. He may even have complained about this a time or two and received a few harsh words in return.

But with time, they found a balance: their union broadened and deepened. Her love sustained him through the dark days, as Martin was taken away and Philipp's world went up in flame. It was the only thing that granted Philipp confidence when everything seemed uncertain—the only healing he knew when he was wounded by his own failures.

Now as Philipp stands in the market square with its ceaseless activity, staring only at his Katharina, he shakes his head in wonder, still unable to believe how God has blessed him.

"What is it?" she asks.

He moves to embrace her in this place of light and life—rests a hand on her belly. Within, he can feel their child moving, shifting against the walls of her flesh. Soon, they will be a family of four, and though he knows not how they will pay for everything or what the future will hold, in this moment, he finds himself just as overcome by Katharina as he was at the first.

She seems to read his thoughts and whispers, "Whatever comes our way, I will be with you. I love you."

He nods and kisses her on the cheek. Though he dare not speak of it, he knows the danger of childbirth. He has seen too many women succumb to death attempting to give life to another. As the day of delivery grows closer, it is a steady drumbeat in his heart, causing him to fear.

Do not take her from me, God, he prays. *Do not let me lose her now.*

25 December 1524
Wittenberg, Electorate of Saxony

Martin Luther walks west along Colleges Street, a lute tucked under his right arm. It is Christmas Day, and the shops are closed, but the streets are still busy with children playing, carolers singing, and people off to see friends and family. The morning service complete, he strides beneath the midday sun to the home of the Cranachs, the closest thing to family he has in Wittenberg. Their second youngest child, Anna, is his goddaughter, so he is invited to all major Cranach occasions. While he cannot always attend, he treasures those moments when he is able to enjoy a feeling of belonging now all too rare.

Sadly, his mood is less than festive. The conflict with Karlstadt endures: Martin has just published a rejoinder to his old colleague's attacks, hoping to limit the damage of what Karlstadt has been teaching. Predictably, it is Martin who is now being cursed for lack of moderation. "How dare you accuse Karlstadt of compromising the gospel!" some have complained, ignoring the fact that it was Karlstadt who first made the same accusation against Martin: "Doktor Luther has thrown the gospel under the bench!" What is more, Martin has received word that his old mentor, Johann von Staupitz, is on the brink of death. Given how long it takes for news to arrive from Salzburg, it is possible that Staupitz is already in the grave.

And if this were not enough, I must also reply to Erasmus, or Philipp will not let me hear the end of it! Martin laments.

Finally, and worst of all, Martin has learned that Heinrich von Zütphen—an Augustinian who studied with them all in Wittenberg and went out to preach the gospel in various places—has been martyred in Heide. Unable to destroy Heinrich using legal means, a drunken crowd stormed his home at night, pulled him outside half naked, and tied him to the back of a horse. After dragging Heinrich for some way, they savagely beat him to death, then tied his lifeless body to a stake and burned it. When the flames failed to consume the poor man's flesh, they dismembered the body, burned the head and limbs, and buried the trunk in a common grave while mocking and spitting upon it.

I knew Heinrich. I encouraged him on this path, Martin thinks. When he considers the poor man's final moments, staring up at the starry sky while the blows and curses rained down, Martin feels positively ill. A shudder passes through his body as if cold metal were pressed against his flesh. *How many more will die? Why are others taken while I am allowed to live? I ought to be dead. Perhaps I soon will be.*

Still trembling, he arrives at the Cranach home: in truth, a complex of multiple stone buildings comprising eighty-four rooms, a print shop, workshops for numerous apprentices and journeymen, stables and animal pens in the anterior courtyard, and the shop of goldsmith Christian Döring next door. Martin's favorite detail about the Cranach residence is that it includes sixteen kitchens producing the best food in Wittenberg: the type of fare anyone would dream of

on Christmas Day. The great feast with all the students and apprentices will be tonight, but the midday meal is only for Herr and Frau
Cranach, their five children, himself, and the former nun Katharina
von Bora, who has taken the place vacated by Ave von Schönfield
upon the latter's marriage.

The largest room in this temple to the arts is the hall, which
serves as both a dining and sitting room. It is here that Martin Luther
is led: a place such as he never saw in his youth, and now he counts
its owners among his dearest friends. There are four marble columns
in each corner of the room, the white veins of the stone fanning out
through a sea of red. On the walls are painted scenes from classi-
cal mythology, usually featuring Venus and an assortment of exotic
foods. A great oak table is on the opposite side of the room, prepared
with Christmas greenery for their feast, but Martin sits on a bench
by the hearth with all five Cranach children—Hans, Lucas, Barbara,
Anna, and Ursula—kneeling on the Turkish rug in front of him,
their parents occupying a pair of cushioned faldstools and sipping
wine from gold-plated goblets. Off to the side, Katharina von Bora
kneels on the floor, folding napkins for their supper. The glow from
the fire behind him dances upon their faces, even as it lends warmth
to his form.

It was the children who demanded Martin bring his lute and
perform for them, so he addresses them particularly. "What would
you like me to play for you?"

Hans, the eldest at eleven years of age, immediately responds,
"One of your songs, Doktor."

"Oh, surely you don't want to hear one of my songs," he protests,
but the children all begin begging and pleading—or more accurately,
whining.

"But Herr Doktor, you promised!" young Lucas protests. "You
promised you would share a song from the new hymn book."

"You wouldn't prefer that song about the donkey?" Martin asks.

"No!" the children proclaim, their parents chuckling in the
background.

"Very well," Martin concedes, and begins fingering the strings
lightly, bringing the pattern back to memory. One by one, the callouses built up by years of friction strike anew, rubbing and chafing,
drawing out the sound. "This is from the new Erfurt hymn book,

based on the Latin *A solis ortus cardine*." When the children look at
him blankly, he adds, "But you will know it as 'Now Praise We Christ
the Holy One'."

This produces something more like the reaction he desires. As
he begins playing, the children all lean forward, longing to hear the
words he will sing—all except little Ursula, who has tired of the pro-
ceedings and begun toddling toward Katharina. He recites the lyrics,
"Now praise we Christ, the Holy One,
The blessed virgin Mary's Son.
From east to west, from shore to shore
Let earth its Lord and King adore.
He who himself all things did make
A servant's form agreed to take,
That he as man mankind might win
And save his creatures from their sin."[1]

On he continues through all eight verses, the children humming
along, their father patting his knee in time, while Ursula sits contented
in Katharina's arms, the napkins abandoned. There is some applause
when Martin has finished, and the children begin demanding further
tunes, but their mother says, "Not now, children. It is almost time to
eat. All of you, come to the kitchen and help!"

With that, the room is emptied of women and children, allowing Martin to set his lute aside and take the chair next to the elder
Lucas. He sinks back and allows his hands to rest in his lap, looking
up at the painted ceiling above him in which angels dance in a field
of golden stars.

"Are you available for hire?" Lucas asks. "We could use some
regular entertainment for the little ones."

"I would have thought there was plenty here to amuse," Martin
replies.

Lucas' laugh is as merry as his rosy cheeks and full gray beard.
He is a genius, a marvel, and a priceless asset, but also a man who
likes good food and drink and has won money off nearly every card
player in town. He is full to the brim of life, intensity, and passion.

---

[1] "Now praise we Christ the holy one", trans. Richard Massie, Hymnary.org,
https://hymnary.org/text/now_praise_we_christ_the_holy_one. Original Latin
version by Coelius Sedulius, German translation by Martin Luther.

Some men are born to make art, but Lucas Cranach was born to make money off art, for his mind tends as much to business as anything else. Always he seeks opportunities: new angles, new lines. He draws not only on the canvas, but the whole of Wittenberg society, shaping matters to his will. A great relief, then, that his will tends to good more often than evil.

"How do you keep up with all those little ones?" Martin inquires. "You're a good decade older than me, and I am not young."

"The children are easy. It's the employees who give me the trouble," Lucas responds, perhaps thinking of the incident a year previous when his printer struck one of the journeymen in the face with an awl, or any of the innumerable times said journeymen have gotten into fights with students. "Speaking of troubles," Lucas continues, "you look as if something is very much troubling you."

Martin nods sadly. "I just received word yesterday—my old mentor, Staupitz, is close to death."

"Ah," his friend murmurs thoughtfully. "I am sorry to hear it. He meant a great deal to you?"

"He did. He does," Martin says quickly. Then a brief pause—a dropping of his spirit. "But not what he used to mean."

"I don't follow," says Lucas, brow furrowed.

Martin pauses to reflect on their relationship. Weeping, confessing, receiving instruction and absolution. Rising, reforming—then breaking and sundering.

"Doktor Staupitz gave me everything," he explains. "He was the one who started it all. But I was wrong about him—terribly wrong."

Lucas takes another drink from his goblet and inquires, "How so?"

Martin shakes his head in frustration and releases words that sting with the effort. "It seems he was driven by avarice just like the rest: greed for the things of this world and the glories of a passing age. Such a terrible misjudgment! Once, I thought him the wisest man I knew. I shared my very soul with him, pouring it out day after day. He set me on the path, but he failed to count the cost, and when the moment of decision came, he turned aside. He abandoned me."

"He must have felt a great deal of pressure," Lucas offers.

"And I didn't?" he responds, indignant at the suggestion. *Where was Staupitz at Worms?!* he broods. *Where was he when I spent a year alone, at war with the devil and myself?! Where was he when I needed him most—when the pressure was beyond human description?!*

"I'm sorry," says Lucas. "I didn't mean to suggest that the two things were the same."

He shakes his head, still unable to make sense of it after all these years. "I thought him a defender of the gospel, but he was unwilling to take up his cross and follow Christ to the end. How could I have been so blind?!"

Lucas nods thoughtfully. "You have been dealt a hard lesson, Martin. He was like a father to you, and you have learned that your father is fallible."

"I learned that lesson well enough from my father of the flesh," Martin grumbles, his hands tightening into fists. "I am not so cold as to condemn Staupitz for his humanity, but his betrayal is a burning ache I cannot escape. I tried writing to him, reasoning with him. I thought he cared about me—that he cared about the gospel. On both counts, he proved himself false. And yet, a part of me still wants to believe in him. I mourn the loss of his company. I had hoped that someday, somehow we would be reconciled. I have lost many friendships these past few years, but none eat at my soul like this one. I confessed everything to him, but he showed me nothing of his true self."

He looks into Lucas' eyes. There is sympathy there, but perhaps not full understanding. Then again, why should anyone understand why this bothers him so much?

"There are few friendships that can be open like that in both directions," Lucas notes.

"Too true," Martin agrees, nodding. "Perhaps it is for the best."

Now they are interrupted by the arrival of Katharina and Anna, who approach them holding hands.

"What is it?" Lucas asks his daughter. "Does your mama need me?"

"Actually, she seeks spiritual counsel from her godfather," Katharina replies quietly, turning her gaze to Martin.

"Of course," Martin replies, looking at his goddaughter. "Anything for my sweet one."

Young Anna smiles broadly as her father vacates his chair and allows her to sit, straightening the thing so she can look at Martin more directly. Muttering something about "getting a drink," Lucas departs, but Katharina asks, "Do you mind if I prepare the table?"

"No, I don't think we will mind," Martin responds, smiling at Anna, who grins in return.

Katharina then moves to a vast linenfold cabinet on the far side of the room and begins retrieving the articles necessary for their feast, while Martin looks his goddaughter in the eye—a young girl only five years old with the same red hair as her mother—and asks her, "What is troubling you?"

Anna sighs far more heavily than any little girl should need to do. She shifts in her chair, attempting to get comfortable, her hands clasped together. Her feet dangle a good half foot above the floorboards.

"The goblin," she finally replies matter-of-factly.

"Goblin?"

"It lives under the floor," she assures him, her expression deadly serious.

"How do you know?"

"Lucas told me!" Here she refers to her nine-year-old brother.

"Did he now?"

"Yes. It's a goblin from the woods. It moved into our house, and now it lives under the floor."

As she speaks these words, her eyes grow wide—her tone deliberate. So sincere is her distress, it seems a greater matter than anything afflicting him. Her shoulders are hunched forward, not unlike a dog caught in its mischief. He attempts to reassure her.

"I think your brother may be playing a trick on you, dear one."

"Maybe. That is what mama says. But I hear it at night. It breathes so loud, the walls shake!"

They may be the words of a child, but the experience seems familiar. Many nights in the Wartburg Castle, he would lay awake at night, imagining that he heard all sorts of things, sensing that the evil one was close at hand. *Do we really grow brave as we get older,* he wonders, *or do our fears simply change?*

"Could it be the wind?" he inquires.

The look on her face is pained. "You don't believe in goblins, Herr Luther?"

"I believe in the mischievous nature of older brothers," he explains with a wink. "I am one, you know."

This provokes a tentative smile. "You have brothers and sisters?"

"Yes, of course, and I used to do the same kind of things to them. Take heart! I believe your room is safe."

Now Anna looks down at her feet, seemingly ashamed. She taps her petite shoes one against another, leather striking leather.

"It's hard," she concludes softly.

"What's hard?"

"I know God watches over us, but I still feel scared."

How I know the feeling, he thinks, offering, "I understand."

She looks up, brows scrunched, lips pursed. "I don't think so," she declares, shaking her head side to side, her plaits swinging freely.

"Why not?"

"You don't get scared, Herr Luther! You're brave!"

"I am terrified every day," he says far more truthfully than she could ever know.

Her mouth gapes in disbelief. "Really?"

"Really."

"But you tell us not to be afraid."

"I am telling myself that as well. It is one thing to know something in your head, Anna. It is another to feel it in your heart. In this life, we pass through trials, temptations. We doubt. But you must know that God is watching over you, even as you told me."

"I guess," she concedes. "I just feel scared. The goblin—it wants to eat me!"

Again, he sees fear in her eyes: they are open wide, glistening in the fire's glow, still innocent of evil and yet just as subject to its curse as anything on earth. He wishes he could protect her from every enemy—even those that only exist in her mind—but he cannot. He must address the one who can.

"Then allow me to speak a prayer against this goblin," he declares, taking her hand in his. As she pinches her eyes closed, he does the same and prays, "Oh Lord who watches over us all, who has defeated the power of sin and the devil, who loves us and gave himself up for us, calm the heart of my sister Anna. May she feel your presence amid the terrors of the night. May you bring her through to the break of day, safe and sound, ready to serve you once again."

When they have opened their eyes again, she squeezes his hand tightly and says, "Thank you, Herr Luther."

"You are a good girl, Anna," he tells her, letting up his grip but finding he is still captured in hers. She seems to cling to him, her stare direct, her desire for comfort strong. "It's alright," he whispers. "It is going to be alright." With this she surrenders his hand.

The room is quiet save for Katharina arranging things on the table. Martin is about to change the subject when his goddaughter suddenly erupts in a burst of laughter. As he looks on in bemusement, Anna leans closer to him, her expression utterly mischievous.

"Can I tell you a secret?" she whispers.

It occurs to him that this conversation could go in any one of a thousand directions and is by no means safe. Nevertheless, he proceeds cautiously. "Only if it is yours to tell."

Sitting up straight and displaying a grin absent two baby teeth, Anna announces, "You should grow a beard!"

Not one of the thousand directions I expected, he thinks.

"That's the secret?" Martin asks.

"You would look handsome, just like papa!" Anna concludes, face beaming with pride.

"Ah! Because your papa has a beard."

"Mama says all men look handsome with beards."

Now he leans in close and whispers, "Can I tell you a secret?"

"Yes, please!"

"I did have a beard once, when I was away."

Not only Anna's eyes, but her whole face is alight with joy. She presses her hands together and declares, "You should have one again! You will be handsome."

He chuckles. "I think it would take a good deal more than that to make me handsome."

"But why don't you have one?"

"Because it itches terribly."

"I don't think so," she insists, shaking her head.

Realizing there is nothing for it, he replies, "I'll grant you this: I will consider it."

"You should do it," she declares, positively beaming, "and then you will be handsome, and then some lady will marry you!"

Here is a topic he had foreseen among the thousand, if only because everyone seems to be asking him about it lately.

"Ah. Well, I'm not going to marry."

"Why not?!" Anna inquires mournfully, her whole body seeming to droop.

How should I put it? he wonders. *How to make a child understand?*

"I am much too busy serving the Lord," he concludes.

"But Herr Luther, wives are very nice. They help you so much."

Surprisingly sound logic, he observes, but nevertheless argues, "I'm beyond the help of anyone but God."

"Then how will you have children?"

"I don't need children of my own. I have all the children of the congregation."

"I don't think so."

"Don't think what?"

She giggles: a magical, musical sound that warms his heart. A snort escapes her nose.

"I don't know," she admits. "I want to get married someday."

"I'm sure you will. You will marry someone wonderful."

"Oh! When you get married, can I carry flowers?"

"I feel like we just went over this," he says, suppressing the urge to roll his eyes.

"Please!" she begs, hands clasped together. "Please, please, please!"

He cannot help himself. He relents.

"Very well. If I get married, you may carry flowers."

"Oh, thank you, Herr Luther! Thank you so much!" she cries, bouncing in her chair.

"Yes, well, it's not much of a promise."

"But you promised! You did! You did!"

"That I did. Now, think no more of goblins. It is Christmas."

The rest of the family enters the room again, and they are all seated at a table bearing breads, pies, plates of winter vegetables, a fully cooked suckling pig, salted herring, and enough sweets to please five children. He finds himself seated with the adults, while the children occupy the other end of the table, bending over steaming dishes to catch the scents and stealing the sweets when they don't think their parents are looking. Katharina is sitting to Martin's left, strangely quiet. As the Cranachs are all caught up in their own conversations, Martin realizes he must address her or seem churlish.

"We have not spoken in a while," he observes.

"No, we haven't," Katharina replies, staring at the empty plate in front of her.

"Are you liking it here?" he inquires, uncertain what else to ask.

"Yes. The Cranachs are very kind."

He can think of nothing to add except, "Good."

Excellent conversation. Truly excellent conversation, he thinks.

Just when he has despaired of the whole thing, she looks up, meeting his eyes.

"That was very sweet of you, comforting Anna like that. I did not know you were so fond of children."

"Thank you," he replies automatically. "That is, yes, I enjoy children."

"Me too. They are so direct, and yet they make me feel more at ease than adults."

For a moment, he simply stares at her, utterly confused. From the time they became acquainted, their sporadic interactions have made him feel ill at ease precisely because of their directness. That would seem to give the lie to her assertion about children.

"I see," he concludes, and with that their conversation fizzles into nothingness as they both turn their attention to the food being served.

The meal is a triumph. It is so unlike what he normally eats: a rejoicing in food for food's sake. He has known many people who would condemn it as a feast of gluttony—indeed, he was such a person in days past—but he sees the joy it brings to the Cranach family, the product of hours of loving labor, and he senses it is virtue, not vice. When they are finished, Frau Cranach pulls him to the side and asks, "May we speak in private?"

"Very well," he agrees, and they walk to a far corner of the room near the hearth.

Making one last survey to make sure no one else is paying attention, she whispers, "It's about Käthe."

He sighs. "What about her?"

"Herr Baumgartner has done her a great wrong," Frau Cranach says earnestly. "She has still not heard anything from him, and it has brought her very low. She is not her usual happy self at all, though she still works as hard as anyone I have ever seen. If he rejects her, people will think something is wrong with her. It will hurt her prospects, even though, from what I can tell, the fault is entirely on his part."

Martin had not realized that Baumgartner was still failing in his duty. *And after I wrote to him directly!* he fumes. It is not as if Käthe is his ward, but he took responsibility for her—for them all—and now this man has misused her.

"I agree with you that he has done her wrong, promising her love and succor and then refusing it," he whispers in return. "My opinion of him has dropped considerably. But you need not fear for her future. Doktor Glatz is quite prepared to marry her should the opportunity arise."

"Ah. Well, that is good news, I suppose," she replies. "But what kind of man is he?"

The question catches Martin off guard. *He is a man who is willing to do right by her,* he thinks. *Let us not get too picky.*

He decides to respond, "He is a Doktor of Theology and an ordained minister."

"Yes, but what is his character?"

"I'm not sure I'm the best judge of that."

Brow furrowed, she asks, "Didn't you used to work with him?"

What do you expect me to do? he thinks. *I am doing the best I can!*

"He will be fine," Martin concludes. "It will all be fine."

She nods. "Alright. You can tell Käthe."

"Oh," he mutters, very much wishing to avoid another awkward conversation. "Would you mind telling her?"

Suddenly, Frau Cranach puts on a look he has only seen her use with her children: a sternness that causes him disquiet.

"Why?" she asks pointedly.

"It's just, I would rather not speak with her directly if I can avoid it."

Now she is positively glaring. "That's not very kind."

"No, I don't mean it that way!" he protests. "Forget I said anything. I will speak with her."

"Yes, I think you'd better. I may not be your mother, Doktor Luther, but I have no intention of letting you behave like a boar."

"Is that not what I am?" he asks, attempting to restore some levity.

"Not if I have anything to say about it!" she concludes.

He is in no hurry to fulfill his commission. Happily, they are so caught up in festive activities that a proper moment does not present himself. At one point, Katharina goes outside to retrieve more wood for the fires, and he sees his chance to escape responsibility, at least for one day. He rises to depart, kissing the children farewell, thanking their parents for a wonderful Christmas meal. Soon he is descending the stairs and exiting into the courtyard that links the adjoining buildings. There he is surprised to find Katharina, not doing anything with firewood, but sitting on a bench alone, shivering in the cold. Her back is to him, so he could easily make an exit without being noticed, but conviction seizes him in the gut.

I must speak with her, he thinks. *I promised that I would, and I am a man of my word.*

He therefore calls out, "Fräulein von Bora!"

She flinches at the sound of his voice, then immediately stands and replies, "Yes, Herr Doktor?"

"I just wanted to say that I am sorry things have not worked out with Baumgartner."

"Ah," she says softly, clutching her arms for warmth. "We are talking about that."

"Yes, it seems so. Listen, Fräulein, I did write to him but received no response."

She nods sadly. A light snow is beginning to fall, and as he watches her standing there alone, with little to protect her from the elements—little to protect her from anything—he cannot help but sympathize with her. There is a heat within him: an anger at what she is suffering.

Before he knows it and somewhat against his better judgment, he finds himself saying, "The man is a scoundrel and what he's done to you is unforgivable! Truly, it angers me. You are an honorable woman and deserve far better."

She inhales quickly, perhaps to hold back tears.

"Thank you, Herr Doktor," she replies with a nod, "but do not trouble yourself. I am quite over it—quite over him."

"I was the one who brought you here—me and Herr Koppe," he continues.[2] "It is my duty to see to your care. Therefore, allow me to set your mind at ease. Do not have any fear for your future! If the Lord so wills, I do believe this is the last Christmas you will spend in

---

[2] Martin Luther and Leonard Koppe worked together on a scheme that allowed the nuns to escape from their cloister.

your present state. There is one who is eager to marry you, though he has said nothing of it before now, keeping his thoughts to himself."

Immediately, her expression changes entirely. Her eyes widen and her lips part slightly, as if gasping. She shuffles her feet slightly in his direction, eyes intent upon his face, seemingly desperate to hear more.

"Really? Truly?" she asks, breaking into a smile.

"If you are still attached to Herr Baum—"

"No!" she cries, then adds more quietly, "That is, as I said, I am not. Please, say whatever it is you have to say, Doktor."

You are so odd, he thinks, *but at least you are feeling better.*

"As you wish," he agrees. "Before he left for Orlamünde, Doktor Glatz, whom I think you know, informed me that he is very willing to make you his wife."

She frowns and asks, "What?"

"Kaspar Glatz. You know him, right?"

"Ah, yes," she replies slowly, as if attempting to process the words. "That is, I had no idea he felt that way."

"Well, I told you it would be surprising. He is not one to discuss his feelings. So, fear not! As soon as it is appropriate to do so, I will write to Doktor Glatz and arrange the whole thing. There is no need to worry."

Shaking her head slowly, she mutters, "I don't know what to say."

I suppose there is a first time for everything, he thinks.

"Well, you don't have to thank me," he assures her, pleased simply to have brought her happiness. "It is all down to your own merit: you have greatly impressed him. Now, forgive me, but I must depart. I have things to do, even on a day such as this."

With that, he turns on the spot and begins walking toward the alley that leads to the main road.

"Herr Doktor!" she calls after him.

He turns back to look at Katharina, her face overwhelmed with—well, what is it, exactly? He would say she looks as much sad as happy. *That must be the pain of love everyone talks about,* he reasons. *Is she still saddened by Baumgartner, or is it Glatz who provokes this emotion in her?* He cannot decide.

"Yes?" Martin asks.

She smiles at him weakly. "Happy Christmas."

"Happy Christmas," he responds.

As he makes his way home, lute slung over his shoulder, he congratulates himself. *Well done, Martin. You made it through without causing a disaster! A Christmas miracle!*

He arrives back at the Black Cloister, his spirit light, the festive mood finally upon him. There are no further activities for him this day: for once, he is free to spend time with his books. A beer, he thinks, would be just the thing to improve matters. He makes his way into the kitchen, where he finds Wolf at work, bent over the wash basin. There was a meal that morning for needy parishioners, and now the mound of filthy dishes requires attention.

"Welcome back, Doktor!" Wolf greets him.

A low fire is burning in the hearth on the opposite wall, and on a wooden trestle table, various foodstuffs are laid out for preparation. Martin sets his lute on the floor and is about to drop his bag on the table when he perceives that there is insufficient space. A large iron pot is sitting empty just in front of him, and he reaches out to move it.

"Don't!" Wolf yells, but it is too late.

Unbeknownst to Martin, the pot has recently been heated. His hand only makes contact for the space of a breath but is immediately seared. He cries out in pain, the bag sliding off his shoulder and hitting the floor. With his left hand, he grasps the injured one at the wrist. On his palm, he sees two places where the skin has turned pink.

"In the water!" Wolf urges him. "Get it in the water!"

Immediately, Martin moves to the basin and plunges his hand into the cool depths. There is a slight lessening of the pain, but he can tell it will be hours or perhaps even days before he has significant relief.

"I was just heating it over the fire," Wolf explains. "Forgive me! I didn't know—"

"You did no wrong," he assures him. "I barely touched it."

"We have some oil of the aloe plant. Let me fetch it!"

With that, Wolf departs, and Martin is left standing alone at the basin. He dares to pull his hand out and looks at it again. The pain comes in unrelenting waves. Such a small thing, and yet it has overwhelmed his senses.

That skin is dead, he thinks. *It will peel soon.*

And then, thoroughly unbidden, tears fill his eyes.

Such a small thing. What happens when they burn it all?

His pulse quickens. It is no longer the pain that dominates him, but the fear that is always there beneath the surface, waiting to spring forth. He has escaped death on several occasions already, and each time a new scar has formed on his spirit to match the eternal wound on his thigh. He thinks of Heinrich von Zütphen—of all the others so cruelly cut down. *How long will the Lord preserve me? Is my time running out?* Despite all the progress he has made, he still doubts.

"Another year gone," he whispers, "and now I must face the next one."

10 January 1525
Basel, Swiss Confederation

Erasmus of Rotterdam lies upon the floor of his study, bent in on himself, longing for death and terrified of the same. It has come again: the stone. Usually, he sees the sign of blood first or feels the slightest tightening of a muscle. Not this day—this day of days. It has come like a thief in the night.

The day of wrath will dissolve the world in ashes. How great will be the terror when the Judge comes.[3]

He twists against the pain, one with the torment of his flesh. He is powerless against the rending, the burning, the catharsis. Every evil he has seen upon the earth and every ache that has tortured his soul is now liquified and running free within him, inflaming his fibers, singeing as it goes.

Death and nature will stand in amazement. Whatever is hidden will be revealed. Nothing will go unpunished.

His mind is purged of thought. All he knows is the pain that has seized him, possessing his body, threatening to annihilate him. It is worse than ever before: a pain so great he can scarcely believe there was a time when he did not feel it. Now a new wave slicing from his back down into his thigh, cutting him open, drawing the breath from his lungs.

"Jezus, heb medelijden! Heb medelijden!"[4]

---

[3] These quotes are from the "Dies irae" portion of the Requiem Mass.
[4] "Jesus, have mercy! Have mercy!"

But why should the Lord have mercy now when he never has before? From his first breath to the one he now struggles to take, what mercy has there been for Desiderius Erasmus?

I tremble and I fear the judgment and wrath to come, when the heavens and the earth shall be moved.

He is no longer alone. Karl Harst has entered the room. And yet, he is intensely alone, beyond any help of God or man.

"Master!" Harst cries, running to his side. "What evil has overtaken you?!"

He can only whisper hoarsely, a fleeting wail from the depths. "The stone! The stone!"

No more: the power of speech is denied him. The man who weaves words into a tapestry for kings is grunting like a wounded beast, and almost he wishes that was his nature, for then death would be the end.

He is being lifted from the floor—by an angel or a demon? *Is the pain itself lifting me?* No, it is Karl: loyal Karl, faithful to the end. Unable to walk, Desiderius Erasmus will be carried to the summit of the purgatorial mount. But here the lie is revealed, a truth savage and cruel: he has ascended not to heaven, but hell.

He is lain upon his bed. His clothes are being stripped from him. Every position, every turning of his body, every touch—unbearable!

"Stop!" he begs. "Stop it now!"

"Am I hurting you?" Harst asks.

He seizes the younger man by the arm.

"Everything!" he bellows. "Everything hurts me!"

Another convulsive wave rips through his insides. He loses his grip. He is falling fast into the welcoming arms of darkness. Harst reaches to grab his shoulders as the contents of his stomach involuntarily release, spewing upon them both, trailing onto the floor.

You disgust me! You hear that? You disgust me!

Harst wipes him off—lays him on his back. Somehow it seems more painful here than it did on the floor, but surely that is a trifle. He has reached the end. The thread of his existence is pulled taut. It is about to snap.

"I will fetch the physician! Do not lose hope!" Harst urges him.

How long until a physician comes? A minute? A year? No, it is an eternity, every second as long as the winter in its silence and the summer in its heat. With one breath, he prays, *Take me, Lord. Free me from this body of death.* With the next, he cries, *My God, my God, why have you forsaken me?* He must die. He must escape the pain, but what pain awaits him in the hereafter? He would tell the physician to slit his throat were it not for the voice in his head.

Son of iniquity! I know what you've done! I know what you are! You are bad!

Past, present, future—they are uniting as one. The words that have tortured him for years and those so recently unleashed are forged into a single weapon that will destroy him body and soul. He hates himself as he hates the pain. Yet, even as there was before, there remains a small portion of his being that clings to pride even as it clings to life.

No! I am free. I can change—I have changed! I will live! Yes, by God, I will live!

Live to endure the threats of his enemies? Live to be the scapegoat for other men's failures? Live to be crucified every day—to see all he loves dissolve into dust?

The physician has arrived. He is lifting a vial to Erasmus' lips.

"Drink this! It is your only relief."

Erasmus opens his mouth to receive, uncertain if it will bring life or death. The liquid slides into his mouth, rushing toward his throat. It robs him of breath—he coughs and sputters—but somehow it descends into the depths of his body.

"It will not take long to work," the physician assures him.

With labored breath, Erasmus bites his lip, sweat dripping from his brow.

"Try counting," he is urged. "One, two, three…"

In his mind, he joins the physician's game. *One, two, three, four.* The darkness is closing in. Behind closed eyes, he begins to see spirals of brilliant color. Something new is surging through his body. Not only the pain is releasing, but everything seems lost, his existence reduced to a vapor. He is no longer in control of anything—even his mind. A force far greater is drawing him to itself. He is floating, flying, soaring. He is nowhere near Basel. *Is this death? Am I dying?* Darkness. Unknowing.

Then, suddenly—something. At first only a feeling as soft as a feather's touch, then a vision wrapped in fog. He strains against a pulsing heat, his sight at last sharpening to take in his new surroundings.

What is this strange, unnatural place?

He is moving through tunnels deep below the earth, buried beneath the ancient fountains. *How do I know that? But surely it must be.* Gasping, he takes in air that is sulfrous and hot. The walls are closing in, if indeed they are walls. *Where am I? What is this?* He feels almost weightless, a figment of being alone in the dark.

Then rising before his captive eyes, a vision of darkest terror: a beast with blackened skin and cloven hoofs, its pupils a burning red, its beard and horns familiar. It reaches for him with fingers like eagle's claws. They tear through his skin and hook into his flesh.

"Come with me, Erasmus!" the beast taunts in a voice thunderous and booming. "Come with me to hell!"

An infinite blackness opens beneath them. Steam rises from the depths, burning as it strikes his skin.

"Breathe it in!" the beast commands.

He has no choice but to do so. He longs to suffocate but cannot. As the steam enters his nostrils, scorching his membranes, his mind is filled with a thousand tortured thoughts. Every evil he has committed and the totality of his shame strikes him like the lash, flaying his spirit to the point of bleeding.

"Please!" Erasmus begs. "Please, let me go!"

The beast pulls him to itself, cradling him against skin that is cracked and hairy, thicker than leather and hard as stone. He can hear the thing's breath—like a legion of horses pounding the turf—but there is no trace of a beating heart. Suddenly, the beast stretches its chest and unfurls a pair of tremendous wings that are somehow devoid of substance, as if they were composed of darkness itself. The two of them begin hurtling into the abyss, the steam growing thicker, Erasmus' body burning. His clothes are instantly consumed, leaving him naked to the heat. He can see his flesh turning black and dissolving. Yes, he himself is melting into the beast. Their bodies and spirits are fusing. There is nothing left of Desiderius Erasmus. He has been annihilated: made one with the beast.

With the last shred of consciousness left to him, he cries with no hope of deliverance, "*Kýrie eléison! Christe eléison!*"[5]

---

[5] "Lord, have mercy! Christ, have mercy!"

Then a change. The beast, the steam, the abyss—all vanished. He sees a kind of glow, first blurred beyond recognition, then becoming clearer. It is a flame upon a wick, which belongs to a candle in the hand of—Froben! Yes, it is Johann Froben! He is back in his own chamber, still lying in bed. It is dark save for the candle, so perhaps it is night. He has lost all sense of time.

"Erasmus!" Froben calls to him. "Erasmus, you are awake. The physician gave you an opium draught. You are coming out of it."

Beside him on the bed, he can see his hand still attached at the end of his right arm. He finds he can raise it and wiggle his fingers. To his great delight, the skin is not charred but perfectly sound, but even this small effort tires him: he allows the hand to drop. Things are blurring again. He is fading.

"Johannes," he whispers.

"Yes?" his friend asks earnestly.

"No more. No more draught."

This is the last thing he knows for some time until he wakes again, having slept a blessedly dreamless sleep. This time it is Frau Froben sitting in a chair by his bedside, a pair of spectacles on her face, reading a book.

"Gertrude," he manages to say.

She immediately looks up, sets the book aside, and removes her spectacles.

"Herr Erasmus, you must drink," she informs him.

"I don't know if I can."

"You will not pass the thing unless you drink."

Before he has fully prepared himself for the effort, she raises him to a seated position, placing a pillow behind his back for support. She then forces a cup of water into his hand and commands, "Drink!"

"I should have some Burgundy wine," he protests.

She tilts her head down and grants him a determined stare. "I tell you 'drink.' You drink."

He acquiesces to her demand and begins to imbibe, but as he does so, a new surge of pain rips through him. Within a matter of seconds, it is so severe that he instinctively curls into a ball, holding his knees, rocking against the pain.

"I will fetch the physician again!" she cries.

One day, two days, three days. The pain continues with only momentary relief. He is offered the opium drug again, but refuses it, begging instead for turpentine and wine. Nine days pass with no sign of the stone. It is lodged deep within him, stubbornly refusing to move. His will to fight is waning. What the pain could not do to him immediately, time is now achieving: his pride is completely humbled, and he has no hope in life.

"Froben," he says to his friend, "send for Bishop Christoph. I am not long for this world."

What fear in his friend's eyes as he speaks these words! Yet, it is as nothing compared to that within Erasmus. He cannot risk another plunge into the abyss, for he might not escape a second time. When the bishop arrives, he will have to confess all his outstanding sins. He will have to speak words he hoped never to speak. *What choice do I have? I am dying.*

The bishop is long in coming, even for his most exalted congregant. At length, Erasmus feels anew the urge to release his water—no surprise given the amount of liquid Frau Froben has forced into him. He calls for Harst, who helps him to his feet. Together, they stumble more than walk. Harst raises the pot with one hand and steadies him with the other. Then Erasmus' muscles release. Pain shoots through him, burning as it goes. He lets out a wail as the last of his water exits. There are tears running from his eyes.

Then suddenly, nothing. The shooting pain is ended: only a dull ache remains. He looks on in wonder as Harst reaches into the pot and retrieves a stone far larger than any he has ever passed, displaying it for him proudly.

"Is that not the happiest thing you have ever seen?" Harst asks with a grin.

He extends his palm and watches as the stone—in truth, no bigger than a pebble—is dropped into his hand. Harst is laughing, and soon he finds he is doing the same. They embrace, then he pulls back to look Harst in the eye and says, "I am risen from the dead."

By the time Froben returns with the local priest, having been unable to locate the bishop, he informs his friend that there is no need for the last rites: not today. He will go on living, at least for a while.

The next day, he is eating solid food again, drafting correspondence, and going for his daily walk, if a bit slower than usual. He is a man restored: snatched from the clutches of death. The family is overjoyed. Indeed, everyone is pleased. Even Œcolampadius sends a note to say he is delighted to hear of Erasmus' recovery.

Yet, there is something lingering: a mark that cannot be erased. The memory of that darkness follows and confounds him, enlivening his fear. Was what he saw real or imagined? Was it a product of the doktor's odd brew, which he swears never to drink again, or a genuine vision? It was as real as his angst, and that seems real enough.

He speaks of it to no one. He attempts to push it from his mind. And yet somehow, he knows. Yes, he can sense it in his being: he has come within a breath of hell, and he can never be the same.

How much time remains to me? he wonders. *That most precious of things—time—and that which binds us to this existence. But there is another existence: a fearsome one.*

He is not safe. Not in Basel, nor anywhere else. He has heard the news of Heinrich von Zütphen's death. *There at least is someone who understands what it is to be in hell. Today, they chase after reforming monks, but whom will they slay tomorrow?* He does not doubt that in Rome and Paris there are those who would gladly subject him to the same tragic fate. And what would lie beyond? Fire giving way to fire, purgation to annihilation in a place that knows no time. For time frees a man as much as binds him, bringing an end to his suffering. But what on earth can bring an end to the suffering of Desiderius Erasmus? He has slithered his way out of many traps, but his doubt holds him forever in chains.

"I am a free person," he whispers in the dark. "Unto my very grave, I believe: I am a free person."

21 February 1525
Wittenberg, Electorate of Saxony

Philipp Melanchthon sits in his study, glass of wine in hand, enjoying a moment of peace before retiring to bed for the evening. His sleep has improved of late, and thus he has reason for optimism that he might, in fact, enjoy the experience. However, there is a knot in his back that will not yield to any amount of twisting and turning. With a sigh, he turns to the book before him: his old student Bible lies open to the forty-sixth Psalm.

"God is our refuge and strength,
A very present help in trouble.
Therefore, we will not fear, though the earth should change
And though the mountains slip into the heart of the sea.
Though its waters roar and foam,
Though the mountains quake at its swelling pride."[6]

He breathes in deeply, his mind filled with images of the breaking and remaking: the irresistible turning of the world as it is molded by the hands of the divine potter. He can see a vast wave, as high as the mountains themselves, rising with the infinite darkness of the deep to cover him and all he loves. He can feel the pillars of the earth shaking upon their foundations, and he senses an hour of judgment is at hand for the deeds of man.

"Come, behold the works of the Lord,
Who has wrought desolations in the earth.
He makes wars to cease to the end of the earth.
He breaks the bow and cuts the spear in two.
He burns the chariots with fire.
'Cease striving and know that I am God.
I will be exalted among the nations. I will be exalted in the earth.'"[7]

A great and terrible passage, he thinks. *I wonder what Martin would glean from it.* His colleague always has a good way of explaining the Psalms.

Suddenly, his thoughts are interrupted by a wail that seems to freeze his blood and melt his heart simultaneously.

"Philipp!" his wife cries from above. "Philipp, help me!"

He is already rushing up the stairs, feet pounding the wooden boards. He reaches the door to their bed chamber and flings it open in desperation. There he finds his wife kneeling on the floor, bent forward, braced upon her hands.

"What's happened?!" he cries, crouching down to steady her. "Are you hurt?"

"My water! Philipp, my water!"

He looks down and sees that he is kneeling in it. The floor is covered in the fluid that is escaping his wife's womb, soaking her

---

[6] Psalm 46:1-3.
[7] Psalm 46:8-11.

night dress and filling her with terror, for she knows as well as he does that the baby is not meant to be born for at least another month. It penetrates the black cloth that covers him, and he feels it upon his skin as the very essence of his anxieties.

"Philipp! I can't…I can't…"

Now she collapses into a ball on the floor, clutching at her stomach, groaning in pain. He grips her hand. *Lord God, what must I do? What must I do?!* After about half a minute—a dreadful space of time in which every second is a life's agony—she is somewhat recovered. He is able to lift her onto the bed before another contraction comes, this one seemingly more severe than the last. From her lungs proceeds a guttural cry, as if it were torn from her by the hands of Beelzebub. Now Anna is awake in the room next door. The screams of both his women are echoing in his ears. Every nightmare, every tortured imagining of the past few months is unfolding before his waking eyes.

Too soon, he thinks. *Too soon! The child is likely to die.*

In the space of a few minutes, his entire world has been called into doubt. Could he have just been sitting in his study, enjoying the fruit of the vine? Was there ever a moment, an existence before this terror?

What must I do?! The midwife will be needed, surely. Who will still be awake? Someone will need to care for Anna. Good God! Will Anna have a mother in the morning?!

Thoughts are pummeling him so fast he cannot make sense of them. He longs to wail with the others but knows he must not. He is the one—yes, he is the one who must take charge, for no one else can.

His heart is jolted again by the sound of banging on the door. Famulus Koch bellows, "Master Philipp, what's wrong?!"

He dares to leave Katharina alone on the bed and meets their servant just beyond the threshold, where he finds Koch hastily tucking his shirt into his braies with one hand and holding a candle with the other.

"I heard yelling—I ran," Koch explains.

Philipp nods. "Katharina has gone into labor. We need the midwife, and Anna needs to be taken to her grandmother's."

Koch's eyes grow large. "She's in labor already? Isn't it too soon?"

"Of course, it's too soon!" Philipp screams directly into his face, the fear pushing him past the breaking point.

Koch places a hand on Philipp's shoulder, shushing him as one would a frightened child—for that is what he is. "Forgive me, Master Philipp. What do you want me to do first? The midwife or the Krapps?"

Another scream is drawn from Katharina, tensing Philipp's muscles anew. He is struck by indecision, frozen in place, striving but failing to act. He feels utterly helpless against the relentless waves of terror. He is ripped apart by the surf! Just at this moment, Veit Winsheim—one of their student boarders and a member of the Akademia—emerges groggily from his room on the other side of the hall, hair a mess, pulling on a pair of boots.

"Do you need me, Professor?" Winsheim asks.

"Yes, you must take young Anna to the home of her Oma," Koch instructs on Philipp's behalf. "Quick now, grab your robe and cap!" As Winsheim rushes off to follow this order, Koch turns back to Philipp and says, "I will go to the midwife, Maria. I will have her back here as soon as I can."

With a firm nod, Philipp rushes back through his own room and opens the door to the nursery, where he finds Anna sitting up in her bed, crying with all the strength in her little lungs.

"Papa!" she cries, extending her arms.

He lifts her up and holds her to his chest, patting her on the back. Their hearts pump fiercely, one against the other.

"Anna, my love," he says, attempting to steady his voice, "I cannot talk long. You must spend the night with Oma. Veit will take you."

"Oma," she repeats, still sniffling but less upset.

"That's right," Philipp assures her.

When he reaches the hall and places her into Winsheim's waiting arms, it sets off a new deluge of tears.

"No, Papa! Papa!" Anna wails, her face scrunched in despair, her tiny hands reaching out to grasp him.

"You will be alright, Anna," Philipp promises, kissing her forehead. "The baby is coming. I have to help Mama."

She does not seem to understand. The weeping continues unabated.

"Just leave with her," he instructs Winsheim. "As long as she sees me, she won't be calm."

With that, the two of them depart. Philipp's insides lurch with each cry from his daughter, but he must set it all aside: Katharina needs him more. He returns to his vigil by her bedside. She is deep in the throes of labor. It is happening much faster than it did with Anna.

"I can feel the head, Philipp," she gasps between contractions. "I can already feel the head pressing down!"

"Hold on," he urges her, pushing the damp hair off her sweat covered brow. "She is coming. The midwife is coming."

Katharina looks into his eyes desperately, her breath heavy. As if her whole existence depended on it, she says, "Philipp, I love you."

"I love you too," he says, kissing her hand. As much as he enjoys exchanging these words, there is something about the way Katharina recites them that seems final, as if she fears she will never speak them again. He clings to her hand with all his might, unwilling to let her go. *You cannot depart. I forbid it!*

Then she lets out another groan, body prone upon the bed, utterly surrendered to the pain. It seizes her by the neck, catching in her throat, taking her for its own.

Lord, please, he prays silently, hoping to hide his terror. *Please, help us!*

After several minutes of this, he finally hears footsteps on the stairs. His heart leaps as he turns to see the midwife, Maria, entering the room: a woman well past middle age with a white veil on her head and the wrath of God in her eyes. Philipp has only spoken with her once or twice before, but they are about to become more closely acquainted.

"Out of the way!" Maria commands with such authority that he automatically rises and steps to the side.

There is no standing on ceremony—no polite use of titles or attempt at deference from this woman. Somehow, it lends him comfort to see Maria so utterly in command.

"How long?" the midwife inquires, pressing on Katharina's belly.

"She lost her water about half an hour ago," he replies.

"I beg your pardon," the woman says to Katharina, reaching under her gown.

Now a new sound exits his wife's throat that sends a chill down his spine. Maria is feeling inside Katharina, arm twisting, face contorting as she whispers thoughts to herself. Then the midwife's eyes bulge and she pulls her hand back.

"Fully open: you are fully open, love!" she informs Katharina.

"Is the baby in the right position?" he asks, appealing to his minimal knowledge of such things.

"Yes, the baby is coming, and faster than any of us would prefer," Maria answers. "Now, grab some cloths!"

Again, he obeys without a second thought. Retrieving the sheets from Anna's room, he kneels beside Maria at the foot of the bed, setting them on the floor. The midwife has pushed Katharina's night dress back and positions one of the sheets underneath her bottom. Crouching beside him again, the midwife speaks softly, even as Katharina lets out another groan.

"Herr Doktor, you must prepare yourself."

"For what?" he asks, the words seeming to burn his ears.

"I have assisted at over three hundred births. Several have been early like this. You must know: this child is not likely to survive."

He inhales quickly, attempting to hold back tears. The words are like a knife penetrating his chest, puncturing his lungs and stealing his breath. He knew: of course, he knew from the first pained cry. But hearing it spoken so plainly, with such certainty, rends him anew. He has seen it happen to so many, but now that it is happening to him, the pain feels utterly novel. *How on earth can we survive it? How has anyone survived the loss of a child?*

"Lift her legs," Maria instructs. "If we get the child out cleanly, we may at least save the mother."

Again, he finds himself frozen on the spot, struggling to do what needs to be done. The fear is total. All his muscles feel stiff.

The midwife takes his face strongly in her hands and cries, "Courage, man! Together, we must do this! Courage, now!"

And so, Philipp prays to the Lord of all, who kills and makes alive, *Be with us now. Be with us in the valley of the shadow of death.*

He nods and springs into action, taking hold of Katharina's legs, allowing the midwife to move into position. She inserts a hand again and proclaims, "The head is in place. You are ready. Push, dear! Push!"

This Katharina does, teeth gritted, face strained, gripping the back of her legs. After a few seconds, she must cease her striving.

"Good!" Maria declares. "We need several more like that."

Another push, then another, and still another. Katharina's tiny body is under so much stress, Philipp fears it will burst.

"God, help me!" his wife cries between efforts. "Lord Jesus, save us!"

"Almost there!" Maria encourages her. "One more push, love! I have the head!"

Katharina looks wearily into Philipp's eyes, the glow of the candles reflecting every drop of sweat on her face—every tear of agony. He is filled with desperate longing, overcome by emotion, uncertain of all that he feels but simply knowing that he feels it acutely. Then she closes her eyes and lets out a cry so loud, he fears it will split the house in two.

"Coming!" Maria shouts. "I have it!"

Philipp looks down and watches as a head, a chest, a pair of legs emerge. So small! Far smaller than Anna at birth. It breaks his heart.

"The cloths!" the midwife instructs, gathering up the child in her arms.

He releases his wife's legs and moves immediately to lift the sheets into position, receiving the child into his arms.

"Boy," Maria concludes. "It's a boy."

A boy? He cannot help it: he begins to weep convulsively, chest heaving, breath exiting in powerful bursts. *A son. I have a son!* The news fills him with a greater joy than he would have thought possible, and yet he is simultaneously crushed upon the wheel of fortune, knowing that this boy—his son, his pride—is very much in danger.

He looks down into the tiny babe's eyes, which he is surprised to see are open wide. They fix on him, perhaps out of focus, but looking at him all the same. For a moment, their pupils seem to lock, and he feels himself captured by something far greater than himself: a bond that must endure through fear and death, war and want, for even after the world is changed, this boy will be his son.

"Philipp," he whispers. "Your name is Philipp."

Then in an instant, the spell is broken. He hears, as if from a distant land, the voice of his wife. "Why isn't he crying? Why isn't he crying?!"

Now Philipp looks upon his son in alarm, for Katharina is right. He is not crying. In fact, he is struggling for every breath. The midwife puts her ear to the boy's chest, then raising her head again, announces, "Fluid in his lungs. He can barely breathe. We must get him down!"

Philipp immediately follows direction, laying his son on the bed. Maria begins pressing and rubbing the boy's chest, crying, "Come on, little one!" She flips him onto his stomach, slapping his back—one, two, three times, skin striking skin. Philipp winces with each collision. Maria flips the child again, rubbing and exhorting, prodding his flesh with her fingers.

With an effort so great Philipp cannot comprehend it, Katharina sits up, leaning over, placing her hand on their son's head.

"Please God, let him breathe!" his wife prays, tears streaming down her face. "Please don't take him, Lord! Please let him live! Oh, breathe, my son! Breathe!"

Maria continues massaging the boy's chest while Katharina strokes his head, but they seem to be making little progress. Philipp bends over to get a better view. The boy's eyes are closed—he does not appear to be breathing at all. He is still coated in the blood of his mother, thoroughly incapable of fulfilling their commands.

"Turning blue," Maria says, not ceasing her work. "He seems blue to me."

Katharina looks up at her husband desperately, worn down by her great physical effort and the torment of her soul. "Do something, Philipp!" she demands. "Do something!"

"What can I do?!" he cries in response, wishing for all the world that there was something, anything within his power that could restore his son.

The midwife lets up her efforts. "It is no good. You must baptize him."

He stares at Maria, heart gripped by terror. Though he knows her purpose full well, he finds himself muttering, "What?"

"He isn't breathing. He will soon be full dead," she replies. "You must baptize him now to save his soul."

Philipp looks at his wife, who is now collapsed on the bed, clutching their son's body, overcome by grief. He feels somehow separated from his own body. *This is not happening. This cannot be happening.* He can sense his son passing through the veil—moving across the chasm from which no man can draw him back.

"Doktor!" Maria chides, breaking him out of his stupor.

"I am not ordained," he whispers, looking frantically from one woman to the other. "Not properly. I have never baptized a child."

"The Lord will understand!" Maria insists. "You must do it! Fetch the basin!" she commands, pointing to a dish of water in the corner.

All at once, in this moment of greatest turmoil, Philipp Melanchthon is caught up in a whirlwind of memory, transported to a moment three years earlier. He was seated in the parlor downstairs, and across from him was their strange visitor: the self-declared prophet, Marcus Stübner. Luther was away, Karlstadt was ascendant, and this former student had arrived with new ideas, claiming to have heard from God, asking Philipp questions he had never thought to ask.

"Why do we baptize children?" Stübner inquired.

"Because it is commanded in Scripture," Philipp responded automatically. "Because it is forgiveness of sins offered to the sinner. Thus, the Church has always baptized children as soon as possible."

How ignorant he was then! He was about to be struck.

"Salvation is not by works of man," Stübner insisted. "When you bring a child to the font and place a bit of water on his head, it is you who are making a choice, taking upon yourself the right that belongs to God. Grace comes to man through faith alone, not through these actions we perform, but on account only of God's sovereign choice. Do you think you can alter the will of God by splashing water on someone? Do you think that the power of election is yours to command: that you can answer back to God and say, 'This child and not another'? You have no such power! The Spirit moves where it will, and you do not know where it is going. Now it is falling with purpose, landing even upon the common man: the young men see visions, the old men dream dreams. A new work is being performed in our day, in which the sun will be darkened and the moon turned to blood! If you confess with your mouth the Lordship of Christ, then will you be saved! No man should think because he has some water splashed on him that he can be certain of his eternal fate. Could Simon the Magus be certain?![8] Hell is full to the brim of baptized heathens! Too

---

[8] Simon Magus was a man who lived in the early years of Christianity. He sought baptism, but then asked how much it would cost to purchase the power to perform the same miraculous acts as the apostles, thinking to use them as magic tricks to win money from his audience.

long the Church has pretended to stand in the place of God, offering salvation to whomever it wills, but the Spirit cannot be contained. It is here and now! You cannot control it! Our God is in the heavens, and he does whatever he wills. Who are you, oh pot, to answer back to the potter?!"

Three years later, Philipp knows how he ought to have responded, but at the time, he was so overcome by the strange spirit within Stübner as to be rendered dumb. Yes, he knows now that Stübner was wrong. He is certain! Yet, within the warp and weft of his person, he feels the needle prick of doubt. It is the very devil's work upon a man in great distress. He looks into the eyes of his wife, which are filled with greatest despair. *What must I do, Lord? What must I do?* He stares at his son still covered in blood. Then, with the very power of the deep, comes another memory from one of the strangest passages in all of Scripture.

"When I passed by you and saw you squirming in your blood, I said to you while you were in your blood, 'Live!' Yes, I said to you while you were in your blood, 'Live!'"[9]

There in the midst of the whirlwind, in the very center of the furnace, Philipp feels something shocking: peace. A parting of the clouds—a shining beam of clarity. He steps forward with authority, bending over his son, placing a hand on his tiny head. He gathers up the air in his lungs, harnessing a power he does not possess, but which has come to possess him. With a voice like the trumpet call of heaven, he speaks the words granted from on high: "Breathe, Philipp! Live!"

A sputter—a cough. The babe twitches.

"In the name of Jesus Christ, live!"

A tiny gasp. More coughing. Young Philipp's eyes open. His lungs are working hard.

"Breathe, Philipp! Live! You will live!"

Then comes a moment that will be imprinted on Philipp Melanchthon's mind for the rest of his days. The muscles on his son's face wrinkle into a frown. His lips pucker and tremble. His eyes pinch shut—his mouth opens! Out of lungs that seemed utterly dead issues an earth-shattering cry. Young Philipp is weeping, wailing, shrieking. His legs are thrashing—hands grasping.

---

[9] Ezekiel 16:6.

"Oh, thank the Lord!" Katharina proclaims, gathering the child into her arms and covering him with kisses. "Lord Jesus, thank you! Father, thank you!"

The joy that fills Philipp is beyond description. Even the midwife Maria is moved to tears. As the minutes pass, young Philipp's breathing continues to strengthen. They are able to clean him properly and place him in the special gown that Katharina has spent weeks preparing, each stitch declaring her love. Koch comes in to assist them. The entire house is awake and celebrating! It is only a bit later, when Maria is preparing to leave, that the mood is punctured. She pulls Philipp aside.

"Herr Doktor, it was my honor to assist at the birth today, and I am so grateful for what happened. The Lord is good."

"Indeed, he is," Philipp agrees.

But the look on Maria's face is not joyful. She speaks in a low voice.

"I must offer you a word of warning. The child lives, yes, but he is not out of danger. He may last no longer than a few days. Even if he does survive, the circumstances of his birth are not in his favor. Children born early—they have problems, Doktor. Some struggle to walk, others to talk. Few live as long as one would hope, and fewer still have what you might call a normal life. I am sure, being the scholar that you are, you wish for this child to excel in the mental disciplines. I am telling you now: you must set those desires aside, for it is quite possible that he will be limited in what he can do. Do you understand me?"

Philipp reluctantly nods, the lack of sleep and emotion of the moment threatening to draw new tears from him. A fierce anger builds within him. *How dare you steal this moment from us?! How dare you crush our hope?!* But he knows she is only speaking the truth.

"May the Lord bless you," Maria concludes, "and may the Lord bless little Philipp."

Then she leaves him there, alone in the passage, in fear and trembling.

Three days later, Philipp is standing before the bronze font of St. Mary's Church, young Philipp fussing in his arms, Anna clinging excitedly to him. Johannes Bugenhagen is beside them in his vestments, waiting to bestow the sacrament of baptism upon the newest member of the church. As he hands the babe to the minister, Philipp breathes a deep sigh of relief. It is happening as it always should have: his son is being baptized in the church, surrounded by his spiritual family. The water is being poured over him. The promises are being proclaimed. It is everything Philipp had hoped for before the darkness seized him in that hour. It seems almost too good to be true: a grace far beyond anything he deserves.

But even now, he feels the sting of doubt. *How long will my son live? What kind of life will he have?* Already, Katharina has struggled to nurse him. The boy has trouble latching and sucking. If he cannot eat properly, he will not grow. There are so many things to fear.

When the ceremony is over, the extended Krapp family celebrates with his children in the far corner of the nave, but Philipp sits alone in a chair by the font, head in his hands, unable to escape the memories: bloody sheets, water poured out on the floor, the sound of his son choking, the terror gripping him in the gut.

The trial is passed. This test, at least, is complete. And yet, for him it is not over. He carries it in his soul. That moment of uncertainty—not knowing if his son would live or die, not knowing if he should baptize him or not—hangs like a shadow over his mind, blocking the light from above. He feels less that he has been delivered and more that his foundation has been compromised, his life now crumbling bit by bit. The trial has changed him: he can never be the man he was before.

The world seems at once more fragile and more cruel, threatening at every moment to destroy all he loves. When he holds his son, it is firmer than it might have been otherwise. When he kisses his daughter good night, it is with deeper feeling. When he clasps the hand of his wife, he feels a desperate yearning for a world less fierce than the one in which they reside. He is haunted by what he might have lost—by what he might still lose. His relief was momentary and fleeting. This is only the beginning of trial.

How on earth can I withstand it? he wonders. *How on earth can I persevere?*

He thinks of poor Heinrich von Zütphen, whom they sent out full of hope into an infinitely brutal world. He remembers that moment in the forest with Landgrave Philipp of Hesse—the meeting with Nausea. *The Lord spared me then. Will he spare me again?* The

Edict of Worms still stands, and he, Philipp Melanchthon, is subject to it. *One day, perhaps not so long from now, they will come riding over the hill. They will make a widow of my wife and orphans of my children.* He fears for the very breath in his lungs. *There is nothing certain in this world—nothing at all.* But even these threats to his body cause him less grief than the threats to his spirit.

Bugenhagen sits in the open chair beside him and places a hand on his shoulder.

"A tremendous day, Philipp. A new child born of water and the Spirit. How proud you must be! Another Philipp Melanchthon: you are born anew!"

Philipp nods wearily. His spirit seems sore, exhausted, overcome, as if the slightest touch will cause it pain. With one hand, he traces the lines on his opposite palm, bidding them surrender the answers he craves. *What can I say to him? How can I possibly speak what I feel?*

"What is it?" Bugenhagen inquires. "You look as if you had lost a child rather than gained one."

Philipp looks at him with moist eyes. "If you could feel what I feel in this moment, if you had been through what I have experienced these past few days, then you would know why the shadow of death hangs over me," he says quietly.

Bugenhagen nods. "I heard that the birth was difficult. I know there are some concerns for his health."

Philipp pinches his eyes shut, shaking his head in utter shame. He fights to hold back his tears.

"Please, friend," Bugenhagen begs. "Unburden yourself."

"What man can possibly unburden himself?" he asks, looking Bugenhagen in the eye. "There is no escape. A moment, perhaps a day, but then it comes again. Oh, Johannes! What I wouldn't give to have those moments back again!"

His pastor's brows lower in confusion. "I don't understand. They said you saved his life."

"God saved his life!" he asserts. "I froze, Johannes! I froze! When those I love needed me most, I was uncertain. I felt the hand of doubt upon me."

"That is what it is to be under duress," Bugenhagen assures him. "Every man has moments when he is overcome. That is why we need the Lord."

You still don't understand, he thinks, then says, "They were telling me to baptize him, but some part of me doubted. What good is baptism without faith?"

"Faith is granted in baptism," Bugenhagen states, sounding a bit alarmed. "It is God's gift to man."

He shakes his head. "So many things I thought I knew, but in that moment, all knowledge was stripped from me."

"So, you are doubting baptism?"

"No, it's not that," he explains. "I didn't doubt baptism: I doubted everything! I longed to stand, but it was as if there was nothing solid to hold me up. I felt myself caught between heaven and hell, and I knew not where to turn. Who am I to stand before God and make demands? I would see his work in our days. Yes, I long to see it with all my being: to know that this gospel we preach will yield its appointed fruit! But that certainty is denied me."

Bugenhagen does not answer, but simply stares, so Philipp continues, releasing the pain within him.

"Now I know what Moses felt when he demanded of God, 'Show me your glory!' Only one thing did the Lord grant Moses: to see his goodness." He shakes his head, practically scoffing at the thought. "What a strange comfort! Little different, I think, than that granted to Job. For he told Moses, 'I will be gracious to whom I will be gracious and have mercy on whom I will have mercy.' What a fearsome sentence! So, the goodness when it comes is a healing balm, but all too soon, we are made to tremble again. Perhaps my faith is weaker than I thought. The more I know of God, the more I feel I know nothing at all."

Bugenhagen sits up straighter in his chair, imbued with a sudden confidence. "It is not the strength of your faith, Philipp. It is the strength of your Savior."

This does not cut to the heart of Philipp's concern, but he accepts it wearily, nodding and accepting a pat on the back. Perhaps it is impossible to make Johannes understand—or perhaps no one can understand. After all, he does not fully comprehend it himself. He craves the certainty of faith, but it seems that his faith must necessarily be accompanied by doubt. He has wrestled through the night with things far greater than himself, waiting for a dawn that never comes.

I am not Jacob.

Rising from the chair, Philipp makes his way over to join the family gathering. His mother-in-law turns to him and smiles, placing the sleeping babe in his arms. As he gazes lovingly at his namesake, clinging desperately to a hope he cannot see, a phrase repeats in Philipp's mind. The words of the Requiem Mass spoken for his father, for his brother-in-law, for Nesen, for poor Heinrich von Zütphen. The words uttered by generations as they placed their loved ones in the care of God alone, praying for a deliverance they could not yet see. The words which seize him now as he holds his son's fragile form, and all existence seems coated in angst.

I tremble, and I fear.

*The story continues in book two,
Face to Face.*

Turn the page for
a preview of Book 2:

FACE
TO
FACE

A NOVEL OF
THE REFORMATION

by Amy Mantravadi

Here is an excerpt from Prologue

…The door opens and Pappenheim enters. No longer standing on ceremony, he simply utters, "Brother Martin, it is time."

Martin nods in acknowledgment—rises to his feet. He feels the tension in his legs but bids them hold him upright. He is moving forward now, as if in a dream, through the same labyrinth of passages as the day before, at the end of which he will find not a garden filled with bursts of color but the table holding his books, and behind it Eck waiting to question him as the Emperor looks down from above, surveying the earth like the Greek gods of old, marveling at the frailties of those who are merely human.

In this moment, Martin thinks of what his life might have been like if he had followed his father's wish and married Anna Reinicke. He would be in his home in Mansfeld now, reading his law books, the voices of children echoing in the halls, comfortable and perhaps even content. Well, he would be alive in any case, and that would be something.

Or if he had listened to Staupitz and risen through the ranks of the Augustinians—if he had just left well enough alone, he might have been sent to Rome and the Church of Santa Maria del Popolo, there to spend his days raising glasses of Italian red to the heavens, one after the other, the weather almost as sublime as the money that would fill his pocket. Instead, he is here, about to accept the fate of a notorious heretic: a fate from which so many have tried and failed to save him.

He is made to wait for two hours. Could this be a strategy to throw him off balance? If so, it is working. His anxiety builds by the minute. The sky grows dark, and all hope seems to fade. He feels a chill in his bones but remembers the words of Christ: "But when they hand you over, do not worry about how or what you are to say, for it will be given you in that hour what you are to say."[1] He clings to the promise.

When the time comes, he enters a larger hall than the day before packed with even more officials. He looks again upon the young Emperor Charles, but instead of fierce majesty, he sees a man too small for his heavy garments, with a comically projected chin and a mind incapable of grasping the higher truths of God. Not a god, but a man, and one who will be subject to divine justice, even as he, Martin Luther, will be. Why could he not see it the previous day?

I have less to fear than you, he thinks.

Eck begins addressing him again. "Answer his majesty's question: Do you wish to defend these books acknowledged to be yours, or do you retract?"

Martin's heart beats strongly, even as before. The surf is pulling him under, but he remembers something a sailor once told him: *You do not fight the current, for even the strongest man will expend his strength. You allow it to capture you—to carry you whither it will—and sooner or later, you will find yourself bobbing up to the surface, free to breathe the air again.*

He chooses to believe it. He pictures himself breathing in the fear and releasing it—imagines the Spirit of God filling him from top to bottom, empowering him to stand. He grips his left wrist with his right hand and remembers that he is one with Christ, and Christ will not abandon his own. Then he looks at Eck with a fierce intensity.

You are not fighting fair, he thinks, *so I will not fight fair.*

Softly but clearly, Martin says, "I ask your most serene majesty and your lordships to deign to note that my books are not all the same kind."

With this request, he sets off on a long explanation, separating his books into categories, holding the room in sway. This is not what Eck expected: Martin can see it in the cleric's lowered brows and persistent frown. *You sought a quick kill. You will not get one.* He

---

[1] Matthew 10:19. All scripture references in this book are from *The New American Standard Bible*, 1995 edition (La Habra, CA: The Lockman Foundation).

continues with his explanation, weaving back and forth, refusing to grant Eck an opening.

He speaks of the tyranny of the pope. He quotes Scripture. He draws attention back to his teachings themselves, demanding that the authorities distinguish between them. Every time Eck opens his mouth to cut him off, Martin launches on a new point. He speaks of his duty to God and his allegiance to the German nation. With each sentence, his confidence increases along with Eck's frustration. The very weight of the room has shifted, and the balance is in Martin's favor. Finally, he concludes, "I have finished."

Eck crosses the space between them, stopping within a single pace of Martin's position. With a look surely intended to obliterate, Eck cries, "You have not answered the question! What is more, you call into question things that have already been either condemned or dictated by councils of the Church. You think you can dismiss his imperial majesty with a horned response?[2] Tell us simply: do you wish to retract, or do you not wish to retract?"

Even as Eck speaks, Martin hears the words of Scripture in his mind. *By faith, when he was tested, Abraham offered up Isaac. He considered that God could raise the dead.*

He closes his eyes briefly. He can feel the tension releasing.

And you were dead in trespasses and sins. He has made you alive together with him. You were buried with him in baptism.

Now as he stares into the scowling face of Johann Eck, Martin feels an inner peace, for he knows he is loved by God and made righteous by his Son. *You do not know that Eck. You are the one who has reason to fear, not me.* The Scriptures are clear and beautiful, offering good news to men. No one can convince Martin otherwise. And though Eck looks upon Martin to kill, he is fighting against the force of the moment. It is time.

"Since your serene majesty and your lordships require a simple answer, I will answer neither horned nor toothed," Martin says.

And in his mind, Martin hears the words, *Let us hold fast the confession of our faith, for he who promised is faithful. Abraham was justified apart from works. Faith was credited to him as righteousness. God was not ashamed to be called his God.*

---

[2] A "horned" response is overly complex and obscure—pedantic.

He speaks again, his voice gaining strength and projecting to the far corners of the room. "Unless I am convinced by the testimony of Scripture or by clear reason—for I trust neither pope nor councils alone, which have often erred and contradicted themselves—"

Oh, the fury in Eck's eyes! He is the one trembling now.

With the strength of voice gifted him from on high, Martin Luther releases the fire that has burned so long within him, concluding, "My conscience is captive to the Word of God." And with a confidence that seems almost divine, he proclaims without hesitation, "I will not, and I cannot recant anything, for it is neither safe nor right to go against conscience." He repeats the statement in Latin. A chorus of whispers erupts.

Then he is seized by his frail humanity. The fear and trembling strikes anew. He concludes not in strength but in that weakness that looks for salvation, speaking in his native tongue alone. "Here I stand. I cannot do otherwise. May God help me."

Applause breaks out, beginning with the Saxon delegation and rippling through the crowd. The imperial herald beats his staff upon the marble floor, while Eck turns a deadly glare upon Elector Friedrich to make sure he is not joining the verbal tumult. There are cries of, "Silence!" in both Latin and German, and the noise begins to taper off, but Martin Luther casts his eyes to heaven, overcome by the grace he has been granted. Against the power of the devil and the principalities of earth, he has done what he came to do. He whispers, "It is finished."[3]

---

[3] This was not the end of the interrogation, though for all intents and purposes, the business was complete. Eck pressed Luther to reconsider his statement, only to receive a repeat of the points already made. The assembly was finally ended on account of the late hour.

Acknowledgments

Thank you to my husband, who when I told him I had no idea if anyone would read this book, insisted, "You should still write it." Thank you to Mackenzie Glenning, my son's much-beloved babysitter, who gave me periods to research and write without distractions. Thank you to my parents, who granted me life and have been so supportive of my writing and education.

Coralie Cowan graciously provided feedback on some of my earliest scenes. Dr. Robert Kolb was exceedingly kind to answer my inquiries—his renown among Luther scholars is rightly earned. He and his lovely wife, Pauline, gave my husband and me a tour of the Lutherhaus in Wittenberg.

I would also like to thank my friends in *The Rest is History* club: you have been a balm to my soul. Our illustrious hosts, Tom Holland and Dr. Dominic Sandbrook, provided writing advice when I requested it, the simple act of which was more meaningful than they are ever likely to know. Tom advised me to "convince yourself it has to be written," and that helped carry me through the darkest periods.

My editor, Kristina McBride, was invaluable to me as always. This was our third novel together, and she has been a great blessing in my life. Katelyn Beaty, Don Pape, and Janyre Tromp helped me to understand the Christian fiction market. I am especially grateful to the writing group The Stories Between Us, which was run by Shawn Smucker and Maile Silva. I first had the idea for these novels while listening to lectures on Church history given by Dr. Carl Trueman, then at Westminster Theological Seminary.

I owe so much to the team at 1517. To Kelsi Klembara, who welcomed me into that world and has edited my articles for the website. To Steve Byrnes, who was willing to consider my proposal for this book and make the case for its publication. To Sam Leanza Ortiz, Elysia Brewer, Rick Ritchie, the brothers Klembara, Mai Choy, and Zach Stuef, all of whom helped to get this book ready for release. To other friends at the organization, including but not limited to Gretchen Ronnevik, Katie Koplin, Ted Rosenbladt, and Brad Gray, who have encouraged me as a writer and a person. To all those involved with the *Outlaw God* and *Thinking Fellows* podcasts, which were helpful to me as I sought to understand my material better. Let us continue to proclaim together the good news that Christ is freely given for us.

Finally, I thank all those who have encouraged and taught me over the years, helping to make me into the person I am today. I owe some part of this to each one of you. And to the Lord Jesus Christ, I owe the whole: everything I am. May this and all my writings be to the glory of God alone.

About the Author

Amy Mantravadi lives in Dayton, Ohio, with her husband, Jai, and their son, Thomas. She holds a B.A. in biblical literature and political science from Taylor University and an M.A. in international security from King's College London. She is a 1517 contributor and author of the *Chronicle of Maud* series of historical novels. When she is not writing, she enjoys geeking out about history and theology, filling the internet with GIFs, and spending time with her family.

1517.

Never Go Another Day Without Hearing the Gospel of Jesus.

Visit **www.1517.org**
for free Gospel resources.